If you have Picke
you are brave
you are loved.

GRIEVE YOURSELF

GRIEVE YOURSELF

a novel

nicky davis

-THE CONVERSATIONALITE PRESS-

LOS ANGELES, CA

Printed in the United States of America. For information, address The Conversationalite Press, theconversationalite@gmail.com. www.theconversationalite.com

October 2020

Publisher's Cataloging-in-Publication Data provided by Five Rainbows Cataloging Services

Names: Davis, Nicky, author.

Title: Grieve yourself : a novel / Nicky Davis.

Description: Los Angeles : The Conversationalite Press, 2020.

Identifiers: LCCN 2020911958 (print) | ISBN 978-1-7353297-0-3 (paperback) ISBN 978-1-7353297-1-0 (ebook)

Subjects: LCSH: Fathers and daughters--Fiction. | Grief--Fiction
Depression--Fiction. | Interpersonal relations--Fiction. | Self-actualization--Fiction.
BISAC: FICTION / General.

Classification: LCC PS3604.A95 G75 2020 (print) | LCC PS3604.A95 (ebook) | DDC 813/.6--dc23.

For Andrea Allen

PREFACE

Every journey with grief looks different. Every family and chosen family looks different. Growing up, I didn't see a lot of stories that looked like mine. When I started writing this book, I had no idea where I was headed. I only knew I needed to see a story about how we grieve for people we love but have often hated. People who have hurt us deeply. People who have let us down. I needed to know how a story like mine would end. I wanted to talk honestly about the intersection of grief and relief, and all the discomfort of living there. I wanted to talk about love, in all its complicated, murky, absurd, and devastating brilliance. About how messily we love our families, our friends and our partners. And about how we must learn and relearn to love ourselves.

It's no secret that Mackenzie Adams saved my life. Writing her honesty, her heartbreak, her imperfection, her fierce love, and her vulnerability, has made it easier for me to bear my own grieving. She has made me laugh at times when I didn't think I ever would again. She gave me ways to articulate fears and feelings I'd never dared to examine. She made me believe that even at our worst, we are worthy. I'll love her forever for that, and it's an honor to get to share her story with you.

I hope you'll love her too.

GRIEVE YOURSELF

PART ONE

January 2018

January 1ˢᵗ

Last night, I set off a firework in a friend of a friend's backyard, at a party I wasn't personally invited to, wearing not enough dress for the even fewer degrees it was outside. I watched it sputter and burst against a clouded-over sky, showering down crumbs of flaming light, and a whole party of friends of friends—strangers, is what they're called—ooh-ed and ahh-ed and congratulated me on my technique. And when another girl, in even less of a dress, skittered across the lawn to drunkenly set fire to another illegal explosive, I nestled into the chest of a guy I'd only just met and thought: *...is this it?*

And then I had another drink.

Something's wrong, but I can't tell what. Strange, how a day can feel broken before it starts. Then again, maybe it's just that patented New Year's Day weirdness, the expectation that somehow overnight everything has shifted, and that life will suddenly be better than it was last year. At the very least, different somehow than it was last night. Burgeoning with stuff people like. Hopeful.

But when I open my eyes this morning, the bedside lamp is still on, and my room is nothing except uncomfortably bright for the degree of my hangover. Thankfully, there's not much sound except the wind shivering through the branches. Across the way, on the windowsill of our neighbor Larry Halburn's apartment, his ferrets are still asleep. If this world is new, I don't see how. Everything is yesterday's leftovers, including the guy sleeping next to me.

It's a new low that I don't remember his name. I'll call him Ben. That I don't remember meeting anyone named Ben, I decide, is irrelevant.

I read once—in a magazine designed to stoke the insecurities of young women desperate to be loved—that the way you sleep with a partner is a major indicator for the future success of your relationship. Not the way you *sleep with* your partner, but actually how you *sleep*. Maybe-Ben has his back to me, curled into the fetal position, perched at the edge of the mattress. This, the article would deduce, doesn't bode well for us.

Which is a shame, probably. Even from the back, he looks like the kind of guy that normal people would want to keep around: all shoulders and skin that glows gold, even in the winter. Meanwhile, I've yet to master how to be a keep-around person. I'm stale and, just like every year, not any closer to passing for normal in the pale January light than I was in the oversweet holiday haze of December.

Not for lack of trying, though. Last night, I got swept up in making resolutions. Started promising myself a ridiculous number of very I-love-myself-I-love-my-life type things from a giddy place in the midst of my champagne buzz, sometime around 12:03 AM. But I already know that that list—*Go to the gym every day! Go to that acupuncturist Mel keeps recommending! Keep a dream journal! Cook for yourself at least three days a week! Try hot yoga!*—won't stick. Not because any of it is particularly difficult, I don't think. There's just only so much I can do to pretend myself into that shiny sort of incandescent happiness.

Still, in quiet moments alone, especially on mornings like this one, I reek of daydreams about being a better person. Or, really, just an entirely different person. Jennifer Aniston, or Penelope Cruz, or Camille Preston from high school.

Maybe-Ben twitches like a happy dog in his sleep. Such a keep-around. No doubt he has a lot of friends who say he's the best guy they know. "He's the guy you call," they tell you, while he laughs like he knows it's true but is too humble to say so.

I slide out of bed, pull on yesterday's underwear and an oversized t-shirt that reads SEAHAWKS SUPER BOWL XLVIII CHAMPIONS, that I got for free once with a haul from Goodwill, and sneak down the hall to the bathroom.

Mel's yoga clothes are hang drying in our shower, as usual. She says it's to "maintain the integrity of the fabric," which I've never understood as I've never thought of spandex as a fabric with a whole lot of integrity. Just in case, though, I whisper "happy new year" to three sports bras and two pairs of leggings. They give me the cold shoulder.

Braced against the sink, I survey the damage in the mirror. My face is more or less the same one I put on last night—granted, the eyes are less artfully smudged now. I clean them up around the edges with a Q-tip, delicate, like I'm restoring a valuable painting. My skin is ashy and a size too small, thanks to me nearly freezing last night, so I slather lotion on my limbs until I brown up again. I get my hands wet and try to twist the curl back into my hair, but it mostly frizzes. Annoyingly, it's still just a little too short to put up since I cut most of it off in another year's desperate grasp at transformation. I rake my fingers through it, trying to tease knots apart until I look like someone I nearly recognize. I think that's the best I can do.

There's a rustle in my room. "Kenzie?"

Maybe-Ben. Awake and not, apparently, mortified to find himself in my apartment in the light of day. Nobody calls me Kenzie, though I have to give him credit for knowing my name, even if it's only the back half. And extra credit for really committing on the nickname, though it doesn't suit me. At all.

"Bathroom," I yell. Not a very sexy way to greet someone in the morning, but things come out of my face sometimes before I can stop them. I scramble for a toothbrush just for something to do.

He's on the move now. I hear the creaking of bedsprings, then floorboards. "Cool, cool. So. Last night was fun... You have fun?"

Mouth now full of toothpaste: "Mmhmm. Fuh!" More creaking. And then he appears in the doorway.

Upright, he's annoyingly handsome. Blonde and blue-eyed and biceped and altogether too handsome. I've been known to make a handsome mistake, but even for me, he's decadent. Quit your job and let him pay for dinner, handsome. And he just sort of leans against the doorjamb and goes, "Hi," in this sometimes-I-think-it's-sexy-to-just-say-hi-to-a-person voice, like: "*Hi.*"

So then, I don't know. I can't think of a clever way to find out his name. And I really should already know it. And I feel a little guilty because it's obvious that he's trying to be cute and maybe if I was Jennifer Aniston or Camille Preston, I would let him, but I'm not, and so I don't want to. And at this moment, it's so painfully obvious to me that I can't accommodate a permanent Maybe-Ben situation.

Not even semi-permanent. I'm not the pretend keep-around person who wrote those resolutions last night with fingers that smelled like gunpowder and prosecco. I'm not the giggling shimmery dress that brought a nameless boy home and whispered nice things against his pulse. *I'm Mackenzie,* I think, and I would say it to him if it would mean anything.

Not to mention, I made up my mind years ago that I'm not much for accidentally falling in love anymore. And especially not with boys with faces too symmetrical to be trustworthy. But then— before I can explain to him about the things I know to be true about us because of the fetal position and the article I read once—I hear "Love Train" playing in the bedroom. And I remember that I spent $1.25 last night buying that ringtone because, according to drunk, pretend me, "I should really have more *love*—just every day. Just like, love every day. *Everydaylove.*" And so, it's suddenly clear that my phone is ringing.

Something is wrong.

I'm answering before I have time to think why the number looks familiar.

And I say, "Hello?"

The voice on the other end is timid, but it knows my name, and it asks if this is Mackenzie Adams, and I tell it that yes, this is she. And then the voice says its name is Beth, and it's calling from the Homeaway Inn Express in Downtown Seattle.

And my voice says, "Oh."

Because I *knew* I knew the number. Because I thought I'd blocked every one of these extensions by now. Because I know all about the Homeaway Inn Express in Downtown Seattle. And suddenly I know what's wrong. This is a phone call about my father.

I want to hang up the phone, but I can't remember how.

In my whole life, I've never gotten a phone call about my father that I didn't want to hang up on. Occasionally there have been calls *from* my father that I didn't want to hang up on. But even that has been a very long time. A chronically unemployed, sporadically homeless alcoholic, with a slew of blacked-out memories, a volatile temper, and a record, he's not the kind of man people are usually calling to say good things about. I stopped answering nearly two years ago. I shouldn't have answered today. The air is heavy, and it laughs at me in his voice.

I'm fine.

The whole time Beth is introducing herself, I'm dazedly watching Maybe-Ben proceed to not get dressed, but instead, get back into my bed. He is working too hard at being cute for someone so good-looking.

And he says, "Kenzie, who's on the phone? Come back to bed."

And I say, "It's Beth." Like I know Beth.

"Who?"

And I say *"Beth"* again. With emphasis this time, like it's *so* obvious.

Then Maybe-Ben smirks and puts his arms behind his head, all loungey and casual. It doesn't look as good on him as he thinks, and I want to tell him so, but I get distracted by the phone.

Beth's voice has lost its earlier formality, and I realize she's long moved on from introductions. "...*unconscious* this morning. Of course, my first thought was to call 9-1-1—but then I remembered how Gerry—or, Gerald—your father—" Jesus Christ. "He's never trusted doctors or the police, and, well, I was raised to respect my elders. So then, I—It's just that it all happened too quickly... Ms. Adams, are you still there?"

"Yes. I'm still here," I say, though I'm not sure I am really.

"Well, I checked him for a pulse and for breath signs—I'm CPR certified by the American Red Cross, you know—and it was clear that even if someone came to take him up to Harborview... well, there wasn't really anything more they could do for him there, was there? Because I determined that he'd stopped breath—he was *unresponsive.*"

"Oh. Wow, okay." I force myself to say. I should be more surprised. I *am* surprised. Or... no. I don't know.

"So, then I thought—well, your number was in his Recently Called, and you're listed as one of his emergency contacts... and oh *god*, you must've spoken to him so recently."

"No. Not really." I wish she would just say it. I've been expecting this call to come for years. For so many years that I mostly forgot I was expecting it. But here we are. It's happening.

The first of the year wouldn't be my top choice of days to die. Though I guess it saves you the trouble of pretending you're finally going to change.

"My dad." My voice comes out eerily familiar, out of a dream. "Gerald. He's dead?"

Maybe-Ben's face goes watery and strange, and I go back to the bathroom, so I don't have to look at it. I'm careful to dodge the mirror, not much interested in my face either.

"I know this must be horrible news to receive over the phone like this. But I wasn't sure—He's always talking about you. I know you two were close." I can hear her throat getting small and squeaky. My throat doesn't change.

"But now he's dead," I repeat, hoping she'll parrot it back. *Tell me*, I think. *Tell me so I can hear it from someone else. Tell me, so I know it's true.* But she just breaks down in tears. Gasping, heart-wrenching sobs. I wonder if I should be crying. What a terrible sort of daughter to have—one that doesn't even cry when you're dead. This isn't at all the way I imagined it. Beth keeps talking.

"I'm sorry, I'm a mess. It's just so *sad*, isn't it? I didn't expect this today. How could anyone expect this? He seemed so well."

"Did he?" I wrack my brain for the last time I saw my dad looking well, but then regret trying so hard to conjure his face. When did I sit down? I stare at my knees.

"Well," she sighs, not answering the question, "We're in Room 313 when you get here."

"Excuse me?"

"Three. One. Three. I've alerted Al who's covering for me at the desk. Just give him your ID when you get here. He'll let you up." The air in the room laughs so loud I think I didn't hear her right.

"No, I'm sorry—You're still with him? No one ever called anyone?"

Beth just wails, "*I called you*," and a voice that must be mine tells her it's okay and that I understand, but I'm sure I do not.

Once I finally figure out how to hang up, there are twenty minutes I barely remember. The laughter's gone, replaced by a static kind of buzz, humming like a fluorescent bulb about to spark out, but the lights aren't even on. I run the faucet like I might be able to just rinse the past few minutes off, but I don't touch the water. Just watch it run out of the room. Envy it. The buzzing swells, and I get so small I wonder if anyone can see me. And then somehow, it's twenty minutes later, and I am in Maybe-Ben's car, headed downtown.

As unopened storefronts drift past the car window, I think that I already knew. That I knew before the phone rang. That maybe I knew as soon as I woke up this morning. The way you know you've forgotten to pack something you're really going to need for a trip. The way you can feel it's missing before you can remember what it is—the hollowness of being without something you're supposed to have.

For the first time, today decisively splits itself apart from last night.

I register I managed to put on jeans to make an outfit, though I didn't bother with a coat. The numb of the cold air is welcome. Shrugging against the passenger side window, I pull at the skin in the bend of my arm, anxious. For a split second, I think I glimpse Gerald in the side view mirror, slumped in the backseat. But it's just me, closer than I appear.

This is not the kind of errand you want to bring a date along for.

As it happens, Maybe-Ben is *not* the guy you call. He's an untrained golden retriever: all unquestioning loyalty and bumbling blonde enthusiasm. I don't know what protocol is for something like this, but I'm sure he's getting it wrong.

"Do they have a parking lot, or is it all street parking?"

"I don't know. I don't drive."

"Oh," he sucks on the silence through perfect teeth. "You don't?"

"No."

"No car?"

"No license."

"Really?"

"Is this—?"

"No. Sorry… I guess we could park in the Macy's garage? You know, if they don't have a lot."

"You don't have to park." I try not to picture walking through the department store sky bridge with Maybe-Ben right now. Past the windows of Williams-Sonoma's holiday display on our way to identify a corpse.

"Well, I don't think you should go through this alone."

"I'm fine."

"You're in shock." He's projecting.

"I'm honestly fine. I'll be fine."

"Kenzie—"

The complete wrongness of the nickname grates. "Really. He's been threatening to die forever. And it's been a long time since I saw him last anyway. Not like we were best friends." I glance at him, and he's turning himself inside out with sympathetic concern. I cringe, pulling my knees to my chest and wrapping an arm around them. "Bummer that he's dead, but… I mean, the world can't stop turning every time someone dies. So. Besides, he's not your dad. Please don't park."

They have a garage. We park. Maybe-Ben holds my hand as we wait for the elevator even though I let my fingers go limp. I wish I knew his name so I could more effectively tell him to stop it.

There's a tourist family waiting with us for the elevator: a mom, dad, and a little girl. The little girl is wearing an "I-Space-Needle-Seattle" shirt, bouncing up and down.

"Can I push the button for the elevator?" she asks her dad, who smiles at Maybe-Ben, and explains that she had a cupcake for breakfast today because it's her birthday.

"Born on New Year's Day? What a special birthday." Maybe-Ben smiles at the little girl, and she smiles back, missing a couple teeth in a very adorable way. I think she must be about as old as I feel.

She pushes every button in the elevator.

"Lily!" Her mother scolds, as though yelling her name will keep this from now being a local car that stops at every floor.

"It's all right," I hear myself assuring them. "We're not in a hurry." Maybe-Ben squeezes my hand and shoots me a pleading look like he's worried I'll spill my dead dad on the birthday girl and ruin everyone's fun. I force my face to smile at her parents and press myself into the wall. I wasn't supposed to have to come back here.

Al, it turns out, is barely past puberty. An acne-ridden part-time bellhop terrified out of his mind about being left in charge.

"Uh, welcome to the Homeaway Inn Express Seattle. I'm Al. Albert. It's Al. Short for Albert." He gulps. "Are you checking in?"

You-Shouldn't-Go-Through-This-Alone clears his throat but fails to make any words.

"Not checking in. No," I tell Al. "We're just here about the body in room 313."

My date is less than pleased with my word choice, and he puts some distance between us for the first time all morning. I'm glad for it. Al is on the phone now, calling up to Beth. He places a hand over the receiver while it rings.

"You're Gerald's daughter?"

"Mackenzie. Yeah. That's me."

"He's very nice. I mean. He *was*." My chest clenches, and I grin through it. "You look like him, you know?"

"All right then, Al. Thank you." I run a hand over my face wishing it would slide off into my palm. He offers to walk us up, but there's no need. I know the way.

The lobby elevators are out of commission, so we have to take the stairs. Two flights up, Maybe-Ben is checking his phone, and huffing a little bit. They're not short flights, and I don't understand what he's still doing here.

"You don't have to stay for this. It's going to be a long, weird day." He keeps climbing like he didn't hear me, so I stop on the step ahead of him and turn. "I'm serious. If you have things to do today—"

"Kenzie. It's no big deal. I wanted to spend the day with you anyway."

It's no big deal. He runs a hand through his flop of blonde hair like that's going to convince me, and I can feel him congratulating his own good intentions. He has all the confidence of a kid in the front row with his hand raised who didn't even do the reading. I wonder what the worst day of his life was before now.

Room 313 is the last one at the end of the hall. The door is propped open with a coat hanger. It reminds me of college, and I try to forget why we're here.

The door hits my father's foot when we try to push it open. From inside, Beth lets out a little yelp.

"No housekeeping! There's a body in here!" She cries. I close my eyes tight and try to wake myself up from this.

"Beth? It's Mackenzie… The body is my dad?" I don't know how to do this. "I can't get the door open?"

"Oh! Mackenzie! I've heard so much about you." Her words run together with tears and snot while Maybe-Ben looks around the hallway, apologizing in a grimace to all the other possible hotel guests. I hope he knows he's not a hero.

"We'll need to move if you're going to get the door open," Beth squalls.

"Well I don't know—yes? I guess. If it's not too—"

"Just hold on!" I can hear the strain in her voice as she wrestles his body out of the way. "All right. Try again?"

I let the boy get the door for me and watch regret fly onto his face.

My father is sprawled on his back on the floor. His long brown limbs crowded between the end of the bed and the minibar. Beth is pinned under him up to her waist, his head in her lap. There are used tissues scattered all over the floor amidst loose tobacco from my dad's haphazard cigarette rolling. The room is dense with the smell of a person who had been hard at work dying long before today. There are more than a few empty bottles of Gordon's on the window-sill. Classic.

Beth is a tiny little blonde thing. Like a country mouse that came to the city looking for her big break. Her cheeks are streaked with mascara, and her nose drips. She's not dressed for work but in a party dress, from last night, no doubt.

Perhaps most distracting is the fact that my father is completely naked.

"*Oh my god*," It's-No-Big-Deal utters as he shuts the door behind us.

"I'm so glad you're here," Beth says to me, leaning over my father's face to shake hands with my date. "Hello, I'm Beth."

"I'm Neil," says not-Ben-but-Neil. "I'm, uh, Mackenzie's... friend. Just here for, you know, moral support." Oh. He's Cute Neil from Mel's gym. There have been other days when this may have mattered.

"He's naked," I say. It seems as relevant a thing to say as anything else, and I'm surprised I manage that much. Gerald's face is the same as I remember but less. He still has my crooked nose, the same haphazard beard. The amber of his skin—the product of his single white mother's clandestine affair with a dark-skinned jazz pianist—has gone sallow, but that was a long time coming. His large brown eyes are closed, a blessing, however small. His lips are colorless and dry, and without thinking, I run my teeth over my own bottom lip, pulling up dry skin and splitting it open. My blood is bitter, and I swallow it. I don't know if I'd thought I would see him again someday. I don't know at all anymore what I thought, but it wasn't this.

Neil excuses himself into the bathroom. He is uselessly polite and tries to cover the sound of him vomiting by turning on the sink, but it doesn't fool anyone. I clamp my arms across my chest, aware for the first time that I didn't put a bra on in my stupor and resenting the lack of support.

"I'm not sure what it is I'm here to do, Beth, to be perfectly honest." Beth starts to form a word, but all that comes out are choked cries. She makes a loud howling noise between sobs like a kid might do. I vaguely remember making those noises in the wading pool once when I skinned my knee, trying to swim. I try to remember the pain, but I only feel tired.

All I want is to go home, so, what has to happen is someone needs to call 9-1-1, explain the circumstances, and then wait here until they come to pick up Gerald's body. I search the room for an adult, only to realize I'm as close as we're going to get.

This will be the last time I clean up your mess, Dad, I think and wish I believed it. "Can I use the landline to call 9-1-1?" Beth nods, still crying all over Gerald's dead face. I step over the pile of them to the phone.

9-1-1 takes forever to pick up. Two weeks ago, a few days before Christmas, Mel had asked me if I was going to call my dad for the holidays. And I'd told her no, not this year, but that I had time if I ever changed my mind. "He's never going to die," I'd whined.

The phone rings and rings.

Cute Neil comes back into the room. He coughs, and I worry he's gonna be sick again, but he reins it in. If that magazine had ranked stories of "awkward morning-afters," this would be the top of their list for the rest of time.

"9-1-1. What's your emergency?" The nasal voice of the operator catches me off-guard.

I do my best to explain my emergency to the nasal voice: Homeaway Inn Express, what appears to be a major heart attack, naked man, sensitive hotel staff, please hurry, etcetera.

They're going to send someone over, and Cute Neil is sitting next to me on the bed now, rubbing my back aggressively in jagged circles. The room is too small, and there are too many bodies. I don't know where to look or how to breathe in here.

From the floor, Beth erupts into another fit of sobs.

"It's just so goddamn sudden," she blubbers. "Gerald was always hanging around in the lobby, keeping us company, cracking jokes…

and now what is he? Just a… a naked heap on the floor that some paramedics are going to scoop up and take back to… to their *lab!*"

Neil's hand disappears from my back as he stifles a gag, and Beth's breathing goes completely drenched and sideways. Before I can think, I'm knelt down next to her, putting an arm over her tiny mouse shoulders. She shakes in my arms. "Beth?" I have to say it so many times it stops sounding like a name. Beth, Beth, Beth, Beth, Beth. She curls her face into my chest, and I cradle her like a baby until she flails away from me, inconsolable.

Her hands stutter in front of her like she's lost all use for them. She gropes above Gerald's face, miming a broken kind of intimacy. She is the picture of grief. I think about telling the paramedics that she's his family. That way, he could belong to someone who still knows how to love him. The light from the Homeaway Inn Express sign reflects off the glass and gives everything this ominous green glow, like a nightmare.

I picture EMTs coming, wrangling his body out of the room. Picture someone tracing a chalk outline on the floor where Gerald lays flopped on top of Beth. And my brain picks up the image and wanders away from here, back to this identity exercise I did in second grade. They didn't call it an identity exercise at the time; they called it "Mini-Me's." But it was an identity exercise.

You lie down on a piece of butcher paper, and the kid you share a desk with traces you in magic marker. And then you trace the kid. And then everyone gets a pair of safety scissors and cuts out their me-size blob. "Mini-Me's" is admittedly a misnomer for something that is actually life-size.

For a while, the teachers just let you color in your blob. Several of the girls insist on starting over so that they can cut out their blob to look like it's wearing a skirt instead of pants. This is allowed.

After about fifteen minutes of this, the teacher says that when you're done coloring, you should flip over your Mini-Me and, on the back, write ten "I Am" sentences.

An "I Am" sentence, the teacher explains, is a sentence that begins with the words "I Am" and tells us something that is true about you. For example, "I am Ms. Lucy."

She encourages everyone to be creative.

"Write them nice and big," she says. "We're going to hang them up in the hallways for the Open House so that all your families can see them."

My sentences were as follows:

1. I am Mackenzie.

2. I am seven years old.

3. I am tall.

4. I am in second grade.

5. I am part Black and part white.

6. I am hungry for lunch.

7. I am done making my Mini-Me.

8. I am bored.

9. I am tired of writing sentences.

10. I am a daughter.

The last one was Ms. Lucy's idea. She even made sure I spelled "daughter" right. She said later that my list was very unique because I was the only kid in the whole class who had managed to not really say anything about themselves at all. I remember hearing her say it in a whisper voice to my parents on Open House night with a lot of creases in her forehead. And my mother just shrugged her shoulders and said, "Well. We're trying with her."

Maybe I was always going to turn out this way.

10. I am a daughter.

It's another thirty minutes before anyone arrives. Al is the one who knocks at the door. He apologizes to Beth for leaving the front desk unmanned so that he could bring the medics up to the room. "It seemed like they might get lost what with the room being all at the end of the hall and everything," he explains, though she's so hysterical it's hardly necessary. Once the medics are situated, he just mutters, "I'm sorry" again and scuttles away.

"This the body?" The first paramedic asks me, and it's such a ridiculous question that I can't form an answer.

"Yes, that's him," Neil offers from the bed. He looks queasy still, but he smiles through it.

The paramedics are shockingly informal. They shuffle around the room, making jokes as they're surveying the scene. Maybe this is standard protocol when there's a dead body in a Homeaway Inn Express. Maybe they do this kind of thing all the time. That's not as comforting as I want it to be. I duck out of the way as the first paramedic helps Beth up off the floor and mutters some kind words to her that I can't quite make out.

"He's naked," the second paramedic notes.

"Yes. I'm sorry about that," I say, like there's anything I could've done.

"Called the family?" The first paramedic is now checking Gerald for a pulse and breathing. I wonder if he's Red Cross CPR certified too.

"That's my dad. I'm the family."

"Oh. Jesus," he says, and then, "I mean, I guess I should've noticed. With the face. Sorry."

"No, that's—"

"Shitty morning," the second paramedic mutters. I look around the room, but I'm the only one who heard.

The first paramedic stands over my father and shakes his head solemnly. "You said natural causes?"

"I was told it was a heart attack?"

"Huh. Young," he grunts.

This can't be how this is supposed to go. "Excuse me?"

"He means he's young. This guy. Your dad. For a heart attack. Seems like a young one," says the second.

"He's fifty-three. Or, he was. Is that young?"

"Eh. Younger than you'd like, probably," barks the first one.

Beth is lurking in the corner of the room, frazzled. She has pulled a small bottle of white wine from the mini-fridge. "He was young at heart!" She squawks, and then suddenly to me, "I won't charge you for the wine." She screws off the top and downs most of the bottle. Cute Neil ushers her into the hallway when she starts to cry again, and, for the first time, I'm almost glad he's still here.

When the door closes behind them, the EMTs forget all about me, talking shop like they're all alone.

"Well, Len. Seems like we ought to load 'im up, take 'im over and have someone declare 'im. Make it official. Get the autopsy paperwork started, always takes a fucking century."

"Yup. You bring a bag?"

"Wanted to have a look at what we're dealing with first. It's down in the car."

"Well. Go get it. And bring the stretcher up too. Looks like a load."

The second one disappears out the door, and the first one looks up over my naked father and locks eyes with me. I'm thinking I've never wanted to be anywhere less, and then, off my shirt, like he's breaking the ice at a dinner party, he goes, "You watching the game this weekend, sweetheart? Seahawks are favored to win big."

I'm fine.

*

PARENT TEACHER CONFERENCE REPORT
DATE: NOVEMBER 15, 2001
STUDENT: MACKENZIE ADAMS
EDUCATOR: LUCY WILSON

PARENTS: ELIZABETH JAMES AND GERALD ADAMS

GRADE: 2

ROOM NUMBER: 406

Teacher Summary of Student Progress: Mackenzie Adams is a gifted student who shows promise in nearly every subject. She has far exceeded third-grade levels in both spelling and reading and shows tremendous improvement in her math and science proficiency. If there is one concern I have about Mackenzie, it is her attitude. She often misbehaves in class, talking to friends during lessons or talking back to both myself and my teaching assistant Ms. Diana. I worry that Mackenzie is not challenged enough by the second-grade material and that this is the source of her "troublemaker" behavior.

Teacher Notes from Conference: Mrs. James and Mr. Adams were half an hour late for the conference. Mrs. James was most apologetic. It was quite evident that Mr. Adams was heavily intoxicated. I attempted to discuss with them my concerns about Mackenzie. Mrs. James seemed unsurprised that her daughter was exhibiting these behaviors in class. Mr. Adams slurred several expletives and referred several times to their daughter as "that little bitch." I found all of this to be very concerning. Mrs. James continued to apologize for her husband's language and assured me that he does not use this language at home or in front of their daughter, which would constitute an abusive home environment. I did my best to continue with the conference. I suggested that Mackenzie might benefit from transitioning into Ms. Dorothy's 2/3 split class so that she might take on some of the third-grade level material, which would be more at her speed. Mrs. James seemed altogether hesitant to relocate her daughter, explaining that the child doesn't handle change well. Mr. Adams laughed loudly at this and then banged his fist down on the table. He then leaned toward me and took my hand, saying—and this is a direct quote—"the little bitch can't handle shit. She doesn't need a different teacher; she needs a thicker fucking skin." This was followed by more laughter from Mr. Adams. It was at this point that Elliot Pollock's parents arrived for their conference, and I was forced to cut the James-Adams meeting short. If I had concerns about Mackenzie prior to this meeting, they were in no way assuaged by her parents. I would suggest that the school keep a close eye on Mackenzie's development and offer her as much help as possible in the coming years. Future educators should be on the lookout for signs of defensiveness or aggression from Mackenzie, as this could be a result of worsening home conditions.

*

Almost everything is closed on New Year's Day except for this one 24-hour diner that's never closed. When I was in high school, Gerald was a regular patron when he had nowhere else to spend the night indoors. Their landline is in my blocked contacts. I've never eaten here on principle, but Neil pulls into their parking lot. For a while, we just sit in the car together, not moving. He's staring at me like I might start crying, and when I don't, he puts his hand on my shoulder.

"You hungry?"

"I don't know," I say, which is true. I'm both starving thanks to the hangover and think I may never eat again after watching Gerald's body bounced down three flights of stairs on a stretcher.

"What do you mean you don't know?" Neil teases as though nothing out of the ordinary has happened today.

"I mean, *I don't know.*"

"Doesn't anything sound good? They have lots of stuff. Waffles, and burgers, and… lots of stuff." Because a lack of menu options was what'd been holding me back.

I look at him, blank, but he doesn't notice.

"Look, if they don't have anything you want, we can leave."

"Do *you* want something?"

"I like their waffles."

So, we go in.

Inside, the diner is a '90s rock time capsule. There are a lot of concert posters on the walls, signed by various guitarists and drummers. The waitresses are all over forty but wearing a lot of dark eyeliner and safety-pinned band tees. It's a completely ridiculous aesthetic for a diner, but it's easy to picture Gerald here, friendly with the staff and telling made-up stories about bassists he'd met when they came to his window at the bank to cash their rock star pay-checks. "Smells Like Teen Spirit" is coming softly through the speakers. Of course.

One of the waitresses, carrying an armload of dirty plates and a carafe of coffee, notices us. "Happy New Year, kids. Sit wherever you want."

"Booth?" Neil points at a table under a Red Hot Chili Peppers poster, and I shrug.

He's being too considerate, and it's making me itch. He sits at a polite distance in the booth, waiting for me to open up about my dad or my feelings. I avoid eye contact and pick at a piece of dried food that's stuck to the table. It looks like a little island on the black laminate surface. I think it was oatmeal once.

"Kenzie?" He's talking in this hushed warmed-over voice that makes him sound like precisely the kind of person you'd want to talk to if you wanted to talk.

"Mm."

"I wanted to—I know this has been a big morning for you. I—a difficult morning. And I know—I mean, I know we don't know each other that well. But I just—if you wanted to—If you want to talk. I'm here." I take my eyes off the oatmeal island and notice that he's leaning toward me in a very caring sort of way. His big blue eyes are all soft and concerned. Girls must fall in love with him all the time.

"I actually thought your name was Ben until a couple hours ago," I barb. "So, um, *thanks*, but I think I'm good."

The problem with me is that sometimes I'm mean just to see what happens. I'm told it's hereditary. People trying too hard to be nice to me makes me go all claustrophobic and clammy. Especially handsome people that think I'm going to be vulnerable with them just because they slept in my bed last night. I shouldn't have let him stay so long. I shouldn't have let him hope I'm someone I'm not.

He doesn't say anything else, just busies himself with searching the menu, which is annoying, because we both already know he's going to order the waffles. And then I'm annoyed with myself for being so hard on him when he's been such a fucking prince all morning. And then I think, no one asked him to do any of this, and barfing in a Homeaway Inn Express hardly counts as being a prince.

And then I remember my dad is dead and, for some reason, I start to laugh.

"It's not funny." Neil looks at me, his wounded ego still visibly throbbing. And even though I don't really care, I don't like that he's mad at me, and I almost apologize, but I'm interrupted by our waitress.

She's like a thick slice of zucchini bread wearing a grimy The Offspring tee shirt. It's got an x-ray of ribs printed on the front underneath big dripping graffiti letters that read "The Offspring." Inside the chest cavity, she has safety-pinned a patch with a dead baby graphic on it. Her hair is stiff and dried out from being dyed too often, most recently a platinum blonde, though her roots have grown in an almost moss-colored brown. Her ears are each pierced at least five times, and she's got a scar above her left eyebrow from where it used to be pierced as well. Her name tag bluntly declares, "I'm Martha."

"What can I get ya? Or do you still need a few?"

"Coffee would be great," says Neil, "and then, well. Do you know what you want, Mackenzie?" He stares emptily at me, so I make a super fake polite face at him. I know he's only using my full name because he's mad, but it feels like the first time anyone's come close to actually seeing me all morning.

"I'll have the Pearl Jam-burger, without mayonnaise," I tell Martha. "And can I have tartar sauce with my fries instead of ketchup?"

"Sure thing, sugar. Well-done okay?"

"Um, medium-well, if that's possible."

"Medium-well... I'll ask for ya. And for you, handsome?" Martha leans her hip against the table, turning her attention to Neil. Oh, good. She's flirting.

"You know, I can't decide?" Neil indulges her. "If you had to choose your favorite, between the Kurt Co-berry pancakes and the Sublime Waffles, which would you go for?"

"You said you love the waffles. Just get the waffles."

"Mackenzie, calm down. I just want to get Martha's opinion."

I have the urge to tell Martha that Neil is being a jerk because I hurt his tiny feelings when the truth is that my dad is dead, and I should get a free pass, but Martha is blatantly Team Neil, so I don't bother.

She giggles all over herself and comes up with an extensive pro/con list for both the pancakes and the waffles. And after much deliberation, Neil orders the waffles with a side of the Limp Biscuits. Gross.

"Look, my parents split up when I was little. And Gerald... he was an alcoholic and an asshole my whole life," I hear myself saying when Martha leaves the table. I don't know if I mean to be telling Neil this, or if it's just something I need to tell *someone*. "So. I'm just saying. It's not the same as if *your* dad died or something."

"You don't know that," he counters, which is obnoxious. Because I sort of *do* know that. His reaction this morning was hardly that of someone who has seen a lot of shit. But being mean to Neil has proven to be more work than it's worth, so I let it go.

"No, I guess I don't know that. I guess I just mean, most people are—a lot of people are *close* with their dads."

"You weren't close."

"No, we were. Very close. Or we used to be. Sometimes... Just... not like most people." I am realizing that this whole thing is more complicated than I feel like explaining.

"*Oh.* Did he..." Neil shifts nervously. "You know... did he, like, ever..."

"No," I cut him off, finishing his half-formed question in my head. "No, it wasn't like that. No." He looks so relieved that suddenly I'm furious. "Also, what the fuck? You can't just ask people that. You can't just *ask* that over breakfast. What would you have done if I'd said yes?"

"I don't—I mean..."

He's a complete fucking dipshit.

"Yeah, so *don't.*" He leans away like I might bite. Good. "It's a long story and... it was just a weird circumstance with him and me, is all. It's just weird and not sad. So. He's dead, but I'm fine." I try my best to look like that's the end of it.

"Well," Neil says after a long pause, "*weird circumstances* or not... he's still your dad, you know? So. I'm sorry."

"Yeah. Thanks." I swallow down the sudden knot in my throat and watch his blue eyes track around the room before landing back on me. I offer him as much of a smile as I have in me. "Thank you."

The food is okay. Surprisingly okay, actually, though Neil says his Limp Biscuits were a little dry, which makes me gag. We don't talk about Gerald again. Instead, Neil tells me a joke he heard from someone at work about waitresses that's pretty sexist. And then we talk about feminism, and he asks me about bra-burning, and I tell him he's a pig, and he looks like he really just doesn't know anything about feminism, and I feel a little bad for calling him a pig, but not nearly bad enough to say sorry, and then I change the subject. I find out that Neil is a full-time personal trainer, and wants to start specializing in athletic training, that he's just finishing getting his certification so he can pivot toward sports medicine, which I pretend to think is very interesting. Then we talk about how I majored in American Studies, and how I think it shouldn't even be a major because what am I going to do with it? I sure as fuck don't know. Maybe teach kids? Or collect weird shit and hope it becomes culturally relevant and valuable at some point so I can turn my sad hermit's apartment into a museum for hipsters? He laughs at a lot of the things I say, which I like because he has a fantastic smile, and it makes me feel like I'm super hilarious. That part is genuinely pretty great.

He steers the conversation toward last night, asking me why Mel wasn't at the party, and I explain she goes up to her family's cabin for New Year's. Then we go back and forth about people who *were* at the party, none of whom I know better than "oh my god, *hi*, yes, *let's* get coffee some time, *for sure*." But then eventually, he is making sort of sweet eyes at me about how it took him a while to get up the courage to talk to me because I always seem so confident. I study the muscles in his arm as he cuts into his second waffle, and I tell him he doesn't give himself enough credit. Flirting is so much easier than honesty; it's a relief. He shifts his tanned limbs a little closer, and I breathe in the smell of his skin—sort of like the ocean, and sort of like the air outside a Krispy Kreme—and I'm almost lost in it when my mind flashes back to the outline of Dad's profile against Beth's party dress. And all at once, tenderness is the last thing I can stomach. I reopen the gap between us, joking viciously about how this has certainly been one of my more memorable one-night stands, relaxing while he winces at the sting.

Still, when the bill comes, he pays for my lunch, because he says it's sort of the least he can do given the morning that I've had.

"You really didn't have to," I say again, and pray he hasn't somehow confused this morning for a first date.

"So, what are you doing now? Do you want to hang out?" We've pulled up in front of my building, and the car is idling because I guess Neil thought it'd be too presumptuous to park. Again. It would have been.

"It's kind of a weird day, I think." I'm very unclear on why I have to explain this to him. "I'll probably have, you know, stuff to figure out. I should call my mom and… clear my head or something."

"Sure, right. Yeah. Well, um. Maybe I'll call you sometime?" We are having the morning-after talk. Now. So that settles that. It is, in fact, inevitable.

"Yeah, you can call me. Or not call me. Or—I guess, whatever you want."

"Oh. Okay."

"Okay." There is an aching pause where I can't figure out what's happening. I don't dare go back for another look at his sympathetic face. I just need to get out of this car. "So, I guess—thanks for the ride, and you know, everything."

"Sure, of course. I, um—sorry, again. About your dad."

"Oh. Yeah, thank you. Thanks. And, you know, sorry you had to see all that." I'm staring into my lap, twisting my fingers like they'll unscrew from my hands, glancing longingly at the front door of my building.

"No. It's fine. I mean… it's not fine. But I guess I don't mind. Or I guess—what are you gonna do, ya know?"

"Right, well. Okay. I should—Have a nice afternoon, Neil."

He's gearing up to say another pointless thing when I make my escape. It takes too long to find my keys, and I can feel him watching me until I get inside the entryway.

As his car finally disappears over the hill, I force my legs to take me upstairs.

*

May 2002

Dear Diary,

I hate everyone. Mom is mad at me all the time for not even doing anything wrong. I think she's just mad all the time now because Dad isn't here. But GUESS WHAT? So am I!!! It's not even fair for her to be mad at me because it's not like I was the one who went and got a divorce from him! So whatever. It's not my fault if she's lonely now. And I don't even know how anyone in the whole world could be more lonelier than me. Dad said he was gonna call today after school, but I waited the whole day and even at night, and he never called.

I checked the messages three times too in case somehow I was maybe busy or something, but I think he just didn't call me. I really wish he would have because I saved a really funny story to tell him from school, and I practiced telling it on my way home so it would be extra funny. He says he's gonna get a phone number soon so I can call him too sometimes, but Mom said she doesn't think so. I know he isn't the best at doing promises. Mom says that a lot. I can get really mad at him when he's like that too, or just other times he can make me really mad sometimes. Like when he gets really mean and stuff. But still, he's still my dad, and also he's my favorite friend I even have. I just really miss him today, and I wish he was here so we could talk about everything like always. I'm gonna practice my story again before I go to sleep, so I don't forget the best parts for the next time I see him. I know he's gonna laugh so much. When I think about that, I feel happier a little bit. Thanks, diary.

Love, Mackenzie

*

It's not fair for death to happen first thing in the morning when there's still a whole day left that you have to keep doing. The apartment is eerily quiet and, no matter how many times I rewind it, nothing about today makes more sense.

"Love Train" starts playing again. It has been either thirteen hours or one hundred years since I purchased that ringtone. I promise myself I'm going to delete it.

It's Harborview. They tell me that they've declared my father and sent him for an autopsy. This can take anywhere from three to five days they say, maybe longer because of the holiday. It seems there's something of a backlog. Unless I need them to rush it, they say, as though it's like shipping something via Amazon. After the autopsy is done, I am welcome to stop by and retrieve the death certificate and arrange next steps for the remains. "Excellent," I say, and like everything else, it is wrong.

I sit down on the edge of my bed. I should make a to-do list. I need to wash my sheets and do some dishes from last night, and then I need to call Mom. These are the only things on the list, so I don't write it down.

Staring at my feet, I spread my toes wide on the rug, and then scrunch the tall pile between them. I could paint my toenails. That might be a nice thing. I add it to my list. Maybe I'll shower first, and then I could soak my feet for a while before I paint my nails. Or I could go to a salon and pay someone else to paint them. I should put the laundry in before I do that. But I don't want to be running the washing machine and the shower at the same time, there won't be enough hot water. So maybe I should take a shower before I put the laundry in before I go to the salon.

An hour goes by like this.

The thing is that if I start doing the things on my list, then, eventually, I'll have to call my mom, and I don't think I can. I should have made Beth call her. Or Al. Even Neil.

Despite living in the same city since I graduated, she and I barely talk as it is, and I already know I'll be so bad at this. I don't know how to tell someone their ex-husband is dead. It isn't fair that even the people we hate leave space behind when they die. But this doesn't change anything. I can't not call just because I don't know what to say.

Jesus Christ. I have to get up.

Flex. Scrunch.

Flex.

Scrunch.

Flex.

My foot starts to cramp. At first, I think it's not so bad, and then it's immediately the worst pain I've ever felt. Not just in my foot, but up through my whole body. I fall back onto my bed, screaming at the top of my lungs. I clutch my foot in my hand, kneading it until my fingers get cramped and achy too. A shiver crawls up my spine, into my neck. Everything goes cold, tense, and crackling; every inch of my body twinges. I roll, desperate, onto my stomach and scream into my comforter. I can't breathe. Clawing at the sheets, I lift my face. My throat feels like someone is standing on it, and I grab at my ribs, trying to pull them apart to make room for air with my hands. The room sprawls huge, with my bed a tiny lifeboat adrift in the middle, and me a fish flopping around on the deck, gasping and writhing into oblivion. I choke out another scream of pain, but my voice breaks off. I feel so miserably alive, with all this fresh-bloomed blood in my heart that works. Each sting thrums through me, hissing *you're still here, you're still here, you're still here.*

Finally, the dam bursts, and the loud kind of crying comes. The kind I'd despised in Beth this morning. The kind I haven't fallen into for years. Everything is stillness, except me and my terrible heart, melting, falling, and flailing. Desolate.

It was a Sunday morning during my senior year of high school when Gerald moved into the Homeaway Inn Express.

A couple weeks before, he had shown up at Mom's house with a busted lip, four more missing teeth, and a face full of bruises, including two grisly black eyes—jumped in a park up the street by some white supremacist dickheads. His shoulder was clearly dislocated, and so Mom took him to the ER where he also got four stitches over his left eye and was told they'd cracked a few ribs. My parents were gone for the rest of the night: hospital waiting room, hospital bed, and then just driving around the city in Mom's truck, arguing about what to do next—what to tell me.

When they came home the next morning, it was 10:46 AM, and Gerald walked right past me without saying a word. Mom said that he would be staying with us until she could find somewhere else to put him. That was the way she said it: finding a place to put him. Like he was an ugly piece of art that she was obligated to keep because it had some intangible sentimental value—to *me*. He never lived anywhere consistent after their divorce. Always crashing here and there with "friends," or mysteriously out of town for weeks, before reappearing with a new girlfriend, none of whom stuck around long. For a little while, he lived in an abandoned RV that someone gave him when the engine died. But it got towed when I was sixteen, and he couldn't afford the impound fees, let alone the repairs. I think, in truth, Mom would have preferred to put him right back in the park he'd come from, but she couldn't bring herself to do that while I was still walking around her house with his face. So, nine years after she'd kicked him out, she put him in her basement.

The two weeks that followed were unbearable. Gerald was in a rage most of the time, and the whole house started to smell like him, seeping in from the bottom up. There was dirt, tobacco, and canned food spilled everywhere. He lurked around every corner, waiting to guilt trip me for not spending more time with him. Using his grisly appearance to threaten that he never knew how much time he had left. Mom would make faces that said, *he's only here because of you*, refusing to even acknowledge him in conversation. After the first few days, I stopped coming home after school, opting instead to go to friend's houses, house parties, coffeehouses, anywhere until it was late enough that I could go straight to bed.

Mom never told me exactly how she'd managed to get him a room at the Homeaway Inn Express, or how she afforded it, and I've never gotten up the courage to ask.

He was only supposed to stay there for as long as it would take his ribs to heal. A month maybe, at the most. "Just until he can keep himself safe," Mom had said to me through gritted teeth that Sunday morning, as I unpacked his things into the hotel drawers. "He's not supposed to be my responsibility anymore, you know," she added, and I just said, "thank you."

The deal was supposed to be that he would go in and out of the service entrance, and up and down the back stairs that let out at the end of the hall on the third floor next to his room. He was not to attract any attention to himself or to cause any disturbance of any kind for any reason. Business at the hotel was typically slow enough that they could avoid booking other guests in the adjacent rooms; much of the time, he had the hall to himself.

But, before long, Gerald charmed them, the way he could charm anyone, assuming he felt like it. He befriended the staff, got into the good graces of the management, shared the occasional cigarette with the janitors, had a beer with the security guards. And so, the first month went by, and then another and another. The hotel bills got smaller, and then stopped coming at all, but still, he stayed at the end of the hall on the third floor. I doubt they'll ever be able to rent out the room again after the way Gerald lived in it; maybe he could've stayed forever.

In the first three years he was there, I would sometimes go downtown to visit him. He liked having a place that was his, where everything could happen on his terms, in his territory. And sometimes, we would sit outside on the hotel roof deck and laugh like we used to when I was a little girl.

But being in that room was awful. It was perpetually full of smoke, reeking of booze, entirely saturated with the worst of him. The kitchenette was stained with residue from microwave meals that sat on the counter unfinished. Nowhere felt clean to sit, nothing was comfortable. And Gerald was always getting worse. He was drinking more than ever, no longer worried about where he was going to sleep. He grew excruciatingly reckless, always in fights in the middle of 3rd Avenue, trying any and every drug that was offered to him by any random acquaintance he happened to make. He was lonely, sad because his body was finally succumbing to the torture he'd put it through, but too angry to let anyone get near him or help. It wasn't long before the calls started pouring in: *Can you come get Gerald Adams from the station? Can you help Gerald Adams back to the hotel from the free clinic? Gerald has broken a leg, an arm, his collarbone, will you come? Hello, is this Gerald's daughter? I'm afraid we have some bad news.*

And he would call too: *Mac, I need a favor. Ms. Mac, can you help me out? Mac, you know I wouldn't ask you if I didn't have to—but, baby girl, do you have twenty dollars? Fifty dollars? Just a hundred dollars? I owe a friend some money. I need to eat. I just need to buy some cigarettes. It's none of your business what I need it for, are you gonna help me out or not? Are you my daughter or not?*

The fourth year he was there, I only visited a couple times. Once for his birthday and once around Christmas.

The fifth year I only went once.

And, in what turned out to be the last year and a half of his life, I didn't go at all.

I still haven't called Mom, and it's almost eight o'clock. It only took until late afternoon to cry myself dry. I've spent the evening staring at the ceiling, mustering my courage. My cheek plastered to my pillow; my face veined with desiccated rivers of salt.

She might not even care. I barely remember the last time she said his name.

I strike a deal with myself that if I get this call out of the way, I can make Kraft mac and cheese for dinner as a reward. Now is the best time to eat it because Mel is out of town and not home to glare at me while threatening to read the ingredients list aloud.

So, I dial.

"Sweetie! What a nice surprise!" She sounds like she always does, like a network TV mom. Like she's doing an impression of a mom instead of just being one. "You know, I was *hoping* you would call today." She wasn't. "Happy New Year! I was just thinking about you." She wasn't. "Tell me you did something fun last night! I was saying to Jimmy this morning that I hoped Mackenzie was having just a lot of fun for New Year's Eve. Oh, tell me you were. Did you have a New Year's kiss?"

"Oh, well, you know. Dad died." I breathe out and brace for impact.

She doesn't say anything, and I wait. I should have gone to the salon. I should have made conversation first. I should have said "passed away" or "left us" or one of those saccharine euphemisms people say to make it feel less like a dead person died. I shouldn't have called. I should have texted. I should've written a letter. *Mackenzie.* I should have done this in person.

I think I should be crying again, but my body disagrees.

"I'm sorry, sweetheart, what… what'd you say? I think your phone is breaking up."

Another chance. "Um, I said, Dad died." Wasted on me. She doesn't respond again, and I think maybe my phone really is breaking up, but now I can't stop saying it, "Gerald? My dad? He died this morning. Or, I guess he was found dead this morning—I think he died last night, or, no, I guess early this morning, technically. He died. Mom, can you hear me?"

"Oh god, I can hear you. I hear you! Just stop it. Stop. My god. My *god*! What do you mean he *died*?"

"He… I didn't know how to tell you."

"So, you decided on *over the phone*, Mackenzie? Oh my *god*. What were you thinking? I need to sit down."

In the background, I hear my stepdad, Jimmy. "Amor mio, ¿que paso?" he coos, and she whimpers, "It's Gerald."

His name sounds like another language in her mouth. "I'm sorry, Mom."

"How did this happen? I mean, where—how did this happen? He was looking so well the last time I saw him." As if she'd seen him recently. And why does everyone insist on how well he looked? It's a load of shit that he looked well.

But then I get another flash of him naked in Beth's stringy arms. And, even though I'm talking to the one other person in the whole world who I know has seen him at his absolute worst, I can't tell her what I saw.

"A heart attack. They think. They think it was a heart attack. But the autopsy won't be done for another week or something, and then I guess we'll know for sure."

"A *week*?"

"Well, there's a delay sort of. Because of the holiday." I hate this.

"Good lord… *Good lord!*" She's starting to cry, and I hold the phone away from my ear and squeeze my eyes shut. I tuck my chin to my chest and whisper, "I'm sorry" over and over. To Mom, but more to myself. When I bring the phone back to my ear, it's Jimmy's voice.

"Mackie? Mackie, you still there?"

"Yeah, hi, I'm here. Sorry, Jimmy."

"Your mother needs a minute." He lets out a sigh. I hadn't thought about what this would be like for Jimmy. He's so kind it's embarrassing.

"I'm sorry to do this to you," I hear myself say.

"You lost your father today, Mackie. There's no good way to do it. *I'm* sorry." I'm tired of thanking people for being sorry, so I just don't say anything else, and neither does he. We both just sort of breathe into the phone at each other until eventually, he says, "Do you want to come over?" And I say, no thanks, and then I don't think

Nicky Davis

so, and then no. And he says, "Well maybe we should talk another time then," and I agree that that'd probably be best.

"I'm going to make macaroni," I say like it fixes anything.

"That's a nice dinner."

"Will you tell Mom that I'll call again later?"

"Listen, maybe we should all have dinner sometime this week." I can't imagine seeing either of them. Seeing the look on Mom's face like somehow this is my fault too. But Jimmy sounds so hopeful.

"Yeah. Sure. Maybe… Just tell her I'll call. Goodnight, Jimmy."

I unfurl my limbs and put an entire stick of butter in my mac and cheese.

*

Dear Alice,

My husband of fifteen years is an alcoholic.

God. It feels good to be admitting that, finally, even in an anonymous letter.

When we first met, he was an entirely different person than the man I know now. We confided in each other about everything. I told him how I had tried to make it as a starving artist, and how burned out I was, and he understood. He knew how to make everything into a celebration. He was always laughing, always stopping to appreciate the sky, or a flower, or a butterfly. He made my life feel joyful again, like he turned the lights on for me. Eventually, we rented a home together in a friendly, quiet neighborhood, and when he proposed, I truly believed that we would spend our lives celebrating together every day.

But over time, he's started to drift away. He's always been a social drinker, sometimes to excess, but it's become a daily occurrence. He drinks to celebrate, and he drinks to escape. He's defensive when I bring it up, tells me he can take care of himself. But something in him has darkened. His happiness has gotten so brittle that it rarely lasts a whole day. I don't know how it happened or why. He won't even say that anything's wrong. I used to think we were a team, but we always seem to be on opposite sides now.

He left his job to stay at home when our daughter was born, but she's in second grade now, and he's still not working. He's tried to find something, but the interviews never go anywhere, and then he's drunk again by the time I get home. I'm drowning, Alice. The liquor store bills are more than we can afford after we've paid the rent and bought our other groceries for the week. I'm cutting costs where I can, but our little girl is growing, and she needs more every day. I'd hoped with her in school it would lighten the load for him, but he only gets further away.

My friends say it's long past time to cut and run—and I'll admit that I've thought about it often. All the signs are there. How can I stay with this man who I barely even recognize anymore? How can I trust this person he's becoming around our daughter? She's only seven years old, and I know she loves him so much. She's never known him any other way, and he adores her. He's almost his old self with *her some days, and she doesn't deserve to lose that. But then I worry that those days are running out... they certainly get harder to find... and I don't think I can bear to live with what's left.*

Please help, Alice. I need guidance. Am I a terrible mother if I kick him out just because he makes life so hard for me?

- Mom In Need Of Relief

*

Dear MINOR,

I hear the pain in your letter, and it weighs heavily on all of us here in the Dear Alice offices. I have spoken to many colleagues about your problem, lauding you for your courage and strength. You are the mother that so many of us would have loved to have had—a true mother.

I want to begin by telling you how proud of you I am—we *all* are—for making the early steps toward a brighter tomorrow in admitting the first of many hard truths: your husband is an alcoholic. And from the sounds of it, you are coming to terms with the second truth here: that he is beyond your help. The joy he has lost within himself can only be his to find again, and it sounds like he is looking in all the wrong places. That fight cannot be yours.

For all of us, there can be no true happiness without struggle. I can feel that you are in the midst of your struggle now.

My advice is not going to be all that different than that which you've already received: it is time to GO. And to go far. Now, if not sooner than now.

Your daughter does deserve a father, one who loves her unconditionally, but she should not be forced to grow up alongside his unraveling, waiting and hoping for his return. Whether she sees it now or not, you both must move forward.

I imagine you are a frequent reader of my column, and so you must know that I am a firm believer in second chances. But there are times when a line must be drawn. This, MINOR, is one of those times.

Break ties. Break free. Run into a sunset of your own creation. There is only one direction left to go: away from your husband. I suggest you start now.

With love and hope for you,
Alice

PS. Expect a follow-up e-mail from my staff about obtaining your home address. We, here at the Dear Alice offices, want to send you a complimentary, signed copy of my newest book: *ME FIRST! Taking the SELFish Steps Toward Your Destiny*

*

<u>**January 2ⁿᵈ**</u>

Sunshine tumbles through the windows onto my bed, spilling to the floor and softening the edges of everything. I feel an almost unwelcome sense of peace this morning. As though, maybe, yesterday doesn't actually have to change anything.

Except for one glitch: my phone has been ringing incessantly since eight o'clock.

I put it on silent after the first couple times. But it's almost eleven now.

And every time it's Mom. Over and over again. I feel confident this is more times than she's called in my entire life before now.

I send her to voicemail another six times before I figure I'm going to have to pick it up. She refuses to leave a message or just send a text like I wish she would.

"*Sweetie*," she says, though the whoosh of relief in her voice gentles it. "Oh, sweetie, I feel just terrible for how our conversation ended yesterday. I really do. But you have to understand that you caught me by surprise. I'm sure you were surprised too. Because it is a surprise, isn't it? In its own way. The whole mess is just so awful. It seems so awful I can hardly even wrap my mind around it, even this morning after a very long sleep. It seems somehow even more awful today. How are you this morning? Did you manage to sleep at all?" She breaks for air.

I don't tell her about the peace she interrupted. "I slept, yeah."

"Did I wake you up? I didn't want to wake you up, and I was worried I might. Did I? Well I guess it's almost eleven, so it's time to get up anyway, but still, if you had trouble sleeping last night—"

"It's fine, Mom. I slept. But now it's good to be awake. Miraculous. Everybody wins."

"*Mackenzie*," she scolds. Among our many unshared traits is a sense of humor.

"I see I missed some calls."

She gusts a sigh. "Well, I've already sent several emails to Aunt Alice." Any remnants of peace evaporate. Shit. How had I not thought of Alice? "I've explained to her what's happened. She says there's no rush for you to come back to work if you need to take some time. Which we assume you will do. We've agreed it's so essential for all of us to honor our grief right now."

"*All of us*," I repeat, but she doesn't seem to agree that this requires explanation.

I was eight when Gerald moved out. The day she told me they were getting divorced, was a rare occasion when she was the one to pick me up from school, and when we got home, he had already disappeared from our house. I don't remember him packing anything or saying goodbye. Just that one day he was there, and the next day he wasn't. Like a cruel magic trick.

Maybe Mom and I should've bonded together then, with just the two of us left in the house, but we very much didn't. Instead, she got very involved in the Self-Help community. She started papering the walls with affirmations and saying things like, "every person, in any relationship, needs to be in charge of their own future." In third grade, I didn't know for sure what that meant, but I tried my best.

It was around the same time that she met self-made Agony Aunt and self-love guru, Alice. Recently relocated to the Pacific Northwest from Texas, the Dear Alice offices opened in the nearby Bellevue suburbs, where Alice lives in a sprawling McMansion with her third husband, Walter. Once my parents' divorce was final, it was Alice who encouraged Mom to set off on what one of her books had termed the "necessarily selfish journey toward starting over"; it was Alice who promised to step in and do the "left behind work" of looking after me.

I became a latchkey kid with a mom in more social clubs than an eager college freshman. During school breaks, I was carted along on Alice's book tours, to conferences and workshops, to signings and speaking engagements. Meanwhile, Mom re-invented herself at open mics, pottery painting intensives, and adult ballroom dance competitions. By high school, I knew the Dear Alice offices like another home. And when, after college, Alice offered me a job as her executive assistant, there wasn't much I was better equipped to do.

But never, in what Mel and I call The Age of Alice, did either of them speak to me about Gerald if it could be avoided. And, for the most part, they found it could be avoided.

It hadn't occurred to me that their policy might change when he died.

"You didn't have to e-mail her, Mom. I could've done that. I would have."

"Oh, Sweetie, don't worry. I'm more concerned about your well-being than I am with who sends an e-mail to Alice. You know, I'm always happy to take care of you." This is new. "And, besides, I was e-mailing her anyway to thank her for the gorgeous afghan she sent for Christmas." *Oh.* "It was so thoughtful, and I am so dreadfully behind on my gratitude greetings." ("Gratitude Greetings" is an Alice-ism, because "'*Thank-you-cards*' has no *pizazz*.")

"Okay, well, thanks, I guess… but Alice is supposed to be at that digital detox retreat in San Antonio until next Wednesday. Things should be pretty quiet."

"No, no, no, no. Uncle Walter changed her travel plans last minute because he has an important meeting with the Gates Foundation! *So* exciting, that. Do you know that Alice might actually go to the Gates' private estate for dinner? I think that's just so exciting. She's exactly the kind of mind that Bill and Melinda need to be spending more time with. The kinds of projects they could work on together! Oh, sweetie, I think this could lead to so many opportunities for you. You should use that Banana Republic gift card I gave you and get yourself something suitable for these kinds of big meetings. Dress for the job you want, you know. Anyway, Alice got back to Seattle late last night."

"Oh." I open my laptop and see a forwarded message from Alice with her new itinerary and another with the subject line: 5 TIPS FOR BECOMING A MOURNING PERSON, which I delete without opening. "I hadn't checked my email."

"No, you wouldn't have, I suppose."

There's a silence, where I think she's remembering what *all of us* are meant to be honoring right now. When she starts in again, her voice is far more solemn.

"I've invited them for dinner tonight."

"That'll be nice for you," I say, and mean it. It comforts me to think Mom will have Alice to tell her what she's meant to feel about this. I certainly have no idea.

"Well, when Jimmy said you were coming over tonight, I thought it'd be nice to have your Aunt Alice there too."

I remember too late that Jimmy can't be trusted to relay a message. You say "maybe" to "next week sometime," and he hears "count me in" for "tomorrow night." Fuck.

"And!" she says, perking all the way up, "Your step-brother Nathan is free as well. So, we can all be together, which I think is just what the doctor ordered, don't you think? At a time like this, it's best to be surrounded by family. That's what Alice said, and I completely agree. Nathan is bringing his new girlfriend, Lana. So that will be a nice distraction, meeting her. Jimmy says she's beautiful, and she works with orphans, which really is God's work. I mean, how often do you meet a woman who works with orphans and isn't a nun? You just don't, Mackenzie. Not in this day and age, you just don't. Nathan is one lucky man. Anyway, I think that'll be nice. And do you want to bring anyone? I didn't hear about a boyfriend at Christmas, so I assumed it would just be you, but I know sometimes you like to keep these types of things under wraps, though for the life of me, I can't think why. I suppose that's another of your choices for me to accept.

Acceptance is a long road, you know. But is there? Someone you'd like to bring, I mean?"

"No, it's just me. But Mom, I—"

"Well, you know what? That's perfectly all right as well. That's perfectly all right. Just you will be more than enough. I've decided I'm going to make those spareribs the way your—" in an instant, her voice goes all static and whispery, "the way your father always liked to have them." I swallow my mouth dry. Nope. No, thank you. I do not want to do this at all.

"Wow, Mom, that's—"

"I mean, I think that's a nice gesture, don't you think so? Alice said she thought it was a lovely gesture. I just hope that Lana isn't a vegetarian because I don't know what to do with a vegetarian. Everyone's a vegetarian now, and I can make a salad, but I'm afraid that the buck stops there, as they say. But I'll go ahead and make a salad, and we can just all keep our fingers crossed that she's an omnivore like the rest of us."

"Well. Fingers crossed."

We get off the phone after she asks me a few times if I'm hanging in there, and I lie that I am going to be fine. To stop myself blowing away, I get in the shower.

When I get out, I have a missed call and a text from Mel that she's in the car, coming home a day early, and that she can't believe she had to hear from Neil about what happened.

I text back that admittedly I don't remember everything about last night, but she was right about him being cute.

Mel replies: *Not about the sex. About your dad. Don't be dense, please.*

The dread of dinner tonight is looming heavily, and the apartment is running out of air, so I resolve to take myself on a walk. This city has too many hills, but anything sounds better than suffocating into a Pyrex bowl of stale mac and cheese leftovers.

The world is oppressively technicolor outside. A beautiful January day, the sun has everything lit up cold and gleaming, which means everyone in Seattle is standing around looking dazedly happy and unsure of what to do with themselves. Fifty degrees is practically a day at the beach for these people, and they're always saying things like, "it was so warm today; I didn't even wear my fleece to the co-op!" I grew up here, so technically, I'm one of them, but I've never felt much like a true Seattleite. I like clothes that fit, I like junk food, I'm more of a cat person, and I've never been a fan of bikes, hiking *or* kayaking. Beyond heretical.

Gerald would always tell me I was a misplaced New Yorker at heart. The same way he thought of himself. He spent most of his early adulthood in Brooklyn. It was clear to anybody, after talking to him for just a few seconds, that even though he'd been born in the Midwest, he'd scavenged his personality from the boroughs.

When I was a kid, we used to walk all over Seattle together. The only Black skin in our yuppie Scandinavian neighborhood, we'd poke fun at the people here and invent stories about them, most of which included multiple trips to the farmers' market and extensive visits to the herbalist.

The sun presses into my cheeks. I remember his face, grinning a warm "good afternoon" at everyone we passed like we weren't doubled over laughing behind their backs at their yard sale Birkenstocks and their "Mothered by Nature" bumper stickers.

Walking past a woman on rollerblades pushing a terrier in a stroller, I nearly take my phone out to call him when the memory of his laugh rumbles under my skin on a breeze. *And for my next trick, Imma disappear.*

I'm just coaxing air back into my lungs, passing the third coffeehouse that has opened their outdoor seating area on account of the "tremendously beautiful weather," when I hear my name and lose my breath all over again.

"Mackenzie *fucking* Adams! Hot *damn*, gorgeous. Happy New Year!"

I turn, hoping somehow it won't be who I already know it is. Rakishly handsome, uncomfortably wealthy, sharp-jawed, heavy-eyebrowed—I'm met by the face responsible for my aversion to pretty faces. Kevin Hudson Wasserman is hopping over the rail of a café patio and near galloping at me.

"Kev. *Hi*—" I eke out before he's on top of me.

"You," he says after holding me too tight for too long, "are only getting more beautiful, is that legal?" He pulls back a bit, my shoulders still locked in his grip as he drinks me in.

"Oh, well, you know. I do what I can," I say, and have no idea what I mean. I pat him on the arm a few times until he lets go.

Getting my bearings again, I get a good look at him for the first time since graduation. Kevin is wearing what looks to be an Orange Crush muscle tee, a denim jacket, and khaki cargo shorts because, evidently, he is still fond of making mistakes. It's exhausting that he doesn't look as absurd in this outfit as he should. Nothing about him has changed, I think, sizing him up quickly. Still only a few inches taller than me, he comes in at probably five foot eleven, though he'd swear on his life it's an even six feet. Still lean, he's muscled in a way that suggests he plays sports, though, in the time I've known him, the closest he's come is seducing the captain of the squash team. He's got one of those faces that makes you want to say yes: megawatt smile with one excruciating dimple on the left side, brown hair that's somehow always perfectly mussed, eyes this bright chestnut color that's almost auburn in the sunlight. He looks like a mischievous prince in a Renaissance painting, all porcelain angles and charm. Disproportionately good-looking. And, true to form, he is leering at me in a way that thins my blood.

"Fucking, *Mack*," he says, stretching the "a" with a laugh and pulling a hand through his hair. He does that thing where he looks at the ground and then flashes his eyes up at me, and I immediately look anywhere else. I can feel him assessing me, surveying the changes that have crept in over the years since we were friends. Then, after what feels like the longest silence in history, he punches me in the shoulder and laughs a big broad laugh. It hurts more than I think he intended (the punch and the laugh, both), but I sort of laugh too, nothing left but raw nerves in my chest at this point.

I met Kevin my first year of college. We hit it off pretty quickly, at least in part because of his face. He's a mistake most girls (and several guys) I knew made at least once while we were in school. Some a few times after.

"So. What are you doing in Seattle?"

"Shit, you know. The uzh." I grin through a shudder, remembering how much I hate that he insists on that abbreviation. "Seeing some things, doing some people." He smirks to himself, shaking his head as his hand flies to his neck. He kneads into it like if he told me everything he's been up to, I wouldn't believe him, and his eyes flicker smugly across my face. I cock my head to the side.

"Sounds gross," I snark, and he laughs again.

"God, it's fucking good to see you. You really do look great."

"So you've said." He's full of shit, but that's not news.

"More freckles… they suit you." His cheekbone tugs his dimple into place, and I do my best to ignore it. "So… what's up? How *are* you? Were you in the 206 for New Year's? How come we didn't party?"

Kevin has all the appeal of fast food. Looks great in pictures, smells even better, and sounds like a very, *very* good idea when you're drunk. He's not the healthy choice, but he's the easy one. I, naively, fell in love with him and proposed to go full *Supersize Me* our senior year, somehow convinced I could survive on Kevin alone. As it turned out, he was less into that idea than I'd hoped.

"I didn't do anything really, just stayed in with a few people," I lie.

"Boring. I've never known Mack Adams to be so boring."

"Well, you know. It's actually been working out pretty okay for me…"

"So, fuck it, what are you doing tonight? Boring shit? Let's grab a drink. My treat." Kevin loves to say "my treat" because his dad is the billionaire bachelor in charge of a massive VC firm in San Francisco who throws money at his playboy bachelor son in lieu of any real parenting. In the years that he and I were friends, I watched him say "my treat" to practically anyone who dared to so much as breathe near him. I would say it worked about 98% of the time, and the 2% of the time it didn't, it was either because they were discovered to be too drunk to need the treat, or they were a happily married professor.

"I can't. I have a thing tonight, actually," and I'm relieved it's the truth. I take back everything I said about Jimmy. Jimmy is a saint.

"What thing? Sounds boring."

"It's a family thing. My... my mom's doing a big dinner thing with Alice... and even my brother's going so—" as soon as I say it, I realize I shouldn't have. Thanksgiving of senior fall, Kevin came home with me and met my whole... everyone. They lapped him up. Particularly my mom, who didn't stop making googly-eyes at him the whole trip. Alice still asks about him. Even Nathan seemed amused by him, which staggered me. Nathan, bless him, barely likes anything.

"A dinner thing at your mom's? Why didn't you say that first? You know I can't resist that woman."

"Why are you like this?"

He bites his lip and leans in to bump my shoulder with his. I sway toward him without meaning to and regret it.

"Kevin. It's just—Tonight's not really a good time." I know if I just tell him about Gerald, he'll back off, but every time I start to say it, my throat closes up. It's an intimacy he doesn't have any right to, and I don't want to talk about it anyway.

"Come on, Adams. You're happy to see me, aren't you?" He pouts, folding his hands under his chin.

"Not particularly." He doesn't need my validation, but my voice doesn't quite sell the dig.

"Liar. Give me one good reason why I can't crash this dinner."

Because my dad's dead.

Because you said the word "uzh" instead of "usual."

Because you're gross.

Because you broke my heart.

Because you're wearing cargo shorts.

Because I hate you.

"I'd have to clear it with my mom. I don't know if there'll be enough—"

"*Rations*, Mack? Really? That's your angle?" He's a dog with a bone now. "Call her."

I don't like how many times Mom and I have talked on the phone in the last twelve hours. She is, as I should have guessed, *thrilled* about Kevin. She won't stop going on about what a "darling boy" he is and how she "always knew we would work things out." I try to hint that I don't particularly want him to come, but she's completely absorbed in how incredible "the universe" is to create beautiful opportunities like this and how having Kevin at dinner will help take the pressure off everyone in "our time of grief."

If I could wake up from this, I swear to God I would never sleep again.

"So that's a yes then," he teases as I put my phone back in my pocket.

"I… yeah. I guess it is."

He says he'll pick me up at 5:45 for dinner, and kisses me on the cheek ("Seriously, these freckles are *good*, and the short hair? It's *working*, Mack.") before laughing like a giddy schoolboy and hopping back from whence he came, yelling, "Mack Daddy Adams! Can you fucking believe it, Seattle? I can't fucking believe it."

On my way back to the apartment, I text Mel: *Declaring a state of emergency. Kevin sighting IN SEATTLE.*

It's less than a minute before she texts back: *NO. What?? EW. Have broken out in hives upon hearing his name.*

I like to pretend I don't know how it happened, but the truth is falling in love with Kevin was easy—made easier by how special it felt to be his friend. By the end of our freshman year, most everyone had either slept with him or had a best friend who had and hadn't been the same since. But with friendships, he was surprisingly more discerning.

We met for the first time in the back of a cheap Thai restaurant that, as a freshman, felt light-years away from campus, though it was really only a couple miles into town. Ten-thirty on a Thursday night, determined to be cool, I slid in at the table beside my roommate Ella's older brother, a senior lightweight crew jock named Josh, and his teammate Damon. They'd been Kevin's hosts when he was a pre-frosh and had taken a shine to him. Even just a couple weeks into the semester, I'd already heard rumors about Kevin Wasserman and what people nicknamed "spending the night on the Hudson." Not the least of which I'd heard from Ella, who took the open chair next to him across the table from me, making big swan eyes, and stealing bites off his plate. Kevin was leaned on the back two legs of his plastic chair, arms stretched overhead, against the greasy mirrored restaurant wall, his t-shirt sliding up to reveal the indent of a hip bone and a hint of soft dark hair on the flat of his stomach. He was generous enough to entertain Ella, offering her a few witty comebacks that she held between her teeth in a smug smile. But to anyone paying attention, Kevin had his wiles focused intently on Damon, undoubtedly sensing in him a sweaty curiosity reserved for late nights in divey restaurants that the rest of campus ignored. The further back Kevin leaned, the more Damon pulled forward. I thought he might put his elbows right into his Pad Thai, trying to crawl over the table into Kevin's lap. My face warmed in a vicarious flush watching Kevin run his tongue under his teeth, a wolfish grin of victory spreading over his face as he reeled Damon closer. When out of nowhere, his eyes snapped to mine, I startled, having forgotten in the thickness of the air and banter that he could see me staring.

"So, what's *your* deal, Adams?" he said, flashing me his dimple and bringing his chair back onto all four legs with a jolt.

"Nothing," I sputtered, unable to peel my eyes off him. I could feel Ella shooting daggers in my direction, and I wasn't interested in turning her against me this early by stealing too much of his attention. "You just put on a hell of a show is all. Lives up to the hype."

He brought the back of a hand under his chin and tilted his head in an imitation of cherubic innocence that looked utterly obscene on him. Ella practically swooned. I could've sworn I heard Damon's blood surge next to me. Then Kevin huffed a laugh and went right back to leaning his chair.

We didn't talk again until a week later when I ran into him looking satisfyingly disheveled and leaving our room as I was coming back from lecture. He asked if I was in the middle of anything, and could I maybe get coffee. I said I wasn't, and I could.

"So… you and Ella, then," I said, watching him rebutton his shirt as we made our way down the hall, not sure how to talk to him.

"For about half an hour this afternoon, yeah," he replied with a wink, and the stark honesty of it made me laugh.

"So… *not* Damon?" I asked.

He turned and raised an eyebrow at me, pushing backward through the door out onto the quad. "Oh. Yes, Damon. Nearly four hours on Monday, bless him."

I thought he was so insatiable that he might try something, but we actually just went for coffee. His treat. He talked less than I expected, and I talked more, though he listened with his whole face, so it didn't feel uneven.

I quickly learned that the effortless charisma he turned on at parties, which seemed to lay him wide open to everyone, was nothing more than a sugar trap. Genuinely being close to him was different. He was like velvet, the way I sometimes thought I could see the prints of everyone who'd ever touched him, and the way they were just as easily smoothed away. The way his softness was a luxury. He'd get far away sometimes when asked too many genuine questions about himself, pulling at his cuticles with his teeth. Answering in long pauses and sometimes just putting on music instead of bothering with words at all. When he did share, it was only ever on his terms, so I learned about him through fully loaded, carefully curated sentences, and over time I managed to fill in the gaps. His mom left when he was still in diapers. "Decided she wasn't much interested in being a parent after all," he said once coolly. His dad's first children would always be his investments, and it wasn't clear whether he'd ever honestly wanted real kids. Kevin had been left to his own devices and a revolving door of nannies. He got too smart early, learned how to persuade so well with charm that by the time his face grew into itself he hardly needed it.

From the way Kevin talked about him, and mostly didn't, I guessed his dad was probably less than thrilled about his son's bisexuality. But, since they were rarely in the same city, let alone the same house, he likely took the same tact he'd taken with most things about his son: pretending it wasn't there. If that was true, Kevin never let on that it bothered him. His easy confidence was part of what made him so addictive. The only time he flagged was when it made waves with people on campus. "I've never had anyone panic as much as the straight girls," he told me lazily one Sunday. "Last week, I was out with this girl, and when she found out I was bi, I swear she turned green. Couldn't finish her lunch. No one thinks they have an ideal of what a 'real man' is until all the sudden they really do, I guess. Fucking shame."

Kevin was the first person I talked to about Gerald that didn't look at me differently after he knew. He never advised me to cut him out of my life, but never applauded me for staying either. He'd just listen until I wore myself out rehashing the latest episode, and then like a breeze passing through the room, he'd say, "And now it's now. And you're still here," the red-brown in his eyes blazing warmth into his whole face. Sometimes it made me feel better, and sometimes it didn't. But it never failed to be exactly the right thing to say. For that, more than anything, I adored him.

By the end of freshman year, we ate all our meals together when our schedules allowed it, studied together, joined the same clubs, and quit the same clubs. We went to all the same parties, me, drunkenly dancing my face off until I couldn't stand, and Kevin taking home anything with teeth. We were magnets that each kept the other from spinning too far away.

"Why aren't they all like you, Mack?" he asked me once over lunch.

"Like what?"

He frowned. "Don't pretend not to know how you are, Adams. It's boring."

But we never so much as kissed. I might have taken that as a sign if everything else about us hadn't been so convincing. In my mind, it was all playing out like a very coy and subdued Austen love affair. *It's so obvious why we haven't kissed,* I told myself. *Because with us it won't be cheap or meaningless. It just has to be the right moment. Not until we know that we're ready for each other.*

It didn't play out that way. It never does when you decide to be in love with someone who doesn't do that. We were standing outside the library, the week before our last collegiate winter break, and he was teasing me for getting excited that they were finally putting the lights up around campus.

"You can't honestly tell me you don't think things are just a little more magical at Christmas time," I was saying. There were a few leafless trees in the plaza that were all wrapped in white lights. Their glow was shining off the little frosty patches on the concrete. The sky was clear, and there was just a sliver of a moon hanging above the roof of the admissions building across the street. It was so late that campus was pretty much dead, and we were the only people reckless enough to stand around outside in the freezing cold.

"Why?" He laughed. "Because there are twinkly lights everywhere?"

"Because, *because*. Look around!" I turned, gesturing grandly at the few spindly trees in front of us.

He put his arm around my shoulder and kissed the side of my head. "You, Mack, are too goddamn precious." My whole body went tingly. I gazed at him as he shook his head, laughing.

It felt like I was outside my body, floating somewhere above, watching us breathe out little puffs of air into the night. This was my moment. It had to be.

"Kevin," I started, unrehearsed though I'd imagined it a million times, "do you ever, like—do you ever wonder about, how it would be if you and I... ? You know..." I wanted him to get there without me having to say it. This, I thought, would cue him to wax poetic about he'd so often thought about us. *Of course* he'd thought about us, but he'd always been worried that he was unworthy of my love or something. And then I, in a sweeping moment, would take his face in my hands and tell him that he was absolutely worthy. That I loved him for everything that he was, not in spite of it. And then, naturally, we would kiss some larger than life kiss, have life-altering sex, get married in a small but sparkling ceremony, and regale all our marvelous friends with our heartrending love story.

Instead, he dropped his arm from around my shoulder and took a step back.

"Oh, Mack. Jesus. I mean… you know I love you. I *do* love you," he said in this weirdly condescending way.

"Yeah. Well, that's kind of what I mean," I pushed ahead, steeped in denial.

"Right, but… *God*, I mean… I'm flattered. Like, really, I am flattered. Fuck. I was hoping maybe you'd get over this, and we could just move on—" And that was it. He knew. And he'd known. The whole time, he'd *known* and was just pretending to be my friend. Calling me sweetheart, and holding me close, and quietly willing my feelings away. It was like having someone slowly loosening my skin from my muscles with a butter knife. I tried to tell myself that I needed to hear him say the rest of what he was saying, but I couldn't stand to listen to any of it. I got so in my head that I don't remember most of what happened. Just fragments. How he hoped we could still be friends. How it wasn't me, it was him. How, sometimes, it just isn't right, but that didn't mean I was any less beautiful or amazing. And someday I would make someone so happy. "God, Mack. I… I really want to hug you. Is that okay?"

I don't remember if I said anything, or if I just nodded. He hugged me for a long time, but I didn't hug him back. The tree lights all blurred together as I squinted hard to keep from falling apart. "Let me walk you home, yeah?"

I wondered if this is what it was like to be one of his one-night stands. He kept his hand on my lower back the whole time we walked, and I wanted to tell him he'd lost the privilege of being close to me. But I didn't. Instead, I tried to make things lighter by talking about the new Carly Rae album, even though my tongue felt too big, and my mouth too small. We got to my door, and I said something conciliatory like, "All right, loser. Good talk." Then I went inside and cried fat, heavy tears into my suitcase.

We made a few attempts to be friends after that night, but they were flimsy at best. A semester later, we graduated, and I resolved that it'd be fine if we never saw each other again. A strategy that had been spectacularly successful, until now.

When Mel comes home, I am upside down on the couch, with my head hanging over the seat, and my legs draped against the back.

"Hi," she says, and her voice is the best sound I've heard in days. "How are you?"

I shake my head. "I hate today."

"That seems completely reasonable," she says. "So, what's this?"

"Preventative medicine. I'm worried about dehydration from over-crying yesterday," I explain. "At least, for now, this seems to have stopped the flow to my tear ducts." She doesn't say anything else, puts down her bag, takes off her coat, and joins me on the couch, her long dark hair dusting the floor. We hang upside down for a while.

"You smell like tree sap," I tell her.

"Ha, come on. You wouldn't know what tree sap smells like."

"Well. If I had to guess." This makes her laugh, and it's so clear and good that it makes me want to cry again, and I'm glad I'm upside down and don't. She searches for my hand, and I give it to her.

"I'm so sorry," she whispers.

I shake my head again. "It was always coming," I say.

She sighs. "It was, and it wasn't." She's right, but she has no idea what the thing she's saying actually feels like, so it still sounds wrong.

I'm out of energy to be annoyed.

"All the blood is rushing to our heads."

"Whatever."

"This really isn't good for you, Kenz."

"I don't care."

"Shut up. Yes, you do. C'mon. Sit up. I'll make you some tea." Mel swings her legs around and stands up. "Oof, yep. Head rush. Take your time getting up, okay? Go vertebra by vertebra, so you don't pass out." I've missed her—even her yoga-speak.

"I'll pass out if I want to," I prod, just to hear her laugh again, and it works. She swats at me as she goes into the kitchen.

"Is ginger jasmine okay? I snagged some loose leaf at the general store out by the cabin, which is so much better because you don't end up ingesting all the crud from the teabag itself. Not to mention the *staple* in the teabag." Mel is a pure, homegrown organic health nut, always learning about the unexplored toxins in everything. Her dad, a gentle vanilla nerd, was at Microsoft at the right time and retired early to open his own fresh-pressed juicery. Her mom, a sturdy Japanese woman, born and raised in Berkeley, used to host naked afternoon tea services and meditations. Their whole painfully idyllic family is skeptical of manufactured anything. I'm pretty thoroughly convinced Mel would have been the perfect hunter-gatherer: getting food directly from the source, roasting venison and rabbit over a spit in nothing but a loincloth. Aside from the fact that no one had a Vitamix, the Mesolithic period would have been her dream.

"Have you eaten today?"

"Um… I had some cheese."

"So, *no.*"

"Cheese is food too, Melanie."

"Uh-huh." I hear her start puttering in the kitchen, clanking pots and humming Joni Mitchell. Mel is the only one of us who cooks real meals. Last year I got her stackable glass Tupperware for all her leftovers in the fridge, and I thought she was actually going to cry when she opened them. "I was gonna make myself an orzo salad for my pre-dinner snack. You want me to make enough for you too?" I swear to God, if I didn't live with her, I would believe she was a space robot.

"Orzo? Is that the weird rice thing?"

"It's the Greek long-grain pasta thing."

"Right, sure. Okay." I start feeling lightheaded and decide maybe it *is* time to move. I transition to lying down on the couch, with my eyes closed while my blood redistributes itself. If there were a drug that could make me feel like this, I would take it every day.

"So, okay, what the fuck? *Kevin* is in town? When did Seattle annul his exile?"

I grin to myself. Mel has never actually met Kevin, which is how she manages to hate him so vigorously. Having only ever heard about him from me, she doesn't do her usual thing of seeing the best in everyone, and he never had the chance to do his usual thing of charming her to pieces. I love when she's vicious about him, so I've promised myself never to introduce them.

"Must've been right before the New Year, because he said he was here for some New Year's Eve party."

"I can't believe you ran into him *today*. The universe is trying to tell you something." I wish people would stop making Kevin a cosmic omen from "the universe." He's a lot of things but, despite my best efforts, fate isn't one of them.

"Well, we'll see," I mutter. "He's coming to dinner at my mom's tonight, so."

Mel drops something in the kitchen and stomps back into the living room. She stares at me for a long time, blinking very intentionally in my direction. She has these sharp hazel eyes like a bird of prey, and so after a few seconds, I turn my head back toward the ceiling and close my eyes again.

"No." She's radiating concern for me, and it itches. "What dinner?"

"Spareribs."

"*Spareribs*."

"I don't know, Melanie. It's a death thing. Or a grief thing. Alice thinks it's a good idea, so Mom thinks it's a great idea, and Jimmy volunteered me."

"It doesn't sound like you want to go."

I exhale sharply to let her know she's being dense. "I don't *want* to do any of this. I want my dad not to be dead, so there is no dinner to not want to go to."

She's quiet a long time, and when I look at her again, her eyes are wet.

"Mel."

She shakes her head, swallowing her whole throat into her stomach. "I'm sorry. I hate this for you, and I don't know the right thing to say. I'm sorry."

"No one knows the right thing to say." She sputters a wet laugh, and my heart grips. "There isn't a right thing to say. Just be Mel."

When I feel her come to sit beside my legs, I bend my knees so she can lean against them. She drops her head back onto my kneecaps.

"How does Kevin have an invitation to this dinner, and I don't?"

"You don't want to come to this. I promise."

"That's not what I meant."

"It's Kevin. He weaseled."

"Seriously?" she sneers. "Into a *memorial dinner*?"

"Well… no." I press my palms over my eyes. "He doesn't know that part."

I sneak a look at her through my fingers, and her gaze is as narrowed as I've ever seen it. I bite down on the inside of my cheek to keep from laughing, and she snorts, prying my hands from my face. "What do you mean he doesn't *know*?"

"I don't know. I didn't want to turn it into a whole thing."

She gives me a sarcastically enthused nod. "A flawless plan. So, what? He thinks this is just regular family spareribs?'

I shrug.

"Kenz. I'm never on his side. Not ever. You know this. But I'd say there's a good chance he's going to find out. If this dinner is Alice's idea, I can't imagine it'll be subtle."

I close my eyes against the thought.

"How was it?" I can feel her glowering, but her tone has eased off a bit. "Seeing him?"

A portrait of his smug face hangs on the back of my eyelids. "He's the same." I blink him away. "Like, *exactly* the same. He was wearing a *muscle tee*. In *January*. Who does that?"

She studies me a while before she says, "You miss him."

I can only roll my eyes at that. "I miss a lot of things I never had."

She doesn't argue, just turns and hugs my knees to her chest.

The teakettle whistles from the kitchen, and, once she's disappeared to silence it and returned to making her pre-dinner, I run my hands over my face, wishing, not for the first time, that any of the ways I'm supposed to feel were the right size.

When I was in 7th grade, Gerald went to jail, and I went to therapy. My parents had been divorced for a few years, and Gerald had been drifting around Seattle ever since. He spent a lot of his afternoons with me at Mom's house because he'd been promised he would still get to see me, but more because he had nowhere else to go. And, though most of the time he was drunk, and most of the time he was mean, and most of the time we fought until one of us stormed out, I didn't have nearly as many extracurricular activities as my mother, and I'd have just been alone otherwise. And so would he.

That year, though, it had actually seemed like maybe things were finally turning a good corner. Gerald had found steady work in a small community bank in the neighborhood and was actually climbing the ranks, having recently been promoted to manager. He was still staying with friends here and there, but he always told me he was saving, that he knew it wouldn't be long before he could get a place of his own. I'd started to imagine a life where I could be like the other children of divorce in my class: two houses, two Christmases, two birthdays, the whole shebang. Then, on Tuesday, April 13th, Gerald got frustrated waiting on savings. Him being a manager, he'd been entrusted with keys to the building and, oblivious to the improbability that he could outsmart the bank's security technology—especially not on a stomach full of Fireball whiskey—he staged a "heist." When he told the story later, he liked to use the word "heist," but in my opinion, it's far too elegant a term for what actually happened.

The security footage was beyond humiliating.

A man living in a neighboring apartment complex was calling the police before Gerald was even in the front door. During the trial, I found out later, they showed the video, and the prosecution stood by while the jury watched my father spend two and a half full minutes fumbling for the right key. First, he tried to use our old house key, which I'm pretty sure he still held onto though my mother changed the locks a couple weeks after the divorce was finalized. Then he attempted to force the key to his old Volvo station wagon into the lock, the whole time alternately giggling and audibly cursing at himself.

I try not to think about how it might have ended if he hadn't already been passed out when the police arrived. As it was, he had to be taken to the hospital to have his stomach pumped before they could even get him to the station, and by then I had been called. Mom was furious at being woken up in the middle of the night, but she dropped me with Alice, and she went.

I remember hearing Alice ask Walter to call in some favors to see if they could get my dad's sentence down. The way she said it was like she was already expecting Sandra Bullock to play her in a biopic about her generosity. It was obvious she pitied Gerald, they all did, which I knew meant they also pitied me, and I resented them for it. I hated that the only time we ever talked about my dad was when he needed to be rescued. I hated how often he needed to be rescued. I hated how he took his life for granted, but most of all, I hated that, over the years, that habit rubbed off on the rest of us.

When he was convicted, I was taking a fifty states pop quiz for extra credit. I scored highest in my class, 98/100 (I forgot what

Arkansas was called and also the capital of South Dakota), but when I got home, there was no one there, so I stuck the quiz on the fridge myself.

Alice, and by extension, Mom, decided I needed help getting my feelings "ironed out" in light of everything. And since neither of them wanted to talk to me, they decided it'd be good for me to spend some time talking to Valery, our school's guidance counselor. Maybe a week after Gerald was sentenced, I got a Request-To-Report slip during homeroom. There was a little heart over the "i" in my name, and I wanted to throw up.

Valery was the first and last time I went to therapy. She didn't like that I called it therapy. "Remember, everyone needs to talk to a friend sometimes, Mackenzie," she condescended at the end of every meeting. But I would never have been friends with someone like Valery. She wore gauchos to work with a braided belt and peasant blouses. It was like she lived her life at an ugly beach resort, except that she worked in a middle school counseling office.

Her office was decorated, not unlike the school nurse's office, with cheesy posters about emotional health. There was one with a bunch of smiley faces depicting different emotions: happy, sad, angry, frustrated, excited, and scared. At the top of the poster, it said: FEELINGS. And at the bottom, underneath a graphic of children's silhouettes holding hands, it said: WE ALL HAVE THEM. SHARE YOURS.

It was that kind of place.

The poster that hung behind Valery's chair was just a picture of a fork in some bumblefuck country road that said, "WE CAN

ALL CHOOSE OUR OWN PATHS" in a squiggly white font at the bottom. I got frustrated sitting in her office looking at the poster because it was so blatantly obvious to me that neither of the paths was going anywhere at all.

Through all of our sessions, we sat across from each other in these very low to the ground orange vinyl armchairs with metal frame arms. Valery would cross her legs and lean forward at me, squinting a little bit like she was trying very hard to see me. Most of the time, I stared over her head at that poster. I didn't like making eye contact with her squinting eyes. The weird smile she put on in an attempt to get me to share cinched my skin.

"What do you feel about your father's incarceration?"

"I don't know… It's fine, I guess."

"Say more about that. How is it 'fine'?"

"Why? I don't have more to say. It's fine."

"So you keep telling me. But sometimes, Mackenzie, we use the word 'fine' to cover up our not-so-happy feelings. Do you think that may be what you're doing?"

"No."

She leaned back in her armchair, and the polyester in her peasant blouse squeaked against the vinyl. She took a deep, cleansing breath before she leaned in again.

"Are you sad that he's in jail?"

"No."

"Do you feel any sadness about this situation?"

"Not really."

Valery didn't understand. She told me that it was okay to be sad, and I told her I knew that, but I wasn't sad. She said, sometimes, when things are hard, we come up with defense mechanisms to help us through them, and I told her I knew that too. But the truth was still that more than anything, I felt relieved, not sad.

And I knew that wasn't how I was supposed to feel. I *knew* jail was bad. But still the whole year that Gerald spent in jail, I didn't feel sad. I was a kid. I was selfish, and I didn't understand any of it, not really. No one was explaining to me what jail would actually mean. What it would really be like. Instead, I told myself that at least jail would mean he had regular meals. That there would be people who knew where he was. People that were in charge of keeping track of him, keeping him out of trouble. And it meant that he didn't come to my house drunk anymore. That he and I didn't have to fight every day. It meant I didn't worry about him freezing on the street in the winter or drinking himself to death in the summer. It meant that when he called, he was never drunk on the phone, and sometimes I could even make him laugh. It wasn't how anyone wanted me to feel, but it meant I could make friends my own age without worrying about abandoning him after school. Without worrying about letting him down. It meant that I knew where he was, for the first time since he moved out, that I knew for sure he had a place to live, and I thought, naive as it was, that maybe he would finally be safe.

But I couldn't say any of that to Valery. Even if I'd known how, I wouldn't have wanted to. I just kept letting her ask me if I was sad, and I kept telling her again and again that I wasn't. She frowned at me a lot that year, looked at me like I was broken, and wrote reports to that effect for my mother.

It was because of my sessions with Valery that I was transferred into fourth period World History and thrown into a geography presentation on Uzbekistan with the Honor Student of the Month, who was expected to be a good influence on me. To her credit, Mel really has done her best.

"Four minutes," she says, putting the tea down on the coffee table in front of me. "You have to let it steep for four minutes so that you really get everything the blend has to offer." She examines my face. "The jasmine will be good for that," she says finally.

"For what?"

"That thing you're feeling," she diagnoses before going back into the kitchen.

"I hate you," I call to her from the couch.

There's a pause, and I'm not sure if she heard. Then just barely over the clanging of the pots, she goes, "Ha. Yeah, well. The jasmine will help."

At 5:42, Kevin buzzes our apartment. He has this insufferable habit of buzzing interminably until you either let him up or come downstairs. I'm only half-dressed when he arrives, and so we have to listen to him play Old Macdonald on the buzzer for a full three minutes because I refuse to let him up to meet Mel.

"You dressed up for him," Mel says, looking up from her book as I put a coat on over my dress.

"No, I didn't." Fuck. I did. "Anyway, I'm going now." I buzz down to Kevin, "You have to stop, or I'll break your hand. I'm coming down," and he finally lets up on the musical interlude.

Mel stands and darts in front of the door.

"What are you doing?"

She just throws her arms around me. When she lets go, her brow is furrowed, and her lips pressed together. Her eyes blink down the small tides rising in them, and she smooths my hair gently.

"You're going to be okay," she says, and I don't know if she's reassuring herself or me, but it's a nice thought either way. "And if you're not, that's okay too. You can call me if you need anything, you know that?"

"I do."

The buzzer buzzes again.

"He's not good enough for you."

I smile. "Obviously."

"*Obviously.*" She's getting emotional, and if I weren't leaving right this minute, it'd be obnoxious. As it is, it's almost sweet, and so I hug her one more time before escaping into the brief seclusion of the hall.

Kevin is wearing a heather grey sweater and black jeans now, denim jacket in his hand, slung over his shoulder, and pristine white converse. He's a dish, only slightly dimmed because of how obviously he knows it. Still, I bite down hard to keep from having to catch my breath when his face lights up as I come through the door.

"Fucking look at you," he says, shit-eating grin all over his ridiculous face. He throws his arm over my shoulder as we walk toward
a small, bright yellow Saab. It's so offensively garish that *of course*
it's what he's driving. "You smell like a goddamn tropical vacation,
Mack," he says, his face in my hair, and I remind myself that this isn't
for me. Flirtation is just his native language.

The whole drive, he gushes at me; how he'd wondered if he
might run into me, how it's been too long, how he's missed me so
much honestly. I'm full of one-word responses, Google Maps navi-
gations, and somewhat coherent grunts. I can barely hear him over
the buzz of my own mind. *You have to tell him*, I keep thinking. *You
should have told him as soon as you saw him.*

But I keep not telling him. The secret looming larger by the
minute. Lodged so tight in my throat, I think I'll choke on it. As we're
pulling into Mom's driveway, he looks at me and says, "Seriously.
We used to have the best time. How come we're not friends anymore, Mack?"

And even though my tongue burns with countless answers,
when I meet his eyes, all I say is, "My dad died yesterday. That's what
this dinner is for."

I'm not getting better at breaking this news.

I watch in real-time as Kevin's ease shatters, and the shock
rolls off him in waves. The air is thin, and, though he tries, he can't
get down enough of it. My face burns. I want to scream because I
don't feel any better, only guiltier and ugly and mean, ashamed of
myself, watching him search for words. We're getting swallowed by
the eddying silence, and I can't stand to be in the car with myself

anymore, so before he finds anything to say, I get out. The adrenaline of my shame propels me up the path, onto the front porch, and I ring the bell, halfway hoping he'll just turn the car around and leave me to make his excuses.

It takes everything I've got left to force a smile when the door opens. Mom is wearing a magenta apron that Jimmy got her for Christmas. It's customized and reads, "Jefe de Cocina: Elizabeth Estevez" on the front in a swirly script. She looks to have planned her outfit around wearing this apron tonight, and, despite the occasion, she is the picture of domestic bliss when she comes to the door, though seeing me rumples her a bit.

"Don't you look just like him," she whispers.

"Hi, Mom," I say, regretting my face.

"Sweetie." She envelops me in one of her signature hugs. Squeezing like a vise with one arm and then using the other for vigorous back-patting. I don't know where she learned it, but it's been the same stilted affection my whole life. At this moment, I find I don't care. I cling to her so tight I hear her back crack. "All right, sweetie, all right," she says, pulling away from me and looking nervously over my shoulder. "Where's Kevin? He did come with you, didn't he?"

I turn, disappointed to see the Saab still in the driveway.

"I'm sure he'll just be a second."

"Well, come in out of the cold, why don't you," she says, but she doesn't move to let me in. "I'm so surprised it has gotten so cold tonight! It was such a beautiful afternoon. Did you get out and spend some time in the sunshine?"

"I went for a walk this morning."

"A walk! How lovely! Such a good way to get some fresh air and some exercise. You know," her voice goes soft, and she leans toward me, "your father loved to go for walks."

I nod, gritting my teeth, irritated that she thinks this memory had escaped me when she's the one who blacklisted his name in our house. Is this how it's going to be now that he's dead? Will she be leaning in to whisper about him for the rest of our lives?

I'm considering self-righteousness when I hear Kevin's car door close behind me, remembering myself just as my mother shrills, "*There he is!*" She bounds past me, down the steps, to inflict one of her hugs on him.

"Liz," he says with his arms wrapped snugly around her shoulders, "I'm so sorry to hear about Gerald. So generous of you to be having us all here so soon. I hope I'm not imposing." He's shifted to using a voice I'd forced myself to forget from late nights in the library or sprawled on the rug in his room listening to live recordings of Billie Holiday. It rolls right through me like a long-overlooked favorite song. Low, warm, and genuine, spreading like butter. Our eyes lock for a second, guilt a lead weight in my stomach, and then he looks back to Mom.

"So sweet of you to say that, darling. You always know the right thing to say, don't you?" He rubs her arm and smiles a genteel smile down into her face. "We've missed you around here! You know, I was so pleased to hear that you and Mackenzie have made amends. She can be stubborn sometimes, but she's got a good heart, really, if you look for it." Sometimes it's like she thinks I can't hear her if she's talking about me.

She sighs this big, heartfelt sigh and puts her hand on his face like she's reuniting with her long-lost son. I clear my throat and list against the porch rail. Finally, she turns back toward the house, taking Kevin by the hand. "All right! Well! Come in, come in, you two. We're just putting the finishing touches on dinner, but there are little snacks in the meantime. Crudités, and that sort of thing if you're peckish."

Inside, the house is still decorated for Christmas, with poinsettias on every available surface, and mistletoe hanging in the archway between the living and dining rooms. Jimmy has put on Ella & Louis and built a fire in the fireplace. The tree is dried out, but still twinkling with lights and ornaments. There are holly wreaths adorning each door in the hall. The stockings are still hanging and, above them on the mantle, is a sea of 3x5 photos of Gerald, the only notable additions since I was here for the holidays. Pictures of him now overwhelm the dining room table as well, where they're surrounded by votive candles. The vigil, in combination with the Christmas theme, makes it look a little like my father may, in fact, have been the baby Jesus.

"Look at this. This house is even more beautiful than I remember," Kevin says as we're taking off our coats. "You have a gift, Liz." Only my mom's oldest friends and Kevin call her Liz.

Mom smiles, saying, "Oh, *you*," and shoving our coats into the closet before vanishing into the kitchen. I start to follow her, but Kevin grabs onto my arm and motions for me to hang back a second.

With my mom safely out of earshot, he scans my face, the auburn in his eyes just embers, and then says, calmer than I've ever heard him, "What's with the ambush, babe? Are you okay?"

I hate his easiness, and I certainly didn't earn his kindness. I don't know what we are to each other, but I'm sure I don't deserve it. Before I can stop myself, everything in me regresses, and I'm nothing more than the bitter teenager that couldn't wait to move out of this house.

"It's whatever," I say, folding my arms, and rolling my eyes. "And don't call me babe. It's gross. Sorry I didn't tell you he was dead before. But… you pretty much forced me to invite you." As if this could all be his fault. I'm so mad at myself, but I can't stop making it worse. Instead, I shrug it off and try again to leave.

"Mack." He steels his hold on my arm. "Come on. Don't be like this. You can talk to me."

"No, I can't! I can't talk to you, Kev. And I don't want to." Bile bites the back of my throat, and I want to yell at him to stop forgiving me, but my head won't make the words. I want him to hold me while I cry, but I know he won't.

Instead, he just stands with me for another few seconds, and I will myself to be stronger than his gaze. Finally, he gives a small surrendering shake of his head and goes into the kitchen. I hear him hugging Alice and telling her what she wants to hear about how thin she's looking. I hear Walter say, "watch out there, son," and laugh heartily to no one. I hear Jimmy asking Mom where I am, and Mom saying she doesn't know but does the table look like the inspiration pictures Alice sent? And the whole time, I just stare at the floor, and stare at the floor, and think about my "I Am" sentences.

I am Mackenzie.

I am twenty-four years old.

I am angry.

I am pathetic.

I am scared.

I am sad.

I am to blame.

I am a daughter.

I am Gerald's daughter.

The garage is stuffy even with the cold air pressing in at the seams in the door. I snag Mom's keys off the hook above the lightswitch and unlock the limited-edition Dodge Ram pick-up that she bought herself after the divorce. There was nothing in her life or mine that required a truck of this size and power. There wasn't even anything that required a new car. The car we had, a 2001 Toyota Camry, was still completely functional. The reason she bought the truck was simply that she'd seen the commercial on TV, and it had "spoken to her."

There's nothing particularly special about a Dodge Ram commercial. It's footage of the truck driving gracefully along some scenic mountain highway. It's the truck doing a montage of very outdoorsy stuff, splashing through mud puddles and hauling through blizzards, the types of things that people who need trucks want to see. And over the action, a lumberjack sounding man details all the car's specs and new features, explaining the deal they're offering on financing that makes it super possible for you, yes YOU, to be a person who drives the thing. But then, and this is the part that spoke to my mother, he says, "Dodge. Grab life by the horns."

She was trading in our Camry within the month.

The affirmation went up on the wall. She said it to herself in the mirror in the morning. If we passed each other in the hall before school she would say, "Sweetie, you have to grab life by the horns!" and "You'll never know what you're capable of until you grab life by the horns!" Every new hobby was explained as her next step toward grabbing life by the horns. Sometimes she would even shake her car keys for emphasis.

In reality, I think grabbing any animal by the horns would prove to be a pretty monumental mistake. But it does have a ring to it.

Brilliant white, with a relatively dainty silver ram logo perched on the imposing grille, the truck is monstrous big in person. The first of her many material declarations of independence from Gerald, it became like a suit of armor for Mom, a mechanical extension of her shining new persona. Announcing everywhere she went that she no longer had any need of my father, it was very loudly not mine.

I didn't learn to drive.

Now she mostly keeps it parked in the garage. Before she met Jimmy, she used to drive it daily, parking it outside on the street like a trophy of her gas-guzzling empowerment. But once she remarried, she didn't need a car to let people know she didn't belong to Gerald. And so, she parked it inside and started to take Jimmy's Honda Civic.

The leather seats are frigid, and, sequestered in the passenger seat, I think maybe I'll turn the heat on, but that'd require starting the car, and I don't know how. So instead, I just curl my legs into my chest and try to feel safe—a nesting doll, tucked into myself, inside the car, inside the garage, inside my mother's house.

No one comes looking for me.

When I was little, after our big fights, after I'd stormed out in a big dramatic exit, after I'd had some time on my own, Gerald would come into my room and sit on the edge of my bed, and say, "Ms. Mac. I just came to check… you're not in here smiling, are you?" He'd watch me closely, and then he'd flash me a silly face, just for a second. I'd bite down on the inside of my cheek to keep from breaking, and he'd say, "You better not be in here smiling Mac, not when things are so serious." And then he'd make another face. "No smiling, Mac!" And another. "I thought we were fighting, Mac, how come you're laughing?" Another face, until I dissolved into giggles and then he would laugh so loud, so hard his eyes shone brighter than anything else I've ever seen. And no matter what had been broken between us, it wouldn't matter anymore.

But he isn't coming.

It occurs to me that sometimes when you push people away, they just go.

It's twenty minutes of cold uninterrupted silence before I hear Nathan and Lana pulling up outside. Nathan is notoriously late for everything and, even when his lateness is of great inconvenience to everyone else, Mom has the same canned response: "That brother of yours! So *fashionable!*" But he's not fashionable. He's just quiet and awkward and largely uninterested in other people. He's five years older than me and was already away at college when Mom and Jimmy started dating, so the first time we met was at the rehearsal dinner for their wedding. He came over to me and said, "Do you know who I am?" And when I'd said yes, and that he was my new stepbrother, Nathan, he just said, "Yup," and walked away. We've only gotten a little bit better at talking in the years since.

But it's Nathan who eventually comes to find me, holding a tiny gift bag in his hand when he gets into the driver seat.

"Good spot," he says, nonchalantly handing me the bag. I look over at him, but he's gazing aimlessly out the windshield. After fussing a bit with the ribbon holding the handles together, I finally get a peek inside. It's an assortment of tiny airplane bottles of booze. He's covered all the bases: gin, tequila, whiskey, vodka, and a tiny bottle of white wine. It is identical to the one Beth gulped down at the Homeaway Inn Express, and a small laugh escapes my lips. "Go ahead. Pick one." He leans against the driver's side door and yawns.

I take the tequila. He goes for the whiskey. It tastes terrible, but I don't care. "Are they wondering where I am?" I ask him after a minute.

"Not really. Think they figure you're grieving." He still hasn't really looked at me. I don't know if he thinks we're bonding, or if he would've come out to the Ram to drink even if I weren't here. I look down at my outfit and fidget uncomfortably when I think about what

Mel said before I left. The neckline speaks for itself. I don't look like a person who's grieving. I couldn't even be bothered to wear black.

"I don't know if I am or not. Grieving, I mean."

"Cheers," says Nathan, clinking his bottle with mine.

I guess we aren't bonding.

For a while, we both drink in silence. Nathan takes the keys from the cup holder where I left them, and turns the car on, flipping on the heat, and adjusting his seat to give him more legroom. "God love a truck," he says to himself. He starts fiddling with the radio and eventually settles on a song with a chorus that's just some twangy voice demanding, "Country girl, shake it for me, girl" over and over. I don't understand Nathan at all, and I wonder if anyone does.

"So," I shift toward him and fold my legs underneath me, attempting conversation, "Mom told me you were bringing your girlfriend tonight. Is she here?"

"Yep." He finishes his whiskey and shifts his gaze to me for the first time. "Kevin's back. Is that because your dad's dead?" He doesn't soften his voice at all. I look away and down the rest of my tequila, tossing the empty bottle back into the gift bag.

"I don't know. I guess." There's a pause. Nathan yawns again and then switches off the radio.

"Welp. You hungry?"

And that's that.

The house smells distinctly of spareribs and barbecue sauce now, and Mom is busying herself with getting the food on the table. It's a real juggling act because she refuses to move the shrine to my father that she has already laid out as a centerpiece, and so the food has to be carefully arranged around all the photos and candles. There are several moments when it seems impossible that she's not going to light the whole mess on fire, but she pulls it off. The final arrangement is cluttered and extremely precarious, but Jimmy comes in and tells her it looks beautiful, "just what Gerald would have loved." As if anyone could know that.

I'm in no fit state to brave the crowd in the kitchen, so instead, I choose to stand next to Jimmy's home aquarium. It's prime real estate: close enough to the dining room table that I'm already in place when dinner is served, and if someone tries to talk to me about shit I can't handle, I can ramble about the fish until they leave.

I am particularly enamored of the Lionfish and am watching him closely when I hear the first of the grievers approaching.

"There you are! My poor lil Ms. Mackenzie! Oh, huh-n*ey* buh-*ny!*" It's Alice. When I turn and look at her, I'm overwhelmed. She has outdone herself tonight, all done up in black, and topped off with a small hat with a tiny lace widow's veil attached. If we were having a competition to see who was the grieviest, Alice would be taking home the gold.

She hurries over to me and throws her arms around my neck. "And look at how beautiful you look! Even in this time of unbearable sadness, you look so beautiful! That is the healing power of youth, y'all! That's the healing power of youth right there in the flesh." She squeezes my face with her giant acrylic nails, and when she lets go, I worry that she may have drawn blood. I run my fingers over my cheek. Luckily, she has not. We exchange pleasantries about her trip to San Antonio, and she tells me what a relief it is to back in a place where the heat isn't having its way with her hair. "You'll never see me without frizz in San Antonio," she exclaims. "That heat won't allow it! And for the love of sweet Jesus, it's *January!*" I offer her my condolences. She tells me I'm a darling and kisses me squarely on the forehead. Then she whispers, "You'll see, muffin. Sometimes death is a blessing." I don't know what to say to that. She just winks at me, bellows that her glass has run dry, and hurries back into the kitchen.

Walter is next, giving me a stern handshake, slipping me a $100 bill, and saying, "Tragic loss, my dear. Tragic." If he had said, "Congratulations, my dear. Congratulations," it would have been exactly the same as my high school graduation. I smile politely at him, but then I realize I don't have anywhere to put the money and hope no one sees me slip it into my bra when he turns his back.

"¡Aqui esta! Mackie! That's my girl." Jimmy comes around the table and holds me in a very long hug. "I was worried you'd back out. I know this must be... with all the photos, and... It's hard for all of us." I hold Jimmy and relax into the smell of cheap Old Spice cologne. For all his quirks, he has always tried his best to connect with me, and at this moment, I think I do love him for it.

"It's harder than I thought," I confide in him. He lets me out of the hug and looks at me, holding my shoulders gently in his soft hands. His bright, smiling face cracks. He takes my hand and squeezes.

"You're a tough cookie, Mackie." He grins, and, for lack of anything better, I grin back. I don't know what it means that I'm a tough cookie, but even more, I don't know what he could have said that would have meant anything.

Nathan doesn't line up with the others. I think he must assume he did his part in bringing me the tequila. To his credit, it was the most useful thing anyone's done so far. He never spent much time with my dad. The few times they were in the same place at the same time, it was tense. Gerald was always asking whether Nathan was my boyfriend. Any boy even close to my age who hung around the house was a potential threat in his eyes—even my stepbrother. "If he's hanging around my daughter, he should know I could kick his ass," he told me. Always surprisingly concerned with me getting my heart broken for the person who did most of the breaking.

Works-with-orphans-Lana glides over, looking more like a praying mantis than a person should. She has very severe and pointy features topped off by large, wide-set, green eyes. She even holds her hands up at her chest, bent at the wrist while she plays with her fingers. The woman is an insect. Her hair is an ashy mahogany color, and she has it all pulled back into a high ponytail. That, in combination with her athletic build, makes me think she must be highly sporty when she's not cuddling parent-less children.

"You must be Natey's sister, Mackenzie." She edges over toward me after Jimmy has gone, and stares into the aquarium.

"I am. And you're Lana."

"Oh! Yes! He—Natey told you about me?" Her whole face lights up, and it loses a little of its bugginess.

"Not in so many words, but yeah. You came up." She half-giggles, and I smile reassuringly at her. I can't help but feel a little sorry for her. What a horribly awkward way to meet your boyfriend's family for the first time.

"I met your boyfriend," she says. "He's hilarious. And," she leans in closer, lowering her voice, "*so handsome.*"

I huff out a laugh. "Oh, ha, no. Kevin's not my boyfriend. Really, very much, not my boyfriend."

"Oh, really?" Her giant eyes grow even more giant. If she actually is a praying mantis, this must be the face she makes before cutting off the heads of her partners. "Are you being serious right now?"

"Yeah, no. Just a friend. Or, really, just a person."

She looks pained. "Oh my god, that is so weird of me, I'm sorry. It's just that he was saying to Alice and me how incredible you are, I just sort of assumed... I think we all did, especially since he's here... you know... *now.*" I'm still shaking my head when her whole demeanor changes as she prepares to broach the subject of Gerald. Her face goes straight from mantis to den mother. She's an Animorph. Her hand comes to my shoulder, "I was so sorry—I mean, I *am.* I am so sorry to hear about your father. Natey told me you two had a complicated relationship."

Lana goes on talking, but I'm only half-listening as behind her, Kevin comes into view, carrying on happily with Alice and Walter. Jimmy joins them, handing Kevin a beer and patting him heartily on the back. *We're not even friends,* I want to yell. *He's just a selfish person feigning empathy for unknown reasons.* He catches me watching him, extending a half-smile my way. The tequila makes it impossible to hold back my grimace.

"Mackenzie? Are you okay?" Lana's enormous worried eyes are scanning my face for signs of mourning. I sense her clicking into orphan-mode.

"Sorry, yeah. I'm just… processing," I say in a far-away voice.

"You know, I work a lot with children who've lost their parents," she says. "And all the adults I know who have been through this tell me the same thing; that it doesn't get any easier just because you're older. It can still be just as traumatic as it would have been at a very young age." She squeezes my arm and awaits my response to this pearl of wisdom.

"I did lose my father at a very young age," I say to her without even thinking about it. "It's just that now he's dead." She shrinks away from me slightly, and then we both just stand there, staring into the aquarium.

The Lionfish swims up to the surface of the water and gulps some air. I wish this was a thing humans could do. I would do it now.

"Everyone, thank you for joining us this evening in honor of Gerald. Let's sit, sit, sit! Dinner is served!" My mother is standing behind a chair at the head of the table. Unexpectedly, her eyes are brimming with tears, though she's spread her mouth into a big toothy smile. Loss makes everyone look like horror movie versions of themselves. "Your names are at your places. And thank you to Alice for the beautiful name card maker she so thoughtfully gave us for Christmas!"

I find my seat next to Kevin and avoid eye contact.

"Where'd you go?" he whispers as we sit down.

"Doesn't matter."

He watches me a second, then leans in and slides my water glass toward me. "All right, well. You smell like tequila."

There's a sharp pull of embarrassment in my chest. I think of Alice, Walter, Jimmy, Lana, all smelling liquor on me and saying nothing, and the parallels are too glaring. My mind churns out a list of reasons this-is-different-because, the way we all lie to ourselves when we start to become our parents. The water is frigid, and I drink it so fast that I hope it drowns me.

Jimmy's still standing at the end of the table opposite my mother. He raises his wine glass to get our attention. "Tonight," he pauses to clear his throat, "Tonight is an occasion for remembrance and reflection." I look over at Mom, who has her head bowed to her chest. Alice is rubbing her back gently and nodding encouragingly at Jimmy, who clears his throat again before continuing. "Yesterday, this family suffered an unspeakable loss. While I can't boast ever having been close to Gerald myself, I think of him often. In all the years I have had the joy of being married to Elizabeth, and of knowing his beautiful daughter, Mackie, I have always thanked Gerald Adams for allowing these women to be a part of my life. Without him, Elizabeth may never have come to Seattle or taken that Pasodoble class. Without him, Mackie would never have been born. So, I would like to be the first to raise a glass to the memory of a man who so generously gave us so much."

"Oh, amen to that!" Alice yelps, raising her glass and sloshing wine on her plate. We all follow suit, raising our glasses as Jimmy takes his seat. It's surreal, seeing Gerald hold court over all of us like this, taking up all our space. Then again, I think maybe this space has always been his. We just weren't supposed to say so.

Dinner is surprisingly quiet at first. All of us just sort of munching in strained silence. Lana is the one to say the thing that people always say when this happens at a dinner party: "The food must be delicious. Everyone got so quiet! A compliment to the chef!" And then we all laugh the obligatory laugh before going back to eating and ignoring each other.

Mom is coming apart. Within the first fifteen minutes, she has to excuse herself several times to go to the bathroom, and, even from the dining room with the door closed, we can all hear her crying. Each time she comes back to the table, she squeezes my shoulders and kisses the top of my head, a demonstration of a closeness we've never shared. Something in me stirs to comfort her, but she's mourning a version of Gerald I arrived too late to witness. So, I just let her go.

I can only get down a few bites of meat, mostly I just push my food around my plate. It's hard to talk over Mom's sobs. Walter keeps muttering "tragic, tragic," to no one. Every once in a while, I notice Lana whispering to Nathan about something to which he consistently shakes his head "no," and I wonder if she's asking whether or not they can leave.

Finally, Alice breaks the ice and begins to talk at length about how she's noticed that they've changed the color of the egg cartons at the Enumclaw Egg booth at the farmer's market. She says she thinks the new dye is rubbing off on the eggs. "I haven't read any conclusive studies," she says, her mouth rimmed with barbecue sauce, "but I'm almost positive that there are food dyes that have caused cancer in lab mice." She swallows another enormous bite of food. "Just something to think about." This sparks a whole conversation about how everything is giving everyone cancer these days, and can you even believe how many people get diagnosed with terminal cancer in a day? Walter says he read a scientific essay about how even grilled vegetables can give you cancer because of the charring that happens on the grill. Jimmy says he hates to think of all those people getting sick and dying, and Lana agrees that she hates to think of anyone dying. And then everyone gets quiet as we all remember what it is we're doing here.

For weeks after I saw my dad for the last time, I dreamt every night he was dying. In the dreams, he would come to my room to tell me he was sick, and sometimes we would fight, and sometimes we would laugh, and every time he would cry, and I would hold his hands. I would tell him not to worry. Every night for weeks.

I didn't know right away that the last time I saw him was the last time. There had been so many afternoons before that when I'd come away thinking I couldn't do it again, but the feeling wouldn't last. I took so much pride in my resilience. I'd have bragged about it if the need for it hadn't been so ugly. There had always been so much pain between him and me. It hadn't occurred to me that there might be a limit. And relative to the screaming matches that had come before, that last afternoon was mild. I remember saying, "I love you" and watching him stare at me like he didn't speak the language. I remember leaving, remember dragging myself down the hall to the elevators in the dazed breathless heartache that became synonymous with spending afternoons in that room. I remember Mel asking how it was to see him and telling her it was fine. I remember going out for lunch later, like it was fine. I remember thinking I could taste my bones and thinking it would pass.

And I remember the dreams. Each one of them. The way his face looked so young and so old at the same time. I remember every time he died. What it was like waking up in the morning, the heavy feeling of knowing it wasn't true. A comfort and a burden at once.

Yesterday was the first time he's died in almost two years. Which almost feels like a punchline, but I'm sure it isn't.

By the seventh time Mom gets up to cry in the bathroom, I hardly even notice her go, except that, this time, Alice follows her. *That's good*, I assure myself. *Alice knows best.*

There's a lull in the conversation, as everyone strains to hear whether any progress is being made with Mom. But we can't hear anything because Alice's Southern belle upbringing taught her that delicate situations like these require hushed tones.

Then Walt says he brought cigars back from his most recent business trip to Venezuela and would anyone care to join him. I've never been entirely clear about what government thing it is that Walt does for a living, and I'm not sure I want to know. Whatever it is, it means that he's always traveling to new places and that he regularly carries a stash of hundred-dollar bills. Jimmy agrees to a cigar, and they go out onto the back porch. Then there are four.

Maybe the third time Mom stood up from the table, Kevin pressed his knee into mine under the table and left it there. Every now and then, I close my eyes and focus in on the warm reassurance of it. This has always been the thing about Kevin. You never know when he'll surprise you and manage to be exactly who you need.

I'm absently transfixed by the portrait I'm assembling, a smiley face crafted from two peas and the rib bone left lying on my plate. Nathan has started to tell the story of how he and Lana first met in an online gaming community where she was a damsel in distress, and he was a warlock.

"Was it love at first sight?" Kevin wants to know.

"I don't know about Natey, but I knew right away," Lana says, smiling giddily. "Natey was the most gentlemanly warlock I'd ever met in the village square. Plus, he gave me a purse full of gold pieces and a basket of eggs, which ended up helping me to defeat the overlord. When I saw him again in the enchanted forest, I suggested that we should meet in person."

I flip the rib bone on my plate upside down to make a frowning face instead, and Kevin nudges my leg, trying not to laugh.

It's not until that moment that I look up for long enough to notice the photo that's parked in front of him on the table—me at three years old, sitting on Gerald's shoulders. It's one of those great disposable camera pictures you never see anymore because everything's digital. The exposure is all speckled with sunshine, just a little blurry in a way that makes us look like we're still moving all these years later. How have I never seen this picture before? Gerald is wearing a tee shirt in a kitschy yellow and white floral print. He has on these fat aviator sunglasses, his beard far less scraggly than it looked yesterday. I'm wearing those little saltwater sandals, and teal denim overalls. We look totally inseparable. Like a father-daughter set you would want to order from a catalog. I don't even notice that I've picked it up or that I'm crying until I feel Kevin's hand on my back.

"Mack," he murmurs, jostling me a little as his arm comes around my shoulder, "Hey. You all right?"

I laugh a pathetic, crying laugh, "Look at us!" I hold the picture out to him. My hands are shaking, and I glimpse Lana's bug face getting panicky across the table.

"It's a great picture," Kev says, taking the picture from my trembling hand and pulling me against his shoulder, my head tucking into his neck. "You don't see pictures like this anymore."

"I *know*, right?" I close my eyes tightly, trying to squeeze the tears onto my fingers to keep my make-up from running down my face into his shirt. I feel him put his face into my hair and take a deep breath. I wish he wouldn't ever go back to San Francisco.

Then I think of Mel saying "*obviously*" with so much tension in her face, and I sit up and put my head in my hands. Damnit.

"Well," he says after another minute, his fingers still lingering on my spine, "it's getting late."

"I was just saying that to Natey," Lana agrees, even though I'm sure she's been saying that for over an hour now. Kevin turns, and our knees separate for the first time in hours.

"You wanna find your mom and say goodnight before I take you home?"

He goes onto the back porch to say goodbye to Jimmy and Walt while I go in search of Mom.

The bathroom door is locked, and so I have to knock and wait for someone to let me in. I hear Alice shuffling around inside and explaining to my mom that she is going to get the door. She opens the door a crack but then hurries me inside once she sees that it's me.

"You're just the girl we were hoping to see, Ms. Mackenzie," she says.

"Oh, my *sweetie!*" Mom howls through a sob. She throws her arms around me, and I fall into her lap on the toilet. I'm too big to be doing this for the first time, and she seems too small to be my mother. She wails, and I hold her head to my chest. I try to push the memory of Beth out of my mind.

It's maybe five minutes before her crying subsides, and when I think the coast is clear, I say, "Kevin and I are gonna go, Mom."

"You're not going because of me, are you? Oh, I feel so terrible I've been such a mess tonight, but how could I have known? I didn't anticipate this being so difficult. Being a hostess...and having all these people here now... And you're supposed to be my *family*. I don't know why I don't manage it better."

I don't allow myself to feel the sting of her word choice. It feels just as true that *she's* supposed to be *my* family.

"No, it's nothing you did. It's just that it's getting late, and tonight has been a rough one for everybody. Okay? This isn't your fault." I look over to Alice for support, but she has removed her hat and is intently tending to her makeup in the mirror. I watch as she peels off a fake eyelash and scratches violently at her eyelid before reattaching it with glue she produces from her purse. What it must be like to be Alice.

Mom's still blubbering. "It's just that you remind me so much of your father, sweetie! So much. The way you smile and laugh and even the way you play with your food. And now that he's gone—looking at you tonight, I just—" She breaks down sobbing again, and I stare blankly into the tub.

"It's all right," I finally manage. "It's okay. I think everyone's just exhausted. This is a lot."

"He loved you so much, Mackenzie," she sniffles. "I just want to make sure you hear me when I say that. He loved you the most."

And I wish so much that there was any solace in it.

It's quiet for a long time when we get in the car. I think maybe Kevin is never going to start the engine, but then he does.

"So. Thanks for driving tonight. It was good to see you," I say, for lack of anything better, as he turns down the street.

His jaw is tight. His face left its politeness at my mom's, and he doesn't answer me. We're hardly three minutes away when he pulls to the side of the road and parks again.

"You're in front of a hydrant. This is illegal," I say anxiously because he's scaring me. He turns on the flashers. Then he slams his hands into the steering wheel, and it makes me jump. His breath is staggered, and when he leans forward, I squint in the light of a streetlamp to see if he's crying. *Please*, don't let him be crying.

"*Jesus.*" I watch while he presses his thumbs into his forehead. He reminds me of Tom Cruise on the verge of collapse. "Why? Why didn't you fucking tell me, Mack?"

And I don't know what to say.

It seemed irrelevant, somehow.

I've barely talked to you in three years.

You were wearing cargo shorts at the time.

You broke my heart.

"I didn't know how." It's the truth that's easiest to get my mouth around. "I still don't. I mean, what would I say? *'Good to see ya, Kev. Hey, so, remember my dad? The career alcoholic? Well, he died yesterday. Wild, right? Wanna come to his weird memorial dinner at my mom's? Nothing too fancy but there might be cigars.'*"

He laughs and then doesn't. "You're an asshole, Mack."

"Don't call me an asshole. My dad died."

"Yeah. I heard."

Kevin doesn't take me home. Instead, he takes me to this craft cocktail bar a few miles from Mom's house, his treat.

"I owe you a drink, at least," he says when we park. I don't see how it's possible that he owes me anything else, but I don't have it in me to turn him down.

The bar is actually sort of cute for being picked out by Kevin. Lots of exposed wood, it's got a very rustic, Scandinavian thing going on. We sit at the bar, I assume because the girl working also has a very Scandinavian thing going on.

He orders us a pitcher of some obscure and expensive IPA he's recently discovered, and I nearly hide my face out of shame at being seen with him.

While we wait for the beer, we learn that the bartender's name is Stace, because of course it is, and that she is working here while she saves money to go back to school. She wants to be a veterinarian, and she leans provocatively over the bar to show Kevin pictures of her German Shepherd. We also learn that Stace gets off work at 1 AM, and was planning on calling her roommate to pick her up, but that her roommate sometimes goes to bed early, and if she could get a ride from someone else...

Her eyelashes basically tie themselves in knots batting at him.

The man is unstoppable.

Finally, the pitcher settles, and Kevin pours himself a glass and then slides what's leftover toward me. "Stace, sweetheart, can I get a straw for my friend here, so she can have her way with the rest of this?" Kevin asks. She blushes all over herself at being called "sweetheart," and I suppress my gag reflex.

"I don't know what you think I'm gonna say," I resist, sucking down IPA.

"Why don't we start with what the fuck happened and go from there." He turns his whole body toward me, leaning comfortably against the bar.

As I tell it, I hear it out loud for the first time. And it all sounds so much worse.

"It was nothing, really. It was—basically, I slept with some random on New Year's Eve. And the next morning, we're standing in my bathroom, and he's, like, being all weird and domestic and stuff, and then I get a phone call, from, you know, the Homeaway Inn where Gerald was living, or squatting, or whatever."

"The Express by the freeway?"

"*Of course* the fucking Express by the freeway. Like he'd have a chance at a regular Homeaway Inn. Anyway, it's this concierge girl, Beth. On the phone. And she's howling and basically tells me she's in the room with Gerald, and he's dead, and she hasn't called 9-1-1 because fuck the police or something, and so can I, like, come ID him, and, you know, call someone to, like, pick him up? And I can't say no. I mean, what do you say to that?"

Kevin opens his mouth like he might have an idea, but no words come out.

"Anyway, so I go. And I have to take this guy—the handsome one-night-stand domestic guy—because part of his domestic thing is that now he's all worried about me. Meanwhile, I don't even remember what his name is, so I feel bad asking him to leave 'cause he's just, like, trying to be nice, I guess? Anyway, we show up, and Gerald's— my *dad*—is um, just, like, naked on the floor. Like, naked on the floor, and dead. And Beth's there. Just, like, crying on his face. She's got his head in her lap, which is so fucking, like, *what the fuck*, and then she's just dripping these huge mascara tears on his face. And the domestic guy just barfs. I mean, he actually barfs because he doesn't know what to do, and he's probably never seen a naked dead guy before, because who has? So, I have to call the ambulance, and then, like, try to calm Beth down a little bit. And eventually, some paramedics show up, these two, like, cartoon paramedics, and they bag him up while Beth is chugging fucking white wine spritzers from the mini-fridge. And then the paramedics haul Gerald down the stairs and take him to the morgue. Or wherever they do autopsies. That's the morgue, right?"

It feels like no one in the bar is talking anymore.

"Fuck." Kevin downs the rest of his beer for emphasis and slams the empty glass down on the bar. "I mean, *fuck*, Mack. Fuck."

"Yeah, I don't know. I'm dealing with it," I say and sort of flip my hair like it's no big thing, which even I can tell is pointless. And it doesn't work. He's looking at me like you might look at a person after they've just fallen off a roof.

"I'm staying at the Express by the freeway," he says after a minute. "Just for a few nights while I'm in town." My face falls open.

"You were *there*, then."

"I guess I was there. Yeah."

"I… I didn't see you."

"*Yeah*," he says, his eyes sparkling at the innocence of this observation. "No shit."

I put my face in my hands, unsure where else to look. "You never think, when you're a kid, that you're going to grow up to be the disaster at the bar, telling their horrifying life story into a pitcher of beer. But here I am."

"How are you doing? I mean, like, Jesus Christ. How are you *doing*?" His voice is soft again like it was when he got out of the car. Like it was at the dinner table. He's asking the most obvious question in the world, but he puts his hand on my knee to do it, and something about it makes everything else goes dark. Like we're spotlit in this one little corner of the bar, just him and me. No more Stace. No more wood paneling. Just me and Kevin. He's looking right at me, into me, the way he used to when we were really friends, and I can't quite breathe right, and I can't lie to him.

"I—I don't—I sort of feel like, like—*finally*. You know? I sort of feel like, *okay*. It happened. The thing I… the thing I used to wish would happen for years… it happened. *Finally, it happened.* And I'm just—empty now. Like, I don't know what to do when I'm not waiting for that."

As soon as I say it, I worry it's too much. It is. Way too much. And I don't trust Kevin. I can't trust Kevin. *Obviously.* And I want to swallow it all back and leave. I shift my leg out from under his hand. We're treading this quiet where I know he must be thinking I'm evil and traitorous and selfish. I finish the pitcher, making that horrible straw slurping sound that soccer moms make with their frappucinos. And then, from out of the silence, he says, "Yeah. I know what you mean. Sometimes I wish my dad would die."

My heart tugs at the recognition, but I want to let him off the hook, so I say, "No, you don't."

His eyes drift over my face, the ghost of a smile in them. "Last summer, I slept with my dad's favorite caddy." He runs his thumbnail under his bottom lip. "Jonah. God, he wasn't even twenty-one yet. I don't know what it was about him. I think I just liked the attention. Or maybe it was just one too many business lunches hearing my dad proudly telling clients about the superior way this kid handled his balls, took such good care of his driver." He does something like laughing, but it looks like it hurts. "Anyway, we were out for a round, maybe a week after… and Jonah winked at me. It was nothing. It was so nothing... but my dad caught it... and... the look on his face when he fired the kid... when he told me he would appreciate if I didn't insist on, how did he put it, 'jeopardizing his reputation with my *lifestyle*.'" He gestures to Stace for another beer. "I know what you mean, Mack. I promise."

If people weren't so afraid of being fucked up, this moment would be the definition of intimacy.

We are breathing the same air at the same time, blinking at the same time, like two things that completely understand each other. We're closer to each other than we've ever been, and we're on separate sides of the world.

I get a pain in my chest like I want to say something. I run through a million clichés, and nothing is right. When I can't make the words come, when I can't find anything to say at all, I have to accept it's because we aren't really friends anymore. And I wonder if that's my fault or his. Wonder if we were always going to end up here. I want to hold him, and I can't. And so, I just keep not saying anything.

The booze is getting to my head. I close my eyes, and I think I see Gerald, but when I open them, it's only Kevin.

This feels like a big deal, but maybe it isn't.

It's quiet forever. Just me and him in our spotlight forever.

Until I flinch, and he catches me studying him. Then he shakes his head, lets out this sort of desperate laugh, and says, "But now it's now, and we're still here."

"Yeah. That's what you always tell me."

"Ha, well. I guess I like to think the worst thing doesn't have to be the last thing."

So, then we don't talk more about my dad, even though that's why we're here, or Kevin's dad, even though his company card is paying for our drinks. Instead, we order another round and gossip about everything we've been up to for the last couple years like tonight is normal, and no one is dead. It's hard for a few minutes, but then it's easier, and then it's fantastic.

Kevin tells me about his crude and explicit adventures in online dating. And I tell Kevin all about working at the Dear Alice offices and writing for her site.

"Alice hasn't changed an inch, I see." he jabs.

"Not true. She's getting into the astrology market," I offer, and I'm rewarded when his eyes go wide with disbelief. "Oh yeah. *Alice-trological* readings."

"You're fucking with me."

"I wish. She has me writing the weekly horoscopes."

He gets this mischievous look in his eye that I recognize from when we were in school. "*You're* writing horoscopes. How much do you know about that stuff?"

"Almost nothing," I admit. "But that's more than Alice."

"Mack, holy fuck. Do you understand that this is a goldmine of possibility for me?"

Of course, I hadn't realized it until now, but I should have. You are, at any moment, one of two things with Kevin: his date or his wingman. It's about three seconds before he has found out Stace's sign, Leo, and written a horoscope on his napkin for me to post this week. I want to throw the napkin away as soon as he hands it to me, but instead, I put it in my jacket pocket and promise to publish it.

"We're even now," I say. "For me crying on you earlier? We're even." He laughs and kisses my cheek, holding my face in his hands for a second too long. I wish he wouldn't, the way it lodges my heart between my ribs, but I'm too drunk to do anything about it.

We sit around the bar talking shit for another half hour or so, before I say, "Well, I'm gonna get a Lyft." Kevin makes a face like he doesn't want me to go, but he doesn't ask me to stay, and he doesn't offer to drive me either. "I think that'll just make it easier... you know... for you and Stace and everything," I go on. He smirks and nudges me to keep my voice down.

He follows me outside to wait, and when we hug good night, he kisses my temple and promises we'll see each other again soon. I nod and bite my tongue.

"We do have fun," he says, looking me dead in the eye, "and I do love you, Mack. But you know that."

My throat tightens up, and so I just look at the ground and get into the car. Kevin runs around to the driver's side window and hands the driver a fifty, even though that's not how this works, insisting it's his treat. I watch him from the back window as we pull away. He stands outside for a second, smiling and shaking his head at no one, before adjusting his shirt, stretching his neck from side to side and going back into the bar.

I do love you. You know that.

I turn around and slump down into the backseat. Do not fall for this again, Mackenzie. Don't do it. It's not worth it.

I take the napkin out of my pocket and read.

"You're on a lucky streak, Leo. You've met that special someone who attends to your needs and makes you feel like the queen of the world. Allow yourself to get swept up in the frenzy of it all. The stars have aligned, and it's not an exaggeration. You're at your sexual peak now, and you should take every opportunity to open yourself up to all this new man in your life has to offer."

It is *so* not worth it.

I don't realize quite how drunk I am until I'm climbing the stairs to our apartment. I fumble around for my keys outside the door, and I think I'm probably waking up the neighbors. Embarrassing. Finally inside, I bump into every piece of living room furniture I can on my way toward the bedrooms. "Motherfucking cocksucker," I blurt out after stubbing my toe on the coffee table. Even I'm surprised that I've been this profane, and I tell myself it's the tequila, wine, beer cocktail in my stomach talking.

"Mackenzie?" I hear Mel's groggy, half-asleep voice as the light switches on in her room.

"I woke you up. M'sorry!" I call to her.

"You're drunk, yeah?" I hear her sit up in bed. There's no fooling Mel. Or anyone at this point. I stumble down the hall and flop down on her bed.

"Kevin made me do it," I tell her as she strokes my hair.

I'm expecting her to be mad at me for going out with Kevin, but she doesn't say anything about it.

"How was dinner?"

I look at Mel's half-asleep face, and I know that I can't lie to her. "It was so sad," I admit. "It was so sad and horrible, Mel. And everyone was just so broken down and miserable to be there together. And Mom—" I remember her face in the bathroom, so tired and confused and upset with herself, and I wish I wasn't me so I could have been more to help her. I hope that Alice stayed with her for a long time after I left. "God, it was just so awful."

"I'm so sorry," she says.

"I think I did the whole thing wrong," I say.

"I don't think so." Her voice is so collected and patient, and I love her so much for always being this way with me. "There's not a right way, right? You just have to be you."

And so, I start to cry, there on Mel's bed, and she just strokes my hair and tells me that it's okay—that I'm going to be okay.

"Would you mind if I sleep here?" I ask, and she just smiles and scooches over to make room for me.

I curl up in a little ball next to her, and she puts her arm around me and coos nice things in my ear. I laugh a little through all my pathetic whimpering and say, "If we sleep the whole night like this, it might mean we're soulmates. I read all about it in a magazine."

And Mel just says, "Shut up, you freak. We *are* soulmates."

*

FILLMORE MIDDLE SCHOOL
NATURAL HELP COUNSELOR END-OF-SEMESTER REPORT
COUNSELOR VALERY MCMANNIS

Dear Mrs. James,

Hello, I hope that this letter finds you and your family well. My name is Valery McMannis, and I'm a Natural Help Counselor at Fillmore Middle School. I trust that you received the take-home notice at the beginning of the semester regarding the school's receipt of your request for your daughter, Mackenzie, to attend weekly meetings with a counselor in order to help her to cope with the difficulties in her home environment caused by your ex-husband's unfortunate circumstances.

I want to begin by telling you that you have a very special girl. Mackenzie is clearly a strong-willed and intelligent young mind. She shows a keen awareness of the circumstances surrounding your ex-husband's arrest and subsequent incarceration, so well done to you on making sure that she is informed of the predicament that you all find yourselves in. I understand that this must be a challenging and turbulent time at home, and I hope you know that you and your daughter are in my thoughts and prayers.

My concern, and the reason for my letter, is that Mackenzie seems to have adjusted to a place of—and I don't say this lightly—unfeeling.

This term "unfeeling" is one I use to describe a student who I believe has evolved into a place of emotional distance that will ultimately, without intervention, become his or her normal. In our sessions, Mackenzie maintains a detachment that is surprisingly steadfast for a child of her age. She is unable to discuss her emotions openly, and she gives very measured and minimal responses that are barely enough to get by on.

I know that one-on-one counseling is not the right path for some, and Mackenzie may simply not be the kind of child who wishes to talk things through. However, her extreme reluctance to engage with me suggests that more than not being a "talker," Mackenzie is struggling with severe trust issues. We are nearing the end of a whole semester of meeting together, and still, she remains so guarded that every session is a battle of wills. This kind of relationship has been exceptionally uncommon in my experience, even with my students with the most significant emotional disturbances.

What has become clear is that Mackenzie is a very angry child. She is holding onto a lot of resentment toward, I believe, both you and your ex-husband for the ways she feels that both of you have failed her. I worry that this resentment is causing her to "grow up" at a rate that is unhealthy for someone her age. My concern is that Mackenzie's anger is so deeply seated that she'll begin to lash out at others. I am sensing some of this behavior in her already, towards myself, especially, as well as toward other faculty members. I have been informed about incidences of back-talking and disregard for authority.

The imprisonment of your ex-husband seems to me to be a single layer in what is a much more complex onion of difficulty, to use a metaphor. I would be sorry to see Mackenzie grow into a woman who struggles with intimacy and emotional attachment, and yet I fear that this is the path she is already traveling down.

Perhaps it would be fruitful for me and you to sit down and discuss the options for Mackenzie so that she might continue counseling outside of school, and maybe even on a more routine basis? For me, the best outcome is an emotionally healthy student, and I feel there is still much work to be done before your daughter is out of the woods for future trauma and dysfunction. If we intervene together, we have a chance to help Mackenzie be the best young woman that she can be, given her situation.

I hope you'll be in touch soon. Again, you truly do have a special child, and it has been my pleasure getting to know her as best I can.

Warm regards,
Valery

*

January 3rd

Mel is already up and making us egg white omelets when I wake up. On her bedside table, she has laid out a tall glass of water and two Advil. She has even left a hot pink Post-It note on the glass of water that says, "DRINK ME." Precious.

She brings in the omelets on her special breakfast-in-bed tray. "I love this thing," she says, setting the tray down over my legs as I sit up. "Okay, so," she points at the plate with a fork. "Egg white, scallion, pancetta, and fontina. I went a little heartier because I figured you'd be hungover, yeah? And then just some fruit. Nothing weird, just grapes and a little melon." She smiles in this way that makes me think she might be about to cut up the omelet herself and feed it to me. Thankfully, she does not. "What are you doing today? Anything?"

"I have to write the Alice-trology shit for the New Year, but otherwise not a whole lot. Sleeping off the last couple days." Mel flashes a judge-y face that I think must have been unintentional.

"Well, I'm gonna go for a run if you wanna come with?" She stands up and starts changing into running clothes. Rain beats down against the windows, and I laugh as a way of saying "literally never," and then focus in on my breakfast. She is wriggling into her spandex when she adds, "And then, Luke gets in tomorrow afternoon. I told you about that, right? I'm picking him up at the airport at 3:12? If you don't remember, that's okay. Because of everything that's going on, you know. I wouldn't expect you to remember."

I glance up from my omelet. "No, I remember."

Before everything went sideways, I was even looking forward to seeing Luke, Mel's long-distance boyfriend who we love. They've been together for almost five years and have lived on opposite sides of the country for two of them. Luke is getting his masters or Ph.D. or something studying Forestry at Yale.

I have asked a few different times what it means to study forestry—whether Luke is going to graduate and become a park ranger like Yogi bear. Mel always says that you can do a million different very important things for the environment with a degree in Forestry, and that, of course, it's nothing like Yogi bear who she's convinced was addicted to pot and probably never graduated from anywhere. And then she goes, "I mean, what does an American Studies degree *mean*? Not everything has to mean something." I think that, really, Mel has no idea why Luke is studying Forestry, and maybe that Luke doesn't know for sure either.

"Well, I wasn't sure, and I just wanted to check and make sure that, like...Is that gonna be okay? I know it's weird because of everything that's happening with you." I wish she'd stop saying "everything" like that. It's not "everything," it's just one thing. And I'm dealing with it.

"You can't exactly ask him to cancel his flight because my dad's dead." This makes her flinch, and I don't know why. It's not *her* dad. "Mel. It's fine. You know I like Luke."

She sighs, "Well, all right. I'm just checking." She laces up her sneakers and heads for the door and then turns around and says, "You know, it's okay not to be okay. The world won't end or anything."

I do my best to see the back of my skull. "I know it's okay. The thing that doesn't seem to be okay is that really *I am fine*."

"That'd be completely okay if you weren't so full of shit," she says. "Eat your omelet."

I spend the rest of the day asleep or half-asleep watching infomercials and daytime soaps in Mel's bed.

The people on the soap operas are an inspiration. Every episode someone else dies, or is dying, or is revealed to be sleeping with their brother's ex-wife's cousin's former lover, and no matter what, they all handle it with precision and grace. One woman, Evelyn Something, is my hero. She found out that her son was dying of the pneumonia he contracted from his ex-wife during the affair they had after she married her current husband, who is also his cousin. Evelyn only cried for exactly fifteen seconds before gathering herself together and writing the most beautiful eulogy I've ever heard. I text Mel that I wish I were exactly like Evelyn because she is perfect, and she texts back that she doesn't know who Evelyn is, and maybe I should get out of bed.

My favorite infomercial is one for a pot that somehow magically cooks every different kind of food perfectly. It's the only pot you'll ever need ever again, the woman in the infomercial keeps bellowing. She threw away VIRTUALLY EVERY OTHER POT IN HER KITCHEN. "Imagine the time I save on dishes! I finally have time to spend with my husband!"

I don't believe that she really has a husband, but I am excited about the idea of only ever having to wash one pot for the rest of my life. So, when she takes a third, perfectly cooked casserole out of the oven, I call in and order one.

I have completely glazed over.

January 4th

Last night was a bust. I barely slept, lying awake instead and reading about the Five Stages of Grief and being alternately irritated and comforted. I'm not sure if I buy into the model entirely. It's almost offensively tidy and cute. I don't believe in emotions that come in five easy steps like that. I've never had one.

So, then I've been thinking about what I think grief is supposed to look like—what I understand about loss, what it is, and what it means—because I received a liberal arts education that taught me how to make everything small and academic.

The shitty thing about being a young person is that everyone is always telling you about how young you are. You say something like, "Life is hard," and everyone within a five-block radius that is even remotely older than you is immediately down your throat about how you don't know anything because you haven't really lived yet. And then they laugh to each other in this morbid and depressing way that suggests that at a certain age all this terrible shit happens to you all at once, and then you're allowed to say that you "get it."

I don't believe in that at all.

I think age is a fucking joke. A person just lives. And you've just seen what you've seen whenever you've seen it.

It doesn't matter if you're an old person or not. It just matters that something happened, and you were there. Because all the terrible shit does happen at once sometimes, but it doesn't wait around for you to be old enough to handle it.

And so, I started to make a list of things I've lost. Already. At my ripe, young age of twenty-four.

Things I have lost:

My luck, or my self-confidence, or both…if I ever had either

My capacity to see the good in people…if there ever was any

My ability to trust any person with a face that I like

My father, if I ever had one

I read the list back to myself, and it all sounds so melodramatic and pathetic, but looking at it again, I'm not sure how else it could sound.

I think about what I said to Lana about having lost my dad at a young age, and I feel the truth of it in my bones. The phrase "I'm sorry for your loss" feels long belated. He's been lost to me for so long that I'd stopped seeing the lines of his face in my own. What I lost has been gone for years: his love, though I'm not sure when, his heart, ages before it failed him, my best friend, in a slur of stumbling days he never remembered. I think of the afternoons I spent in his company, desperate for his help to find the parts of him I'd already lost. The days I picked fights just to feel something from him. I want so much to remember a time when everything about us wasn't loss. Some way that it doesn't have to always end up the same: with him leaving, and me alone.

And yet, if anything, death has made him less lost than found. He turns up everywhere; my cruelty is his; I still hold his temper, his spite. I make his jokes. I laugh his laugh. I smile with his mouth. I spread my arms across the bed, and thumb over my freckles like they're constellations that might offer me some sense of direction. This toffee skin I inherited from him too, and him from his father, an even bigger mystery. Maybe loss is just part of our lineage.

My head hurts. The sun is coming up, I've been awake all night, and nothing is solved. I have to get out of this bed.

"Is this what Denial feels like?" I am talking to Mel through the bathroom door. She is in the shower, getting ready for work, but I can't be alone with my brain for even one more minute. I want to get her opinion on some of these ideas I've had.

She shuts off the water. "What are you talking about?"

"Kubler-Ross. Five Stages of Grief. Do you think I'm in Denial right now?" Mel comes dripping out of the bathroom, wrapped in a Yale towel that Luke sent her. "It's the first stage, so I kinda figure I must be. But your other options are Anger, Bargaining, Depression or Acceptance, if one of those sounds better," I add. "What do you think?"

Mel looks confused as she wrings her hair into a hand towel, and squeezes by me in the hallway. "I think," she calls from the bedroom, "that you should come in today before I pick up Luke, and we should have an appointment, is what I think." She reappears in the hallway in her underwear. I should have known she would say this.

"That's not really what I asked," I try to steer us back in the direction of my Denial. She shrugs, going back to the bathroom to brush her teeth.

"I don't know enough about psychology to give you an opinion on that, Kenz." Her mouth is all foamy, "But I do think"—spit—"that I could really help you through whatever stage you're in if you came for an appointment." She cups her hands under the faucet, gathering up some water before gargling for altogether too long, spitting again, and looking at me, her hip leaned very seriously against the sink. "I won't have this kind of time in my schedule once Luke is here, so then you'll have to wait 'til after he goes back to school." There's a long pause where she just raises her eyebrows in a very peer-pressure-y kind of way. I figure that we aren't going to talk about my theories on grief.

Mel works at her parent's juicery, Juice & Harmony. Their flagship Seattle store opened a few years before Mel was born, and, because of the amount of success they've seen, they now have opened several more storefronts around the Pacific Northwest. Mel started at the bottom of the ladder as a "Juice Slinger" in high school because it was all she could fit in around her cross-country schedule, but since college, she has really focused on her work and now has invented her own unique brand of juice therapy. Her official title now is a word she coined herself: Jutritionist.

It's entirely impossible to take her seriously sometimes.

"You wouldn't believe it, but usually diet is a huge factor in determining your mood," she's always saying to anyone who'll listen. "And so really what I do is just common sense. By balancing out the internal state using specific juice and smoothie blends, I can help people to see a difference in themselves and their lives. Even within the first day." Someone should give Melanie an infomercial. She could take over the world.

Peer pressure works, and I agree to come in at one o'clock and sit down with her to figure out a juice plan to help me "battle my grief." I'd never tell her that really, I think the whole juice thing is a little bullshit. But the larger reality is that if Mel can help make any of this make more sense, I'd owe her big.

Not even fifteen minutes after she's left for work, I get a text from Kevin that reads: *Threesome w/bartender thx 2 u & ur whoroscope. LOL. But seriously, where r u, babe? Lunch?*

The place we agree on for lunch, this cafe next door to Mel's juice bar, is by far the most Seattle-y place in the city, meaning that the Wi-Fi password is kale_chips, and there are four, count them, *four* different white adult males inside with dreadlocks.

I get a curried tofu sandwich that I don't want and grab a table to wait for Kevin.

He is twenty minutes late and hungover.

"Mack," he says my name like he's just found an oasis after weeks in the desert.

"You look like shit, Kev." It's an understatement. He keeps his sunglasses on indoors, and he's wearing an all-black velour tracksuit that I think he must be borrowing from someone since it's several sizes too big in addition to being tacky as shit. He looks like he hasn't slept much, but I lean across the table to crackle some dried drool from his cheek with my thumb. When I'm done, he kisses my hand and slumps back in his seat.

I am painfully aware of everyone staring at us.

"You wouldn't even believe me if I told you," Kev starts. "The last couple nights have been *out of control*, Mack." His voice is far too loud for the room.

"Oh, I can see that." The third dreadlocked man glowers at us from across the cafe. *We* are disturbing *him*. Shame is with me in abundance.

Kevin begins to detail the first night's escapades with Stace and her roommate, a Chinese acrobat named Henry. It is precisely as explicit as the dirtiest thing I've ever heard, and I'm annoyed when he gets a laugh out of me. From time to time, he throws his head back and runs a hand along his throat like he's trying to coax the words out. He's just describing how to get into a sexual position called "The Reluctant Organ Donor" when I hear a familiar nickname from the vicinity of the counter.

"Kenzie? Shit. Hi."

And before I know what to do, Neil is standing at our table, blinking a lot of boyish innocence in my direction.

"*Hello*," Kevin drawls, lowering his sunglasses at Neil, coming out of his sex-tired haze for the first time today. The pull at the corner of his mouth betrays that the symmetry of Neil's face hasn't escaped him either.

"Neil. Hi." I swallow audibly. My "hi" sounds all gaspy and windswept as if I were seeing Neil for the first time in years on a cliffside after a torrid love affair, which is to say, entirely inappropriate.

Then nothing. If there were supposed to be more words at this moment, everyone forgot what they were. I sit staring at Neil, who shifts his gaze from me to Kevin and back, blinking the whole time. I assume Kevin was doing about the same, albeit with less decency, but I couldn't bring myself to look at him.

Finally, Neil looks around, trying his best to be casual and says, "I didn't know you liked this place. It, uh—doesn't really seem like you."

"Oh. Well yeah. It's not really me," I say.

"Fuck off, Adams. *You* suggested it," Kevin teases.

"So. How are you?" Neil ignores him, getting this very intense look on his face. "I've been thinking about you a lot the past couple days."

Kevin's face shifts as he puts together how I know Neil, and he leans back in his chair, now laser-focused on my face.

"Neil, this is my friend, Kevin." I hear myself use the word and regret it, but it's too late. "And Kevin, this is Neil. He's um, a trainer at my roommate's gym. But he likes sports. So, he's gonna be a sports trainer… or… something. Soon." This is my worst introduction ever. The two of them shake hands.

"I'm just," Neil looks impatiently to the counter for his food. "I was in the neighborhood because I was talking to Mel about some of her clients… she has a couple athletes she might want to refer to me. You know, once I level up."

Kevin makes a sharp noise, trying not to laugh, and I can't breathe.

Neil only shrugs a little, and then lowers his voice, "I'm not really—this isn't really my kind of place either."

"*Okay,*" snorts Kevin, and I kick him under the table.

"Sure, no, I know. You're more the waffles type," I say in this weird voice I didn't know I had. Neil laughs this funny tiny laugh and then, all of a sudden looks shy about it.

"Well, anyway," he says, "It was good to see you, Kenzie. You look good… *better.*"

Better? The word rattles around between us, and I don't really make words back, just nod. He puts his hand on my shoulder, and I flinch. Kevin exhales a small shuddering laugh, and Neil goes, "Right. Okay," and then goes and waits at the counter for his food before disappearing out onto the street.

Once he's gone, Kev's eyes get all bulgy-eyed and excited. "*Kenzie,*" he gapes at me. "*Very* cute."

I beg him to not.

He gathers his mouth into his fist to suppress a massive smirk and then asks a bunch of questions about Neil that I don't really answer. He gets bored when I don't play along and eventually goes back to detailing his exploits. I'm half-listening, but mostly I stare out the window, replaying that run-in over and over. It has left this jangling feeling in my chest, and I want to understand what it was about being with Neil again that has me so undone. When the only time we've ever really spent together was with a corpse, I don't know what I expected. That we could just go ahead and be normal friends? I sort of wish he would come back, and I also really don't. *We don't actually know each other at all*, I keep reminding myself. *You don't know him.* But I can still feel where he put his hand on my back. *Why did he say I looked better?*

"I don't even know him," I say aloud to Kev, who has just finished saying the word "wetness," which no doubt made horrifying sense in context.

"Who? The… what'd you call him the other night? The domestic guy?"

"Neil."

"Sure, okay, Neil." Kevin looks wholly uninterested in learning his name, and I don't really blame him. "All right. You don't know him. Got it. I didn't say you did."

"I'm just saying." Kevin's eyes glimmer like I'm full of shit, and he reaches across the table and smooths my forehead with his thumb.

"Just trying to get your face to match your words, *Kenzie*," he mocks. He knows me too well—the best and worst thing about Kevin.

I glance up at the clock, 12:46. "I have that appointment, actually, so I should—you know. I don't want to be late."

"Hey. Seriously. You okay?"

"I just don't like to be late is all." I'm already getting up from the table—my body shifts into autopilot. I don't know what it is, but I can't be here anymore. My ribs are too tight, and I need to not cry here, not in front of Kevin. I've already let him back in more than I meant to.

"I thought you said it was right next door."

I'm putting on my coat and my scarf, stuffing my wallet into my bag. "I did, but you know. Early is on time, on time is late, blah blah blah." I lean in to kiss him on the cheek and then think better of it and straighten. I pat him on the head instead, which feels… very weird.

"Your treat, yeah?"

"Mack," he starts to say, but I am walking away and out the door before he can finish.

The fresh air is good, but it's not what I'm after. I immediately search the street for Neil, though despite my desperation, he's nowhere, because why would he be. I feel so shaky and weak that for a second, I think I should just sit down on the curb and get my shit together, but then I start to worry that Kevin will come out looking for me. So, I practically run until I'm inside Juice & Harmony. I close the door and then press my back against the wall next to the Juice-To-Go fridge and close my eyes.

When I open them, the high schooler behind the counter is watching me, nervous.

"I have an appointment with the Jutritionist," I tell her, as though that sentence makes me sound more reasonable.

She shrugs and says, "Ohhhhkay," like she doesn't believe me, but she goes into the back to get Mel.

In the few minutes when I'm alone, I can't tell if I'm going to cry or laugh. I try both but don't really manage either.

"Everything is just so fucking fucked up," I whisper to the ceiling fan, and it totally agrees.

Mel is wearing the Lululemon equivalent of a pantsuit. She has her hair swept up into this perfectly imperfect bun, and she's wearing a little more make-up than usual because of her impending boyfriend. She looks absurdly healthy.

"How's your morning?" She asks me while we're getting settled in her office. She has a bowl of fruit on her desk, and she offers me a banana. I take it, but then I don't want it and just sort of play with it while I talk.

"Weird. I don't know," I say and wonder the last time I felt anything else.

"So. Talk to me." Mel says, "Why are you here?" Then she goes all quiet and patient, and she makes this see-how-professional-I-am face.

"You told me to come in," I say because I'm a brat. She takes a deep breath and then smiles heavily at me.

"What are your goals for our time together?"

I squint at her, trying to get her to break focus, but it doesn't work. I sort of wish Mel would be more Mel right now, but then I think this is about as Mel as she ever is.

I start like nine different sentences, trying to figure out what it is that I need to say. "I guess... I don't know... I guess I'm having a..." Until finally I come out with it. "My dad died." Mel blinks at me a couple times, then nods, closing her eyes like she understands anything.

"I'm sorry," she says in this very neutrally, compassionate voice.

"Yeah, well. Yeah." I wonder if there's more, but it doesn't seem like it. My mind is just this low buzzing static. My eyes wander around her office. There are a lot of charts and diagrams and food pyramids, and all of them make me feel like I am never eating anything right.

"Grief can be a complicated emotion," Mel says next. "It's one of the hardest emotions to prepare yourself for because it's so often brought on by the unexpected." I love that she says this. I love that she wasn't an expert on grief when she got out of the shower this morning but, now, she has all kinds of thoughts on the subject. I laugh a little, and she takes a bite of an apple and then pulls a clipboard out of her desk.

"So, to help us to get started, I want you to fill out this client intake form." She hands me the clipboard. The form is my least favorite kind of form: lots of big spaces for writing in paragraph-long details about things like your goals, hopes, and dreams. "The first half of the page is the required client information, and then you can look over the other questions and decide what you think it'll be helpful for me to know while we're working together." She hands me a pen and gets up from her desk, heading toward the door, so I can fill out the form in solitude as though she believes privacy will help me.

From behind my chair, she says, "The back of the form is just the billing information. You can skip that stuff."

I don't want her pity. "I can pay you, Mel."

"I know you can. But you're my friend, and I don't want you to."

And then she's gone.

*

JUICE & HARMONY

Melanie Itzhaki-Sweet, Jutritional Specialist

Initial Client Intake Form

FULL NAME: Mackenzie Elizabeth Adams

AGE: 24

HEIGHT: 5'8"

WEIGHT: ~~A lady doesn't tell~~. 145ish? I try not to keep track.

ALLERGIES: Penicillin (?)

DIETARY RESTRICTIONS: I hate tuna fish and tuna fish casseroles. I also try to avoid stringy greens like okra and stuff. I prefer sugary food, but I guess that's not a restriction. Oh! No goat's milk. Too weird.

REASON FOR APPOINTMENT: Death in the family. ~~Grief~~. Bossy roommate. ~~Weird boy stuff~~

WHAT ARE YOU HOPING TO GAIN FROM THIS EXPERIENCE:

To be more in control of ~~everything~~ my feelings? Or to understand them better. Just to feel better, I guess. Can that be a goal?

WHAT WOULD BE A SUCCESSFUL OUTCOME FOR YOU:

Feeling less like shit would be ideal.

WHAT ARE THE WEAKNESSES OF YOUR CURRENT DIET:

All of it.

How much shitty Mexican food I eat in any given week.

HOW WOULD YOU CHARACTERIZE YOUR RELATIONSHIP TO FOOD:

Life partners in an open relationship.

HAVE YOU EVER WORKED WITH A JUTRITIONIST BEFORE:

Are there even other Jutritionists in the country? In the world? I honestly thought you were the only one.

IF YES, WHEN? WHERE? WHAT WAS YOUR EXPERIENCE LIKE?

Like I said, I didn't even know there were more. But I'm sure you're the best one.

*

When she comes back in, and I give back the clipboard, she rolls her eyes, scanning over my answers.

"Do you actually want my help?" She puts the clipboard on the desk and looks at me like Mel for the first time. It makes me feel like a total ass.

"Yes," I sort of murmur. "Please."

She sits down and waits for me to talk, and I think about how many times people have done this to me in the last four days.

"I saw Neil?" It comes out as a question even though it isn't one. Mel looks up, surprised.

"When? Today?"

"He was at that place next door to you," I say, looking past her at a chart about the average Americans caloric intake, which is maybe the most depressing chart I've ever seen. "I was having lunch… with Kevin." Whenever I say his name to Mel, I think this must be what it feels like to go to a confessional.

"How was it?" She takes a piece of paper out of her desk and makes a little note on it, then looks up at me before writing something else.

"Kevin's the worst. You know that." I shrink down in my seat because I know that too, and, thinking back about his text, I'm ashamed of myself for going to lunch with him at all. "But you know. He loves me. In his own way," I add, and I'm disappointed to find that it sounds just as pathetic out loud as it does in my head.

"I meant how was it to see Neil," Mel goes on like she didn't even hear Kevin's name.

"Oh. It was fucking weird."

"Weird bad?" Mel makes more notes.

"Weird… I don't know." I wish she would stop trying to Valery me. I don't care about getting Valery-ed, especially by Mel.

"I think you do know, and you don't want to say," she says. I don't believe that any of this is what a Jutritionist does under normal circumstances. But then again, I suppose Mel sets the bar for that.

"It's not a big deal. It's just... he—" I make eye contact with Mel, and then immediately divert my gaze back to the calorie chart. "He, I don't know. Seeing him... it reminds me of everything." She leans back in her chair and nods. "He reminds me that Gerald's dead... and of the stale smell in the Homeaway Inn... just of everything." I can tell by Mel's face that this is the kind of breakthrough she was hoping for, though I'm not even sure if it's real. Some of it feels true, but mostly I feel like I'm not even in my brain anymore, like my mouth is just going while my brain runs into walls in the background. All these pie charts are overwhelming.

Mel scribbles something else on her piece of paper. "That must be hard," she says, finally.

"I don't know. I guess so." Between 1970 and 2003, the average American increased their caloric intake by 523 calories a day. "Can we talk about the juice?"

"Kenz, it's important to work through—"

"I really just want to talk about juice now." I hold her gaze until she looks away and out the window.

"Okay." She sighs and puts her pen down. "I have a lot of ideas about things we can start you on." Her eyes pass over my face a couple times, and so I press my mouth into a happier looking shape and nod. "And I warn all my clients that the sudden shift in diet can have a pretty intense effect on your moods in the first couple days." She gets up from her desk and grabs a "My First Month with Juice" form.

"That's fine. Intense is fine."

"Okay, then. Well. Let's get started."

My pockets are stuffed to bursting with vitamin supplements and fancy organic powders when I leave Juice & Harmony. Mel has written me a list the length of my arm that tells me what produce to buy at the co-op. I am lucky because I can use her fancy blenders and juicers, so I don't have to shell out for my own. She even sends me home with a bookmarked smoothie recipe guide for beginners.

Riding the bus equipped with all this stuff makes me feel healthier already. I'm humming a little to myself as I prance around the store looking for a series of unfamiliar fruits and veggies. I think maybe I'll become a person who could seriously use the word "veggies."

The more things I've never heard of that I put into my basket, the giddier I get. By the time I get to checkout, I'm basically dancing.

"Is that your phone?" The checker, seemingly amused by my delirium, has started looking around, confused.

"What?" I'm initially caught off guard, and then I remember that I changed my ringtone a couple days ago, to the default ring, which I now don't recognize. "Oh, god. Yes, that's me," I say, picking it up without looking to see who's calling. "Sorry." I'm pretty sure I make this "eek" face that I've seen Alice make whenever she receives a phone call in the middle of a transaction.

Beth sounds different than I remember her. She sounds younger or blonder or something. And she's calling from a new number. "I didn't think I'd actually get you. I thought maybe you'd be at work or somewhere," is what she opens with. There's a palpable amount of fear in her voice.

"Well, I'm at the grocery store," I say, trying to look nonchalant to the checker, who mouths, "do you need a bag today" at me.

"I didn't think I'd get you," she says again. "I wrote down notes for what I was planning to say in a voicemail."

I shake my head at the checker, and hold the phone between my shoulder and my ear as I try to fit all this produce into my tote bag and the reusable grocery bag that Mel insists I take with me everywhere for "emergencies."

"Well, you can just read me your notes if you want, I guess," I say. The butternut squash is not fitting on top of everything else, and I realize I probably should have packed it first.

"Is that all right?" Even more like a mouse is really how she sounds.

"Let's hear it, Beth," I say, dumping everything back onto the grocery conveyor belt and starting again. Doug-the-checker tries to help me. There's a strange silence on the other end of the line, and then I hear her take a deep breath before launching in.

"Hello Mackenzie, this is Beth Bruce from the Homeaway Inn Express downtown, calling you from my personal number. I am calling about your father, Gerald Adams, who recently... *passed on.*" She gulps down tears. Putting the squash at the bottom of the bag has made it so that now that farro doesn't fit and Doug says he'll give me another bag, and he won't even charge me the five cents, but I shake my head, intimating that I don't want another bag. What I want is for everything to fit into these two bags that I already have. "Your father left behind several personal items in his hotel room," Beth goes on, "including a letter that is addressed to you, Mackenzie."

And then I drop the phone, or maybe it wasn't very well balanced to begin with. Either way, the phone is now on the floor, and I am standing there holding a large bunch of bananas and a bag of farro and not picking it up.

I think a million things at once. I have so many questions for Beth. Like, who the fuck is she? Like, why the fuck is she calling me and expecting me to be at work? Like, why does she think I even want this letter? Like, what does this letter even say?

Doug asks me if I'm okay, most likely because my face has gone all rubbery and blank. When I don't respond, he offers to re-bag things for me so that I can finish my phone call. He has put the "lane closed" sign out on his conveyor belt, and I really hope he didn't do this just because of me, but I didn't see him do it, so I can't know for sure. Regardless, I set down the bananas and pick up my phone.

"Are you there? I heard a bang or something... Mackenzie!?" Beth has gone totally hysterical.

"I'm here," I close my eyes and clench my jaw tight before asking, "You were saying that there's a letter?"

"Well, um, yes. Among... other things. Yes." I hear her sorting through, finding her place in her notes again. She clears her throat. "In the interest of respecting your father's memory, I would like for us to meet at your earliest convenience so that I might pass some of his effects onto you and deliver the letter. In-person." My head is swimming. I look over at Doug-the-checker, puzzling over how to fit all my shit into my two bags.

"Why didn't you tell me before?" My voice is sharper than I intend, but I'm suddenly so angry I can't breathe. "Why didn't you tell me that there was a fucking letter when I came for his body?" This grabs Doug's attention, and I will him not to make it weird.

Beth starts to sob. Her voice is close to the phone and then far away, and I gather that her hands are doing that graceless uncontrollable wobbling thing. "I just," she wails, "I didn't want to upset you more!" People around the supermarket are starting to watch me. I glimpse Doug-the-checker out of the corner of my eye, giving me a meek thumbs up after having figured out the bagging situation.

"For fuck's sake. Pull yourself together," I hiss at Beth. There are another few moments of whimpering before I hear her sniffle and reshuffle her notes.

"I am—" she clears her throat, "I am available during the day tomorrow for a meeting. I understand that this is an incredibly difficult time and won't pretend to know the trauma you're going through—" her voice breaks off, and I think she might lose it again, but she holds steady. "Please feel free to contact me at this number to arrange the details. I will wait to hear from you." And then she hangs up before I can say anything else.

I pick up my groceries and thank Doug for his patience. He asks me if everything is all right, and I give a half nod before leaving the store.

The sky is a clear, bright blue, but there's no warmth in it. Instead, it's all biting cold that starts to numb me as soon as I'm out the door. Maybe it's not the cold. Maybe I'd be numb in 80-degree weather too. I don't honestly know.

For a long time, I just sit on a bench at a bus stop, looking into the street, thinking abstractly about getting hit by cars. The buses going by me are headed in the wrong direction to take me home, but it doesn't matter. I'm not waiting.

I have this fantasy that Neil will be going by this bus stop for some reason and see me. That he'll have gone to the store to pick up some useless thing he buys, like protein powder, and then, through an act of fate, he'll pass by this bus stop and ask me what's wrong. It makes no sense that I want to see him so badly when seeing him was so strange. And still, I feel myself smiling as I play out what we might say to each other, and how I might make a bad joke that we have to stop meeting like this, and how his perfect teeth would part in a little laugh. I imagine that this is the kind of thing that would happen if I lived in a movie where life was consistently romantic in its sadness. But I do not.

What happens instead is that a homeless man comes and sits next to me and asks if I can spare any change for the bus, and when I give him a dollar bill, he smiles and says "bless your heart." Without warning, my chest clamps tight around my lungs and my face gets hot from tears I can't bear to cry. Instead, I just smile back and say, "yours too," before getting up and walking toward anywhere else.

Once I'm walking, I don't want to stop. And so, the afternoon ends with me walking the two and a half miles back to our apartment, weighed down by produce that I don't know how to eat.

Luke is in the living room, eating Oat Bran and listening to a podcast when I come in. When he sees me, he takes his headphones out, drops the cereal on the coffee table, and insists on taking my bags so I can sit.

"I see Mel told you," I guess, relinquishing the bags and flopping down on the couch. He gets a very guilty look on his face and sets the groceries on the floor instead of taking them to the kitchen.

"Anything in there gonna melt?" he asks, and when I shake my head, he sits down next to me. "How are you?" I don't move, and he looks me over with his very soft and sympathetic brown eyes. "It's good to see you."

I look at him and laugh pitifully. I can't think of anything eloquent to say, so I don't bother. I slump against him on the couch and close my eyes.

"Oof," he says. "That bad, huh?" I feel his arm come around my shoulder and squeeze, and I just laugh some more to keep from crying.

I forget sometimes, when he's on the other side of the country, how much I really do like Luke. Another Black kid from a vastly white town, he and I bonded quickly when we first met. He's the kind of guy I'd want to see coming in to rescue me from a fire. This big, broad-shouldered, mountain man from Maine, with a beard that suits him beautifully, he wears a lot of rugged plaid flannel as I presume is required by his Forestry major. It amuses me that the tiny hipster men of Seattle dedicate hours of their lives to trying to look as effortlessly handsome and outdoorsy as Luke. He's one of those rare boyfriends of my friends who I would be happy to be friends with regardless.

"Where's Mel?" I ask, calmed by the ease of being still for a bit.

"Gym," he says, smiling at the mention of her name. "I figured I'd stay here, get settled, shower, have something to eat, and then we'll go out when she's back." Even at my most jaded, I am buoyed that couples like Mel and Luke exist. I sigh, and he looks warmly at me. "And then, of course, I wanted to see you." He rubs my arm and sits forward, reaching for his cereal and stirring me from his shoulder. "You gonna be okay, slugger?" I roll my eyes and laugh, running my face through my hands.

"Eventually."

He nudges me in the ribs gently, his mouth now full of oats.

"Hey, um, since you're here… do you mind sitting with me for a little bit while I make this weird phone call?"

"Anything you need, Kenzo."

So, we sit together while I call Beth and arrange the details.

January 5th

My inheritance is, in reality, a cookie tin full of old photos of me and even older photos of Mom, an invitation to Mom and Jimmy's wedding, envelope and all, a half-smoked carton of Marlboros, a water-damaged old painting that Mom did once of a cherry tree, his clothes, his keys, and the letter. All stacked very neatly in a cardboard box.

Beth sits across from me in a Starbucks downtown, in no make-up, and a very simple black sweater dress. She looks as though she hasn't slept in days, and she fiddles with a too-big-for-her ring on her thumb every time she speaks.

"I didn't read the letter. Just your name on the envelope," she says, as I sort through the contents of the box. She isn't looking at me even when she's looking at me. Her face is vacant, ghost-like, and her eyes are these enormous empty saucers. Her skin is pale, almost translucent in the winter sunlight, and her lips are chapped. She is drying herself out, mourning my father.

"How old are you, Beth?" She would look young if she didn't look so dead.

"Twenty-six," she squeaks.

"Hmm." I open the cookie tin and pick up a tear-stained picture of Mom in a sarong. It must have been taken on their honeymoon. Beth slides the ring off her thumb and puts it on the table. Then she twirls it back onto her thumb. I should give the pictures to Mom. In her new state, she might like them. Or they'd just end up in another forgotten box of old things—stashed away in her attic or molding with the rest of his stuff in the garage. But still, knowing she had them, that he'd held onto them all those years later, might give her some kind of peace.

"I didn't call sooner because I didn't want to upset you is all," Beth sputters, and it breaks my focus. I had forgotten she was here for a moment. I glance up at her face, and the hollowness of it makes me feel like apologizing too—for snapping at her over the phone in the supermarket, for being too callous at the hotel—but I don't.

"No, it's all right," I tell her.

"It's just… These things—his things. They belong with you." Her eyes dart from crumbs on the windowsill out onto the street, watching an old man playing saxophone for spare change on the corner outside Tiffany & Co. The expression on her face softens as if she can hear his melody over the trendy folk song on Starbucks radio and the 6th avenue traffic. I lay the photos back in the cardboard box and check my phone like I'm expecting to hear from someone. Nothing.

The ring clinks when it lands on the table again, and I stare a while as she fiddles with it. It's his wedding band. I would know that ring anywhere; the way the gold has worn down with age, the little scratches in the metal, the amateurish inscription on the inside.

Sometimes, sitting in that tiny hotel room, on the days when Gerald was at his worst, I would stare down at that ring while he ranted. I would try to distract myself with it, a little fleck of gold, jammed onto his knobby, weathered hand. Part of me was always angry that he still wore it so long after the divorce as if it gave him some lingering rights to our family. And at the same time, I would have hated for him to have taken it off. *He loves you, and he loves Mom*, the ring told me. *Even now, even though he can't say so.*

But now here it is, hanging off Beth's tiny thumb. "You two must have been close," I say, while she twists the band around and around.

Twist, clink, twist. Clink. The ring falls still on the table, and she notices my fixation.

"I'm sorry." Her face crumples for an instant, but she irons it out and doesn't cry. I put my elbows on the table like I want to say something, but then I look out the window instead.

I hate thinking about them—how she was already there, and how she knew before me, before Mom. She was the reason he'd called for room service. She was the reason he was naked when he died—little, twenty-six-year-old Beth. He must have told her he loved her, too, given her the ring so she could be sure of it. Was she wearing it that morning? Was she wearing it when the paramedics came? I can't remember now. Everything is a blur. Then I wonder if Beth is short for anything. For Elizabeth, maybe. And I think of Mom.

Maybe I'll just light the letter on fire.

"He was a gentleman," she says, after what feels like years of silence, and somehow, it's almost funny.

"Go ahead and keep the ring," I say, without looking at her. "It doesn't mean anything to anyone anymore." I don't know if that's true, but I couldn't bring myself to touch it now, even if I did want to take it from her. Sitting up in my chair, I am overwhelmed by the desire to climb out of my skin, his skin, and I know it's time to leave. I glance back over the contents of the box. "Is this everything?"

"Yes." Her voice is hoarse from grief, and I almost envy her that.

"Good." I get up from the table, and for the first time since we sat down, I catch her eye. "Please, Beth. Don't call me again." She blinks back tears, bites her lip and nods, her chin tucked down onto her chest. I pick up the box and walk outside. My heart feels like it could beat right out of my chest. But it can't think of anywhere else to go… and neither can I.

I keep getting lost in the middle of places I know well. I wander through the middle of downtown like it's a corn maze. The streets all blend into each other, and everywhere the air is fraught with the latest Abercrombie & Fitch cologne that smells just like the last one. I bump into people, but no one pays me any mind. Even the Green Peace workers, who usually ambush me with their clipboards and good causes, leave me alone. They let me wander aimlessly past them, probably assuming that my signature on their petition wouldn't be worth anything. My fingers are freezing, clinging to the rough cutout handles of the cardboard box, but after a while, I don't feel them anymore.

Luke and Mel offered to pick me up from downtown this afternoon, but I told them no, and even though I can't imagine getting onto a bus right now, I'm not sorry. I don't want to see anyone, especially not two people who look so healthy and happy and *together*.

Eventually, I sit down at a picnic table in front of a hot dog stand. The man running the stand gives me a look for loitering and not buying a hot dog, so I order one and then let it get cold because I'm not hungry.

I close my eyes, hoping that when I open them, I'll know what to do next. Whether or not to read the letter. Whether or not to throw the box in the trash and forget the whole thing. I'm so past my limit I nearly forget what it was like to hurt.

"You're stalking me now?" It's Neil, suddenly standing in front of me, holding a hotdog and chuckling. At first, I think he's a mirage, but when I blink, he's still there. My throat is dry from the cold, and it doesn't make any sound when I open my mouth, but it doesn't matter because he keeps talking. "What are you doing down here? I mean, I guess you have just as much right to be downtown as anyone.

I just wasn't expecting to see you again. Not today, anyway. But it's a small world, I guess."

Nothing he's saying means anything. His manner is completely new. Like he's forgotten everything, and now I'm just another girl he knows. I wonder if he thinks I look so much better that he needn't be so delicate with me anymore. Then I wonder if he's really looked at me at all.

"Oh, Mackenzie, this is Sadie. She's another sports trainer. Or she will be. We've just been studying for the certification exam together. Just taking a break to grab some food."

I shift my gaze and notice for the first time that we're not alone.

Sadie. She's got jet black, wavy hair that's in this very messy and elegant fishtail braid over her shoulder, and these absurdly beautiful, dark Kardashian features. Her build is slight, but very toned, and her all-black exercise gear highlights it. She's also holding a hot dog, smothered in cabbage, relish and mustard, and then a diet coke. Even I want to make out with her a little bit—what a bitch.

"It's nice to be meeting you," she says in a very thick accent from somewhere sexy. She reaches out to shake my hand, tucking the can of coke under her arm.

"Mackenzie is a friend of Melanie's from Juice & Harmony," Neil explains to her, and she just keeps smiling at me.

"We *love* Melanie," she beams like I'm a child that needs convincing that she's in the company of friends. "Ooh! What have you got in this box? Shopping?"

"Oh. The box. Um, no. It's nothing. Just—I'm just donating some things… to a charity. I mean, well, just to GoodWill, really. Salvation Army, you know. It's just a box of things my friend Beth brought by… that I can't use." I glance at Neil to see if he's caught on at all, but he's just contentedly eating his hot dog, doing his vacuous blinking at Sadie.

"This is very, how do you say? Generous?" She looks to Neil for confirmation that she got the right word, and when he smiles reassuringly, she oozes pride. "Very generous of you."

"Well, I do what I can."

She takes a huge bite of her hot dog and gets mustard all over her face.

"Look at me, a total chaos!" Her loose interpretation of the phrase "such a mess" does not endear her to me any, but obviously, Neil is tickled pink and grabs some napkins, trying to help her get cleaned up.

"We should probably get going," he says when they've stood there giggling over mustard for basically an hour. "Good to see you, though. Hang in there, Kenzie." He pats me on the head, like a dog, and then smiles at Sadie, and I remember patting Kevin on the head the same way, and it makes it worse.

As they're walking away, he puts his hand on her back, and she leans her head on his shoulder, laughing. It feels like getting stabbed for a second, and then it feels utterly irrelevant.

I take out my phone and dial Mel, but then hang up. My teeth start chattering, and without thinking, I get one of Gerald's sweaters out of the box and put it on under my coat. Then I force myself to eat the cold hot dog because I decide I'm probably starving. It mostly tastes like rubber. I sit for another few minutes and then get out my phone again.

Alice says she can be here in twenty minutes if traffic's good.

The Bellevue house is colossal for two people. Alice has it decorated like she expects it to be chosen as the set for a modern remake of *Gone With The Wind.*

We leave the cardboard box in the car, and immediately she takes me up the stairs to their guest room. "What you need is a good rest, and someone to take care of ya," Alice says, squeezing my face like that *someone* is her. "I'm makin' you some of my grandmomma's special recipe chicken. No ifs, ands, or buts. Some hot chicken and a big ol' cuppa tea is what you need." She's built her empire on the belief that there's a right answer for everything, and she has it. Acknowledging that even she has no idea how to comfort me could render her fraudulent in a way neither of us can afford, but I notice that she's gone extra-strength Southern in her discomfort.

Still, she draws the shades, and confidently turns on a sound machine, setting it to "Waves." I sit on the featherbed and kick off my shoes. The feather down swallows me up, and, in an instant, I'm a little kid again, being tucked into this room when there wasn't anywhere else for me to go.

"Give me that phone of yours." She holds out her palm, and, reluctantly, I hand it over. "I don't know what kind of no good woman bothers a little girl with her mess. But I'll tell you: if she calls again, I'm going to give her a piece of my mind." I don't think Beth really counts as a "no-good woman." She's only two years older than I am. As hard as I try, I can't get her grief-stricken face out of my mind. I wonder what her close friends must have thought about her getting involved with some vagrant guest twice her age. And then I think that maybe Gerald was her closest friend, and that is the most terrible realization.

"She won't call again," I assure Alice, and I hope, for Beth's sake, that I'm right.

"Well, she'd better not. No need for the likes of her around our Mackenzie."

Alice is still busying herself around the room, straightening knickknacks, and uselessly fussing. I try to push the afternoon out of my mind, settling under the covers and closing my eyes. I didn't realize I was so tired, but I feel like I could sleep for the rest of the day. For the rest of the week, even. Then, just as I'm drifting off, I have a thought and start awake again.

"Alice?" I manage to catch her right before she leaves the room. "Could we maybe not mention any of this to my mom? I think the whole thing with Beth would just upset her more." She comes back over to the bed and plops down next to me.

"Of course, we won't, sugar. Of course, we won't. But don't you go worryin' for your momma. She's a tough bird. So just close those pretty eyes of yours and let Aunt Alice fix your chicken."

She bustles out the door, and I try to nestle down and get back to a tired place. The guest room decorations are nautically themed. Alice has mounted a series of display shelves over the bed and then filled them with miniature sailboat models that Walt loves to build in his spare time. "It's becoming very chic to use art in place of a headboard," she told me, and I had agreed with her, though I don't know that this counts exactly. The drawer pulls on the dresser are designed to look like tiny Captain's wheels, and she even replaced the windows with these little porthole style lookouts that make it feel a little bit like you're in Martha Stewart's submarine. All of this, with the addition of the waves coming over the sound machine—I decide that I have to go to sleep to avoid getting seasick.

The next time I wake up, Alice has left a plate of fried chicken on the bedside table with an enormous buttermilk biscuit and a glass of milk. I take a few bites, but, delicious as it is, I can't get interested in eating.

When I was five, and my parents were still under the same roof, fighting all the time, I used to build myself a blanket fort in the basement and then sneak half gallons of ice cream downstairs to my new headquarters. The blankets, I discovered, blocked a lot of the yelling, and the ice cream took care of the rest.

But now food just seems wasted on me. Everything tastes like sand, and I hardly notice the difference between empty and full. I'm always cold, always tired.

Picking the skin off the chicken, I force myself to swallow some of it. It's mostly grease, and for a few minutes, I think it helps, but then I just feel queasy. I pull the biscuit apart into fat breadcrumbs, and set a few of them on my tongue, one at a time, letting the bread go all soggy and dissolve. I'm completely disgusting, but I don't care. Disgusting feels better than nothing. I run my greasy fingers along the plate, writing my name in chicken fat cursive, and then I wipe my fingers on Gerald's sweater and pull the blankets back over my head.

It's been dark out for hours when Alice comes in to tell me that she used my phone to call my boyfriend; that he's on his way to pick me up and take me home.

"There's nothing like the safety of a man's embrace," she says, and I restrain myself from throwing leftover chicken bits at her.

I should have called Mel.

Kevin arrives a little past eight. Today he is driving a red Jetta, much more understated than the Saab, though it has a vanity plate that reads "IM SASSY." I wonder, pointlessly, who he borrowed it from, and how he explained why he needed it.

I watch him from the porthole as he waits for Alice to answer the door. The color has come back to his face, and he's in his own clothes, thankfully, but he looks uneasy. I hear her greet him, but then their voices get dimmer and further away. It's easily a half-hour before he knocks on the door, and by then, I'm back in bed.

"Yeah?"

He slides into the room, reeking of concern. "It's me."

"I see that."

He stares at me a long time, his throat working over words he doesn't say, and I start to overthink my breathing like I'm performing it for him.

"You want a ride home?"

I shrug. "Since you're already here."

Alice packs up the remains of the chicken so I can take it with me. Kevin moves Beth's box out of Alice's car and into his backseat. No one asks me to do anything, so I don't.

When we say goodbye, Alice nearly squeezes all the air out of me. "See?" she says, tucking a soft curl behind my ear. "Things are better already." They are definitely not, but her eyes go all watery, and I say "thank you" in a voice I hope sounds sincere.

My head is pounding, making everything blurry and dizzy from the passenger seat where I adjust the air vents once, and then again, and a third time.

"You okay?" Kevin hazards a glance at me, and I wish he'd just watch the road.

"Just a weird day. I'll be fine," I say, but my mind keeps going back to the letter. I don't know what I'm hoping it'll say. Could be nothing. Could be just a piece of paper with *I love you* scrawled on it in my father's nearly illegible script, maybe someone only assumed it was written for me. The idea of that climbs inside my heart and explodes. My cheeks start to burn, and soon I'm gasping for air that isn't coming. I adjust the vents again like it helps.

"Mack?"

"I'm *fine*," I croak, but now I'm choking on what seem like lethal levels of new car scent, the air too hot and dense with it. I roll down the window to gulp down as much fresh air as I can, but all it does is bite my skin and pull tears from my eyes. "Actually, can you pull over?" I'm lightheaded. "Can we pull over for a second?"

When the car stops, I spill out onto the curb and throw up on the front lawn of a big, stately Bellevue townhouse, gagging on the nothing in my stomach.

Kneeling, doubled over on the sidewalk outside this house for what feels like an eternity, I hear Kevin get out of the car. He doesn't come near me, just stands curbside, leaned against the back door, watching me.

"Sorry. I hate that you're seeing this," I bleat, but he doesn't stop looking. Gravelly concrete presses into my knees, and I want to stand up, but I'm too woozy to manage it. Instead, I look through the front window of the townhouse. It doesn't look like there's anyone home, but the light fixture hanging in the dining room suggests a happy, yuppie family with dogs and Ivy League aspirations.

"I'm supposed to be going back to San Francisco at the end of the week," Kevin says, in a cloying voice I hate. I try to stand up but fall forward onto my hands, and it's all I can do not to lay down in the grass and give up.

"Yes, Kevin. I know that," I say feebly.

"I'm just telling you because I want to make sure you to have a plan for when I'm not here to—"

"Not here to *what*? Come to the rescue? You didn't have to come get me. I mean, thanks for coming and everything, but honestly, you didn't have to. I'm fine." From all fours in a stranger's front yard, this is a bad and blatant lie, but I want it to be true. I hear him moving closer, and I force myself onto my feet, pressing my eyes shut to stop the world spinning.

"You don't seem fine, Adams." He closes in on me, putting one hand on my back, the other on my shoulder, and steadies me against him. My muscles relax without my permission, settling into his chest. His voice is soft in my ear. "Alice and I were talking, and we agreed you're not in a good place to be by yourself."

I eke out a half-laugh, forcing my legs to hold me up straight as I step back. "Oh. Oh, is that what you agreed?"

"Mack."

"You and Alice think I shouldn't be alone. Okay. And so, who's she putting in charge of me, then? You?"

"I'm just trying to be a good friend."

"Since *when*?" He pulls further away, and all my empty spaces fill up with fury. "Look, I know you want everything to somehow magically be fine between us, but it isn't fine. It isn't fine that you let me pine after you for years, and just hoped it'd go away so you wouldn't ever have to talk about it. Especially when all you ever did was flirt with me and tell me how beautiful I was and how much you loved me. You should know that's not fine. That's *really* fucking shitty, Kevin."

"Okay, I—"

"Don't—I don't expect you to apologize for it now. It was college, and whatever, I don't need you to apologize, I don't care. I honestly don't care because my dad is dead, and he wrote me a letter I don't want, and I can't even remember the last time I knew for sure that I loved him…" My voice breaks off, and I swallow back tears to repair it. "And no matter what you think you've decided with Alice, I'm in this alone. I always have been. Mom has Jimmy, and Nathan has Lana, and Alice has Walter, and Mel has Luke, and Neil has fucking Sadie… and you—you have anyone in the world who isn't me, I guess."

"I'm here. I'm trying to be here for you."

"You can't be my in-case-of-emergency person. Half the time, *you're* the emergency." My heart keeps breaking smaller and smaller, and I can't stop it. I notice for the first time that I'm shaking, and I don't know whether or not it's the cold. "*God.* There were so many days when I felt like my dad was the only person I had. And I thought it felt like having no one at all… but it wasn't. It wasn't even close." Kevin makes like he's going to step toward me, but I shake my head, too exhausted for any last-ditch gestures of kindness. "I just… I just want to not be standing here with you, in his clothes, and my vomit. I just want to go home. So. Can you just take me home? And then you can go back to San Francisco or New York or fucking Siberia if you want. I don't care where. Just take me home, and then you can go."

We get back in the car without another word. He keeps breathing in like he wants to say something, but he doesn't say anything until we're in front of my building, and then "Okay, Mack," is all.

After he drives away, I stand outside for a while, looking up the street where his car has long since disappeared up and over the hill. I'm not waiting for anything, and yet it seems like if I go inside, I'll miss it… whatever it is.

Next door, Larry is coming home with arms full of ferret food and sawdust bedding. He gives me a nod, and I give one back, like neither of us is devastatingly lonely.

January 6th

Alice has called Mel about my fragile state. I can tell by the way she and Luke are tip-toeing around me. They're constantly offering to get me whatever I want and then bringing me whatever they think is actually best.

Luke brings me a bagel, with cream cheese and a butter knife, and then stays in my room and watches me eat it. When he leaves, he is careful to take the knife with him.

Mel makes me a smoothie with papaya and beet greens and gives me two Vitamin D supplements because she thinks they might help my mood. She checks my mouth to make sure I've swallowed them.

The apartment is turning into a psych ward.

Radio silence from Kevin, though I don't know what I expected.

Last night I put the letter with its envelope into another, larger envelope and then put that envelope into a shoebox that I duct-taped shut. Mel agreed to keep the whole thing in her closet until I decide I want it.

I think I will never want it.

She stands in my room and makes me watch while she puts her phone on loud before they go to lunch, and she instructs me to call her in the event that *anything at all* happens.

Nothing does.

When I can shut my brain up for long enough to sleep, I dream about Beth and Gerald. I dream that Beth is pregnant and that Gerald vows to stop drinking so that he can be a good father. I dream that he faked his death so that he could run away with Beth to New Hampshire and live in WASP-like bliss. I dream that Beth stole his body from the morgue and is dressing him up in fancy outfits in her living room.

I turn the volume up on the TV to keep myself awake.

January 7th

The autopsy concludes what we already suspected: massive heart attack brought on by living like shit.

"It's best if you make the necessary arrangements with a funeral home or crematorium of your choice within the next twenty-four hours," says the mortician woman on the phone.

"All right. And, um… just in case, what happens after twenty-four hours?"

"Well, to be blunt, the body doesn't hold up." There's a pause, during which I think she realizes that there was no need to be blunt because she elaborates: "What I mean is, that he will start the natural process of decomposition." I nod my head, but of course, she has no idea I've done this, and so she continues. "And the time is especially important, in this case, I believe, because the autopsy was delayed by the holiday." Her voice is so monotone that I imagine she doesn't really hear the words she's saying.

"I understand," I say, mimicking her drone. "You're saying that he'll rot."

This disrupts her. "Well, no. I don't like to use those terms, Ms. Adams." Gerald would have gotten a kick out of this. "But, yes," she continues, clearing her throat, "it's best to make the arrangements as soon as possible. I'm afraid your father's remains are already beginning to show preliminary signs of decay."

"Oh, I doubt it. That's just how he looked."

We hang up, and I laugh, but it doesn't last. My heart contorts under the strain of hearing Gerald's laugh echoing in the belly of mine. Then, I'm so angry that I can't move. I clutch the phone in my hand until I think I might break it with Hulk super strength. I wish I could. I hurl myself around the room, furious that I'm too scared to break anything. I fall onto my bed and tense the muscles in my arms and legs until they start to cramp. I grind my teeth. My throat aches from breathing in like I'm going to cry. Then it subsides, and I go limp.

In a sea of nothing else to do, I run a Google search for Seattle crematoriums and find out that there's a place in Fremont that vaporizes the dead bodies. No smoke, no odor, no ashes.

Vaporizes.

I heard Mom tell Alice once—when one of his worse episodes with me had forced the subject—that she wished sometimes he would just evaporate. She didn't want to hurt him, and she didn't want him to hurt himself—but if he could just disappear? That would be a relief to everyone, she'd said. It was the first time I thought maybe I could see a little of my mother in me after all.

Maybe now we both get what we always wanted.

The admission of it makes me sick with guilt. I get up and look at myself in the mirror, half-expecting to see some horrible monster that's taken me over, nauseated to find that I look exactly the same.

I've been given strict instructions to text Alice on the hour, every hour, one of four messages: Yes, No, Sleeping, Awake.

"Yes" means that I'm in crisis and require help. "No" means that I'm all right. The other two are self-explanatory, though how I'm supposed to text her "sleeping" if I actually *am,* goes unexplained.

From the way she laid it out for me, it sounds like she has set up a phone tree of people who can rush to my aid if need be. If I send a "Yes," I'll receive a response with the name of who is being sent for me within three minutes.

You'd think I'd received a kidnapping threat.

I spend a couple hours (No. No.), just floating around the apartment from room to room with no real purpose. I have the whole place to myself, and the wandering feels good.

Mel and Luke have gone out for the day, "hitting up a few local climbing walls and maybe even getting in a hike if the weather keeps up." Mel tried to convince me it was a better idea for me if they stayed home, but I encouraged them to leave and enjoy themselves for a change. The best thing about Luke being here is that he is an excellent distraction for her.

Besides, if I really need her, I'm sure that Mel is number one on the phone tree.

My loop of the apartment is pretty straightforward. I walk next to the walls around the perimeter of the living room, down the hall into the kitchen and around the kitchen island, back into the hall to my room, then diagonally across the hall to Mel's room and finally make a pitstop through the bathroom before going all the way back up the hall to the living room again.

I'm on my twenty-second spin around Mel's room, when I take a detour past her closet and notice the duct-taped box jutting out of the top shelf. I don't know how long I stand there, just looking at it. Long enough that my legs get tired, and I sit down on the edge of her bed. One "No." Maybe two.

It might say nothing at all. It might say nothing. Maybe it's just an envelope with my name on it and a blank piece of paper inside.

Yesterday I considered that maybe it's a suicide note. But the autopsy declared heart attack, and Gerald didn't understand suicide.

Besides, if he'd wanted to die, he could've taken one of the millions of other chances he got.

It will not be a suicide note.

Maybe he thought if we couldn't talk on the phone, we could be pen pals.

Maybe it's his will.

Maybe it's a grocery list.

I use a box cutter to get through the duct tape, tear through the first giant envelope without thinking, and then sit for a while with Gerald's envelope in my hands, doing nothing, because I can't bring myself to rip into it.

So, then I'm in the kitchen. Standing over the stove, boiling water in a frying pan so I can steam the letter open. I ease the paper apart, as the steam loosens the adhesive. I am more delicate in this work than I've ever been—like I'm trying to reassemble an egg-shell. My hands are steady, though my breath is quick, and my heart is quicker.

Another hour.

No.

*

HOMEAWAY INN EXPRESS
1763 Minor Ave
Seattle, Washington 98101

Ms. Mac—

You know my handwriting ain't shit anymore. You probably figured out that this ain't me writing. Friend of mine at the front desk offered to take down a letter for me. I've got some people here who said they can get me some stamps, so I can put this thing in the mail. I'll just send it to your mom's since I don't know where you live anymore. Hopefully, it'll get to you.

~~You know, I am sorry.~~

Well, my dear, my dear. It's been a long time now since I saw you. Things here are the same. I imagine you're grown now. Still beautiful, too, I bet. You have a boyfriend? Someone who makes you happy? I hope so.

I'll tell you, Mac, there aren't many things an old fool like me hopes for anymore. Life is what is. You get dealt what you get dealt, and then you just play the best you can. But I still hope that you and your mother are happy. I hope that you get everything you want. You know I love you. No matter what I say or do, remember that that's the truth.

And other than that… here I am. Still alive. Don't know why but seems like someone up there thinks I've got something left to do, I guess. Not that I'm complaining.

Maybe now that I've told you that I love you no matter what, maybe I'll die tonight. I hope not, but maybe. Life's too short already.

I don't know if what happened with us is all my fault. Usually is. But I do my best with you. Always did the best I could. If you think my best's not good enough, well then—

And I couldn't have messed up too badly. Seems like you turned out okay, am I right?

Still, I know it's never been easy between us. And you'd tell me there's nothing I can do about that, I bet. Probably there's not. I miss you, though, Mac. I do miss you.

So, here's what I'm gonna tell you, and I tell you this for your own good: it scares me to look at you sometimes. Think you're too much like me. Maybe that's why you don't like talking to me. I hate looking in the mirror too.

What was I saying? I tell you, my brain ain't working anymore. These days I can't hardly even talk or take a shit by myself. Ain't that just life.

But know this, Mac. You're lucky. Me and you both, we're luckier than we know. What we got, even when it's not working quite right... it's a rare thing, ain't it? We got love.

I don't get out of here much. Can't go too far since I fell a couple months ago. Now I barely get across the street.

Damn though. I'll tell you, this morning I was thinking how much I'd like to go up to the mountains again like I used to do with your mom. Swim in the river and just feel the fucking cold and fresh air for a minute. I keep dreaming I'm up there in the woods, just me and the trees and the water.

Promise me somethin', Mac. If you go up there, bring back a rock for me. You know where to find me.

You're young, my dear. Make sure you see the world and enjoy your life. I'm tellin' you. It's short. So, make sure you live it. And come see me sometime. Really. We don't have to talk. I just want to look at you, see my little girl. See your smile and hear your laugh. You still smile sometimes, don't you?

I love you. I love you. I love you.

That's the truth, Mac.

That's the truth. No matter what.

— *Pops*

*

"Hey now, hey now. Slow up there, Mac! The way it works is this..." He picks me up off the ground, my little Keds swinging in the air for a second before I land on his other side on the sidewalk.

"Why?"

"Because Ms. Mac. An adult walks on the outside, and the little girl walks on the inside."

"Yeah, but why?" I am at the age where I just love the "but why" game.

"Because. It's safer."

"Yeah, but *why* is it safer?"

"Oh, it's gonna be like that, is it? Well, Ms. Mac. You see all these cars hurrying down the street here?" We stop and watch a few cars go down the hill. A Honda, a Honda, a Subaru, a Honda, a Subaru—Seattle is nothing if not consistent.

"Yes, I see."

"Well, now imagine one of these drivers gets distracted. Just a little distracted, and their car swerves and comes up here onto the sidewalk." I squint, trying to imagine what that would be like.

"That'd be silly," I say.

He shakes his head, disapproving. "It'd be stupid, is what it'd be."

"We don't say 'stupid,' Dad."

"We do when people are being stupid. And if a car came up on the sidewalk here, where you and I are walking, it'd be stupid." His tone is steely, and I decide not to argue anymore. I hate it when he uses his serious voice on park days.

"Okay."

"Now, if that were to happen, I wouldn't want the car to hit you, would I?"

"Ouch!"

"Exactly. Ouch. I'd rather the car hit me because I'm big and I'm tough...and I've had a pretty good life."

There's quiet for a minute, and I hold tight onto his hand while we walk. Now I can't stop watching the cars. Every one that whizzes past us seems threatening. I glare at the strangers in the driver's seat, warding them off.

"Dad... Would you *die*?" Now I have on my serious voice. Five years old, and suddenly I'm aware that at any second, my dad could be taken away. The question makes him laugh.

"Why would you ask a question like that, Ms. Mac? I'm not going anywhere. Do I look like I'm going somewhere?" I feel like I'm going to cry thinking about it. I don't want to look at him, but he tugs my hand and asks again. "I said, do I look like I'm going somewhere?"

I turn my head and look up into his face. He has this broad irresistible smile, and his eyes are glimmering in the sun of the afternoon. I can't help but smile back, looking at him, and I shake my head. He picks me up and sets me up on his shoulders.

"Dad!" I squeal, feeling the warm breeze on my face, and reaching up to grab low hanging leaves from the trees. "Dad! It's so high up here! You should see it! Dad!! You have to see it!" I hear him laughing, and I laugh too.

"Look at you, Ms. Mac! Flying through the trees up there."

Everything is green and leaves and sun. I forget about the threat of distracted drivers, now hearing the whoosh of passing cars as sound effects to my high up adventure.

I breathe in all the spring I can take in my lungs at once. The whole city smells different from up here, and I am invincible as long as I am with my dad.

When I wake up, I am hollow. I can't stop crying. I scream into my pillow. The car came, and I wasn't even paying attention.

January 31st

Death eats away at everything that isn't dead.

And for weeks, I let it.

The rest of the month bled into itself. Some days stood out more than others, but in my life now, every day is somewhere on the spectrum of "my dad died," and so everything is about that. Even the things that aren't at all.

One of the first things I learned about being unhappy with any regularity is that the world is not interested in sad people. Other people's sadness has a certain novelty at first, when there are brownie points to be earned for being a shoulder to cry on, but extended bouts of sadness are widely considered a nuisance. Pretty quickly, people stop asking how you're doing and start asking if you're feeling any *better*. And if the answer is too often no, you can be sure they'll get exasperated.

There are all these rules no one ever says aloud—like that the window of time allotted for your feelings is always shrinking as you get older, or that the more times you're hurt by the same thing, or by the same person, the less time you're allowed to feel bad about it. This unspoken rubric seems to suggest that we should all be on a path in life toward learning how to feel less.

I had started converting my sadness about Gerald to vacancy by fifth grade. I trained myself to gather a full-scale meltdown into a flinch. If I had to cry, I did it without audience and often without sound. And over and over again, people around me commended me for my strength, my maturity, my resilience.

I joked once to Melanie that it's like switching my brain into Airplane Mode—keeps me non-disruptive and incapable of connecting until it's safe again to use my data. She laughed but said, "You don't really do that anymore, though, do you?" and I shrugged as a way of changing the subject.

A long time ago, Valery told me that it's not good to put on a show of normalcy for other people; that it's a form of self-harm, which I told her was a bit dramatic. But then every time I made the switch, I wondered if something inside me was dying back—if I'd come out the other side with a little less.

Now I've stopped bothering to come out the other side at all. Not just because other people need me to be fine, but because *I* need me to be fine. Feeling nothing is more survivable than feeling everything, and I think I've passed being able to do anything in between.

Lately, though, I get this pull like the tide is coming in on the banks of an ocean that's been spreading between my ribs for years.

And that if I were to risk wading into it, even just a little past the rocks, the ground beneath me would drop off, and the impossibly strong depth of it might steal the air from my lungs. When I can't sleep, I catch myself researching the mechanics of reinforcing sea walls.

Despite what she told Alice, Mom couldn't stand the vaporization idea. She didn't understand it, and she was made uncomfortable by the idea that there wouldn't be any remains.

"How would we grieve?" she kept asking me, and I didn't know what to tell her because I didn't understand the question.

She made it clear that she no longer trusted me to make this decision, though, of course, she didn't say that. And so, I was taken off the case, and eventually, she called a more traditional crematorium and scheduled an appointment for Gerald. If that's what it's called—an appointment.

But then she called me again because she needed my opinion on how we thought we would like to receive the ashes.

There are a variety of options, I was told, depending on how much we'd like to spend on our charred loved one. There are a series of urns of increasing value and visual appeal, and once we've chosen one, they place the ash into the urn, and the whole thing is delivered very tidily, right to our front door.

Out of curiosity, I asked what happens if we didn't choose an urn, and Mom said that in that case, they just put all the ashes into a cardboard box.

"A cardboard box? Like a shoebox?"

"I don't know what kind of box it is, Mackenzie. Please. Don't be morbid." But I'm me, so I pressed her for more details on the box. "Whatever kind of box it is, it's free. I think it's just a default. It's included in the cost of cremation." This impressed me since even grocery bags cost an extra five cents in the state of Washington.

"I want to do the box," I told Mom after some thought. I could tell by the tone of her silence after I said it that she was disappointed in me. But I think Gerald would have liked that it was free. He told me more than once that he thought the amount of money people spent on coffins was bullshit. I don't see why an urn would be any different.

Mom called the crematorium again, and, consoled to learn that the box is more of a sleek black gift box than an old shoebox, she was persuaded. So, we got the box.

It took several days for them to get the ashes back to us after the appointment. I don't know if it takes a while to gather everything up once they've burned it, or if it takes several days to get the box properly prepared. There are all kinds of logistics to dying that I don't understand. Even now.

But, after the required three days, they delivered the ashes to Mom's house because they wouldn't deliver to an apartment building.

After having them in her possession for forty-five minutes, she insisted that I come and pick them up.

"It's too much," she said to me desperately over the phone, and I sort of laughed at that. I wanted to ask her when *exactly* this all became too much for her.

The tide never turns, and all I do is run from it.

I am no longer even remotely myself.

It's bizarre to take the bus with a cardboard box full of your father's ashes. I couldn't escape feeling like I was hauling around a dead body, probably because I was. Not to mention that ashes are heavier than you'd expect. It turns out, a whole person's worth of ash is a lot. I tried to be inconspicuous, like if someone found out what I was carrying, they'd report me. But there's nothing illegal about carrying your dad's dead body on the bus. It just *feels* fucked up.

That I now have two cardboard boxes worth of Gerald seems exorbitant.

When I got home with the box, Mel was curled in a ball on the sofa crying. Luke had gone back to Yale that morning.

I walked straight past her and into my room. I put the box on the floor and slid it under my bed with my big toe. I knew I wouldn't be able to sleep with him under there, but I couldn't look at him anymore.

I came back into the living room and plopped down next to Mel, putting an arm around her and hushing her as gently as I could manage.

"It's not fair that it's always so hard," she sputtered. "The day before, I think I'm ready, but then it's just so hard all over again." I nodded softly like I gave a fuck, and she cried some more. I tried not to hate her for feeling something when I couldn't.

I sat on the couch with her and listened. I told her that it'd get easier, and nothing is forever, and she'd see Luke again soon. That she'd made it through before, and she could do it again—that she's lucky that way. And after a while, she said she felt better, and I hated her for that too.

Gerald was planning on dying every day that I knew him. He used to ask me sometimes what I'd miss about him when he was gone. Talk to me about what kind of memorial to have in his honor. Tell me who to invite and what kinds of music to play.

"I might be gone tomorrow, Mac," he used to say when he was leaving after long, tortured visits. "I might be gone, so make sure you're happy with the way we leave things."

Once, when I was eleven, I got so sick of it that I said, "Go ahead and die then, Dad! Go ahead. You're always saying you'll do it, but you never do. We're still waiting!"

I was so sure that day that he would outlive me.

I wish he had.

The memorial we had is barely worth mentioning. Mom and Jimmy hosted some of Gerald's old friends, most of whom had stopped speaking to him before I was born because he owed them too much money or because he'd told them to fuck off too many times. Mom bought a bunch of pre-made frozen hors d'oeuvres from Trader Joe's. I told her we should just serve malt liquor and hand-rolled cigarettes like Gerald would've had. She didn't think this was funny. It wasn't.

Everyone wore black, but we played Paul Simon's *Graceland* at full volume like Gerald had told me he wanted once. It was uncomfortably loud and sad, and as the title track played, I told no one in particular that he was right. It *is* the best album.

No one really told stories about him, though Jimmy kept trying to encourage it. No one eulogized. Nathan came, but Lana "couldn't make it," and I didn't blame her. Mel stayed for an hour, but then she had to go back to work because it was Tuesday afternoon, like it is when you have a memorial service for someone no one liked.

I spent the whole thing staring at Mom, not recognizing her on the brink like this. I wished I had something to offer, something to help her get through it, but every time she looked at me, she only cried harder. So, I just watched while her little paper plate of pigs in a blanket and crudités shivered in her hand. Guests offering their condolences were met with a very shaky smile and a deep sigh. Her only relief came when Jimmy would find her and gently place his hand on her back. Then I could see the tension fade from her shoulders, and she would look at him softly with the gaze of a baby bird being tucked back into the nest—the consolation of seeing his face, neutral territory, not tainted with memories of my father.

Alice ran out of patience to "honor my grief" after about two weeks. She says I have until February first to get back to work, or else she's going to promote some girl she found at her country club into my job. The girl's name is Charlotte Something, and apparently, she's a fast learner, a joy to work with, and her dad is very much still alive. This month I've just been writing weekly horoscopes from my room, which barely makes me enough money for food, let alone rent. Mom begrudgingly helped me make ends meet this month but made sure it was clear that she and Jimmy aren't going to keep enabling this behavior. Mel has started glaring at me when she thinks I'm not looking.

I've graduated from nuisance to burden.

I've read all the symptoms of depression and have diagnosed myself. This is a supposed stage of grief too, but it doesn't feel like grief. It feels like being half-dead.

In the movies, depression always looks very sexy. It's brooding and full of chocoholism and punch-bowl sized glasses of wine. It's satisfyingly messy, with half-eaten Chinese take-out containers scattered everywhere and unwashed clothes in piles. Depression in the movies has a very distinct air of wallowing to it. You don't bathe, and you watch the same classic black-and-whites over and over while your body melds with the couch.

This is nothing like that.

My depression is sterile. Everything in the apartment is clean, bleached, and re-bleached. To people who don't know me that well, I think I must seem healthier than I've ever been, adhering strictly to Mel's juice regimen. I am drinking less coffee and more green tea. Sometimes, when I wake up around sunrise, I'll go out for a run. I run uphill until I can hardly breathe. I don't try to run far, but I run fast. Fast like I'm running from someone.

In the hours I'm awake, I whir around the apartment, trying to do everything at once. Not to keep busy, like people like to think, but trying to get the death out of all the corners and creases. Some days I do several loads of laundry and scrub the soap scum out of the shower. Other days I iron and vacuum and dust and then vacuum again. When we're up at the same time, I'll vacuum behind Melanie as she comes in the door, catching every piece of dirt that she might track in with her shoes. In between meals, I vacuum all the furniture.

I read extensively about the best ways to polish metals and have polished everything silver and brass that I own, which isn't much. I have polished Mel's hammer and all the nails. I am working on taking the rust off an old bike lock I found in the closet, for a bike Mel sold two years ago.

My sleep schedule is fucked. There are long nights when I can't sleep at all and days when I can't lift my head. I've resigned myself to sleeping whenever I can manage it, and once you get used to it, exhaustion starts to feel like being alive.

On weekends, I eat all the raw vegetables I used to hate and watch the news. I have become obsessed with the 24-hour cable news cycle. There is news all the time. The world is a disaster. Everyone is fucking terrible. Half the time it's just pundits arguing with each other over things that shouldn't be up for debate, but those are the times I like the most. Nothing should make any sense. People think it's depressing, but the news is the one thing that consistently makes me laugh.

About a week ago, I think, I bought every book on Astrology I could find at the used bookstore. It cost me $37.53 for the whole stack of 13 books, and I posted the receipt on the fridge so that Mel would know what a bargain I'd gotten. She was incredulous that I was throwing away money I don't have on books I'm never going to read. I turned on the vacuum to drown her out.

I am learning everything there was to know about Sun signs in the 1980s, which is a lot. I wanted to get more current intel, but there were no contemporary volumes available for the $2.68 I had left in my checking account.

And now somehow, it's the 31st. I had to check the calendar twice this morning to be sure. This month is ending, finally. It's hard to tell if that means something.

It is okay to grieve however you grieve, so long as you're not harming yourself or others, the internet says. I have no idea anymore what counts as harming myself.

I've read Gerald's letter twelve million times, like the next time I read it I'll know what to do. Like the next time I read it, I'll understand why he's dead, why he had to die before I could read it. I read it again and tell myself that if I'd only gotten the letter sooner, I'd have gone to see him. But it's a lie and knowing that is worst of all.

Mel takes me out for happy hour to celebrate me going back to work in the morning. She's dressed up like everything is normal, and when she finishes telling me over appetizers about how brave and amazing I am, she complains about Luke being so busy all the time. And I nod, because, in Airplane Mode, not only can I play brave and amazing, I can also do selfless and supportive.

I feel so much nothing that I get bored. Mel says she's so happy that the juice is working, that I'm starting to feel better, and I smile because it takes fewer muscles than frowning.

The tide laps my ankle, and I look for higher ground.

Maybe this is just what normal looks like from the inside.

Mackenzie, please. Don't be morbid.

PART TWO

February-June 2018

TO: khwasserman11@gmail.com

FROM: mackenzadams1377@gmail.com

SUBJECT: hi

SENT February 2, 2018 1:06:07 AM PST

kev, you can delete this if you hate me now. for what it's worth i sort of hate me now. i read that letter from my dad, which was a bad idea and has made everything worse, but it made me want to write to you and say i'm sorry. it was nice to see you, and i know you were only trying to help, and a lot of that stuff was years ago, and some of it isn't even your fault… i don't know. i guess it's just, i don't know how to rewind things, and it started to feel like my entire past was coming back to haunt me at the same time. and i wanted to think i'd sort of made my peace with everything and moved on but actually seeing you, on top of everything else… well. you were there. obviously, it went super well. everything about this is harder than it was ever supposed to be. also, people keep sending flowers to my apartment with little notes about how they're sorry to hear about my dad, and then i just have to watch the flowers die too. anyway, i'm sorry i said you were the emergency like i'm not. i am. and people in glass houses should shut the fuck up or whatever. so, i'm sorry. really, really sorry. i don't know if we're still allowed to say this to each other or not, but i love you. honestly, i'm not even sure that means anything coming from me, but it's not the worst thing someone can write to tell you. unless it is.

- mack

*

February 7th

Alice Facetimed me on Wednesday so I could be part of the champagne toast for Charlotte's promotion.

I didn't go back to work on the first.

I didn't even get out of bed or turn off my alarm. I let it go off every fifteen minutes until my phone died, which took until 4:30 PM.

I have been demoted to occasional contract work (there wasn't a champagne toast for this announcement), which really means that I will keep writing horoscopes from my bed. Mom called yesterday to tell me again that my behavior is unacceptable, and she is insisting that I come to her house this afternoon, "to discuss my future options." She says it is fine to be depressed as long as you're functional.

"And *you* are becoming dysfunctional, sweetie. Do you know what I mean by that? What I mean by that is that you are no longer acting like the educated adult woman that you are. I'm not trying to be insensitive, dear. It's just that—you know. Well, you must know this can't continue. And it's not that—It's not that we don't miss Gerald. Of course, we all miss your father… and we've taken time to honor our grief. But, Christ, we have to remain functional. I mean, for the love of God, Mackenzie. You don't think I'd like to throw in the towel sometimes? Because, of course, I would! But I don't. I do not. I look myself in the face, and I say, 'Elizabeth. You are a strong, educated adult woman with all the potential in the world. And today, you have to keep going.' You know that's the mantra that Alice and I created together a hundred years ago. And it really helps me… to remind myself of that. It helps me to keep myself functional. Have you thought about a mantra at all? Did you get my email about those? I think it might be helpful to you. Getting on your feet again. Because, I mean, have you thought about what you're going to do for rent money? Have you considered that at all? Because, you know, we've turned your room into Jimmy's home office, you know that. And, I suppose, there's the futon in my pottery studio, but, *no*. Mackenzie. You're going to be twenty-five. Two, five. That's a quarter of a century. Is this what you envisioned for yourself?"

I said I would come over.

Winter is no longer pretending at crispness. February's streets are full of brown sludge and littered paper cups from Starbucks in sickly shades of red and pink, festive. I remember that, of course, Valentine's Day has not been canceled.

My first bus is twenty minutes behind schedule, and when it comes, there is only room to stand and drip on strangers.

I take this bus and then another and finally a third to get to a few blocks from my mom's house. On the last bus, I sit next to a hairy-eared businessman in a three-piece suit who is listening to his Katy Perry Pandora station on his phone. He stares at me until I smile at him, and then he keeps staring. When I lean to pull the cord, he tells me in a raspy whisper that I smell like springtime, and it makes me so angry that I laugh. Functional people are a myth.

Mom is all business. She has taken the day off of work to look for jobs with me. She makes no secret of the fact that this is her "going out of her way." I nod and say thank you, but don't mean it.

She has the dining room set up with her laptop and Jimmy's sitting across from each other, each with a legal pad next to them, and a large whiteboard at one end of the table, which she tells me is for brainstorming and for sketching my "life map."

"I emailed you the top ten postings I've found so far, sweetie. Do you want coffee? There's a Costa Rican blend regular and Jimmy swears by this Venezuelan decaf he got from that new, hip place on Market."

"Costa Rican is fine, thanks."

Four hours later, I've applied for two junior copy-editing positions for local tech companies, even though I'm totally underqualified for both. And then a series of jobs listed under "miscellaneous." Miscellaneous is a bunch of stuff that's so vague it makes you think you'd be qualified, but just detailed enough to convince you it's not a scam.

Mom is not satisfied.

"Maybe you should take resumes around to a few places, sweetie. You know, restaurants and things. Somewhere probably needs a hostess. Or maybe they could train you to do some cooking. You might be surprised. Maybe you could be a chef. At least that would be something."

I tell her I want to get going before I get stuck in too much traffic.

I'm getting my coat on when she says what she really means—what I suspect she always means. "I'm sorry if I'm pressuring you too much, sweetie. It's just—you know I watched your father give up on himself for so many years. And I did my best to support him, but I—well, I'm hardly eager to do that again, am I."

On the ride home, I scrutinize the faces of children and their parents. Try to pick apart which feature came from where. Wonder how their personalities line up.

Sometimes, in the flicker of a burnt-out light bulb, I think Gerald and I are almost twins. Same nose, same strong, clumsy jaw. His eyes were smaller, thinner, and a brown that looked black too often. I got Mom's fat, doe eyes in an only vaguely more inhabited shade of brown, but still. The bones of Gerald are all there.

I know it's not a good sign that more than anything, this makes me want to drink.

February 20th

"Hey, so guess who came in yesterday?" Mel is juicing carrots and beet greens and listening to Sheryl Crow like she's starring in a commercial for herself.

"I don't know. Who?"

"Guess."

I never want to play this game. If I would ever actually be able to guess, then she wouldn't be asking me to guess. I jump down off the counter, where I'd perched, and get out a countertop spray from under the sink. I wipe down every open surface I can find, going over some places twice.

"Would you not do that when I'm cooking, Kenz? I hate the idea of getting those cleaning chemicals in my food." I want to ask her why it was that we had to switch to organic, probably totally ineffective, cleaning solvents if she's still so afraid of their chemicals. But I don't.

"I don't want to guess. Just tell me. Who came in yesterday?"

"Ugh, you're no fun," she sulks, and I think this is a very obvious thing for her to say. "It was *Cute Neil.*"

I say nothing but, without thinking, start in with the counters again.

"Kenz, seriously. Chemicals."

I put the spray back under the counter and then lay down some paper towels before jumping up again, sitting next to the sink.

"Anyway, he asked me about you, wanted to know how you were doing and everything." Mel has this smile on her face like I should be really over-the-moon about this news.

"Cool," I say, even though it isn't.

"I think you must have really made an impression on him," she smirks.

Of course, I made an impression. I know that. I also happen to know that the impression had practically nothing to do with me. It's not every day you sleep with someone and see their naked, dead dad all in one go. It would make an impression on anyone.

But Melanie keeps talking. "So, obviously, I told him you're doing a lot better, and that he should call you sometime."

"What? No. Not 'obviously.' Why would you say that?"

"*Because,*" she gets a little glass off the shelf and tastes her juice concoction. Her face twists up, dissatisfied, and she goes to the fridge for the agave nectar, "you deserve for something nice to happen." She licks some nectar off her finger and closes her eyes like it's the most delicious thing ever to happen. Refined sugar would blow her mind.

"Did he and Sadie break up?"

Mel's face twists again, this time at me. "Sadie?"

"Super fit, foreign accent, trainer? I don't know her last name."

"Yeah, I know Sadie. Are they a thing? I don't think they were ever a thing."

I roll my eyes and laugh, like, "it's no big deal, and I've known basically forever, but yeah, *duh.*" Mel goes quiet for a while, and her brow furrows, like a fourth-grader puzzling through a tricky long division problem.

"I mean, I know they're friends... but I'm pretty sure Sadie has a boyfriend."

"I never said she didn't. I just said that her boyfriend is Neil."

Melanie is unimpressed by my wit.

"I, like, really don't think so," she says and turns on the blender like that is the final word on the matter.

February 24th

There's a prolonged silence hanging on the end of the word "dinner." I think Neil is holding his breath waiting for me to respond, and so, to keep him from passing out, I answer his question with a question.

"Is this like a date?"

"Yeah." Blunt, but to the point. Then another silence. I'm getting ready to say something else when his sentence starts again. "Or. I don't know. Do you... I mean, would you want it to be a date?" Quiet. No breath signs.

"I was just asking."

A silence filled with anxiety on his end, and disinterest on mine.

"It doesn't have to be a date." Fumbling, and that throat echo that happens when you open your mouth, but nothing comes out, followed by: "We could just... it could just be a friends thing."

"Sure. If that's what you want."

"Well, that's not what I said. I mean, Kenzie—"

"No, fine. It's a date. That's fine too."

"So, a date then?" A pause, wherein I consider that this is likely a huge mistake for innumerable reasons, and then:

"Yes, a date. Sure."

I hate talking on the phone with boys: too much breathing and expectation. Whatever confidence was there in Neil's voice that day downtown with Sadie has gone now. He sounds just as uncertain as I remember him.

Mel has been watching this phone conversation with a level of excitement that should be reserved only for Beyoncé sightings. I think that if Neil had called when she wasn't at home, beaming at me, I probably wouldn't have said yes.

"I knew he would call you," she squeals when we hang up. I nod and try to get past her to go to the kitchen, but she needs details.

I tell her that it's just dinner. He's picking somewhere, and we'll go and eat, and maybe I'll let him kiss me, but probably not.

"You already slept together," she protests, and I'm not sure what she thinks that's supposed to mean. I raise my eyebrows to express as much, and she says, "I'm just saying it doesn't seem like a kiss is so out of the question."

I don't humor her but choose instead to smile and continue on to the kitchen.

But I don't stop at the kitchen. My legs take me all the way down the hall to the bathroom, and thoughtlessly I begin to peel off my clothes. Once inside, I lock the door and breathe a long sigh.

"Are you getting in the shower?" I hear Mel ask through the door.

"Yeah," I answer, but I don't turn on the water. I'm distracted by the mirror.

For a while, I stand in just my underwear, watching my stomach hollow out on each exhale. But after a while, I unclasp my bra and slide my underwear to the floor. As the straps slide from my shoulders, toilet paper falls from my chest and into the sink. I am an embarrassment, stuffing my bra like a pre-teen girl, desperate to hide how much weight I've lost since the start of the year. When I'm alone, it's clear that my new health is a weak façade. So much so that it's almost laughable. Juice isn't a food group. At this point, I'm ashamed to be completely naked, even alone with myself. I clasp my arms around my torso and thumb my ribs. I know I should be eating more, but food just sits on my tongue most of the time, and I'm so rarely hungry. Hugging myself this way, though, I see that my bones are sticking out at odd angles. I look jagged and ugly, like a stack of broken coat hangers. I resolve that I've got to start eating, even if I can't taste it.

I sit down on the edge of the tub, and when I feel myself starting to cry, I turn on the shower. For a while, I let it run while I stay perched on the porcelain edge, watching it gather and the swirl down the drain. Not until my teeth start chattering do I swing my legs around and slither down into the bathtub. I sit with my knees tucked to my chest, letting the showerhead beat down on me.

It reminds me of a project in my 3rd-grade science class on erosion. We spent a week building these elaborate models of riverbeds in plastic storage tubs. Then we were supposed to be able to watch, over the course of a single class period, the way that our rivers eroded the ground around them, changing their course ever so slightly, widening their path. Except for the one built by our teacher Ms. Dorothy, the models turned out to be mostly a mess of sand and water that turned into a grainy sludge and sloshed around in the storage bins. We ended up crowding around the table at the front of the classroom, trying to see erosion in action and scribbling "experiment notes" in our composition books.

The way I feel now, I think I understand erosion better than ever before. I imagine myself wearing down under the rush of the shower—swirling down the drain little by little—with just traces of me left behind on the walls of the tub.

As far from myself as I am now, crying simply comes and goes—passing through as unnoticed as breathing. My chin doesn't scrunch. My brow doesn't furrow. Only a gentle flush before thick saltwater streams run down each cheek.

Limbs knotted on the floor of the tub, I don't let myself in on whether this is mourning for Gerald or myself, and when I think about it for too long, I can barely tell us apart anyway.

I keep thinking that an answer must be coming. That someone will call with another letter from Gerald. That Kevin will write me back. That Mel will think of a vitamin that she forgot I need. That Neil will remember some detail from that morning that makes everything make sense. But there's been nothing else yet. So, I take long showers and wait to dissolve.

February 27th

My room is the messiest it's been in weeks, as I try to get ready for this date. There are piles of discarded clothes on the floor, and Mel, sitting on my bed rating outfits as I try them on, is eating a gluten-free scone and getting her wheat-less crumbs everywhere. A project for when I get home, I tell myself to keep from banishing her and pulling out the hand vac.

"I don't know why it matters so much," I call from the closet, wriggling out of what must be my twenty-ninth outfit option. I wish Mel wouldn't sit in here with me while I change. I don't want to be undressed with anyone.

"It matters because you haven't done anything fun for yourself in ages." I can hear the crumbs flying out of her mouth and onto my sheets as she tries to enunciate with a face full of scone.

"I think this is more fun for you than for me," I say. Outfit Thirty is a no go: another pair of jeans that have gotten too loose not to look dumpy. I don't even bother to show Mel. I pull on a dress I haven't worn since college, a long-sleeved black sweater dress. It's very business casual, and, aside from the fact that it fits, there is nothing particularly date-like about it. "I found a winner," I say, adjusting the stuffing in my bra to make my boobs look even.

"Ooh! Let's see!"

I put on heels before opening the closet door, so it at least looks a little like I'm making an effort.

"Oh. It's very... black," Mel says, her cheeks bulging.

"Little black dress is still a thing, isn't it?" It's clear from the look on her face that this does not meet the criteria, but I'm not changing again. She shrugs and says something like, "Yeah, no, it's cute," and then gets up, picking through my jewelry in the hopes that bangles will fix it.

I end up with just a gold pendant necklace as an accessory, because Mel tells me it's understated and sexy. I don't bother with the mirror.

"You know, Neil is a real catch... Everyone thinks so." Her voice is defensive like I'm not nearly excited enough to be going on a date with someone who *everyone* thinks is a *real catch*. "You could at least smile."

There are a million nice things about Neil, from what I can tell. The fact that he still wants to see me at all is at the top of the list. But the sound on my life has been turned down so low that I'm straining to even pretend at excitement. I dig deep to make myself smile for

Mel, even though she just rolls her eyes, dissatisfied, and texts Luke that I'm being a sourpuss.

The buzzer goes right at seven o'clock. Add it to the list: the man is prompt. Mel acts like a helicopter parent on prom night, insisting that I go back to my room while she lets him up, so I can "make an entrance." I don't know why, but I do it.

I sit down on my pillow so as not to get crumbs stuck to my ass and scan the room. I consider cleaning up, but I'm already so exhausted from playing healthy that I just sit. I hear Neil come into the living room, laughing with Mel about something that shiny, happy people laugh about. I check my email, a compulsion I've developed ever since I wrote to Kevin, but of course, nothing.

"She's almost ready, I think," I hear Mel lie. "Kenz! Neil is here!"

I refresh my email again. One new message from Twitter that @UnderpantsEdgar794 is now following me.

I get up.

Neil is undeniably handsome; his blond hair has been moussed effortlessly to the side, the smell of his cologne drifting gently through the room. I vaguely remember craving his company once. His face brightens when I come around the corner, and I notice him straighten his shoulders.

"Wow. You look…" his voice trails off, and he turns bashfully toward the floor.

"You don't clean up so bad yourself," I flirt, pleased I remember how, and his face reddens. He's now comfortably inside the living room, but I'm not sure what kind of greeting is appropriate, so I stay on the other side of the couch.

Mel gets a call from Luke that she takes into her bedroom, and once she's gone, Neil moves toward me.

"Hi," he says in a way I recognize immediately. I think at first that he's going to hug me, but he just sort of puts his hand on my arm and squeezes, biting his lower lip with his clean, perfect teeth. "You really do look incredible. You ready to go?"

It's like a static shock after so much time feeling nothing at all. I'm caught off guard by how badly I suddenly want him. The touch is innocent enough, but it promises a closeness I'm desperate to binge until I'm full. Swallowing the impulse to drag him into my room, to beg him to lay on top of me, I manage a nod.

He helps me into my jacket and opens the door for me, and I don't let myself stray too far from the warmth of him, let myself be intoxicated by it.

"So, I have a confession," he murmurs from over my shoulder as we head downstairs.

"Oh?" My voice squeaks out several octaves higher than its usual pitch, and I clear my throat in an effort to bring myself down. I turn toward him once we're out on the sidewalk, and he takes the hint, sidling up to me and taking the lapels of my jacket in his hands to pull my collar up around my scarf.

"Yeah," his face cracks into a shy smile. "I, um—I'm sorry. You should know that you're very beautiful, and it's a little distracting."

My hands find his waist, and I pull him closer, laughing. My head spirals toward a five-alarm fire, the heat a relief to my water-logged bones. I wonder how close I can get without burning. When he smiles, I think it might singe my eyebrows off, and I don't care. I remember what hunger feels like.

"Was that your confession?" I do my best to sound coy.

"No, that was unrelated." He puts his hands into his pockets, drops his head and scuffs his foot on the sidewalk like a little kid admitting to a schoolyard crush. "No, my confession is that I didn't actually choose anywhere for dinner." He laughs quietly, as though he has cleverly pulled a trick on me.

"*Oh.* So, we have no plan?" I think about skipping dinner. I imagine him pulling me back up the stairs, my fingers in his hair, his breath on my neck.

Neil takes my hand and traces shapes on my palm. "Not an official plan," his voice is a dull growl that forces me to lean in to hear, "but I figured, between the two of us, we might be able to come up with some ideas." I feel my lips fall open slightly, and a quick dizzy giggle escapes. He leans so in so close that his lips graze my ear. "I mean, you must have favorite places to eat around here, yeah?" I let out a deep breath and smile, shoving him gently, but not letting him get too far. Dinner it is.

We go to this only somewhat unbearable hipster brewpub a few blocks from my apartment. Both of us look overdressed, but every-one else is too ironically disinterested in everything to notice us. The hostess puts us in a corner booth, and Neil scoots into the corner, so I scoot with him. We may as well be sitting in chairs on the same side of a two-top, like couples I hate so often do, but next to him, I forget myself.

We share a single menu because two would be too crowded, and as we peruse it, Neil points at things that sound good and says he can't decide. Nothing on the menu actually looks that appealing, and I know he's just being sweet because I said I like this place.

"You smell nice." It flies out of me as soon as I think it. He smirks this gentle kind of self-satisfied smirk, and I can't tell if it's sexy or kind of obnoxious, but he puts his arm around me, so I don't care.

"Thanks." He's looking more at me than the menu now, with most of his focus on my top lip, and I'm pretty sure he's finally going to lean in and kiss me when our waiter comes over with bread.

Was it like this before? I find myself wishing I could remember the first night we met. Has he always been this dizzying? Or is this just what it's like to go on a date with a guy who watched you identify your father's body?

We make conversation, and I think I manage to be intelligent and funny, but as he's talking, I'm constantly distracted by the way the cotton of his shirt stretches across his chest, and I laugh too much. I had been worried we'd have to revisit the subject of Gerald, but we never do. He is so effortless and light, I almost feel like nothing from the past two months is even real. It's like starting over on a clean page. Addictive.

The whole meal is basically sex. By the time we get a dessert menu, we are so close to each other I'm surprised anyone can tell that there are two people at our table. Neil's hand is toying shamelessly with the hem of my dress, and, when I lean forward for my water glass, he slides his fingers underneath and around the inside of my thigh. I feel like I'm seventeen. My brain races with a million things at once: fear and curiosity and self-doubt and lust and need. For the first time in weeks, I feel in control of something, like he wants me so urgently that he'd give me anything I asked at the bat of an eyelash, and I revel in it. I glance at him and bite my lip, full to the brim with this new power.

"I wanna go somewhere. You wanna go somewhere with me?" I ask, even though I already know the answer. I hold his gaze while his hand explores the skin of my inner thigh, and he nods, leaning in close, his breath scorching the curve of my ear.

We don't order dessert. Neil throws way too much cash on the table, and we leave before he can get change. It's less than an instant before we are in the back of a Lyft and then in his house, and his shirt is off before we can get upstairs. Between breaths, he tells me that his housemate is out of town for a bachelor party, and so we have the whole place to ourselves. Convenient. We don't bother with formalities and stay in the living room, where I let Neil undress me.

"You're so fucking gorgeous," he says, through the two or three beers he flew through at dinner. I just breathe as his fingers work their way up my body, sliding my underwear to the ground first, the skirt of my dress hiked up around my hips. He touches me like he's discovering something sacred, kissing all the bones that protrude where there used to be smooth flesh, but he doesn't mind. Doesn't even notice. His hands are warm, and they hold me together, and I'm flooded with relief at not having to do it myself even for a few minutes. I get goosebumps, and my spine vibrates, but my mind wanders. And then I remember the toilet paper stuffed in my bra.

"Wait," I gasp, as he kneads what little of me still clings at my waist. "No, wait. Hold on." I push him away with more force than I mean, suddenly cold and aware of the sweaty, teenage reality that is this moment. I yank my skirt down with shaking fingers and try to catch my breath.

"No, hey, come back," he pleads, his voice barely more sophisticated than a mumble. He's a puddle of want, with that sweet flop of hair.

"I'll be right back," I try to tease over my shoulder, but I'm sure I'm too flustered to pull it off, and I'm basically out of the room already. I scramble to the bathroom and lock the door. I feel the sting of mascara in my eyes, and lean heavily against the door, eyes pressed shut to keep all the black mess out. My legs buckle, and I sink to the floor, relieved to find myself splayed out on the cold tiles. Peeling the toilet paper from my chest, it's sticky with sweat, and I use what little of it is salvageable to wipe my eyes. They threaten to cry, but I push it aside. Making it back to my feet, I think I'll take a moment to compose myself in the mirror. I tuck a few stray hairs behind my ear, a hollow gesture in the face of everything.

The moment turns into five, maybe ten, and then Neil is at the door. First, I just hear the padding of his feet on the carpet in the hall and think maybe he's walking by for something, but a few minutes later, he knocks.

"Kenzie? Babe, you okay?" I feel like I can see him through the door. *Babe.* The word sticks in my chest, and I cough like that will dislodge it.

"Yeah, no... I'm fine. I just... I'll be out in a sec, okay?"

"Is it," he is small again, full of a nervous self-consciousness that can't help but impede the nonchalance of his sex appeal, "is it something I did? I'm sorry if I was—you know. If I pushed you too fast... I thought—"

I squeeze my eyes shut, and when I open them again, I have switched back on. I catch a glimpse in the mirror—Airplane Mode. The water is calm.

I open the door.

"It's nothing you did," I hear myself assure him. "I'm fine. Don't I look fine?" I throw him a coy smile, and he relaxes some, falling back into his earlier confidence. I hop up onto the edge of the bathroom sink, easing my dress off over my head. "Now, please. Come over here and fuck me."

And he does.

February 28th

When I was a little girl, I loved playing house. I had one of those Fisher-Price kitchens that Mom bought me as appeasement during the divorce and custody proceedings. I cooked elaborate fake meals on my little plastic stovetop before I went to work at my job as a unicorn veterinarian. My dolls assured me that I was the best mommy in the world, and I knew they weren't just saying that. I *was* the best mommy in the world. I made fluffy pancakes every morning, and we always had a balanced dinner together at night, where I made huge salads that I would never actually touch if they'd been real. I was the mom I didn't have.

In my imaginary life, I was happily married. My husband's name was Sam, and he worked as a lawyer for fairies who were suing over unfair land usage. Sam and I were always very romantic with each other. We knew everything about each other, the way you do with a husband you made up.

The best thing about playing house is that everything always goes according to plan, and if it doesn't, you get infinite do-overs until it does. When I played house, my parents weren't getting divorced. Gerald wasn't homeless. Mom wasn't moving on without me. I wasn't always on academic probation. Everything everywhere glowed with the kind of perfection kids think will be attainable once they're adults who can do whatever they want.

I used to dream that I would be that perfect adult. Always clean and organized and beautiful, with lipstick that stayed put all day and hypoallergenic pets.

Most of my life, I think I've only been getting further and further away from her—until this morning.

The sun is shining in through Neil's IKEA curtains, and a note on the pillow next to me explains that he ran out real quick, but will be back soon, and not to worry, just to make myself at home. It ends in a smiley face, which I would usually hate, but right now, I find oddly soothing. I take in the bedroom in the light and am pleased by the tidiness of it. Everything is just as shiny-happy as Neil. The way I imagine Sam's first place might have been.

I'm scanning the contents of his bookshelf—*A Heartbreaking Work of Staggering Genius, Infinite Jest, War and Peace*—when he comes home. Before I turn around, he's behind me, his arm snaked around my waist, face nestled in the crook of my neck.

"You're up," he purrs in my ear. "I didn't know what you liked, so I got you three croissants." He produces a series of pastry bags from behind his back, and I flounce onto the bed like an overeager puppy. I don't recognize myself this cute.

He plays it up to be this grand reveal, "In bag number one… " he tosses it to me, and before I realize it, I'm playing along.

"Ooh! A chocolate croissant!"

"Not just any chocolate croissant, a croissant filled with a homemade chocolate ganache."

"Oh, come on. You're spoiling me," I grin.

"Just wait." He is beaming now, pleased with himself for being so fairy-tale perfect. "In bag number two… "

Toss. Catch. Reveal.

"It's… is this just a regular croissant?"

"Ah, see, at first glance, I can see how you might think that. But in fact, it's a croissant filled with Margaret's famous raspberry jam."

I feel a sudden urge to kiss him, so I pull him down onto the bed with me, an easy feat, and bring his face to mine. He smiles into my lips, kisses my cheek.

"Who's Margaret?"

"Why? Jealous?" His mouth makes its way to my ear. "She's the baker at my coffeehouse," and then, for good measure, he adds, "she's happily married, thirty-nine years."

"She sounds lovely."

"She's got nothing on you." I close my eyes as he kisses me again, his hands sliding down my waist. The earnest stability of him feels so good, I think I'd like to lie in bed with him for days, and we haven't even gotten to the third croissant. Maybe everything happened exactly like it was supposed to, so that now here I am. If I ignore the echo around the edges, I decide this could feel like happiness.

I'm determined to absorb as much of his fresh-baked goodness as I can, when he says, "How is it possible you're single?"

"Oh." My skin shrink-wraps to my bones. "I don't know. There are plenty of reasons."

"Like what?" He laughs an easy laugh. "I can't see any."

He's naive enough to think he wants to know me, but I know better. Instead, I promise that I can't wait to try all the croissants, but that I need to get home and change clothes because I'm supposed to help my mom out with some stuff this afternoon. I shove the pastry bags into my purse, and after he kisses me a few more times and tells me he'll call to set up something in a few days, I leave his place, go out onto the street and try to breathe.

It's not more than a few miles, so I decide to walk home because I need the fresh air. There are three texts from Mel on my phone from between midnight, and 2:30 AM last night, which are all variations on a theme: *Oh MY GAWD, are you still with CUTE NEIL???? He's such a CATCH, riiiiight??*

No emails.

I walk past a 24-hour grocery store, and an old man outside asks if I can spare some change so he can get something to eat. I only have my debit card, so we go in together and after I buy him a sandwich I ask him if he likes croissants.

March 14th

Two years ago today, I saw Gerald for the last time. He asked me what day I was born, and maybe I even told him. I said, "I love you," before I left, and it sounded like a lie. He didn't bother saying it back.

And now I let Neil touch me all day long.

Like I am still here to be touched.

Like I ever came home to myself again.

March 21st

Neil says he would like to be my boyfriend, and I get water down the wrong tube and cough myself blue in the face.

Not that I don't like Neil. I do. There's objectively nothing *not* to like about him—which is actually maybe something not to like about him. I try not to think about it. The first few weeks we've spent together so far are enough to make maple syrup look bitter by comparison. And I feel closer to better when I'm with him than when I'm on my own. We order side salads instead of fries and make jokes that aren't offensive to anyone. We smile walking down the street and say thank you to strangers even when they're being complete assholes. It's not that I don't want him to be my boyfriend. I would be the most sparkly girl in the world if Neil were my boyfriend. I would be a walking sequin.

It's just that every morning when I wake up next to him, for a split second, I think I'm in a nightmare where I'll have to live the first of the year over again, and my whole body goes numb.

But relative to how good things are the rest of the day, that's hardly worth mentioning. Except that it happens. Every morning.

I'm working on ignoring it.

He wants to be my boyfriend, and I know that should make me happy, so I tell myself it does, and when I finally say yes, his eyes go so bright, it makes me almost believe it. Like his smile will somehow reflect off my face.

There is close to nothing in my bank account by the end of every week. I know I should be stressed, but I can't make myself feel like it matters. I've turned it into a game where if I make it from Friday to Friday without overdrawing, I get a treat.

Sometimes buying the treat results in overdrawing. But I pretend it's an accomplishment that that's only happened once. I put this month's rent on a credit card.

I have $846.00 left in a savings account that I tell myself I am saving for an emergency. Since my life this year has been more or less a constant state of emergency, I don't know at what point I will actually break the glass and pull the handle. But I figure I'll know it when I see it.

Mel keeps hinting that I need to get a real job. She says that, eventually, I will actually need to fix things for myself.

But I have a new boyfriend. And he's so handsome. He thinks I am perfect.

I am a sequin.

March 28th

Being under twenty-five and virtually unemployed means you rarely need a convincing change of clothes, and so it's been almost a week since the last time I came home from Neil's. Honestly, I probably could have made it another week, but Mel called and said she needed to talk to me, and where was I, and how come I was never home anymore. So, I came home.

She's sitting on the edge of my bed when I come in, and she's got a very important look on her face.

"Hi," she says, all excited and flustered.

"Oh. Hey. You're in here," I say, but she doesn't offer a reason. I let it go. "So, listen, sorry I haven't been-"

"Happy one-month anniversary!"

"What?"

"You and Neil. It's a month now, right?" I can't tell what's happening to her. She doesn't quite seem mad, but she's definitely not fine.

"I don't—what day is it?"

"The 28th," she says, matter-of-factly. And then adds, "Of *March*," which embarrasses me.

"Oh, yeah, no, I know. I just meant—I haven't been keeping track of like—like, we just—"

"He's obviously your boyfriend, though. Seems like you guys are serious. I mean, you're happy with him, right? You seem happy. Happier."

None of this is like Mel at all. I sit down next to her trying to get a closer look.

"You're happier, aren't you? Being with him makes you—What? What are you looking at?"

"You're being weird, is all," I say, unable to diagnose her.

She smiles a big creepy smile before her body sort of relaxes, and her face flips into this anxious horrible face I've never seen before.

"Okay, yes. I'm being weird, sorry. It's just—So something kind of unexpected happened," she says, taking my hand, "and I super wanted to talk to you about it as soon as I found out, but I wasn't for sure that it was even gonna happen and then when it did, you were always at Neil's, and there wasn't really ever a good time—"

I drop her hand and squint again. "Christ, if you're pregnant, Melanie—"

"What? No. God. No. I'm not preg—how would I even suddenly be pregnant? I haven't seen Luke in—no. No."

I flop back onto the mattress. "Well thank God, I was gonna say—"

"Kenz, though. Okay, ugh, um, okay. Here it goes: Um, they—my parents? They decided—they're taking my advice, finally, and they're opening a Juice & Harmony on the East Coast."

I roll over and look at her. She's biting her lip and raising her eyebrows, very anticipatory-like. "Is that it? That's great, Mel. Congratulations." Her face doesn't relax, even at all.

"In New Haven. They're um—they're putting the East Coast location in New Haven. They got a really great storefront close to campus, and they think Jutrition will be a huge hit with the Ivy League undergrads, especially around finals and midterms and stuff? And they—well, they were hoping I'd—you know, because Luke is there for Forestry school anyway, so they thought I could—"

I catch up with her, and it must show on my face because hers goes all loose and undone. "You're moving to Connecticut? You want to *move* to *Connecticut*?"

"I know it's sudden—and I wouldn't even think about it, you know with everything you've been through already this year, and losing your job and everything—"

"It was a demotion."

"Right, no, I just mean—with your dad and—but then lately… I don't know, it seems like things are so good with Neil, and you're almost never here anyway—"

"No. I mean, whatever, things are good, but no. I—You can't just leave. You can't move 3,000 miles away and just…Just *move*. What would I—? I mean, I can't move in with him. It's been like five minutes."

"A month."

"Same difference."

"But if you're spending most of your time over there—"

"Yeah, *this week*. But that's just this week. And with the understanding that I can leave. That I can go home if we change our minds about each other. Which we totally might. Any minute. One week doesn't mean that we're moving in together. God, Mel, it doesn't even necessarily mean we *like* each other."

She shrugs and sighs and does this fake walking away thing that makes me want to throw something at the back of her head.

"Don't—"

"I'm not going anywhere! I just don't know how to—you're being impossible!"

"I'm not—I'm—*Jesus*. It's been one fucking week, Melanie. You're acting li—"

"It's been a *month*."

I hate talking in circles. But we keep at it. For hours. For what feels like days. She makes excuses and throws her head back in a fake, angry laugh. I break a plate, mostly by accident, but kind of not. She tells me I'm being a baby. I tell her I'm an adult. She asks why I don't act like one, and I ask her why she acts like such a raging bitch if she isn't one. She says she's sorry that my dad died, and I break another plate entirely on purpose.

She crosses the room, frustrated and flailing through the air.

"It's not like you actually have nowhere to go! You could—I don't know—you could go to your mom's or to—even to Alice's if you really needed to. I mean, even if you just keep your stuff there—"

And, in a flash of pain, I can see it. That she's been taking care of me since seventh grade, and she's tired. That she worries I'm only getting worse. I *am* getting worse. And I know this isn't really a conversation. It's a fight. And it's one I'm going to lose. I remember the day I told Gerald I was moving away for college. The look on his face like I'd betrayed him. I wonder if I look like that now.

I should have given up. Because I recognized the way she was looking at me—begging me to give her permission just to go and not worry. Because I'd felt that same heartbreaking urge to be free from caring for someone set on destroying themselves. But I didn't. Instead I screamed and guilt-tripped and locked myself in the bathroom for hours until she fell asleep crying outside the door, and then for hours after that.

I slept under used bath towels, curled up in the tub like a junkie.

I don't know what time she left.

*

Mackenzie Adams
Personal Growth - Mrs. Klein
Letter to My Future Self
10/17/2009

Dear Future Mackenzie,

~~Congratulations on your super awesome hover-craft and your brand new robot dog!~~ (Mrs. Klein says I can't write that because this is a "serious assignment," so I crossed it out, but I hope you can still read it.)

Um. Okay, so, right now, I'm a sophomore in high school, which pretty much sucks. My best friend is Melanie, who you probably remember. I hope you're still friends with her. I don't have a boyfriend, but I've done everything already. ~~And besides, boys are actually so boring and disgusting and only want blowjobs all the time, so that's whatever.~~

I feel weird about this assignment. I don't know what I want to tell you—like, you already know everything about me because you ARE me. So, it's not like having a pen pal. It's weird. I'm sorry this is so boring.

I guess, like, I don't know. Are Mom and Jimmy together still? She seems happy with him, I guess. Not like she would tell me if she wasn't but still. I don't know if we're allowed to ask questions in these letters. Probably not cuz it's not like you're gonna write me back, but whatever. I guess, if we're allowed to ask questions, then I have to ask: Is Dad dead yet?

I told Mrs. Klein that I don't know what else to write, and she said to tell myself about some of my hopes and dreams for the future. So, like, I guess I can do that, but just promise you won't be super mad at yourself if you haven't done any of them when you read this.

I guess it'd be cool to be… I don't know just, like, doing my own thing. Like, to have a cool job where I get to travel and to have an apartment and stuff. It'd be cool to have, like, my own dishes or like, to like, buy art and get to hang it up wherever I wanted. And, I guess I could be in love or whatever. But also, like, it doesn't matter. That's not really what I'm worried about. I just want—I guess I just want to be, like, less fucked up. To feel less fucked up. Like, less depressed. Cuz I'm just, like, I don't know. I just feel like everything sucks and like it's not getting any better or easier. It's just really sad. I'm really sad because things are just not really what I thought they were gonna be at all—like, growing up and stuff isn't how I thought. It's pretty much exactly like being a kid except for that now magic isn't real, and all the people you thought were superheroes are really just fucked up human monsters like you are. I guess I don't know if that'll ever feel different or not. But I hope that you at least, like, figured out a way to deal with it. Or maybe that you found a way not to feel like that anymore.

This is fucking depressing. This assignment is so depressing. You know what I really hope for the future? I hope you never ever read this letter.

Love,
Past Mackenzie

*

April 1st

"No, it's not—it's—Mom. It's not an April Fools. I'm asking you. I— it'll just be for a little while when Mel leaves in May..."

Breathing. Breathing. The beginning of crying. Jimmy's voice murmuring. The middle of crying. The clumsy shifting of the receiver against a sweater set.

I try not to think it, that there's nowhere else to put me. I tell her I'll be at Neil's most of the time. That it'll only be a few nights and just storing some boxes while I look for my own place—that it's temporary.

But the disappointment in her voice when she agrees weighs more than I do.

I wonder how long it will be before she stops saying my name in her house.

April 30th

I didn't date in college. I moved halfway across the country and started over with new people, and I didn't want to talk much about my life before I got there. I didn't want to tell people about Gerald getting arrested, or about losing my virginity in a Quizno's parking lot at 4 AM on a Wednesday. I think I imagined that I would meet someone like Neil in a poetry seminar, and he'd be wearing glasses to distract from his obvious underlying hotness. Then we'd end up in some debate about Chaucer that ended in lattes and impassioned parallel careers and, eventually, grandchildren. Instead, I met Kevin.

Neil told me on our third date that he thinks it's "adorable" that I haven't seriously dated anyone before. I couldn't tell if it was condescending and could tell even less if I cared. I'm constantly chasing that uncomplicated floaty feeling he gave me on our first date, and I find I'll take anything I can get for even half that high.

I am sitting across from him at lunch, watching him eat a turkey burger, when he tells me that he's been thinking.

"So. She's going to Connecticut," he says with his mouth full.

"Who?"

He swallows too much food at once, coughs, and then says, "What do you mean, who? Melanie. Your roommate."

I've been avoiding talking to him about it because I don't want my living situation to be his problem. I just nod a little nod.

"Timing," he says, and I wonder if he thinks we are one of those sparkly couples that can read each other's minds. We're not.

"Yeah, no, I know. It's not great timing. But you know…"

"No, Kenzie, I mean, I think it's kind of—I don't know. You don't think it's kind of like… I don't know. Fate?"

"Fate?" I turn my mouth down at this. Too much, probably. "No. I mean, I don't know how it would qualify as—" I'm caught off guard when he starts to lean across the table. And then it clicks, and I know where this is headed. I know because he is leaning so much and looking at me like he just found something he thought was lost forever. I can tell that he is feeling a gooey flood of nice things at once, and it makes me remember that I haven't always been this empty—that I felt that flood once standing outside in the winter with Kevin. I taste salt at the back of my throat, remembering the flood and the lights on the trees, and the blur, and I have to close my eyes for a second against the hollow ache of not being able to feel it anymore—of feeling nothing. No flood, no lights, no blur. Just Neil, looking handsome near a sandwich.

"Oh. Fate. You mean fate… for us."

"Well, when you say it like that it sounds… God, no, that sounds—sorry. That sounds way cheesier than I meant. I just meant, like—Okay. Forget I said that. Can I start over?"

"You don't have to—"

"No, I want to. I want to. Look, okay. It's… I've kind of been— I've been thinking about getting my own place? I mean, with the extra money I'm making now as a trainer, it's—I realize that I just don't really need to be living with a housemate. And so, I was gonna look for a one-bedroom anyway… um… and I—" His face flushes pink, and he takes my hands in a very serious way. As soon as he's touching me, I realize I'm sweating, and then I think about how my palms are sweating, and suddenly my brain is screaming to stop the production of sweat, and I get this weird chill and make a shuddering "brrr" noise. I'm a giveaway.

But Neil doesn't let go of my hands.

"You alright?" He sort of laughs as he asks the question, and I try to laugh too, but I only produce this awkward sputtering hiccup.

"Yeah, I'm fine." I clear my throat. "Sorry, I don't know what that was, I'm—Sorry. *Sorry.* You were saying that you want to get your own apartment."

"Well, I was thinking about it, but now I—I mean—what I wanted to say was just... Kenzie, you are... I... I like you—a lot. I really, really like you. And I feel like you—I mean, I know it's soon, but I feel like you... well, look, you need a new place and I was thinking about a new place anyway..."

I nod, and then close my eyes again for another second and wait for something—for anything. No flood. No lights. No blur. But I think how easy it would be to love Neil—how reliable and stable and easy it would be. Anyone could do something that easy. Even *I* could do that.

"You want to live with me. You want us to move in together. Is what you're saying," I ask, and I try to smile as I say it. I think about how it could solve so many of my problems. How it would mean not moving home again, not being an embarrassment to my mom. Maybe I could move on and not be so fucking damaged all the time. Have a healthy life with my hyper-athletic, handsome, well-defined, live-in boyfriend. I could start eating a balanced breakfast and drinking enough water. I could be Melanie.

Neil is still holding my hands, but his face is starting to get worried in all my silences. He tugs at my arm and jolts me back into the moment. "Hey, listen, do you think it's too soon? It's okay if it freaks you out, I know we haven't been together that long and you're still—"

But when I smile at him, he stops talking and looks at me like he can't actually see me at all, like I'm some beautiful glowing thing with no pores and no scars, and I have a glimpse of how much simpler it'd be if that were true. And it feels almost like if I let him look at me long enough, it could be. I'm hungry for the peace of it, and so I push toward it. "No, shut up, no. It doesn't freak me out. I think it's… I think that's what I want too. I think—no, I do. I do. I want us to do that."

The first and only time Jimmy and Gerald met was the weekend after my high school graduation. Mom and Jimmy had gotten married not too long before. Jimmy had been at my graduation in the Mackenzie Adams cheering section, and Gerald had not. They met by accident. I was at Mom's house alone with Mel, panicking about college roommates and choosing a major or something useless, and Gerald showed up at the door. It'd been years since he used to come over every afternoon. But I knew it was him without needing to look—I could hear him fumbling with his old set of house keys, trying to fit them into the new locks. The telltale jangling of his key fob made my stomach drop. I don't know if Mel heard it too, or if she just saw it on my face, and knew to disappear downstairs somewhere. I'd wanted to follow her. Pretend it was no big deal to ignore him. But I was frozen with the guilt of not wanting him. And, unable to face it, I just laid myself flat on the living room rug, stone still, and prayed for him to find some other place to go.

And then I heard the car door slam outside. Jimmy was home.

Gerald never did come inside that day, though I didn't move from the floor either. I just lay there, swallowing sobs, while he tore into Jimmy on the front porch. I listened while Gerald belched slurs and obscenities for what felt like hours. On and on about how he couldn't be replaced—not by a truck and not by some "ballroom dancing son of a bitch." He demanded to be let into the house, demanded to see me, demanded to talk to Mom. And when none of it happened, he threatened to beat Jimmy to a pulp, to break the door down, to smash the windows. His voice was raw, his desperation burning into malice.

But what I most remember was that after Gerald left, Jimmy came through the door and said good afternoon to me like nothing had happened. He smiled and asked me what I wanted to have for dinner. He laughed as he told me about a woman he'd seen at the post office paying for stamps with exact change. He never said anything about Gerald, never asked me why I was on the floor, dripping mascara into the carpet. He just let it be. And I thought then, what I have so often thought since: *I know why Mom loves you. You let all the ugly things disappear. You let Gerald evaporate. Just like she's always wanted.*

I think Neil can do that too. For me. I think Neil can do that if I let him.

May 8th

"You have that look again," Neil says. I look at him and shrug. He loves to do this thing where he comments on my face. I think it makes him feel like he really knows me, and so I don't tell him otherwise. We're laying in his bed, staring at the ceiling the way unhappily married couples do in the movies. But we aren't unhappy. Maybe *I* am sometimes, but I'm working on that. And together we aren't ever unhappy at all.

"Sorry, just thinking."

"I know. That's your thinking face." I roll over and smile at him. Sometimes, I think he's like a dog that loves me so much I want to be mean to him just to see the shock on his face. But that's wrong. I stroke his hair instead.

"I think I really liked the last place we saw today. The one with the window seat?" I hum. Together we are happy all the time. Together we see window seats and imagine breakfast nooks.

"It's a great location," he says, and I worry that we are boring.

"I know, so close to the farmer's market too. And it's only a few blocks from the bus, which is great. Did you like it? You liked it, right?" We are boring. He smiles and kisses my forehead. We are excruciatingly boring.

"If you liked it, I loved it."

So, I think we will apply. I close my eyes and imagine that this could be my real life for the rest of forever. And Neil asks what I want to have for dinner, and I suggest that we go out to celebrate our new apartment. I say I feel like celebrating because everything is perfect.

I decide not to tell him that I quit my job at Dear Alice today.

I decide that can wait.

May 15th

My old place is mostly empty. Mel has shipped a lot of her stuff to Connecticut already, and sold the rest on Craigslist or Etsy or somewhere. I realize that most of the prominent things in the apartment were hers: the couch, the bookcases, the dishes, the pots and pans, the vacuum. There's a lot of dirt and dust and nothing to clean it up.

Mel and I are going through whose books are whose today. I told her she could just take whichever books she wants, and I'd take the rest, but she insisted that she really wanted to spend the afternoon together.

It's been four hours of, "you take this *Complete Works Of,* and I'll just keep *Collected Essays.*" We're getting down to the last section—reference books.

"We have three Oxford English dictionaries," she says, holding them up. "Did you buy these? I've only ever had a Merriam-Webster's."

"I bought them in college, yeah."

Mel's face twists around a little, and I figure she's waiting for an explanation.

"I got the first one on purpose, and then a couple years later they'd added a bunch of slang words, you know, like 'crump' or 'froyo,' or whatever. So that year I bought two of the new editions because I thought I'd give one as a gift, but I couldn't decide who would like it, and then I didn't know whether I could recycle the first one, so now I have three."

Her face doesn't go back to normal. She wants to say something.

"What is it?"

"What? No. Nothing. It's nothing."

I consider not begging because I don't really care. But, in the spirit of our days being numbered, I give in. "No, come on. You can tell me. What's up?" My voice won't engage all the way, so I sound bored and pissed off. But the message is right.

"Well, I—" She sighs loudly, puts the books down, and, out of nowhere, sits down on the floor. "Look, I'm starting to, um… okay. Do you wanna sit down?"

"Not really. The floor is disgusting right now."

"Well, okay. But I actually think it'd be easier…" Before she can finish her sentence, I'm sitting on the floor. I can't sit cross-legged anymore because I've lost enough weight that my ass is pretty much just skin stretched over my sit bones. So, I'm sort of kneeling. Which also sucks.

"Hi," she says, making a lot of eye contact. There's sugar in her voice, and it reminds me of a flytrap.

"Okay. So. What's the deal? Why are we on the floor?"

"Um, okay. Honestly? I'm starting to worry about you. Like *really* actually. And I'm worried that this is sort of, I don't know… maybe that it's my fault… you know, because I sprung all this Connecticut stuff on you, and suggested that you and Neil should… are you comfortable like that?" My knees are digging into the floor. I shift around, trying to take the pressure off my bones—nothing works.

"I'm fine." She grimaces at the lie. "Seriously. It's fine. Go ahead."

"Okay. Well… okay. Okay. I guess, so anyway, I just feel like this is kind of a mess. And, like things with us have been weird. Weird, but also just really bad. And tense. I feel like you're mad at me a lot of the time. And maybe I deserve that. Probably. Because

I feel like maybe I wasn't the most... like maybe I didn't really take enough time off to spend with you after... you know, with your dad and everything. And now it's like... I'm leaving, and you're kind of, I don't know, Kenz. I'm freaked out about leaving. Like I'm freaked out that... Jesus, I don't know—that I'll get a phone call from Alice or something that you just, like, killed yourself or something. Because you keep saying you're fine, and for a while, I thought maybe you actually were, but lately, it's like you're *so* fine that I don't think you are. I really don't think you are. And that scares me a lot..." her voice breaks off, and she looks away from me and tries to breathe. Part of me wants to comfort her, but I don't, so it's quiet for a long time, and we both just listen to her breath stuttering around. Finally, I think of something to say. And it's terrible. I think maybe it's not what I mean to say. But I also think it is, so I say it.

"But you're going anyway."

Mel doesn't move for a while. She looks at me, and her eyes don't move. They don't even flicker. She just stares. And her breathing gets so calm and still—it's like it's barely happening. We stay like that for hours, maybe. Or maybe it's only five minutes. Then she moves. She moves, and in an instant, she's all over me. It's a hug like I haven't had in years. The kind of hug I used to give Gerald whenever I caught glimpses of the dad I thought he could be. The kind of hug that breaks you. She hugs me and hugs me and says, "Do I need to stay? I will stay. If it will save you, I will stay."

"It wouldn't save me," I tell her, but when I hear it, I realize I'm also telling myself. My throat goes dry and full of lumps, and no more words come out when I open my mouth. Instead, it's just a loud sob before I crumble. There are a million things I want to tell her—my best friend in the world—but I don't. I don't want to know them myself, don't want to hear them said out loud. So, I just cry and cry, and she strokes my hair and whispers that she's sorry again and again.

I heave big loud sobs out of my chest, like shoveling snow, but everything just feels heavier. "It's okay to still be grieving," Mel says, and it occurs to me that everything about this moment is Valery's wet dream, but I can't care. There's a hole swelling in my gut that threatens to get bigger and bigger until it swallows me, and I know it's the void left by my own absence.

I don't know how long I cry. Past the usual point where it feels silly or unnecessary. Longer than I let myself cry alone. And the more I cry, the more helpless I feel to stop. Mel says she'll order in food and we'll just stay together in my bed tonight.

She asks if I need to let Neil know where I am, and I forget who that is.

May 24th

The realtor's office is quiet, and glimmers like the set of a primetime network drama. I am wearing pointy shoes and a skirt of a respectable length. I cling onto Neil's arm in a way that is neither comfortable nor usual for either of us but has been taught to me by fictional women as a way to indicate belonging. I hold onto him even when we sit down. We're told that Fran will be right with us.

Neil places his hand on my knee and squeezes. "This is a big deal," he murmurs into my ear, and I smile into his neck and think about all the empty spaces in this new apartment that will become full of things that are ours. Ours. Ours. Ours, ours, hours. Hours and hours and hours. And all of them together. I look at Neil, and he is still smiling.

"Fran's ready for you."

We go back into a broad, stark conference room with an oblong table that is decades across. Fran is a small woman, perched on the far side of the table. Her lips press tight together when she's pleased about something, and they are particularly inseparable when we come in. I imagine she's had a sex dream or two about Neil, the way her eyes sweep over him, and although it's only in my imagination, I dig my talons deeper into his arm.

"Did you have a chance to review the lease I sent over?"

We nod, and I float out of my body to watch as a whole part of our life begins.

We sign a lot of pieces of paper, with Neil reassuring me that things are going to be okay. I really believe him. Believe *in* him. I feel peaceful like everything has finally been ironed out the way Alice always wanted for me. Neil's voice is so sure as we go over details, I want him to talk forever. His fingers settle into the grooves of my rib cage, and I feel a placid warmth settle inside me where I am missing. I catch his eye and think quietly, *I would like to marry you*. Hours and hours and hours. I would like to be yours.

"What do you want to do now?" He smirks as we get back to the car.

"You're very sexy when you talk real estate," I tease. "Has anyone ever told you that before?"

He pulls me in close and brushes the hair from my face. "You know, Kenzie. I think you might just be the first." The kiss that follows is sweet and then intense, desperate. I want to be closer to him, to this perfect feeling. I want to belong here. I claw at his shirt, fingers in his hair, and down his neck, across the breadth of his shoulders. *This is strong enough to hold me*, I tell myself. *I want to belong here.* He presses me against the car door, his hand quickly underneath my skirt. I feel around behind me for the door handle and fall into the back seat, peeling my clothes off.

"Tell me I'm yours," I whisper as he climbs in on top of me. He pulls my skirt off, and I wait. He kneels, unbuttoning his jeans, never taking his eyes off me. "Tell me. Tell me I'm yours, Neil. Please." I try to make it sound sexy, but my heart is racing, my face hot with fear.

"You're all mine, Kenzie," he says finally, both his hands finally between my legs. He soothes my loneliness like a gravity blanket, but it only works if he's right on top of me.

"Tell me again," I sigh.

"You're mine. You're all mine." I grab his hands and pull him towards me, my back sticky against the fake leather of the back seat.

"Show me."

"Kenzie," he says, his breath hot on my collarbone. "I love you." I look him in the eye, feel him inside me, think how tired I am.

"I love you too," I whisper. "I love you too." I close my eyes and relish in feeling full of someone who isn't me.

*

Dear Alice,

This is my first time writing to you, although I've been a reader of yours for a long time. I'm embarrassed to say that I don't know where to begin.

I guess I don't know why I'm writing. Things are fine. Things are good, even.

I just—do you ever feel like maybe you're missing something? Like, as a person? There's just some part you don't have? That's what I feel like sometimes. More lately. The part that understands why I'm here. The part that feels like this life wasn't just a huge mistake.

Probably that's fine. Right? Probably. Because I'm young. No one knows what they're doing. No one understands anything. Even the people who really have it together. Even you, Alice. Right?

But I can't shake feeling like something's wrong. The happiness in my life… Sometimes it feels more like a trap. Like something I haven't earned, but that I'm just being given as a test. And I'm failing because I don't understand how to have it, but I don't want to give it up.

I'm sorry to be so vague. I get nervous about the idea of my personal details being published. And really. Things are fine. Things are so, so good. Really.

I'm just paranoid.

But please. Help.

-Missing Piece

*

Dear Missing Piece,

My dear. I will ask you simply to stop lying. Stop lying to yourself. Stop lying to me and those around you. My sweet pea, it's clear that you are not fine. Things are not good. You are hurting, and you are lost.

Your letter did not say what this "happiness" in your life is… but my instincts say it is not happiness. It is a crutch. Genuine happiness will fill you up. It will not hold you back.

I know what it feels like to be missing something. I have loved and lost and wandered. I have been young. But, Missing Piece, please trust that when we feel something is missing, it is a signal to go out and find it. We cannot do as you are doing now and pretend that this is something to be accepted as given. We deserve to be whole. You deserve to be whole—to know why you're here, and to feel that you're enough.

Now, finding our whole is not easy. Sometimes it will mean separating from what we know. Sometimes we must get more lost to be found. But my advice? Do not wait for someone else to find you. They are not coming. They could not possibly know this place you're being swallowed into, Missing Piece.

We, here at Dear Alice, have listened to your pain, though you mask it with pleasantries and kind words.

We have heard your cries, but we cannot help, as you've asked us to do. We can only urge you to help yourself.

You are alone. But ask yourself, why must that be a scary thing?

With all love and hope for you,
Alice

*

May 25th

I'm watching Neil sleep when it happens again; the awful déjà vu that I keep hoping will go away if I am patient.

"We are both okay," I breathe as it comes. "We are together and happy. Today is May 25th. Today is May 25th. Gerald is already gone. We are both okay." But my breathing is growing shallow, and I start to feel dizzy. I stagger out of bed and into the bathroom. My body in a cold sweat, my hands tingling. I am buzzing. Like I might ignite—like I might suddenly disappear. I take off all my clothes and press my body into the floor, and the cold hurts—burns through me so fiercely that I let out a panicked sob. "*STOP. STOP!!*" My voice is a dull screech, broken by bursts of saltwater in my throat. My teeth start to chatter, and Neil is at the door.

"Kenzie? Babe, what's happening in there? You're scaring me."

I wrap myself in the bathmat, leaned against the toilet. He knocks again before he tries the knob. I remember I didn't lock the door, and then I turn and throw up. Neil is next to me, holding my hair, rubbing my back. Doting.

"*Kenzie.* God. What happened? Hey. Hey, you're okay. What can I do? You're okay. Just breathe."

I let him hold me. Let him clean me up. And the whole time, I think of Beth. I think of her holding Gerald in her lap, dead and naked and alone. I think of my own body, too pale, writhing in scrawny cowardice on the bathroom floor over a fear I won't name. Grieving for something I've always been losing. Neil says again and again that I'm okay, and as long as his hands are on me, I know I haven't evaporated, but he touches me as though, for the first time, he suspects I'll collapse without him. I think I would.

He carries me back to bed and puts me in one of his t-shirts. He brings me water and fruit to pick at. He kisses my forehead. And the whole time I don't say anything. I just watch him doing the very best he can, doing everything right.

I lay in his bed, and the sound of birds outside lulls me away from here. Maybe I'm just tired... maybe if I sleep...

<u>May 26th</u>

His hand is already on my cheek when I feel myself coming back to life.

"Hi," he says in that way he does. "You wanna talk to me about what happened yesterday?" He searches my face with a pout. Somehow, he is no more than a delicate child.

"I don't know. Panic attack or something. Is there water?" He doesn't answer or move, and so I get up and go to the kitchen. The house is so quiet today, so still that as I turn on the faucet, I can hear him sitting up in bed. When I come back with water, the air in the room is different.

"How's the water?"

"I don't know. It's water. It's wet." I try to laugh, but there's no room for it.

"A panic attack about what? About us? About moving in?"

I sit at the foot of the bed and gulp down water so I can save on time to think. "Neil, I don't know." He leans back against the headboard but doesn't take his eyes off me. Something has fractured in his gaze, and I realize it's me.

"Well... okay." He's inspecting me like he's never seen me before. I guess he hasn't. "Was this your first panic attack?"

The hole in my chest starts to yawn. "I don't—I... I need more water." I leave again, but this time he follows me to the kitchen. The house is filling with the echo of silence pulled too tight.

"Was it your first?" More quiet. He's unraveling, and I am revealing myself to be the nothing behind the curtain. "It wasn't, right? It wasn't." I don't want to look at him. "Fuck, I know it wasn't. You don't want to tell me, that's fine. Because I already know."

My jaw tightens at hearing his resentment. Like this is something I was supposed to solve before he got around to noticing it—like this is all too inconvenient for *him*. "So, fine. Okay. What do you want me to say?" I turn on the tap, but the water won't get cold enough, and I turn it off.

"You could tell me the fucking truth. Were you having a panic attack that first night?"

No. I don't want to talk about that. "Why are you so angry?"

"Were. You. Having. A. Panic. Attack." The way it feels when the current pulls the sand out from under your feet.

"When? I don't know when you're talking about."

"You know when. Why are you playing dumb when you know when? That first night. Before we had sex."

I flinch. It's so blatantly obvious that he knows the answer. That he's known this whole time. That I had imagined this elaborate, innocent lie for us, and now it's crumbling. I think of Kevin and Gerald, and I wonder how many more times I'm going to imagine a love that isn't there. I open my mouth, but it's dry.

"*Oh my god*, Kenzie. Why did you let me touch you?"

I cough up a laugh. "I'm sorry? Why did I *let* you? I don't know, why *did* you? You didn't have to. I didn't force you. And what? Like you wouldn't have touched me if you'd known? What do you even think?"

"No. Of course, I wouldn't have… Not if I'd known you weren't okay. If you'd told me you weren't better, or… or—"

I throw my glass on the floor, but it doesn't break.

"God, what is this? Nothing breaks in this house except me?"

"It's plastic."

"How could you think I would be *better*?" I sit down on the floor in front of the sink. "You don't get better. This isn't like getting sick. This isn't like breaking a bone or... or getting over a headache. It's—"

"Well, then why didn't you say anything?"

"Because you *knew*. You're telling me right now that you *knew*. Or, god, or at least you suspected. You wondered whether I was okay, but you didn't *ask*." He picks up my glass, sets it on the counter, and then pulls up a chair at the table. I glance at him, but his head is in his hands.

"Are you waiting for me to tell you that's bullshit, Kenzie? Or are you going to get there on your own?" The tone in his voice startles me, scathing in a way I didn't think he had in him. "I can't even count the number of times I've asked you if you're okay. And you always say yes. You insist that you're fine. So, what am I supposed to do, not trust you? Read your mind? Pressure you until you crack and start to fucking hate me?"

I'm quiet for a long time, paging through a Rolodex of next sentences, unsure where to land. I crawl to the end of the counter and around the other side, so he can't see me. I want to hide for a long time. I begin to think there is nothing left to say, and then my mouth starts talking.

"Of anyone, I thought you knew the best what it was like because... you were *there*." I hear my voice shake. Every time I blink, I am back in that hotel room, Neil vomiting in the bathroom and Beth a pile in my lap, with my father's head in hers. "You *saw* him. You saw everything. I thought you would know. I thought—I thought it sort of happened to you too. That in some weird way, maybe we were going through this together. And so, I could distract you, and—and you would distract me. Until eventually, we would forget."

The air melts, and we are swimming. Just treading water near each other, bobbing around like unanchored buoys with nothing to keep us together, but nothing to pull us apart. Then I think, who knows if he's even still here. Maybe he left the room or fell asleep. Maybe he died while I was hiding on the other side of the counter.

I hear the floor under his feet as he comes closer to me. He sits under the breakfast bar, just around the corner, and holds my hand. "He wasn't my dad. It's not the same for me. You know that."

I let out an astonished puff of air. "He was barely my dad anymore. Not in the way you mean. You don't... you don't know everything all the time. You have this idea that the word 'dad' has some magical meaning for everyone. But it doesn't for me. For a long time, it's just meant trouble... or fear, or, not fear... just... I don't know, just dread."

Neil's quiet gets all stiff, and I know I've made him uncomfortable. He doesn't know what to say, and he tells me so. He does the weird muttering ask about physical abuse that people always do, even though he's already asked. I wonder if he's hoping for a different answer this time. If maybe he thinks that'd make me easier to understand. In a tired voice that is trying not to snap, I say no again. Not ever physical abuse. Sometimes threats, but never any follow-through. And he says that that's good, that's really good, and I wince, and he goes all starched silence again. After a while, I say the only thing I can think of, which is, "It's okay not to know what to do in this situation. It's a fucking weird situation."

He squeezes my hand and kisses it like some sort of nobleman. I am out of sadness and anxiety, so all that's left is anger. I think about digging my nails into his hand, but I restrain myself.

"I'm in this with you, but... I don't think I can save you, Kenzie. That can't be my job here." I wait for more, but it doesn't come. I want to take my hand back, but it doesn't come either. The floor hurts.

"I don't want—I don't want to need saving. I want this to be fine, and I want to feel good. And I want to want to be here. I want to love you and be here with you and move in with you, and instead, I'm—" I steal my hand back to cover my face. "Fuck."

"Kenzie."

"Fuck. I'm so fucking tired. I'm always tired." He's all over me now, cradling me, breathing into my hair, arms clasped, and clinging like he can keep me from vanishing.

"I love you," he murmurs, and I'm too angry to give a shit.

"No, you don't," I say, and the cradling stops.

"What?"

"I don't know... I—I said, no, you don't. Love me. I think—I think you want to, and I want you to, but you don't. Because genuinely, how could you? When I'm pushing you out and having fucking panic attacks all the time and—"

"No. You don't get to decide that I don't love you."

"Christ! Look at me, Neil. This is me. This is who I am. Fucking half-dead and empty. I'm barely even here most of the time. And I love the idea of us. I love it, and I want it, but I feel so… so sure it's not for me. Not actually. Like I've been window-shopping a life with you that I know I can't afford. I'm not making any sense—"

"Look, if you don't want to be with me—"

"*Of course* I want to be with you! Are you fucking joking? Of course I want to be with you. Look at you. You're here on the kitchen floor, holding my hand and telling me you love me… even though I'm throwing dishes and screaming and crying… you're this perfect… completely amazing guy who wants to be with me, for reasons I don't get. I mean, you… you saw my dead naked dad on the floor and still wanted a second date. You're like a… a superhero or something. Of course I want to be with you… but I—or I *want* to want to be with you—"

"But what? There's a 'but,' right? Because you 'just can't,' right?"

"What I can't do is *this*. I don't want to do this to you. I don't want you to think you're getting someone who doesn't exist."

"Stop deciding what I can and can't handle! I love you, Kenzie. Stop deciding for me."

"You don't even *know* me. I'm not *Kenzie*. I'm not your fun, sexy girlfriend… I'm Mackenzie Adams, and I'm a mess… I—I quit my job. With Alice. I quit. Three weeks ago, but I didn't tell you. And I, um, I haven't been eating… I feel like I'm dying, and I'm scared. Waking up next to you scares me—like every day is gonna be—I'm scared. Terrified. All the time." All my strength has abandoned me.

I am Mackenzie.

I am undone.

I am ashamed.

I swallow audibly to keep myself from losing it again. "I'm not happy. I haven't been happy." I close my eyes. I will myself to wake up from this.

"Oh, so you're just not happy." His tone is gruff like he's just figured out the punchline to a joke that offends him. "You're not happy. Huh. She's just not happy. You just haven't been happy. Okay." He stands up suddenly, paces the kitchen. "So, okay. So, then... what the fuck, Kenzie? Or I'm sorry, *Mackenzie*. Like... What the fuck? Did it occur to you that I might be, I don't know, getting attached to you? Or to the... what'd you call it? The 'idea of us?' God, I mean, if he was 'barely your dad' then... I'm sorry, but what the actual fuck? I don't get it. I'm sorry, I don't. I don't get it. What are we doing here? If you're not happy... if you haven't been happy, then what the fuck are we doing here?" He stares at me, but I can't think of words, only sounds, and tears. And then he goes out the front door.

So much of this is wrong, and I can't stand myself for letting it get this far. Inside, I'm a cavern of lack. I try to stop myself crying, and it hurts. I take deep panic breaths and smooth my spine.

It's probably twenty minutes before Neil comes back in like a hurricane.

"Okay, so where can I take you and all your stuff? Because you can't stay here."

"Neil, I—"

"Get your stuff. Come on. You're not happy, right? So, let's keep it honest. I don't want you here. This fucking hurts, and I want you somewhere else, okay? So, where can I take you?"

He drives me to Mom's house since the apartment is no longer mine. Mel flew to Connecticut last weekend. I picture her on the plane, at the baggage claim, far away.

He parks across the street.

I unfocus my eyes and let the blades of grass run together into a green blur. It hurts to turn my head away from the window. When I manage it and catch his eyes, I feel myself fall cold. Some small voice in me says: *I don't mind if this is ruining his life. I don't mind hurting him. I don't mind. If it means I can breathe, I don't mind.*

"Can I say something before this is over?" He looks different, hollow somehow. *I did that*, I think, hating myself for not regretting it more.

"Okay."

"I love you, Mackenzie. Don't tell me I don't, because I do. And I'm sorry about your dad. Whatever kind of dad he was."

"Oh," I say in a voice that seems too small to be mine.

"Get out of my car."

Mom is on her way to her car when she sees me walking up the driveway.

"Oh, sweetie! I'm just heading out to yoga! What are you doing here?"

I shrug and then collapse in the driveway, sobbing. Through a flood of tears, I watch as Neil screeches out across the street and disappears down a hill.

"Oh!" Mom inches toward me and hovers. In all the years I didn't have her there to hold me, it never occurred to me that she wouldn't know how. She grazes a hand over my shoulder, and I cling against her leg. "Jimmy! Jimmy, get the door! Honey! Mackenzie's here, and she needs breakfast."

May 30th

They put me in the basement.

I sleep on a folded-out futon next to shelves of my mom's pottery, settled in the scent of wet clay. The basement doesn't have enough windows, and the ones it does have are up high so they can peek out over the edge of where the house is buried. All the air tastes recycled from a past life. I wonder if this is what mausoleums taste like, and I think it suits me.

I'm sure I don't miss Neil as much as I should for someone I loved. I vaguely remember a time when loving someone felt like more than pretty words recited in the right order. When it felt like competing in one of those egg and spoon races, where your hands shake, holding tight to a silly fragile thing that should mean nothing at all, but somehow feels like holding your own breakable heart outside your body.

Mom doesn't come downstairs much. I think how she talked about taking Gerald in, like a stray she couldn't bear to sit back and watch die. I wonder if she thinks about getting me a hotel room somewhere. Wonder if I'd let her.

She calls down the stairs when it's time for me to surface again and push food around a plate while she and Jimmy run through new ideas on what to do with me.

"There's always that group that meets at the Ballard Community center on Fridays," she says tonight, piling sweet potatoes onto my plate.

"What kind of group?" I try to sound curious, even though the pit in my stomach already knows.

"Well, the flyer said it's for people going through loss, or grief, that sort of thing, but you know, I think anyone could attend. I mean, they posted it right there on the bulletin board for anyone to see." My mother is afraid of me.

"Group therapy," I say.

"You know how Mackie feels about therapy, querida," Jimmy offers without looking up.

"Oh, don't you start pretending she doesn't need help too," Mom snaps. Her face is a shape I've never seen before, and her whole chin is dimpled and shivering. Her enormous wet eyes lock on me. "This isn't a life, Mackenzie. You must know that."

"I'll be okay. Break-ups are hard, that's all."

She laughs a sharp, dangerous sound, and, in a flash, I think I see exactly how she and Gerald were married to each other once. "I have time on Friday afternoon," she says. "I'll drop you off myself."

June 1st

It's a wide room with overstuffed couches, and the woman who met me at the door, Marla, is wearing horn-rimmed glasses and comfortable walking shoes, sitting with her legs folded under her on the sofa opposite me. She is not smiling, and I like that about her most.

"Um, how many people are we expecting?"

"Oh, it changes week to week. Sometimes it's only three or four. Sometimes it's as many as ten." She stretches her legs and gets up, moving towards a small coffee cart in the corner. "Can I get you tea or something? Some people find tea to be very soothing for their first session."

I nod and force myself to sit instead of disappearing out the door while her back is turned. I try not to think what Valery would say if she could see me now, all her worst fears about me come true. Marla brings me a mug with a large cat's face printed on it.

"Here. Jasmine with honey," she says as I inhale the steam. It reminds me of Mel, and though my gut is churning, I make up my mind to stay.

This is a slow week. There are only two more people by the time the session starts, Lydia, a forty-five-year-old woman who just lost her husband in November, and Terrence, a high school gym teacher whose son died four years ago in a boating incident. Marla encourages them to speak first because I'm new.

Lydia tells her husband's whole story and only cries once. She tells us about how it wasn't sudden, how she had sat by his hospital bed, and watched him get worse for months. How as soon as they got the diagnosis of late-stage pancreatic cancer, it had been like he died right then. And then she was just waiting for him to leave. "Sometimes it was like waiting for the bus," she says, "I'd think I most certainly saw it coming right up the street, and I'd get myself ready, fare in hand... and then it would be something else. Just a semi or a school bus. Or maybe it'd be a bus, but it wouldn't be mine." Then she cries, but it's graceful. She has done this before. I think I want to ask her if she ever felt guilty. Like she shouldn't have been waiting but praying instead. For some kind of miracle that would change the truth she already knew. But I don't ask her because, no matter what the answer is, the story ends the same way.

Terrence talks about his son like a god. How everything he touched was blessed and beautiful, how selfless he was, and how much everyone loved and adored him. He even uses the word Christ-like. I think about how a boating accident couldn't have killed Jesus because Jesus could walk on water. I do not say this to Terrence.

Marla's hand is on my shoulder, and everyone's eyes are wide.

"Would you like to talk with us about a loss, Mackenzie?"

I try smiling, but only half my mouth goes along with it. "Um. I was supposed to be living with my boyfriend... but we broke up."

Marla nods at me like this isn't what I was supposed to say.

"Uh... and my dad died."

Terrence closes his eyes, and Lydia leans back into the couch, and I wonder if it relaxes them to know why I'm here—if they're relieved that I'm officially one of them.

"When was that?" Marla's voice is beige.

"January. He had a heart attack on New Year's, I guess."

I hate this feeling. Like everyone wants me to cry when I know I won't.

"And how did it make you feel?"

"It didn't... I mean, it's complicated, you know? He and I... um, we used to be close, I guess when I was a kid, but um... he's... he can be difficult. It was never easy between us." Their eyes are like lasers. "He drank all the time. Which I guess doesn't sound like enough, but it... I just, um, I didn't... everyone agreed, you know, that it was better if I didn't, um... I was the last one. Still talking to him, and uh, it was just... it was too much. It got to be too much, and so I stopped."

Marla leans back now. Everyone looks so fucking relaxed.

"You weren't speaking."

"No."

"For how long?"

"Um, two years? Things kind of... it was pretty soon after I graduated from college. So... yeah... two years." It sounds like more time saying it out loud.

Terrence has opened his eyes. My heart is racing like I'm being chased, but absolutely nothing in this room is moving. The clock gets louder.

"I don't... is there something else I'm supposed to say?"

"Is there something more you'd like to share?"

"I don't know... I'm sorry, I feel like I shouldn't even be here."

Marla frowns. "Why's that?"

"*Because*. This is for people who *lost* people, and, like… I didn't lose anything I hadn't already given up, so I don't… I mean, I shouldn't be here. I should be fine, right?"

There is no noise in the room for what feels like it must be half an hour, but I can't be sure even though the clock is basically scream-ing now.

Then Lydia's voice cuts in, so clear it's like a song. "Is that what you think happened? You gave up, and so he died?"

There's no sarcasm in her voice, but it still sounds like a joke. Marla says something else, maybe to try to keep the peace, but I don't hear it. All I can hear is waves crashing against my ribs, and Lydia's eyes searing right into me, and I don't know how but I can feel her seeing everything: the way Gerald looked that last day, the nothing behind his eyes when I said: "I love you." How everyone thought I was so strong and so brave for finally ending things when the truth was really that there'd been nothing left to end.

If she sees it, Lydia doesn't say anything. Still, I feel her eyes holding onto me even after I look away, even after Marla and Terrence thank me for sharing and after Marla makes announcements for next week and after we close the session with a prayer circle, and I drag myself out the door and down the stairs and onto the sidewalk. Somehow, I feel like Lydia's still there, seeing how completely noth-ing I turned out to be.

I was supposed to call Jimmy to pick me up, but I can't hold still.

I walk, so fast it starts to burn. It's warm out, and my face is so slick with sweat that I don't notice when I start to cry. I walk like if

I walk far enough, I can get away from myself. I walk the two miles back to my mom's house like I remember the last meal I ate. I walk and pretend my lightheadedness is relief and not my system failing. I walk until I'm back in the dark, cool, quiet of this same fucking basement. And when my legs finally give way, I think they'll never hold me up again. And I don't care.

June 2nd

I stay home all day and don't want to talk to anyone. I sit in the basement, staring at the kiln and thinking how I fucked everything up. How Mel is far away, and Neil hates me, and Kevin is ignoring me. How Mom wants some magician therapist to fix me, so she doesn't have to worry anymore that I'll turn into Gerald, and Alice has replaced me with Charlotte. How Dad is dead, and no one is coming for me. And I think of Lydia's face. I don't know how it is that strangers see you best sometimes. My mouth waters like I might throw up, but I know all too well that my stomach is empty. And now, down to the very guts of my heart, I believe that I am at the bottom. And what's more than that, I have no desire to come back.

I think about lighting the kiln and climbing in. About how warm it might be, and wouldn't it be nice to feel warm. I think about how clean it would feel to burn off all my skin. I think about being rid of my hair, my clothes, my fingernails. I imagine the shapes my bones would leave behind. I think of shoveling myself into a gift box. I think of Gerald. And sometime—I don't know when—I fall asleep before I can find a match.

June 7th

It's either been a week or an hour.

I am too weak to get out of bed again. Mom brings me soup that I don't want. I didn't eat yesterday and can't remember the day before. My body has forgotten how to tell me it's starving.

My eyes are so dry they itch. I've forgotten how to cry even.

I watch the kiln all day.

It does nothing but wait to burn.

June 17th

I can't remember the last time I went further than the bathroom, but I text Mel and tell her I went back to work. I think if I am going to die in this basement, that she should believe it wasn't her fault. I spend hours thinking of the lies I could instruct people to tell her. Then I think of lies for Kevin. For Alice. I think of lies for Neil.

I think everyone should have their own lie. No two should be the same. So they could be sure that I loved them each, specially. Uniquely. So they wouldn't ever wonder about that. Then I wonder when exactly Gerald wrote my letter. I wonder if he was waiting to die, or if I was the only one waiting for that.

June 28th

"It's been nearly a month, and she isn't even moving anymore," I hear my mother whimper into the phone. She stands right at the top of the stairs so her voice will carry, but she doesn't even pretend to know how to talk to me directly anymore. I know it's Alice on the other end, and if I had the strength, I would laugh. My mother is in tears again, and I hear Jimmy try to breathe the life back into her. Bless his heart.

They shuffle around the kitchen and then go into a bedroom to talk about me where I can't listen in. That must have been Jimmy's idea.

I haven't bathed since before grief group. Mel keeps texting with regular questions about how I'm doing, and I just lie and lie. I am glad for her. She sounds happy in all her messages—lots of very intentional punctuation.

I am letting myself rot and growing into a strange kind of loneliness. Something that doesn't just come from being alone too long or being misunderstood. A loneliness that just descends and stays. Convinces you that no one can see you, and, if they could, it wouldn't be enough—that you were never enough, not built to last.

I am always between a dream and a nightmare, and even I don't know when I'm awake.

June 29th

"You're really still down here." Nathan is sitting on my bed when I open my eyes again.

"What are you doing here?" My voice is cracked and shriveled in my throat.

"Your mom said you don't ever move. Wanted to see." He is eating a sandwich. Roast beef, I think. The smell of it is the size of the whole room.

"Here I am."

"Yeah. Still down here. Just like she said." He shrugs.

"Sandwich?" He holds it out, nonchalant. "I'm done if you want it." I stare at him, hoping he'll go away, but he just keeps trying to hand it to me. "Mackenzie. You're kind of my sister, so," he says, opening my palm for me and putting the sandwich in it. "He won't be alive again if you die, okay? None of it will change. You'll just be dead too." He closes my fingers around the bread. "Is that what you want?" He watches me not answer, shrugs, and goes upstairs.

I wonder if I will eat. The sandwich gets heavy in my hand and my palm sweats.

And then I'm screaming. My fingers tear through the bread, and I pulverize the meat in my fist. I scream like I'm being murdered. Like all the air is rushing out of the room. I scream like I am on fire. Everything slows down. Mom comes running into the basement, but I see it in slow motion. She hurls herself at me, clutches me as I gasp in her arms. I think, for a moment, I remember the day I was born. The two of us there, somehow surprised to meet each other though we've already been introduced. So desperate for each other, without Gerald anywhere to be found. She combs my hair with her fingers, and murmurs, "You're okay—sweet, sweet baby. You're okay—my sweet, beautiful girl. You're okay. We're okay. We are. Here we are, and we're okay."

June 30th

Mom is still in my bed when I wake up. I curl myself into her side and cling. She blearily turns her head and peels an eye open.

"Hello, sweetie," she grogs.

"Hi," I whisper.

"Today," she clears the sleep from her throat, "I was going to go to yoga today. But maybe... would you like to have lunch with me?" She pulls my head to her chest, and even though we only fit together awkwardly, it's nice to feel warm.

"Okay."

"It's just lunch," she adds. "And then it'll be done. And we can come right back."

"Okay, Mom. I said, okay." And for the first time, I think I don't want to fight her. I think I want to go. "I don't want to be like this," I confide in her. "I hate that I'm like this."

"Oh, sweetheart. You can be any way you want," she says in a voice so natural I barely recognize her. "Any way you want to be, you can. If this isn't it, then you can try something else."

"This isn't it," I say, and it's as much a revelation to me as anyone.

Mom looks at me and smiles for what feels like the first time in ages. "Well. I am very glad to hear that."

But we don't go to lunch. I can barely get up. I have no endurance after a month in bed on next to no food. My muscles don't work for more than a minute. Jimmy has to carry me upstairs, and I see myself for the first time in weeks in the mirrored door of the linen closet as we pass the laundry. The bright light of the summer sun is startling, and I see it glint off my bones through my skin. I thought I'd look sick, but I look dead. He puts me on the couch in the living room, wrapped in blankets, and goes to the store for more groceries. Mom, in over her head, calls Alice and demands she come over this second as she gets a hot water bottle ready for me. I feel like a feral animal that has chanced on an open door and a kind family.

Alice arrives within the hour, her saddlebags full of romantic comedies and self-help books. She puts me in the shower to rinse and then immediately runs me a bath. "There's clean, and then there's calm, little lady. And you need both," she titters on, as I slump my shoulders into the hot water. "You get it all out, hmm? You get it all out, and then we'll have dinner and talk. Maybe see if Meg Ryan can find another way to fall for Tom Hanks." And she bustles out.

I hug my knees to my chest. The room is still—just me and the water. I wait to fall apart but don't. Instead, I let go, slide back into the tub and slip my head underwater, but only for a second. When I come up, gasping, I hear myself whisper, "This isn't it. This isn't it." Being alive is a decision you have to keep making.

It's another hour and a half before I pull myself out of the tub—the water long gone tepid. Standing in front of the mirror, I examine my body, withered, and sallow. I pull on clothes and lean into the mirror, right up close, and out of the corner of my eye, I see Gerald. Standing so close, he's on top of me—standing so close that he *is* me.

"I love you. I love you, I love you, I love you," I say to us. To him. To me. "That's the truth. That's the truth. No matter what." Again. "I love you." Again, and again, "I love you, I love you, I love you. I love you, I love you, I love you. I love you, I love you, I love you. I love you, I love you, I love you." My voice sort of rattles around the room at first, but then it catches, lands somewhere. "Dad?" I wait. "I love you. I love you, I love you, I love you. That's the truth." I wait. He'll say something. I know he will. He'll say something if I just wait.

"Mackenzie, sweetie? Is that you?" Mom's voice startles me when it comes through the door. "Dinner's ready. You clean, sweetie?" I wait, but he's not here. I'm just me.

"Yeah, Mom. It's me. It's just me. I'm clean."

PART THREE

July-November 2018

TO: mackenzadams1377@gmail.com
FROM: khwasserman11@gmail.com
SUBJECT: RE: hi
SENT: June 27th 2018 4:23:18 PM PST

Mack—

What the fuck? Nate called me last night and said he heard you aren't eating or moving? I didn't know it was still that bad. I honestly thought it'd be better if I just stayed out of your way, but I should have written you back. I feel like a dick. Will you call me, please? I've been calling, but your phone is never on anymore, and I don't want this to be a thing where you're dying, and I'm just fucking sitting in San Francisco, leaving you a shit load of desperate voicemails. Nate said he'd update me when he knew something, but you know it's fucking impossible to get any information out of him. Could you just call me and tell me you're okay? I'm like one panic attack away from writing a fucking letter to Alice.

I love you, and I know you don't owe me shit, but I'm not interested in giving your eulogy, okay? I love you. Fucking call me. Please.

- K

Sent from my iPhone

*

July 13th

It's my birthday. I've been trying not to think about living under the close and constant surveillance of my mother, but the fact that I'm turning twenty-five today seems to underline it a bit.

Mel asks if we can FaceTime, and I ask her why she would make me do something I hate on my birthday. It works and gets me out of having to explain why, despite a week of vaguely consistent meals and walking up and down the stairs without entirely running out of breath, I still look like an antique ghost.

She settles for sending me a series of increasingly ridiculous gifs and a voice memo of her and Luke singing a full-length, though pitchy, karaoke rendition of Stevie Wonder's "Happy Birthday".

Mom has already been to a bakery to acquire massive cinnamon rolls and is jamming candles into mine when I come upstairs.

"Sweetie, wait. Don't look!" She straightens out the candles, and I see they're those hulking numerical candles, a sparkling purple two and five, which she ignites with a comically long lighter. The whole thing reeks of Alice.

"Please don't sing," I say, as she brings the cinnamon roll toward me, the five tilting lopsided and dripping wax into the icing. She pouts, so I turn up the volume on my phone and play the voice memo aloud to fill the silence. Mom rolls her eyes, but she's smiling before the first chorus.

"So, what should we do today, sweetheart? It's your big day," Mom's voice goes up at the end of her words, in a sing-song way that she likes to use on special occasions.

"I actually thought I might go out… you know, kind of, alone for a little while?" I see her jaw tighten at the thought of it. I'm twenty-five, and I have to beg for my mom's permission to leave the house.

"Oh? Really? Where?" Every word is an octave higher than the last, and I feel guilty she's so on edge, even if it's nice to have so much of her attention finally.

"I thought maybe I would take a walk. Just get some fresh air. Reflect. Try some of those breathing exercises Alice is always talking about. I just want to feel like I'm still my own person." Her face levels out, and when she smiles at me, I smile back, pleased to be making her happy, even if I had to lie to do it.

I'm early, and the session isn't finished yet. I stand on the asphalt of the parking lot, baking in the sun, and waiting. I curse myself for not wearing shorts and remember that, when I was eating more, I didn't ever get so woozy in the heat. It is an eternity of ten minutes before people finally start filing out. I try to stay inconspicuous as I scan the group for her.

Lydia is wearing a sundress today. She looks light and happier than I remember her, and I worry for a second that she has forgotten all about me. But I'm on a mission, so I start towards her as she's heading for her car.

"Mackenzie, right?" She says over her shoulder, catching me off guard. The way I'd imagined it, I'd be the one to speak first.

"Yeah, hi. Sorry to—"

"You didn't come back to group."

"No, I—no."

She gets to her car and turns toward me, leaning against the trunk. "Are you stalking all of us now, or just me?"

Her gaze settles familiarly into me, and I wonder what else she sees. I'm realizing I don't have a plan. I'd just hoped she might talk to me. Maybe tell me something I haven't been able to figure out myself, though I have no idea why I think she would know.

"I—um… Today is my birthday," I stammer, by way of explanation.

"I see." Her face doesn't change for a second, and then it's overrun by a grin. "Do you like crab cakes?"

I look around like she might be talking to someone else, but it's just us. I manage a nod.

"Come on and get in the car," she says, turning and beeping the doors open.

The restaurant looks out over the marina, and Lydia gets us a table right by the window because she knows the waitstaff.

"My husband was a fish broker," she smirks as we are seated. "That's a real job."

"I believe you," I assure her, surprised by how intimidated I feel sitting across from her, like a 12-year-old spontaneously invited to sit at the teen's table.

She picks up the menu, opens it for ten seconds, and puts it down with a flourish. "Everything here is amazing, so get whatever you want, on me, birthday girl. I'll be having the crab cakes, which, if you've never had, I highly recommend."

I open the menu to look, but then feel her staring at me and stop. "You're being very kind," I say like it's a question.

"I'm very kind," she laughs brightly. "Is today really your birthday? How old are you?"

"Yes. I'm twenty-five."

"Twenty-five. Hmm. Look at you. Still a baby and already so ready to be done." This brings me up short, but she just looks out the window and sighs. "C'mon and pick something to eat. I'm starving."

We both get crab cakes even though I try to insist I'm not hungry. Lydia orders us gin and tonics without asking if I want one, and when they come, she lifts hers to toast.

"To the birthday girl." She clinks her glass to mine and giggles into her first sip. Maybe she can tell how nervous I am, because she doesn't wait on me to make conversation, but instead talks fondly about her husband and the restaurant business for a while. She says she thinks it is funny to be forty-five and starting her life over, and she says maybe it's a blessing to get to start all over again so late. Then she sheds a couple tears over a small laugh and says she's honestly not so sure about blessings.

I ask her if she's spent any time with other people from grief group, and she says no. "I don't really identify with grief in my spare time," she says.

The waiter brings over our food, and another round of drinks we didn't order. He smiles dotingly at Lydia like she's his favorite aunt, and I get a pang of jealousy that she has this place, with all its warm, comfortable nostalgia.

"So, what about you?" she asks like she's reading my mind.

"What about me?"

"I don't *know*, Mackenzie," she says. "I was hoping you'd tell me."

"I don't know, I'm fine. I don't want to ruin a perfectly nice birthday meal."

"What'll be ruined? Birth, death, grief, joy, it's all part of the same story. You'd hardly even be changing the subject." Resting her face in one palm and gazing at me over the drink in the other, she sucks air in through her teeth like someone who has spent a lifetime talking shit over cigarettes. "Out with it then."

My throat clenches my vocal cords, as I try to think where to start. "Do you like coming here?"

Lydia squints and chews her lip, looking around. "On good days, I do. It's nice to be around people who remember David."

I nod, pushing food around my plate.

"Is there somewhere you can go? When you want to remember your father?"

I look up at her. "Anywhere. There's no room to forget him."

She leans back in her chair. "Ah," is all she says next.

We eat quietly for a while, and she's right. The crab cakes are excellent. Outside, the wind picks up the waves and throws them against the sides of houseboats. I lose time watching it. Something pulls taut between my ribs, and before I can think what I'm going to say, I'm talking.

"I didn't do my best," I hear myself tell her. "That was always his thing. Telling me to do my best. He used to say nobody could get mad at me if I'd done my best. He'd drop me off at school and say, 'Have a good day. I love you. Just do your best.' And I think I did. For a long time with him, that's what I tried to do... It was never enough to change him or to help him... but I always told myself I was doing my best. Trying my best." The roof of my mouth aches for me to breathe out or to cry, but I only press my tongue into it and close my eyes. "And then, one day I was looking at him and I just... couldn't anymore. All those years, I'd tried so hard... and it was just over. And the world kept turning. And I was still here. But I think... I don't know. I didn't do my best that day. I think maybe I stopped doing my best at all. And then he died."

I wonder what she sees, watching me now, but I can't bring myself to look at her. I stare out over the water and feel so small, or maybe just as big as I am.

"You know, David spent months in the hospital," Lydia says after a while, pulling my attention back to the table. "Months that felt like years to me. Towards the end, he was unconscious a lot of the time. He was exhausted. Everything at that point was a fight for him. I'd sit in that room for days, just for a smile that wouldn't last more than a second." She smooths her napkin over her lap with her palms, like wrinkles are the problem. "Anyway, a while after the funeral, David's mother invited all his doctors and nurses to a dinner, to thank them for everything they'd done for her boy." Her head shakes, her focus going soft. "And I couldn't go." I catch her eye and feel like we could swallow all the air in the room. "I couldn't be around those people—the people who had watched me praying for him to die. They'd only ever known me when David was sick, and I was so ugly then. They were kind people, good doctors—who knows what they really thought of me—but it didn't matter. In those last months, I hated myself. I hated myself because I hated David. He would give me that tiny smile every few days, and I should've been grateful for it, but I wasn't. It wasn't enough. I hated him so much for leaving me; a smile wasn't what I wanted. I liked to think I put on a brave face for him, but there I was, praying for it to be over for weeks before he was gone." She swirls the ice cubes around her glass and shrugs, but under the weight of the room, it barely shows. "I didn't do my best, either."

She stretches her palm out to me, and I take it.

"Mackenzie," she says, "I don't know everything that happened between you and your dad, but I think if it were true that you hadn't lost anything, we wouldn't be sitting here."

Swiping at tears, I clear my throat. "I'm not coming back to group," I snark, and she laughs a bigger laugh than I expect, so big it brings everything around her back to life.

"Then don't," she smiles. "But if you want my advice, and I'm guessing you do since you've tracked me down on your birthday: you're only twenty-five. Your life has hardly been long enough for you to decide whether or not it's a good one."

"Is that advice?"

"Maybe not. How's this? If you're mad at yourself for giving up once, then don't do it again."

July 19th

There's a banner outside Elliott Bay Books that reads, *"Alice Knows Best: Twenty Years of Questions, A Lifetime of Answers."* I haven't been back to my old neighborhood since Mel left, but I promised Alice that I would come to the anniversary party tonight. It's weird how little it's changed, same cracks in the sidewalk, same hipster coffeehouses and karaoke bars, same rainbow crosswalks. Unlike the quaint yuppie district of Ballard where I've been holed up with Mom and Jimmy, Capitol Hill seems to scream at me that I'm supposed to be young, that I'm supposed to be having fun. When I first moved back to Seattle after college, finding our place on the hill felt like claiming my own little corner of the city. Not Mom's 1930's craftsman, or Gerald's chain hotel suite downtown, or Alice's hulking suburban Versailles, but somewhere all my own. Now though, it only reminds me of how empty I let myself become, and I feel so far away from the girl who thought she would grow into belonging here.

Inside the bookstore, Patsy Cline is playing over the speakers and, in the center of a swell of fawning middle-aged readers in their REI formalwear, Alice is dressed head-to-toe in twentieth-anniversary platinum. It's… something.

Mom is immediately swept into a conversation about ethically sourced wool with a woman she knows from a knitting class, and I duck through the masses and head for the bar.

"You're her," I hear over my shoulder after ordering myself a mint julep, tonight's signature cocktail. I turn around to find my replacement, a ruddy-cheeked strawberry blonde with saucer-eyes and a gingham dress. I wonder if she made it herself.

"Charlotte," I say, smiling automatically to mediate any awkwardness.

"You're *her*," she says again, and she sounds so awestruck like she's meeting a celebrity, that I think she must have me confused for someone else until she says, "Mackenzie Adams."

"Hi," I try.

"Can I hug you?"

I open my mouth to answer, but she's already got her arms around me by the time I'm saying, "I guess, if you want." She smells like the inside of a Bath & Body Works.

"Sorry, I feel like I know you. You're kind of, like, a *legend* at the office. I mean, you wouldn't believe how much Alice talks about you. But I guess that makes sense since you're, like, basically her daughter." I don't know what to say to that, so I don't say anything. Charlotte lets me out of the hug but doesn't let go of my shoulders. "Big shoes to fill," she says. "Massive."

"Oh, I'm sor—"

"But I'm up for it, you know. I've been reading Dear Alice since I was in middle school. She's why I started my blog… I mean, she's basically *why* I started writing." She blushes, making her red face go even redder. "I'm babbling, sorry."

"You're fine," I assure her.

"So, what are you doing for work now?"

"Um, well—"

"I mean, no offense or anything, but I can't imagine ever wanting to leave Alice's office. I mean, she's such an inspiration, isn't she?"

As if on cue, I hear Alice's howling laughter, undoubtedly at one of her own stories. "She's... yeah."

"So, are you going into advice?"

"Advice? ... No. No, I'm not, um, I'm not going into advice."

"Something else in self-help?"

"Um, no, I don't think... no."

"Oh. Wow." I'm disappointing her, not turning out to be the second coming of Alice that it seems she was promised. "Well, I guess it makes sense why you quit then." There's an air of judgment in her tone, and she looks past me, scanning the room for other people to talk to, presumably. "So, what *do* you want to do?"

"Um, well. I got a degree in American Studies," I say to fill space.

"What's that mean?"

"Well, I don't... I mean, it's sort of—you can use it for a lot of different things."

"Oh. Cool," she says. "Like what?"

I sip my drink and try to remember if I've ever had an answer to this question. If I've ever known what I wanted to be. The silence stretches thin.

"My girls! Together!" Alice foghorns, hurtling toward us. She kisses us both on the cheek and basks in our compliments on her outfit. "Charlotte, sugar, they're getting ready up front to introduce me for the reading. Will you make sure there's one of those little bottles of water, no labels unless they're sponsoring, please. And check that my reading glasses are set? You know how I like things."

Charlotte's spine straightens, and she's radiating pride and purpose as she hurries toward the podium.

"Julep?" Alice asks, and I barely have time to nod before she's gulping down the rest of my drink.

"Impressive turnout," I offer, and she smiles knowingly.

"Well, honey, you know, deep down, everyone just wants someone to tell 'em what to do next." I bite back a laugh. "It's only a few of us know there aren't really right answers. Just what you choose, up against everything you don't." She hands back my empty glass. "All right, now. Do I look wise?" She fusses with her dress, and I re-affix her rhinestone fascinator.

"Very."

"Twenty years," she sighs. "Amazing how all that time can go by, but I never get any older, ain't it?" She kisses my cheek again. "But, I suppose some things never do change." And then she turns away, swallowed back into her swarm of adoring followers, just as Walter takes the stage to introduce her.

I stand on the edge of the crowd and listen while Alice reads an assortment of greatest hits from her replies over the last two decades, most of them I've heard her read a hundred times if I've heard them once, though even the newer ones sound familiar somehow. And her audience is familiar too, captivated like they always are, hanging on her every syllable. They are blue-blooded Seattleites through and through with their PCC Market bags and Smartwool socks. As the evening wears on, I think I know everything there is to know about this place, except what I'm doing here. I've never known how to do anything more than survive in this city. Now, standing here, it occurs to me that striving not to be dead isn't the same thing as living.

And so, as Alice opens the floor for questions, and a sea of flannel-clad people raise their hands at once to ask her what they ought to do next, I make up my mind that I have to get out of Seattle.

July 26th

"Wait, so, explain to me how this plan works?" Mel is sweating in a sports bra in front of a fan. At this moment, I don't understand why she moved to the East Coast or why she always so desperately wants to FaceTime.

"I'm gonna apply for jobs kind of everywhere, and anywhere that's not here and see what bites." She makes a face that looks half inspired, and half mortified.

"What kinds of jobs?"

"I don't know. Anything that sounds like it might be interesting."

"Ohkayyy," her face is going more and more skeptical by the minute, "And then what?"

"Then I move to wherever the job offer seems the coolest, and I don't know, try to figure out who I want to be from there."

She laughs at me. "Have you completely lost your mind? Or are you sort of okay?"

I laugh too. "I don't know. I actually think maybe I'm sort of okay?"

She squints and leans her sweat glistened face toward the camera. "You're a little pixilated, but you do seem sort of okay," she says. "You'll forgive me if it takes me a second to wrap my mind around this... last time I managed to get you on the phone, you were moving in with your boyfriend, and now..."

I nod and look away from her. "I understand." I've still only given her a heavily abridged recap of the last couple months. I haven't told her about nearly dying in Mom's basement, and I don't get into details about why things didn't work out with Neil. I've mostly just told her I need a fresh start and hope she'll get on board.

"What happens if the job is somewhere horrible or boring? Like Wyoming... or—"

"Or, where? Connecticut?" She rolls her eyes at me. "I don't know, Mel. I just know that right now, I feel like I'll take anywhere that isn't Seattle."

Her face softens. "I didn't know you wanted to leave so badly."

"I don't know if I did either. I think I used to make sense here. When I had a job, and you were here and my dad—" I sigh. "I don't know. I just feel like I don't know who I am anymore."

"You're *Mackenzie,*" she says.

"But, like, what does that *mean,* though?"

She looks confused. "What does it *mean* to be *you?*"

"Like, did you know I have no idea what I actually want to do? I'm twenty-five, Melanie, and the only thing I'm qualified to be is Alice."

She lets out a half-laugh. "Well, no. I mean, I love you, but you'd be a terrible Alice."

"Okay, so, not even that then."

"But lots of people don't know what they want to do, Kenz."

"Yeah, but it isn't only that." I try to think how to explain. "It's like... like I think for a long time, so much of what I believed about myself was wrapped up in everything with my dad. And then, when I stopped talking to him, it was wrapped up in the fact that we weren't talking. But now... I don't want to be the girl whose dad died forever. And lately, Seattle makes me feel like that's all I am."

She looks as deep into my face as she can through the internet, and finally says, "Okay. So, then you need a new place. It's... it's a pretty good plan, honestly." I watch the tension fall out of her shoulders. "You know, I'm on your side, Kenz. Always."

"Even if it means I move to Wyoming?"

She dismisses me with a shake of her head on a sigh. "Yes. Anywhere." She grins.

"Oh God, don't look at me so earnestly, it stresses me out. Can we talk about something else? What's happening with you?"

"Mmm... Luke strained his groin the other day during sex," she offers after some thought.

Aaaand we're back.

July 31st

I've been summoned to Bellevue. I got a call from Alice last week telling me that if I want a recommendation from her for some new job in some new city, I'd better get my tail to her office and ask nicely. By that afternoon, I'd received a calendar invitation for "Groveling, July 31, 1-1:45 PM."

On the 8th floor of a tall, generic office building in downtown Bellevue, the elevator opens into an expanse of glass surfaces, rose gold fixtures, decorative chandeliers, and indoor plants with massive glossy leaves. The Dear Alice offices. The most recent time Alice brought in decorators for a "seasonal refresh," I heard her tell them she wanted a Bottomless Mimosa aesthetic.

Charlotte is in head-to-toe polka dots today, and she puts me on the crushed velvet waiting chaise, telling me Alice will be right with me. Looking around, I wonder what the rest of the staff has heard about what happened, about where I went. Still, the Pacific Northwest tendency toward passivity and avoidance means none of them acknowledges me much beyond a few waves and smiles from a distance, and a nearly sincere, "gosh, we miss you around here." I fold my hands in my lap and wait for Alice.

Alice's office is a big glass box that looks out over an LA fitness and a Ruth's Chris Steakhouse. She has a big vase of peonies on her desk next to a framed photograph of herself on her wedding day. "Walt took that, you know," she bragged to me once. "Such an eye."

Today, she plunks down in her tufted desk chair across from me, her eyebrows knitted tight above her big false lashes, and her lips pursed. "Well? Come on now. Sit," she barks, and so I do.

"All right, Miss Mackenzie Adams," she sighs.

"Alice, if you don't want to be a reference for me," I start, "I respect that. I know I didn't leave in the most—"

"Hush. Would you mind?" She leans back and studies me. "I just needed to get you in here. I'm not expecting you to grovel." She aimlessly straightens some things on her desk. "No elegant way to do it, so I might as well just tell you, I s'pose." Her computer pings that she's gotten an email and she silences it, but still scans over the screen. I hardly register that she's still talking to me when she says quietly, "it was Walter and me. Paying for that hotel room."

"What?"

"The hotel room." Her focus snaps back to me. "Sugar, you didn't think your momma could honestly afford it, did ya?"

I'd mostly tried not to think about any of it, but no, I hadn't thought that. I don't know the details of what I thought, just that they'd just stopped bothering to charge us because they liked him enough that they didn't mind having him around... It sounds ridiculous now.

"Now, she paid for as long as she could, of course, but it wasn't free, darlin'. And she thought it was helping you, him being there. You did a little better in school. You made friends. She didn't want to put him back out on the sidewalk."

"Oh my god." My face burns with embarrassment, and I wish I could disappear. I wish all these walls weren't windows. "Oh my god, I'm so sorry, Alice, I didn't know. You shouldn't have had to—"

She holds up a hand. "Walter and I had been saving for a while. We decided a long time back to help your momma with tuition for you since you'd been such a part of our lives. And we'd planned to surprise you for your eighteenth birthday, but then with things being what they were... well, your momma and I agreed you could probably get some financial aid to help with college, and there's no financial aid for something like your daddy. So, we agreed that money would go toward his hotel bills 'til it ran out, and after that, we'd just have to see."

My heart is under my tongue. I feel sick. My brain scrambles to calculate how much it must have cost them. I can't bring myself to look at her.

"There's no point in telling you any of this at all, 'cept now he's gone, and there's still a little money left."

My head shakes automatically at the thought of it.

"I talked with your momma about it a while back, but she didn't want you wasting away on that money the way he did."

I try to blink back my tears, but they fall into my lap. "I can't take any more of your money, Alice."

"This money was always supposed to be for you, sugar. And you're gonna need somethin' to get yourself started, wherever it is you wind up, ain't ya?" I feel her watching me a while, and then she takes a check out of her desk and slides it toward me. "Take it. So your momma doesn't worry."

I shake my head again. "I'll talk to her. I'm sure she'll understand."

"I was talkin' about *me*, darlin'. Please. It's not as much as it should have been, but all the same, it's still yours. Take it."

I glance at the number: $7,438.24. I nearly choke on my next breath. "Alice. It's too much."

"Psh, how would you know? You don't even know where you're goin' yet. Best case, it's a flight, a security deposit and a few months' rent. Maybe some furniture." She frowns. "Don't tell me you're thinking of not taking my advice." She laughs softly, and I try to be light, even though my lungs are lead.

"I just… it's a lot and I… I don't know how to say thank you."

"You just said it," she shrugs. "Now, send a list of any places you're applying to Charlotte, and she'll make sure I'm on top of it if they reach out for a reference, all right?"

"Yeah, I can do that."

"Good, then that's that done." And then she's engrossed in an email, and back to work. I stand to leave, and she looks up again with a seriousness that's foreign on her face. "You're the only Adams left, Miss Mackenzie. It's up to you to decide what to do with that legacy now."

I slide out of her office and, after exchanging pleasant enough goodbyes with Charlotte, climb back into the elevator. With each drop between floors, my stomach lurches, the check folded in half and gnawing at my wallet.

August 7th

In an effort not to "waste away," all I've done for the last week is hunt for jobs. I've applied to six different things so far: two executive assistant-type gigs in California, a research librarian posting in Maine, an office manager job in Virginia, a docent job in Illinois, and a personal assistant position for a parenting blogger in Texas. After consulting Mel, I've been assured I should, at the very least, be able to fake my way into success at any of them.

I haven't talked to anyone about the money, though I can tell by the way she's watching me that Mom knows Alice gave it to me. As much as I try to be grateful, there's guilt in knowing I wouldn't have it if Gerald were still alive. Maybe it's always been mine, but that's hard to believe when I didn't even know it existed before now. I can't convince myself to deposit the check.

A few weeks ago, Jimmy asked if I wouldn't mind moving some of my things out of his office and downstairs with me since Mom isn't using her pottery studio much at the moment. At the time, it hadn't seemed like a big deal. But now, in the corner of the room, under boxes of winter clothes and bedding still packed up from my old place, is the box of Gerald's things Beth gave me and, tucked inside that, is the box of Gerald. I tried to hide it away behind a crate of books, but I know he's there. All his clothes and his keepsakes, his letter and his ashes and me—every last piece of him stored in this basement together.

We're crowding each other, and I wonder if it's really Seattle's fault I can't let go of him, or if it's mine—if my shadow will be just as long in another city. I'm not sure I know the difference between starting over and running away from yourself.

"I am going to move away to someplace new," I hear myself telling him. "I am going to move to somewhere else, and there won't be room for you there." I don't mean it as a threat, but it sounds like one. My voice shakes with the same fear I remember from our fights when I was little. The kind of fear that you feel the first time you stand up for yourself. Those beats of silence where your brain just spins with *Don't back down* and *Stand up straight*. "There won't be room for you there," I say again, this time more certain.

He says nothing. But in a flash, I think I see his face so clearly: all silence and air and nothing except the quiet knowing of how completely wrong I am.

I drag myself upstairs to get away from him and tell Mom and Jimmy I'm going to the bank.

I sign the back of the check and push my mouth into a smile, telling the cashier it was a birthday gift.

August 23rd

Two phone interviews, a Skype call, and several dozen emails later, I got a job offer from Virginia. And, after googling, "I'm Black, will I die if I move to Virginia," in a panic, scouring the internet for stories and finding countless women of color who've moved from one of the coasts to the South and actually *loved* it, and learning that Loudon County, where I'll be living, actually swung blue in the last election, I decide this can happen. I text Luke, and he says: **Do they have cities** *named for confederate generals? Sure. But there are far more Black people in Virginia than in Washington, and you grew up there. Live where you want to live.*

I am set to start training in October. It would be September, but since I have to move my whole life across the country, they were kind enough to give me some extra time. My new boss, Andrea, is lovely, soft-spoken, and direct, with a biting sense of humor. The kind of person I think I'd like to be. She's been running a small independent press that publishes primarily short fiction and poetry, though they have also worked on a few novels. She'll be expanding thanks to grant-funding and needs an office manager who can also occasionally help out as a reader. The funding comes at the beginning of next year, so she was excited that we'll have a few months to set up a new digital system, get started on overhauling the site, and get a hiring plan together for the expansion.

I told Andrea about my time working with Alice on her online presence, about the growth initiatives I helped implement during my time there, and my (slightly exaggerated) editorial background. I didn't tell her about Gerald, or that, despite what's on my résumé, I've spent the last eight months in various states of decay.

I am flying out on the 16th of next month for the weekend to look at apartments in person, and I think it can't come soon enough. Mom has already been thumbing through every furniture catalog that comes in the mail and asking me which sofas I like. Alice sends me guided meditations that tell me to picture myself as a blank slate or an empty garden plot. I stay awake late, looking up restaurants and attractions in Waterford. I tell myself that Virginia Mackenzie is going to go to the drive-in on weekends and see old movies. Virginia Mackenzie will see fireflies and summer thunderstorms. Virginia Mackenzie will be better.

August 29th

On Monday, Mom and Jimmy left for a weeklong couple's retreat that Alice is hosting in Vancouver. With the time to myself, I decide to spend the week doing all my favorite things around Seattle, so I can at least try to remember this place as more than just the city that tried to kill me.

Today, I've wandered through the arboretum before getting Mexican food at this place Jimmy loves and eating my burrito in Volunteer Park at sunset. Everywhere I go, people are smiling at the sun, and, knowing I'm leaving it all behind, I don't bother making fun of them for it. It's nice.

By the time I get back to the house, I'm practically vibrating with the anticipation of a new version of myself. I draw the blinds, strip down to my underwear, and dance to Motown in the living room. I sing along to Gladys Knight and The Pips into a wooden spoon. I throw on a robe before making myself a Manhattan, and everything about life makes me laugh.

"I am moving to Virginia, Gerald," I announce, tipsy as fuck and spooning leftover guacamole into my mouth. "I am going to become a Southern belle, and you can't fucking stop me." I try out a Southern accent and don't hate it. I start to watch *Sweet Home Alabama* and fall asleep on the couch.

August 30th

I'm buzzed and half-asleep, with the music still playing loud when someone starts banging on the front door at 3 AM.

I do a quick scan in my brain of who it could be. Mom and Jimmy are out of town. Nathan has keys. A noise complaint? Shit. I turn the music down. The banging doesn't let up. I reason that it couldn't possibly be a burglar since they wouldn't announce themselves by knocking. Still, I grab the fireplace poker before even looking through the peephole and then drop it with a clang when he turns around to knock again.

Kevin.

*

MEL

Mon Dec 7th, 2015, 4:30 PM
Wait, what do you mean Kevin doesn't like you?

4:32 PM
I feel so pathetic.
I've literally been crying for like a day.

4:35 PM
You're not pathetic, Kenz.
Ugh. I'm so mad I'm in a review session right now
What did he say?

4:57 PM

Um basically that he loves me, but he doesn't like me?

Whatever that means.

Oh, and also that he knew I was into him but didn't say anything

I feel so pathetic.

4:59 PM

I'll be out in like 20 minutes. Can I call you?

5:00 PM

Yeah.

Mon Dec 7th, 2015 11:17 PM

Fuck, he just texted me.

11:18 PM

EW!! What the fuck???

11:19 PM

He literally JUST texted me: what r u doing?

11:19 PM

Wait WHAT?

11:20 PM

Like I guess he thinks we're just like friends again now?

11:20 PM

I'm gonna murder him.

11:20 PM

Ugh, I just want it to be break.

Should I text back?

11:22 PM

I mean, do you want to?

11:22 PM

I don't know. I kind of want to talk to him, but I also like… I
don't know.

Also, if this is super annoying, we don't have to keep talking
about it.

Like, I'm fine. It's fine.

He's literally the worst, and I'm so over it.

I'm over it.

11:23 PM

I mean, I think you have to do whatever feels right to you.

It's just like, I get tired of him taking you for granted.

And like he really hurt you. it's so ducked up that he can't give
you space.

*Fucked ugh. phone.

11:23 PM

No, you're right.

I'm not going to text him. Because like, fuck him.

11:25 PM

OKay, yeah. If that's what you want to do.

But dont do it just because I said you shoudl

Should*

11:25 PM

Ugh. It sucks that you don't know him really.

Because like he is kind of a good friend.

Or he was.

But also I guess whatever. that wasn't real.

11:25 PM

I'm so sorry, Kenz.

I wish I was there.

Tues Dec 8th, 2015, 9:58 AM

How're you doing?

Also, sidebar, but I just read a blog post about how people in long-distance relationships are secretly just bad at relationships.

That kind of thing is bullshit, right?

12:01 PM

Sorry, just got out of a final.

OMG, so I texted him.

Which I shouldn't have done. But I felt like it wasn't fair that like,

I always have to be the person who is feeling all the feelings, and he

is just around.

Like shouldn't he have to feel something sometimes?

Right?

Like isn't that the fucking idea of being friends with a prson??????

But also fuck.

Because it was a bad idea to reach out.

Because then, he fucking came over.

IDK maybe you were right.

Like I texted him and was basically like, listen, you really hurt my feelings, and I just feel like it's gonna be hard for us to like stay friends and stuff because Idk like what you wnat at this point right?

So then hes like completely silent like doesnt say anything. So I think it's over & I go tot he vending machine just to buy like every snack I can even think of to eat alone in my bed.

And when I get back hes like outside my door, like just ducking standing there. And is like, Mack, I still wanna be friends. So we talk for like ever about a bunch of kind of irrelevant stuff and of course, i end up crying. and now i guess he thinks things are better?

But... idk.

I still feel like shit kind of.

Like this was actually all about him, and like i dont feel better.

Like. I still dont feel like we can be friends because nothing is really differnt.

What do you think?

Ugh. Sorry, this is so long.

This all so fucking sucks.

And like, no, Melanie. You're not bad at relationships. HAVE WE MET????

*

August 30th

I don't know how long I watch him through the peephole before he starts talking. He's pacing back and forth to the door, muttering.

Drunk. My mind is a million places at once, and not a single one of them is new.

"MACK? Someone open the fucking door. Come on! *FUCK!*"

I sit down on the floor on the other side of the door and try to breathe in patience. I wrestle against the part of me that sparks at seeing his face on my front porch.

"No one is home," I hear myself say to him through the door.

"Mack? Is that... is'at you?" His voice is sloshing out of him, wasted and broken. I hear him press his body to the door, and think I might feel the warm, pathetic weight of him against my back. I put my cheek against the wood and close my eyes.

"No one is home," I say again. The door creaks as he really leans into it. He shifts and bangs a fist, sloppy, and sad.

"You're okay?" He wilts, and I hear him slide down to the ground. I don't want to hold his infuriating face in my hands. I do *not*. "I thought maybe—Mack... Say something else." He's crying—like a little boy lost in a supermarket without his mom.

I lift my cheek from the door and press my hand into the wood, where I think I might meet the center of his spine on the other side.

"Hi, Kev."

He whimpers on the front porch, and I don't open the door, like that'll keep him out. When his crying subsides, we just sit together. I don't hear him at all, except for the occasional snuffling. I'm so tired, and I wish so hard that I was stronger than I feel now.

"I came back for you, Mack," he manages after a long time, and against my better instincts, I feel my heart lift. Like some little part of me had been waiting all this time to hear him say that. But I swallow it.

"I didn't need you to." I let my breath sink all the way out of me. Until I feel completely full of the space it leaves behind. "I'm fine."

I hear him cry again. And stop crying. His nose is running, and he snorts like an ugly toddler.

"Open the door, Mack—" he slurs.

"No," I give back firmly. "I'm okay. Just go to sleep."

It is my mother's kind-but-too-invested neighbor Roger who calls the police, describes Kevin as a "vagrant" and insists that they come to the scene. The knock on the door is violent, and Kevin isn't all the way sober yet.

We slept the rest of the night pressed to opposite sides of the same door, together and not. It's 8 AM.

"Mrs. Estevez? Are you in there? It's the police."

Shit. For a moment, I'm surprised to hear Jimmy's last name but then remember in a daze that my mom changed hers for her second wedding, though she couldn't have been bothered for her first. Probably for the best.

"Mrs. Estevez is out of town. I'm her daughter," I say, sleepily, crumbling leftover mascara from the corners of my eyes, and trying, quickly, to look like I belong here . I unhooked my bra in the middle of the night, and I can't get it fastened again because my right arm is asleep.

"Well, miss, can I ask that you open the door? There's a man out here who is claiming to know you—and he's causing a disturbance in the neighborhood."

I pull my robe closed tight, put the chain on the door like I'm in an episode of *Law & Order*, and crack it open, blinking blearily into the bright daylight. Kevin lurches forward at me, a lost puppy reunited with its family after months away. "Holy fuck, *holy fuck*," his face breaks into a marshy smile. "It's *you. Look at you.* Let me look at you." He's still slurring a little, and the cop keeps him at arm's length, frowning heavily at us both.

"Ms. Estevez, do you know this man?"

"It's Adams."

"You're Adams?" The cop says, addressing Kevin, who reels and looks sick.

"No, *I* am. I'm Adams. Mackenzie Adams, I'm not an Estevez… I'm Gerald's daughter—it's fine. I live here. That's Kevin. And, yes. I know him. Unfortunately." I close the door to take off the chain so that I can open it all the way. "Here, okay, just… just give him to me, I'll just take him," I offer the cop, and he lets Kev fall into my arms. Over Kevin's shoulder, I wave good morning to Roger, who is watching all this unfold from his porch across the street. The cop seems to relax some when Roger recognizes me. Fine.

"You smell old," Kevin murmurs into my neck.

"Well, that's a gross thing to say." I breathe in, trying to pick up my scent.

"No. I love it. I love you," he says, clutching my waist. "You're all bones, Mack. We should eat, huh? Will you eat with me?"

The cop is still lurking, and I notice that he's young, maybe thirty. This might be his first time dealing with this sort of thing. I wish it were mine. He's still grimacing, unsatisfied somehow. "Well, if you have this under control," he says.

"Yeah, we're fine. I can handle it from here…"

"Your guests should be sleeping *inside,*" he reprimands, clearly pleased with himself for thinking of it.

"Yeah. *Thanks for that.*" I don't bother waiting for him to get off the porch before closing the door.

When Kevin finally lets me go, I put him to bed on the couch. He's asleep again before I dig up a blanket.

There's a chenille throw from the foot of Mom's bed that I tuck up around his chin. I sit on the edge of the coffee table a while and just watch him sleep.

There've been a handful of times in the last several months when I wished for someone, *anyone,* to come to my rescue. And admittedly, more than a few times when I've wished that someone would be Kevin. But not now. Not when I'm making an honest attempt at rescuing myself.

"What the fuck, Kev," I whisper, but he just drools on himself and snores, his soft dark hair a mess. Shit.

Alone in the bathroom, I strip the robe off and shake my hair out until it's nearly a mane. I lay down on the bathmat. The low piled plush of it is loyal to the back of my head. I spend too much time this way. Staring up at the ceiling, I count the spots where the cheap paint is peeling from humid showers. Count them again. Run my hands over my chest and feel acutely made of flesh and bones. My skin has deflated, aged a million years in this grief. I am older, faded and fractured, trying since January to rebuild myself stronger in this same frame. But inside, the pattern of my heartbeat is still so familiar it aches. I wonder how many of us ever really manage to get a fresh start in our lives—if it's even possible.

Three showers, and between them I just lay in the tub until I'm shivering—littered in goosebumps, my teeth clattering together. After the third, I feel raw, and still not quite clean. But before I can start a fourth, I hear Kevin moving around the house.

I wrap myself in a towel.

The air in the rest of the house is harsh without steam to soften it. Leaving wet footprints on the wood floors behind me, I make my way to the kitchen, where I stand in the doorway. Kev's wearing one of Jimmy's aprons now, studying the recipe on the side of a Bisquick box with a frying pan in his other hand.

He looks up at me, and his face combusts into one of his unmatched grins, beguiling and dangerous. He leans against the island, posing. His apron of choice says, "Bésame, I'm a chef."

"What're you doing here?" I wonder aloud.

"You like this? Very domestic, no?"

It feels like a jab at Neil, and I bristle. "That's not an answer."

"I'm making you pancakes."

"I meant why are you in my house, Kevin?'"

"Technically, this is Liz's house."

"What. Are. You. Doing here?"

Finally, he takes a breath before answering. Sets the pan down and looks at me squarely. "You didn't call."

I tighten my arms across my chest. "I'm fine. I told Nathan to text you."

"Yeah, thanks for that," he says, taking a step toward me. "He fucking texted me '*nevermind*.'"

"Well, it stopped you calling all the time."

"What's the point in calling if you weren't gonna answer?"

"So, you assumed you should get on a *plane*?"

"I needed to make sure you're okay." The distance between us is closing as he comes closer, and I back up against the doorjamb.

"Like I said, I'm fine."

He looks me over, frowning like I'm missing parts. "You always take three showers in a row?"

"Oh, fuck you." He's seeing me, and I hate it. I back into the hallway. "Do you always clean out the minibar before making out-of-state house calls?"

He shrinks back toward the counter, "Look, I don't want to fight with you, Mack. If I make pancakes, will you eat them?"

"*No.* You can't just show up wasted in the middle of the night and segue it into a pancake breakfast."

"I'm sorry, okay? I drank too much on my flight, I was scared—God, Adams, of anyone, I'd think you'd understand how terrifying it is to love someone and have no idea whether or not they're okay."

The fear in his voice catches me by the throat and won't let go. My lungs are sandbagged. "I can't—" I shake my head and tears swamp my vision, guilt climbing up my back like a ladder. "I can't do this with you. I don't want to, and I can't."

"Mack."

"Will you go, please?"

"Have breakfast with me."

"I'm going downstairs to get dressed. Please don't be here when I come back up."

I'm a flood rushing down the stairs. My body forgets its bones and spills out over the mattress. A whole storm shudders through me, and I can only weather it, wait for it to pass. After a while, I hear the front door shut overhead, feel the house shudder.

"Why wasn't it enough," I beg as if Gerald could hear me. As if he would answer. "Why wasn't it enough that I loved you? Didn't you want to be better?" My nose runs, and my face is so hot it hurts. "Dad, why can't I be better?" The recognition throbs in my gut, and I cry until my anger dies back into a well-worn loneliness. Until the cold of it lulls me to sleep.

By the time I wake again, the day is mostly gone.

When I finally put myself back together in sweatpants and an old t-shirt, and peel myself out of bed, it's pitch black and quiet upstairs. I stub my toe fumbling for the lights in the kitchen.

There's batter Kevin left sitting out on the counter and I drag a finger through it, swish it in my mouth. Still good.

Without thinking, I turn on the stove and ladle perfect circles into the pan. Make a stack of pancakes for no one.

Eat one.

And then another.

And then more.

Before long, I've eaten them all, with barely space between to breathe. They are the most delicious pancakes anyone has ever had, and then they are only okay, and then they taste terrible, but there's only a few left, and nobody wants leftover pancakes.

Sprawled on the kitchen floor, I digest them into the parts of me that feel emptiest. The backs of my knees and the soles of my feet. The hollow of my chest, the base of my spine. My forehead.

Just like him, he rings the doorbell. Twinkle, twinkle little star.

It shrills while I get back on my feet and feel the brick of pancake in my stomach sink. There's no animosity left when I answer the door. Just Kevin, standing there, empty-handed, shoulders slumped, waiting for me.

His eyes flicker in the porch light. "Can we try this again?"

I give a small nod.

"I'm really sorry, Mack," he says.

"Yeah. Me too," I say, moving out of the way so he can come inside.

We sit together on the couch, and nobody talks. Minutes of silence turn into an hour of silence, and we inch closer together with just the light from the kitchen coming in around the corner. Eventually, I curl up into the side of him, and he puts an arm around me. I lean into his chest and listen to him exhale. I sync our breathing the way I used to do with Alice on trips when I'd slide into her bed after a nightmare.

"Have you eaten?"

"I had pancakes."

He huffs a laugh, and I relish the sound, letting it settle over everything.

"Where'd you go today?" I find that I want to know.

"Just walked around. Until I was as far away as I thought you wanted me. And then some more, until I was back here."

"Thanks," I whisper. "For coming back."

"Had to," he says. It's late enough that the heat kicks on and sighs warm air up through the floor—the house stretches and creaks.

"Where is everyone?"

"Mom and Jimmy went to a couple's convention in Vancouver."

"Alice's?"

"Who else."

We fall back into a comfortable silence. I shift to keep my legs from falling asleep and fold them out onto the coffee table. He copies me, shaking out the arm he'd draped over my shoulder, and setting his hands in his lap. I try to find faces in the geometric pattern of the rug.

"How long have you been living here?"

"Mel moved to Connecticut this spring." My fingers find the hem of my t-shirt, and I pick at it so determinedly I think I could unravel it.

"And what about the domestic guy? He didn't swoop in to save the day? I've got to say, that seems a little off-brand for him." Kev leans into me, trying to coax a smile, but I don't have one.

"No, he tried." I shake my head. "A lot of people tried."

His banter dries up, and I feel him just watching me a while. "Well. I'm not here to try saving the day."

I scoff without meaning to, "No?"

"No." His voice goes soft. "No, I just wanted to see you."

I finally look up at him, and for the first time since I've known him, he looks almost genuinely shy.

"Hi, Adams," he says.

"Hi." For a while, we just stare into each other, like we're the first people either of us has seen in years.

A smile threatens at the corner of his mouth. "The first night we met, you threw me off my game. You remember that?"

I laugh. "No. What are you talking about?"

"You don't remember? I was juggling between that crew kid with the alt-right haircut and your roommate, what was her name?"

"Ella."

"Ella, fuck, that's right. Remember this? I thought I was on a fucking *roll* that night, and then I look over, and there's Mackenzie Adams, just seeing right through me. You were laughing at me like a bad joke."

I swat a hand against his ribs. "That's absolutely *not* what happened."

He just grins. "You're still the only person I've ever met that can do that. It's like you see all of people when you look at them, not just what they want you to see. Nobody'd ever looked at me like that before. I fucking loved you immediately."

I shake my head, ignoring the sound of my heart racing in my ears.

"Mack, listen. You're one of the strongest people I know, and if you're telling everyone you're fine, I have to believe that you will be. But I'm here because I wanted to see you like you always did for me. The parts that are fine, and the parts that aren't. I just wanted to see you."

I sit up, resting my head on my fist to look at him, sitting next to me in the dark, and he looks exactly like the love of my life, which, I think, unfortunately, has always been true. "Did you write that little speech while you were on your walk today?"

He elbows me. "It was *good*, wasn't it?"

"It could stand to be workshopped a bit, but it was pretty good." I lean back against him and take a deep breath. We rise and fall together, and it starts to feel like we're just one body. "Kev?"

"Hm?"

"I'm moving to Virginia in a few weeks."

I'd expected a bigger reaction, but he just asks, "Like the *state*?"

"Yeah, the state. I got a job there."

"Is that a good thing?"

"I think so. I want it to be."

"Okay."

"And," I take another breath, "I think I have to scatter his ashes," I add, not realizing it's true until I've heard it come out of my mouth.

"Okay," Kevin says again. "Where should we go?"

"I didn't mean… You don't have to help."

"Oh, did you *want* to do it alone?" He pulls his shoulder out from under my head and twists his face in mock curiosity.

"You're so obnoxious."

"*Yeah*. So, where should we go?"

It takes forty-three hours total to drive from Seattle to Waterford. Kevin estimates we can probably do it in a week comfortably, maybe a little longer, since I don't drive. He says he should teach me on the way, and I tell him to go fuck himself, and he laughs a big wide-open laugh I'd like to build a house in. I don't know where I'll scatter the ashes between here and there, but Kev says we'll figure it out. He tells me he got a hotel room not that far from here, and he can stay there tonight, and I say okay, it's getting late. But, still, for a long time, neither of us move.

I don't know what time it is when I wake up against his shoulder, but I just pull the blanket back over him and dismiss myself downstairs to bed.

August 31st

Around the time that Gerald got out of jail, I got very into the Worst Case Scenario survival board game, a game where you draw from a deck of unthinkable life or death situation cards, and you have to guess from a list of multiple-choice options which solution you should choose to survive. Sometimes you guess right and it's exhilarating. And other times, you choose wrong and you die. I loved this game. I wanted to play it at every sleepover, every family dinner, every recess. I would lie in bed at night, reading all the cards and memorizing the various survival tactics. I became a wealth of knowledge about venomous snakebites, bear traps, hurricane preparedness, and quicksand. *Whatever is coming*, I thought, *whatever happens next, I will be ready.*

I wake up to the sound of Kevin on the phone upstairs.

"No. No, for—no, for the love of God, that is so fucking irrelevant to this—" he's saying. I creep up to the middle of the stairs, so I can hear better. "I'm not *soft*, you asshole. I'm being a fucking human being. Someone needs to go with her. And now I'm here, I'm not just gonna leave. Can't someone else lead the meeting with Kline?" It must be his dad.

Kev sighs, and his voice breaks into something that would be a laugh if it wasn't so hatefully angry. "This isn't one of your fucking deals. I'm not negotiating. There's nothing to negotiate. I'm taking her. So, what else? Have Jason call Kline and push the meeting a couple weeks; it's just a quarterly. They'll love the extra time. God knows Hank won't care, and he doesn't even need to know I'm not in the office. I'll be on email. I can take calls. Just move the meeting; I don't know what the fucking problem is. You've met Mack, remember? At graduation? I'm telling you she's more important."

Listening to him, the scale of what he agreed to last night seems totally irrational in the light of day. I straighten out my t-shirt and head up into the kitchen to try to take it back.

Kevin set the phone down on the island, his father's yelling on the other end nothing more than a tinny hum in the background. He has his head in his hands. Very brooding and business-y and… *hot*. Everything about this is a bad idea. I shake it off.

"Good morning," I whisper. He looks up at me, and his annoyingly perfect dimple is all *good morning*. He mutes the call, grinning at me across the island like it's nothing.

"Did you sleep okay? I know the couch is kind of—"

"No, it was fine. Very hospitable. This bullshit didn't wake you up, did it?"

"No. I mean, it's fine." We stand, looking at each other a minute. "Look, Kev –"

"Don't do the Carrie Bradshaw thing," he says, and then off my confused look, "Don't do the thing where we make a plan and it's fine, and then you go away, spiral out about it in secret, and then come back and fight with me like I'm an asshole."

I bite down on a laugh at this. "I didn't realize you were calling that the Carrie Bradshaw thing."

"Watch the show; she does it *constantly*." There's silence from his dad suddenly, and I realize he must've asked Kevin something.

"I've gotta deal with this, but I meant what I said yesterday: we're gonna do this, and it's gonna work out. Okay?"

"Okay."

He picks up the phone again, while I pretend to look for something to eat. "Yeah, no, I'm here, I was just thinking," he says to his dad, and then kisses the side of my head before he takes the call into another room.

I slump against the fridge. I'm trying not to spiral, but my brain hasn't stopped spinning since Kevin got here. I'm a total chaos. I scribble a note that says, "Went out," and decide to take myself outside, even if it's just to walk around the neighborhood.

But then I don't go around the neighborhood. I get on a bus and ride until my stop, and when I get off the bus, there I am, across the street from Neil's gym. The big glass doors slide open and closed with every pedestrian who walks by, and he's there, easy to spot right away; Apollo, with his back to the door. He's talking to a client at the front desk.

At first, I think I don't know why I came. I don't have anything to say except that I'm so desperately sorry, and that won't mean anything to him since nothing else has changed. But some part of me needed just this much. Just watching him, hoping that whatever damage I did was temporary. That even if I ruin things, I don't ruin them forever.

He looks okay.

"Please be okay," I whisper. "Please, *please* be okay."

I stand there for what feels like hours—staring as the doors glide back and forth. And I keep remembering a fight with Gerald when I was fourteen. Another afternoon when I'd told him I hated him, and he'd stormed out of the house and told me he was never coming back. But that day, as angry as I'd been when he left, the more I thought about the very real possibility of him never coming back, the more scared I got. Because, *God*, what if it was true? What if he left forever thinking I hated him? Thinking I'd never really cared at all? It woke me up in the middle of the night, pulled me out of bed, and dragged me out onto the front porch at one in the morning, barefoot in my pajamas. I don't know what my plan was. To wander the neighborhood, calling his name? But I didn't have to look. He was already there too. Standing across the street, looking at the house, waiting for me. The speed I ran down the stairs—I can still feel the asphalt under the soles of my feet.

I remember us standing in the street together for an eternity. How I clung to him and told him I loved him. Told him again and again so that, just in case it was the last time we saw each other, he would know.

Neil has been out of sight for a long time before I notice.

I'm embarrassed at myself for thinking he might run outside like I'd done, relieved to see me, to forgive me.

"Even if we were always going to end up like this, I'm sorry I didn't do it better," I say, and hope somehow it finds its way to him.

As an alibi, I go into a corner store and force myself to buy something, like this was an errand that I ran on purpose. I circle the store three times and end up with hot Cheetos and a pocket pack of tissues. Super believable.

It is almost dinnertime when I get back to Ballard, and I'm exhausted from trying to hold an anxiety attack at bay all afternoon. I'm still looking for my keys when the front door swings open. Jimmy. I didn't even notice his car in the driveway.

"There you are!" He says, half-relieved, half-hysterical.

"I left a note," I counter like my note explained shit.

"Well, come on, we're all in the kitchen," he continues, pulling me by the elbow into the house. I put my bag down in the hall on the way. "San Francisco should be beautiful this time of year," he's saying over his shoulder, "not so much fog as there is in the spring." They sound like words, but I can't make them make sense.

And then we're in the kitchen, and there's Kevin, relaxed and a little unbuttoned, standing over a map of the US on the kitchen island next to my mother, pen in hand, circling landmarks. She looks up at me, beaming.

"Sweetie, hello! I told Kevin not to worry about renting a car for your big trip, of course, you can take the Dodge," she says.

"You told them?" I ask. Seeing him alongside my mom, I am very sure that all of this is moving too fast to end well.

"Was it supposed to be a secret?" Kevin says, and I wish so much that he would just read my mind sometimes.

"I don't know, I just… I've had kind of a weird day," I try to explain.

"There are so many great stops between California and Virginia," Jimmy chimes in. "I've always wanted to do one of those cross-country road trips. Even if you take the coast down to San Francisco, you can get there in time for Kevin's meeting next week. And you'd love the coast, Mackie. It only adds an extra day or two, but you can just leave a little earlier."

"San Francisco?" I say, and Kev opens his mouth to answer, but he's cut off by Mom.

"It's miles on the Dodge, but you know what, who cares?" She chirps. "That's what I said to your aunt Alice, and she agrees. Who cares about some old truck? Plus, it'll save you a fortune, only a little extra gas." Everyone is so full of kicky optimism that I think I'm going to pass out from the strain.

"I'd love to take a look at it, actually," Kevin says, suddenly beside me. "Can you show me where it is, Mack?"

"Keys are on the hook!" Mom calls as we duck out to the garage.

Kevin laughs an apology about how he didn't know they'd be so excited, once we're out in the hall, and I just shrug that it's fine. "Look so, after the call with my dad this morning," he's saying, as I unlock the car and climb into the passenger seat, "it seems like the best way for us to pull this off is if we make a pitstop in SF—just for, like, twenty-four hours so I can take this meeting. I know it's not ideal, and I tried to get out of it, but—"

He's barely got his door closed before my anxiety wins, and I blurt out, "I can't fall in love with you again."

"I'm sorry, what?" He smirks, looking around like he's checking for hidden cameras.

"This is a very 'fall in love with me' thing you're doing," I say, "going on this Gerald Adams memorial tour of North America with me. I think you're too smart not to know that. And I haven't figured out yet *why*, aside from being a very arrogant nightmare of a human person sometimes, you'd *want* me to fall in love with you again… unless," I squint at him, and he laughs, folding his arms across his chest.

"Unless? Oh boy. Three guesses, first two don't count," he says.

"This isn't funny."

"It's not?"

"Kevin."

"*Mackenzie*," and the warm, bright way he says my name makes it all so painfully obvious that I can't look at him anymore. My heart climbs up my throat, and I press the heels of my hands into my eyes, and all I can see is Neil's brokenhearted face, and the part of me that didn't mind making it that way.

"I need us to just be friends," I say into my wrists. "Honestly, I'm not even sure I'm cut out for that much at this point."

He pulls my hands off my face, and I blink a look at him. He's smiling at me, and I wish he wouldn't. And I don't. "Believe it or not, Adams, I *want* to do this with you. Even if you refuse to fall in love with me again."

I should say thank you, but instead, I say, "You're growing up."

The air between us is so still it disappears. "Is that what this is?" he says, holding my eyes a moment too long before moving to get out of the truck. "Huh."

You get stuck for a month with only enough water for three days. You realize you're in piranha-infested waters. You are confronted by a hungry mountain lion.

Nothing ever goes the way it is supposed to. Make a choice. What are you going to do to survive?

*

TO: khwasserman11@gmail.com
FROM: mackenzadams1377@gmail.com
SUBJECT: notes from Amira's class
SENT: November 2 2012 7:29:17 PM PST
hi you beautiful, beautiful boy. did you take notes on today's lecture? i fell asleep… please send help and notes. also… food? xoxo mack

―――――――――

TO: mackenzadams1377@gmail.com
FROM: khwasserman11@gmail.com
SUBJECT: Re: notes from Amira's class
SENT: November 2 2012 7:38:55 PM PST
Adams, you know you don't have to sweet-talk me for favors. Notes are attached. I have dessert plans later lol… but dinner is free. What sounds good? My treat.
- K

―――――――――

TO: khwasserman11@gmail.com
FROM: mackenzadams1377@gmail.com

SUBJECT: Re: re: notes from Amira's class
SENT: November 2 2012 8:41:35 PM PST
fuck. my dad called, and it was a whole thing. done crying now. sorry. you still around? ps. thanks for the notes. your thoroughness never ceases to impress. xo mack

---

TO: mackenzadams1377@gmail.com
FROM: khwasserman11@gmail.com
SUBJECT: Re: re: re: notes from Amira's class
SENT: November 2 2012 8:43:21 PM PST
Legends of my thoroughness will live on long after I'm gone. You've got no idea. ;) Canceled the thing I had later. I'm ordering in. Come over. You can even cry here if you have to.
- K

*

September 3rd

Most of my stuff is still in boxes from moving out of my place with Mel, so there's not a lot to pack. I want to call her about all of this, but I think she would have a lot of questions I couldn't answer, and then I'd second guess it all, and now I'm in too deep for that. Kevin has been loading things into the truck bed for a couple days now, and my room is emptying out. I have expressed several times my concern for what might happen if it rains, or if we leave all of my possessions in an open truck bed overnight in a motel parking lot. But no one else is worried about it. Probably because I have a paltry amount of stuff. "There is nothing worth taking," seems to be the unspoken agreement.

And now, here we are. Today is the big day.

I'm back in the passenger seat, adjusting it to see how comfortable I can get. "I want to drive straight through," I'd told Kev a couple days ago. "I'm not interested in sightseeing. I just want to get there. Besides, you have a job to get back to...I don't want to take you away from your life." I'd even suggested we sleep in the car, to save money, time, and most importantly to watchdog my things, but he shot this down because he's doing all the driving and wants to sleep in an actual bed to avoid killing us both out of exhaustion. Fair.

Mom and Alice are flying out to Waterford to meet me once I get there, and they'll help with the apartment search. I've kidded a couple times that it'll be a miracle if I arrive at all. At this, they have both said, "Oh, *stop!*" and shushed me with a giggle.

The seat has all kinds of weird adjustments. You can get it to tilt your pelvis every which way, and the passenger side lays all the way flat even though the cabin doesn't look like it should be big enough. Once all my bedding is packed in around me, it's practically a featherbed. "I will sweat," I announce, but am assured, to little avail, that we will just turn up the A/C.

Gerald goes under my seat. The gift box fits snugly, so there's no risk of it coming dislodged or spilling out onto my things down there. It feels weird and entirely inevitable to know he'll be at my ankles all the time.

The freedom I'd imagined would come with leaving Seattle behind is far from reality. I am irritable and anxious. Surprise, surprise.

I hear Kevin throwing the last of the stuff in the back, and then he comes around and opens the driver's side door.

"Is there room for the snacks and stuff to go by your feet?" He asks, but he is already handing me a large grocery bag filled with crackers and chips and bottled water.

"Last chance," I offer. "You can totally still back out now, and I won't blame you," but he rolls his eyes and goes to hug Mom good-bye. She's our whole farewell party since Jimmy is gone to work for the day already. I hugged Mom yesterday, which is recent enough for us, so she just waves to me through the window, as Kev gets in and starts the car.

The garage door peels open, the light of this otherwise regular autumn day flooding in. I wave back to Mom, but my arms are so weak with disbelief that it's more of a gentle flail.

We pull out onto the street, rolling through the hum of the neighborhood and onto the main thoroughfare that'll take us to the highway. I stare out the window and try not to think too hard about what I'm doing. It seems impossible our friendship will get through this intact, tenuous as it is. It's only been twenty minutes, and already every time I look over at him to start a conversation, my throat closes up in fear that anything I might say could be the wrong thing.

At the next light, Kevin breaks the silence, "Hey, I packed a tarp for your stuff—so it won't just sit out or get wet. I know you were worried." I have never been in the middle of doing something I understood less.

"Well," I breathe, "it seems like you've thought of every-thing then."

"Yeah. Don't fall in love with me," he says, and we merge onto the freeway.

I try to ignore him, and curl into my pile of blankets, watching the city go by; see my elementary school in the distance, the sky-line of downtown, the people out in their boats on the water. Seattle, with its maze of bridges and hills, shrinks and eventually disappears behind us as we crawl south.

We run into traffic maybe forty-five minutes out and get stuck behind a Honda Odyssey packed full of kids under the age of six, it seems, and one very tired chaperone. Through the back window, we can see her constantly turning around, trying to maintain some semblance of order and peace amidst the mayhem in the backseat.

"Sucks," I say, without meaning to, and Kevin sort of laughs and nods. The next time she turns around, he holds up a fist to her in solidarity.

"I put some CDs in the glove box since we couldn't find an AUX cable," he offers, glancing me out of the corner of his eye. "Just, you know, if you don't want to sit in mildly tense silence for the *whole* trip."

I shoot him a look he doesn't see over his smug smirk when I pop the glove box open to see what we have on deck.

"They don't have cases," I grumble.

"Oh, don't be a dick yet, sweetheart. It hasn't even been an hour," he says. "They'll be fine. Some of those are your mom's, too, I think."

It's a surprisingly large assortment of CDs. I sift through the top layer and pull out Sufjan Stevens' *Illinois*, one of my all-time favorite albums when I was in college. I slide it into the disc drive, and when the piano comes through the speakers, the corner of Kevin's mouth tugs up.

"Figures," he says.

The Odyssey Chaperone has unbuckled her seatbelt, since we're at a dead stop, and is fully turned around in her seat talking to the kids. She appears to be breaking up a fight over something... maybe an iPad, which she confiscates. She gives a faint smile to Kevin before she returns to the steering wheel, shaking her head.

"You made a friend," I say.

He shrugs. "I was getting lonely in here with you and your cold shoulder."

I tuck my legs under me and lean on the door; my cheek pressed into the windowpane.

We're supposedly driving all the way to Ashland today, down in southern Oregon, but I wonder if traffic will let us make it that far. I picture sleeping through the night in the truck while we inch forward. And before I know it, I am asleep.

I dream I am in an enormous house in a town I don't recognize. The front door was standing open, so I let myself in. For a while, I just wander the foyer, enjoying the sound of my shoes on the glossy marble floors. Then, at the top of a grand staircase, Beth appears in an evening gown. She looks like I've never seen her, glamorous and poised. She wears Gerald's wedding ring around her neck on a fine gold chain, and as she descends the stairs, I find myself curtseying, which makes her giggle. She comes toward me and holds my face in her hands without saying anything. She takes me into a back room, where a dress is laid out for me on the bed. She softly closes the door, and I begin to change clothes without hesitation. The gown feels far too small at first, but when I look in the mirror, I find that I am much younger, only nine years old and that it fits just fine. There's a knock at the door, and it is Gerald. He is done up in a tuxedo and walks with his old confident ease. His smile is broad and white, not yellowed and sparse like I remember it. *He looks well*, I think, and he laughs with delight to see me. He scoops me up in his arms, swings me around in a circle.

"*Daaad*," I squeal. He starts to say something, but I realize I can't hear him. I strain for his voice, but it's muted. He sets me down, urgently trying to get through to me, shaking my shoulders, as I try desperately to read his lips. "Dad, I can't hear you," I work to make him understand, trembling and crying. "I can't hear you. Can you hear me?"

And then, through the agonizing silence, I finally hear my name. "Mack. Hey. Mack?"

But it's Kevin. We have stopped. The car is parked, and Kevin has come around and opened my door. He has his hand on my shoulder, gently shaking me awake.

"Mack, we're in Portland. You wanna get out? Stretch? Get some food?"

Half-awake, I say the only thing I can think of: "What am I doing in Portland with you?"

Kevin leans over me and unfastens my seatbelt. "All right, gorgeous. Come on. Let's get something to eat."

I sort of stagger up the block behind him, trying to wipe the sleep out of my eyes and re-orient myself. *We really left*, I find my mind repeating as I look around Portland. Kevin turns into a little place with a sandwich board out front identifying it as The Brunch Box, serving burgers starting at 8 AM.

"Gross," I whisper on a reflex, but when I get in the door, the smell of grease starts to win me over. I sidle up next to Kevin in line, uncomfortably aware of just how much I like him.

He glances over at me, as I glare up at the menu. "We can go somewhere else to get you something, if you want," he says.

"No, I'm fine with a burger, burgers are good, I like burgers," I assure him, fixing my face and bored by my redundancy.

"Alright, cool." He's hungry and tired, so I decide not to prod him too much.

He gets a double burger with two waffles where the bun would go. I settle on just a regular cheeseburger and fries. Kevin doesn't get fries, but he eats mine.

We sit at a bar table, chewing in harmony, and not talking. When he's eaten more than half my fries, I kick him under the table, which makes him wince, and then laugh. It's an open-mouthed laugh, and I can see all the chewed up waffle and beef on his tongue.

"You're disgusting," I say, averting my gaze.

"Aw. You wish," he chides. And he's right.

On the road again, I ask if we heard the whole album, and Kevin says, yes. All the way through. Twice. I take the hint and go to the glove box for something else, and in a flash of nostalgic adoration, I go with Weezer's Blue Album.

Kevin is immediately singing along. I cover my ears in protest, and he just gets louder. "You know how I feel about this album, Mack. What'd you expect?"

"That you would know you can't sing to save your life," I say lovingly, but it doesn't stop him. He air-drums in stop-and-go traffic, and my face aches from grinning at him. I roll down the window, and start to sing alongside him, which only eggs him on. We alternate turning it up until the guitar is ear-splitting, and we're catching strange looks from passing cars, trying to outdo each other singing instrumental interludes. We crack each other up with increasingly bad dance moves. Kevin comes up with a scoring system of points earned for different reactions we can get from other drivers, and we go track-for-track in a sing-a-long Olympics. The scenery is a total bore going through central Oregon along I-5, but we hardly notice. The album plays through twice, til my sides hurt from laughing too hard.

As "Only In Dreams" starts again, I hunt for another CD, and Kev pulls off the highway toward a gas station. Car parked, he goes,

"Mack," in this sort of moony voice, and when I look at him, his face is slack, leaned dreamily against the headrest.

"What?" I ask as he fixes his jaw in an uneven bite, pouting a bit.

"What am I gonna *do* about you?" His brown eyes scan me up and down, and my heart goes very loud. I politely tell it to shut up, and mirror his lean, reaching over the console to smooth out the creases in his forehead with my fingers. He tilts his chin up, kisses the inside of my wrist, and I snatch my hand back.

"Do you always get this sloppy with girls who won't fall in love with you?"

"I wouldn't know," he sighs, and his dimple applauds his cleverness.

I make a show of rolling my eyes. "C'mon, let's see if they have good ice cream sandwich options."

We roam the aisles of the Good Mart. Kevin picks out more ice creams than the two of us can put away before they melt, watches me sort through Pringles flavors, and I feel myself wishing it could always be like this, that I didn't go dark sometimes, that I knew how to love someone up close. But happiness has always been so fragile, and I'm clumsy with it at best. At least, as friends, we can stay in each other's lives without me going nuclear. Friends. On opposite coasts. With separate lives. I go to the bathroom, to splash water on my face, get my head around it, and when I come back outside Kevin's leaned casually against the truck, halfway through a Drumstick cone, sun shining on his broad shoulders through his The Strokes emblazoned t-shirt, and I want to devour him whole. So, it's going well.

"What do you think?" he calls, shaking me out of my daydream.

"About?"

He gestures widely at the surrounding nothing.

I shrug. "Lot of dirt," I answer.

"I'm realizing," he says, offering me a bite of his ice cream, which I take, happily, nestling up at his side, "there's not a casual way to say, would you like to scatter some of your father's remains here?"

"Mm," I snort, taking another look around. "Not very scenic, though, you think?"

"Not very, no," he admits. "But, given the departed…"

I turn on him, eyes wide. "Oh, *please* finish *that* thought."

He takes an oversized bite of Drumstick, raising his eyebrows with a shrug. I shake my head disapprovingly, though I can't help laughing.

"It's whatever you want, Mack, honestly." He says through a too-cold mouthful. "I'm just checking in."

I take a deep breath. "Could be okay, I guess. I just feel kind of like… weirdly nervous to start?" And I realize how true it is once I've said it. "I hate having the ashes, but it's also… if I still have them… at least I still have *something*. I don't know. Does that sound creepy?"

"No." He puts an arm around me.

We go through another round of ice cream sandwiches weighing pros and cons (Pros: No one will see us or care, the ashes will blend right in. Cons: It's a gas station off I-5 in the middle of Oregon) and finally climb back into the car. It's not until the ignition revs, and he says, "Okay?" that I think, *fuck it, I have to start somewhere,* heave a big sigh and wriggle the box out from under my seat and onto my lap.

Kev turns the car off, studying me carefully. I start to open my door and then turn back to him, anxious. "I'm right behind you," he says in that velvet voice, and I think there's no one else I'd rather be with to do this if I have to do it. I climb carefully out of the truck and start to wander up a little way from the gas station—into a patch of nowhere next to the road. Kevin stands at my side, sets his hand on my shoulder, and presses a kiss into his fingers. I wait to know what to do next.

"Should I hold that?" he offers after a minute, taking the box. I haul in a deep breath, and slide my hand under the lid. When I pull it out, it's greyed with ash.

"Fucking weird," I squirm.

"Totally fucking weird," Kev agrees. "But still. Here we are."

I close my eyes and clutch my fist. Then, when a breeze comes, I hold my arm out and open my fingers. We watch the ash take off into the dust—past us onto the concrete and out into the wasteland.

"And now it's now," I say without thinking, and Kevin smiles this secret smile just for me.

We get to Ashland later than we wanted and check into a weird little roadside inn that does most of its business during the Shakespeare festival. I'm surprised there's still someone at the desk. It's twice as much for a room with two queen beds, so we get one bed, and ask for a rollaway cot, which he takes without argument, and I almost tell him he could just share the bed with me, but thankfully I don't get the words out. Kev falls asleep pretty much immediately, but I lay awake and look at the ceiling for at least another hour. I think about the dream I had that afternoon, about Drumsticks and best friends and shitty timing, about which part of Gerald I let go today, about what I'll have left when all of this is over.

September 4th

I think I've barely been asleep at all when Kevin wakes me up at 5:30 AM.

"If I'm supposed to show you the coast on the way to SF today, we have to get going, Adams."

The morning is scarcely half-lit through the too-thick motel curtains, but a shaft of light washes over me when Kevin goes out onto the breezeway to take a work call. I climb out of bed and pull on a clean t-shirt and yesterday's jeans and find a bakery that's already open where we can stop for breakfast, and with any luck, coffee.

"I found breakfast," I say, holding out my phone when Kev comes back in.

"It's out of the way," he says, even though it's only ten minutes from here.

"Still not a morning person, I see," I tease, but he doesn't laugh.

"You ready?" I nod, and he's out the door again to deal with checkout. He's obviously in a mood, and I hope it's work and not regret.

The ten-minute drive is tense, but the bakery itself is charming, and our barista is all smiles, even when Kevin grumbles at her for asking if we'd like our food to stay.

"Sorry about him," I find myself whispering over the counter, as though I'm the mother of a fussy toddler. "For here is great. It's hard to eat a cinnamon roll on the road," and then she and I share a tight, awkward laugh about sticky fingers because conversations with strangers are necessarily strained and polite.

Kevin is already at a corner table, wadding up chunks of croissant and gulping them down. I slide into a chair across from him, and when the giggling barista brings over my cinnamon roll, I burn my mouth, trying to get through it quickly, while Kev just stares.

On the table between us, his phone buzzes, and he glances at it. "Fuck," he says at his phone, and then "fuuuuck," again, this time in no particular direction.

"Everything okay?" I ask like the answer isn't obvious.

"You'll be in my apartment tonight," he says after a long pause, and I agree, waiting for him to make a point about it, but all he says is, "fuck" again. It's definitely weird, and I try to think if I've ever seen him this agitated.

"Can you tell me what's going on so I can stop worrying that you've finally realized this is a huge mistake?"

He takes a deep breath and then just goes, "Do you have something nice that still fits?"

"What? Like clothes?" He nods, plainly annoyed at the question. "Um, I mean, probably something. I don't—define 'nice.'"

"Black tie."

"Do I have something *black tie*?" I find I'm looking around the bakery for confirmation that I've heard him correctly. "Kev, all my possessions are currently under a tarp in the bed of a truck. What about that screams 'black-tie ready' to you?"

"Okay. Nevermind. We should go." He stands up and sighs.

"*Kevin*," I say, but he just strides out of the bakery, and I have to grab my stuff and chase after him, squeaking a quiet "thank you" over my shoulder to the barista. He's in the car with the engine running before I can even open the door.

"Nope. We're not doing this," I say, leaving the door hanging open, with my leg dangling out. "You're talking to me, or you're gonna have to drive to the Bay like this." He backs the car up a couple feet, and I smack him hard in the chest. He parks again and takes another deep breath, leaning his head on the steering wheel. I wait, still chewing icing off my fingers. "*Guy*," I plead. "Start fucking talking, please."

"I forgot that I have to go to an event tonight for a client, and I—I mean, you can come," he says, tenuously.

I squint at him, trying to understand. "That's it? That's why you're pitching a fit? Because you need me to be your date for some gala?"

"I don't need you to be my date," he sighs. "I have a date."

"You *have* a date," I echo like it'll make more sense coming out of my mouth. It doesn't. I let it hang there for a while like if we leave it alone, it'll turn into something else, but it doesn't do that either. "*Who?*"

"This, um… fuck, this sounds worse out loud… This girl I was sort of seeing?"

My mouth falls open, and I look at him and let out a scoff. "Oh, the girl you were sort of seeing." I'm nodding a lot. Too much, but I can't stop. "And does the girl you were sort of seeing know about the girl and her dead dad you're bringing home with you?" He puts his head in his hands. "Actually, you know what, don't answer that. There's not an answer I like." My ears are ringing a bit, though I'm not even sure I'm surprised. "This is, without question, the most Kevin thing you have ever done. Ever."

"I know."

"I hate being friends with you sometimes."

"I know."

"Like, I really fucking hate you right now, for example."

"I know," he breathes. "I'm sorry."

"Okay." I suck down a bunch of air and keep it, yanking my leg into the car and closing the door. "Well, let's go. I don't want you to be late."

We get onto a highway that winds through redwood forests toward the ocean. The trees are so tall and dense, it's like meandering down a narrow corridor, and the intimacy of it feels all wrong. No music today—I decide that nothing would sound good.

I want to fall asleep. I close my eyes for a while. Try hard to focus on the sound of the tires on the pavement, and… nothing.

Kevin is breathing too loud, I determine. And for a while, I will him to stop breathing at all. I'm angry.

It took forever getting over him the first time. I'd told everyone, especially Melanie, that I was over it at graduation. But then I took his picture when he walked across the stage for his diploma, so he'd have one for posterity. And I invited him to dinner with my family during commencement weekend when his dad had to cut out early. And I insisted we help each other move out one last time. And that last afternoon, when he came to my dorm room, and picked up a box labeled HEAVY, and made a dig at me for keeping my textbooks, I still looked at him and thought we'd wind up together someday, making space for those same books on shelves we'd share. He'd hugged me too long the way he does, told me he loved me too many times the way he does. And I'd let him. *Everyone's wrong about you, even you*, I thought.

The box under my seat grazes my ankle, and I wonder how much of grief is just the ache of having too much love leftover for someone and nowhere to put it.

There's a break in the trees ahead, and the Pacific sprawls out in front of us. I take a deep breath, and Kevin looks at me over his shoulder for the first time in miles. He turns off the highway.

"What's going on?"

"You haven't spoken to me for more than two hours," he says. "And now we're getting in the ocean."

"What?"

"You heard me."

"I'm not getting in the ocean."

"Well, you definitely are."

"No. I'm not. It's like sixty degrees out."

"I don't care."

"*Kevin.*"

"*Mackenzie.*"

He pulls into a parking lot in the center of a wide beach that arcs toward the horizon at the far edges. There's no one much around. It's still too early in the morning. The waves froth on the sand, and wind ripples the tarp in the back. He unbuckles his seatbelt and turns toward me.

"Look, I know you hate me right now, and I get it. I do. This sucks. But I really need you to know that I'm sorry," his throat works over what comes next. "I didn't mean for you to get hurt. I'm actually trying really fucking hard *not* to make things worse for you, so... I'm sure you can imagine my disappointment when I realized that I'm supposed to go on a date tonight. *While you're staying with me.* But I also don't feel like I should cancel the date because you've asked me very explicitly to just be friends. Which, by the way, also sucks." He reddens slightly, and swipes a hand over his face. "Not like I was planning to just show up at your door like, 'Hey, I heard you're not eating or moving, but lucky for you, my dick and I are here to solve all your problems,' but—"

I can't help laughing, and he grins.

"This is a fucking weird thing we signed up for, Mack. And sometimes it's hard, and I can promise I will continue to get stuff wrong. But I don't regret it. I don't wish I was anywhere else. And I don't wish you were anyone else."

I look out at the beach, the blue-gray expanse of the waves melting into the blue-gray of the sky, and I know I wouldn't trade any of it either.

"Oh my god," I say, sitting back against my door. "I think it's possible you're my favorite person." The beauty of his laugh is all-consuming. "You have no idea how much I wish that weren't true."

"You've been my favorite person for a long time." He shrugs through the blush rising in his cheeks. "It's a pain in the ass, but you get used to it."

He gets out of the car, and the wind pulls at his hair. He beckons to me through the windshield, walking backward toward the crash of the surf. I shake my head like there's no way I'm getting in, but I'm powerless not to follow him. I slide out into the parking lot, and Kev takes off at a sprint for the water, doubled over laughing when the first wave smacks into his shins.

"You're in all your clothes," I shout, and he just laughs harder. I kick off my shoes and set off down the beach. The water is too cold, and the sun has disappeared behind a cloud, but Kevin grabs my hand, and we wade in up to our waists, screaming curses and cracking each other up. A wave knocks him sideways, and he bobs up behind me, teeth chattering in the goofiest smile I've ever seen. When I turn away from him, there's nothing but water as far as I can see, and for the first time, the vastness of everything I'm feeling all at once seems to scale.

It's something like peace.

The current tugs and I let myself lean into it. It doesn't care about me, I know. It would just as soon pull me under as keep me afloat. But if I surrender to just my feet in the sand and the shoreline at my back, I feel, for a moment, not as alone facing the unknown of what's next. Instead, I'm in the company of all this depth, both of us coming and going at time's whim, steadfast and stubborn and endless. The breeze is pierced again with Kevin's laughter when he topples against me, and I duck below a rising crest. Underneath, everything is muted, swirling chaos familiar as my reflection. Then I'm surfacing again, on the back of a wave, spitting saltwater spray, and can't do anything but gasp a laugh back at him. Bound together as we are, we're free as we've ever been.

We're nothing but water-logged denim and salt when we crawl back to the beach, and I track half the shore back to the car with me. We stand on opposite sides of the truck, getting into dry clothes, wrapping all our drenched things in one of my towels in the truck bed. Without a word, Kev watches me let a fistful of ashes dance out over the water. They're gone a long time on the wind before we wash our hands and climb back into the car.

"Thanks," I whisper, and he nods, both of us still shivering. And then we're back on the road. The coast is beautiful, all rocky cliff faces and spilling views of the ocean on one side, and thick with redwoods on the other. The road clings to the curves of the landscape, and I forget we're ever supposed to be anywhere but here.

"I think I got it from my dad," I muse, as much to myself as to Kevin. "The way I look at people. He was like that too. I always felt like he could see everything about me without having to ask."

Kevin sneaks a look at me. "Do you miss him?"

I shrug, not sure why I brought it up. "Some days more than others."

"What about today?"

I weigh it in my heart. "I don't know," I answer honestly. "Sometimes I think I do, but then it feels weird to miss him now when I didn't even try to see him before he died."

Kevin chews his lip a bit. "You never told me," he starts, cautious, "what happened the last time you saw him."

My throat catches, and I press my mouth into a line, realizing that I never actually told anyone the whole story of that day. Mel was too gentle to press for details, and I think Mom and Alice were just relieved it was over, though neither of them ever said anything about any of it to me. It had felt like so much nothing, I'd just swallowed it down and tried to forget it. It's suddenly heavy on my tongue.

"I went downtown to see him, and when I got there… sure, he was drunk again and deluded, and maybe it was just that one afternoon… maybe it was. But… he didn't remember me. Not even my name. He called me Mallory." It feels harder to breathe, but I push through it. "I've never felt anything like that before… someone who used to know me better than anyone, just not knowing me at all. It's like… it's like having all your organs vacuumed out. Like losing everything into nothing at all…" I shake my head. "And I still tried. I tried to make conversation. He asked me inane things like what my favorite color was, and what kind of ice cream I liked, and I gave him bland answers… it was like a bad first date. And then he started to get tired, and so I made an excuse about needing to get home… and

I said, 'I love you'… and he said nothing. And I went home. And I didn't go back. I just didn't go back."

The hole in my chest gapes, and my breath echoes over it. I feel Kev reach across the console and take my hand. It sounds so blank, this little secret story I've been keeping. It sounds like static, like a bomb going off.

"Sometimes, I think more than I miss him… I miss *me*. The way I was before everything I thought we had got lost. It's been almost three years since it happened, but there are still days when I don't feel like anyone anymore." As terrifying as it is to admit, I think it's better than pretending it's not there, and Kevin doesn't flinch.

"Well," he says after a while, "I think you're a fucking miracle." And for just a minute too long, I forget not to fall in love with him.

It's getting dark by the time San Francisco erupts from the horizon in front of us, buzzing and crowded in too many gentrified pastels. Kevin's building is just as massive and pristine as it would be in my nightmares, and it looms over us, glinting in the moonlight. "No, you don't live here," I say, and he just swipes into the underground garage. We put the truck in a parking spot labeled Penthouse Guest, and I nearly throw up on him.

The elevator opens right into his living room like he's the villain in a spy movie, and the back wall of the place is floor to ceiling windows overlooking the Bay. I think the furniture and everything in here must have been picked out special for him; it looks like a catalog ad for getting laid. And as if he's auditioning for the role of the insufferable rich kid, Kev barely looks up at the panoramic view when we walk in, so I keep my mouth closed because his ego doesn't need encouragement.

He jumps up and sits with one leg folded under him on his gleaming kitchen island. "I'm thinking I'll order Chinese for you, and then get in the shower. Sound good?"

It is altogether too much. "Kevin."

"Yes, darling," he says, not looking up from his phone.

"Your apartment is obscene."

He looks around with a smirk, and then his gaze lands on me. "Suits me, then," he says.

Unsurprisingly, I opt out of third-wheeling the black-tie thing. Instead, I sit in Kevin's room, picking at fried rice, watching him primp.

He looks nearly pornagraphic in a tuxedo, his face clean-shaven, and his eyes gleaming copper in the lamplight. I can only look at him in short shifts.

The date, I've now learned, is the daughter of one of his dad's major investing partners. Hailey. It was a set-up for a launch party a few months ago, and she's been his plus-one to work events ever since. His dad loves it. "Good optics," Kevin winces. "But it's okay. I like her. She's fun."

She's supposed to be here by 8:30 PM. At 8:15, I am standing opposite Kev in front of a mirror, tying his bowtie.

"You should know how to do this," I scold, though I hardly mind.

"I've done it myself before… it's just… you offered." He has me there. "Where'd you learn this anyway?"

"A woman should know how to tie at least three different classic knots and a bowtie," I recite, and he grimaces. "Alice."

"I should've guessed."

Finishing the bow, I straighten it so that he can check in the mirror. I see us standing together, him all suited up, and me, undone, but not quite the mess I always imagine I am. Our reflection shakes through me, and I look away, flopping back onto the bed and stuffing an entire egg roll into my mouth.

"You look good in that suit," I tell him because, in all today's honest sharing, not saying it was starting to ache.

He looks me over, and I'm suddenly too aware I'm sprawled on his bed. "How dare anyone forget you," he says.

And then the elevator dings in the living room.

Hailey is tall and regal and painfully cool. Her dress is backless and low cut in the front, with this scandalously long slit up one side, but somehow, it's still demure. She has a lot of hair, and all of it is perfect.

"Oh my god, *finally*. I get to meet one of Kevin's real-life friends," she laughs with lots of beautiful teeth. Her voice is one of those raspy, sultry voices, and it makes you want to tell her all of your weirdest secrets. "We're always at work stuff. This is rare," she opens her arms to hug me.

"Hailey, right?" I say, smiling through the hug and, *of course*, on top of everything she smells good.

"Yeah. Hi. I can't believe I'm actually meeting you. You're Mackenzie."

"I'm her," I put my hands up, joking in a way that's not remotely like me, "What have you heard?" She laughs again and puts her French-manicured hand on my shoulder to reassure me. Her hands are warm and not at all clammy.

"No, oh my god, please. Nothing but amazing things. He adores you."

I laugh and try to act unfazed. She doesn't even fake jealousy, and I can't decide if it offends me.

"Hey," Kevin's voice croons in from behind me. "I see you two have met. Hailey, this is Mackenzie, and Mack, this... is Hailey." He kisses her cheek, and she beams at him. It pains me, but they're cute.

"I was telling her how many stories I've heard about you guys in college," Hailey says right into his ear.

"Were you? Good. Sometimes Mack doesn't believe how much I love her. It's good for her to hear it from someone else." I feel as though I'm shrinking. Am I shrinking?

"You look incredible, as usual," he says with all his usual charm, and she moons at him. I feel him glance at me, and I try to pull a rogue hair out of my leg with my fingernails.

"All right, ready?" He asks with a deep breath, and Hailey nods. "We should get going then." He calls the elevator, and we each give a small wave as the doors glide shut, and they disappear.

I stare out at the Bay for a long time after they go, let myself fall into a daydream where instead of all this messiness, I had a regular dead dad and just grieved like a regular girl. Spent days inside looking at old photos and telling sweet stories from my childhood. A very practical black dress and a heartfelt speech at the memorial. The long elegiac Facebook status with lots of likes and condolences. And then maybe a trip for me and my mom to the Greek isles or somewhere. It'd be something we'd always planned to do as a family, that his death had re-inspired. There'd be albums of photos: me and my mother, blue and white tiles, lots of large platters of seafood. Several candid photos of me staring out into the Mediterranean that conveyed I was processing my loss. And then I would come home all bronze from the sun and refreshed. I would tell people that I felt my father had graduated from guardian to guardian angel—that I felt closer to him than ever. And my friends would marvel at how well I handled everything, and I would say that I was just lucky to have had as much time with him as I did.

And then my phone rings.

"Kenz! Hi!" Mel's voice is bright and chirping. I completely forgot that we'd agreed to a phone date today. Things were very different when I'd said yes to this two weeks ago.

"Hey." I try to match her upbeat timber, but it comes out gravelly and dry.

"Uh-oh," she shifts, "What's happening? You're not back to vacuuming at 2 AM, are you?"

"No." The question grates, and I have to remind myself that she means well.

"Okay, good," she breathes this breath full of expectation, and I don't feel like talking, but I don't feel like being alone either. "So," she says after a while, "are you packed?"

"San Francisco," I eke out like that's a sentence.

"San Francisco?"

"I'm, um, in, like, this penthouse thing in San Francisco," I explain. But it's not an explanation. I'm annoyed at myself for being a tease. I don't want to play guessing games, and I'm giving her no choice.

"Mackenzie, can you use your words, please?" She's doing that thing where she talks like Valery, and I think she knows she's doing it, which only makes me hate it more.

"You're gonna be weird about it," I snap.

"Can't be weird about it if you don't tell me what it is," she snaps back.

"It's Kevin's." There's this long silence where I know she's making up her mind about what side to take on this.

"The penthouse?" She's being dense on purpose.

"Yes. The penthouse is Kevin's." Another lull. After a minute, I hear Luke in the background asking what's happened, and I hear Mel say, "She's in San Francisco... Hold on..." and then she's back, breathing on the other end of the line. "Is he with you?"

"Kevin?" Two can play this game.

"Yes, Kevin. Is he with you?"

"Right now?"

"Mackenzie."

"He's on a date."

She guffaws, and then swallows it. "*Cool for him*," she mutters, and then, "So you're alone in Kevin's penthouse in San Francisco while he's on a date." She wants me to hear it out loud, and she wants Luke to hear it too. I have to admit it doesn't sound very good.

"I'm not entirely alone," I counter. "Gerald is under the front seat of my mom's truck in the garage."

"Shit… Kenz—" her voice breaks off. I am so often right on the edge of me being entirely too much for her. "What are you doing?"

"I don't know," I tell her, honestly. "I don't know. It's just… life used to feel like more, I think, and I'm trying… I want to feel that way again."

She pauses. Probably looking for patience with me, and she finds a little. "And? Is it working?"

"Sometimes," I start, but I'm suddenly too tired to try explaining the ocean. "I don't know, Mel. Can we… can we just talk about you for a while?"

Once we're off the phone, I peel myself up and find my way back to the guest room. The only art in the room is a map of San Francisco.

"Condescending," I grumble to no one.

I lay down, and as I sink into the memory foam, I think I will still get up and change into pajamas and wash my face. I'll get ready for bed so I can really relax and let all of this weirdness go.

I don't.

September 5th

It's 9 AM, and I smell coffee.

I'm crusty and gross, the way it is when you sleep on top of the blankets in all your clothes and all your make up. I take my bra off and wriggle around in my t-shirt to give my ribs a break—air out my boob sweat. I wipe the mascara from under my eyes and brush my teeth before waddling into the kitchen.

It's Hailey in a t-shirt dress.

"Oh, you're up! Yay!" She has a ridiculous amount of energy for someone who was at an open bar event the night before. I don't bother thinking about the fact that she's still here this morning.

"Hi. Yeah. Up. Is that coffee?" I make my way to the counter and rummage in the cabinet for a mug. Everything in this kitchen is so sleek and modern; it makes me want to go back to bed.

"Yeah, please. Also, listen, I was gonna make eggs or something, but since you're up... do you wanna go out? We could get brunch? There's this amazing place not that far from here. Their French toast is unreal." There's something utterly fascinating about her effortless friendliness. I don't trust it, but I like looking at it.

"Sure, yeah, is Kevin up, or—?"

"Oh, yeah, he already went in for that big meeting... my dad, and his dad and negotiations or pitches or something. Whatever. Boring." She rolls her eyes and gives me a conspiratorial smile, "He's not gonna be able to leave for a while still, so I thought maybe you and I could hang out a little. Sorry, is that weird? If that's weird, I totally take it back." I can't tell if I hate her or want to make out with her. At least he has a type.

"No, god, no. Not weird at all," I bluff. "Let me, um… I'll get dressed… or changed. I'll change, and then we can go."

It's kind of dreary fall weather outside, hasn't decided if it's going to rain or not. But Hailey says the place is just a few blocks and it's not worth it to drive, so we walk.

"I don't know if there's like, a super tactful way to do this, but um…Kevin told me about your dad," she says as we set out. "And I just wanted to say that I'm really sorry. That's really hard."

I breathe into the discomfort of it. "Oh. Thanks. It's—we don't have to talk about it."

"I, um," she continues, "I lost my mom when I was sixteen. And it's just, like… I mean… it's not the same thing for anyone… But… you know, I'm just… I'm sorry."

I look at her, and she glances back with a half-smile. "What happened?" I ask, even though it's the worst question.

"Oh, um, it was cliché. Freak car accident."

"Mine was a heart attack," I offer, and she nods like, *neat story.* "Did you, like… go to therapy or anything? Sorry if this isn't—"

"No, I don't mind—grief counseling. I probably should've stayed in it longer than I did. But I was a kid, and I was pissed off." She sort of kicks at a piece of concrete jutting up in the sidewalk.

"I tried group. Like a sort of grief group… my mom read about it on a bulletin board, and everyone was so desperate for me to be better. And you know, I was too. Desperate. And so, I went and… I don't know. I don't think I regret it, but it sort of just… like, I got this false sense of security from it. Like I was going to fix myself somehow by going, but then afterward, I just felt like more people knew how fucked up I was. I don't know. Maybe I should have gone back."

"It's not ever really fixed, I don't think," she says after a minute. "I don't know if it even gets better, really. I mean…God. That sounds sad. I just mean it always feels weird and not quite real. At least that's how it is for me. Like, even ten years later, I still don't quite believe I'm never going to see her again. That just seems absurd. And I still tell stories about her like we just live in different cities and I'm overdue for a visit. Maybe, if I'd stayed in counseling, I would have learned better tactics for moving on, but—This is the place."

I look up and see we've arrived: a very cute little corner cafe with big windows and a chalk art menu.

"After you," she says, holding the door.

We get a little table near the kitchen and busy ourselves with menus and drink orders and the usual brunching things. We watch other tables get their food and decide which dishes look too good to pass up. We get coffees, and home pressed lemonades and mimosas and waters. There's barely room on the table for anything but cups. I order the French toast, and Hailey orders the Eggs Benedict, so I order a side of eggs, and she gets hash browns, and we decide we will also share a fruit plate. She says she never orders this much food, as though I might think it means something about her, and I just smile and say, "Food's great."

"What was she like?" I find myself asking between sips. "Your mom?"

She sighs and settles into her chair, glancing up at the ceiling like she's checking in with her mom to remember.

"Smart, super smart. She read all the time, magazines, newspapers, novels, biographies. She'd read like ten different things in a day, and somehow retain it all. It seemed like she knew everything about everything. It was like living with an encyclopedia." She laughs the kind of laugh you do when you really love someone and can't help smiling just talking about them. "What about your dad?"

I think maybe she's already heard a Gerald synopsis from Kevin, but then I think maybe not. And suddenly I decide to skip it. "He was, um, just really funny. Made me laugh more than anybody. That's what I miss." She just smiles at me and nods.

It's too much food, and we sit there eating it for hours. She asks me about my new job and Virginia. And I tell her I sort of have no idea what I've gotten myself into but that I needed to do something new. She says she thinks about doing that sometimes. "I've been in San Francisco for like four years now, and sometimes I think I still love it, and sometimes I think I want to get out of California. Like, it sounds crazy, but have you heard about the dirt-cheap houses you can get in Detroit right now?"

I laugh at her before I realize I'm doing it. "My dad hated shit like that—people moving into cities they've never cared about just because it's a good market. I mean, think about it, go to Detroit if you actually want to live in Detroit, but even the cheapest house in the world won't automatically make you happy to wake up in Michigan every day."

"Explain to me how that's different than what you're doing." And when I can't answer her, she just raises her eyebrows and smirks into her Benedict.

I get a text from Kev around noon, wondering where I am and if I'm almost ready to get on the road. And I say maybe we should ask for the check, and so we do.

"It's weird to meet someone who is exactly as great as they've been made out to be," she grins, signing her receipt. "Like, when Kevin talks about you, it's like, *okay, I get it. She's amazing.* But, like, you really are."

I shake my head and shrug it off, "I mean, thanks, but I don't know."

"There's just, like, you *glow*. You know?"

I laugh out loud.

"I'm serious! You're very cool, Mackenzie. And it's like... I don't usually open up about this kind of stuff. I mean, Kevin has no idea about any of that stuff."

"What stuff? You mean, about your mom?"

"Yeah, or Detroit. No way. And part of that is, like, we're just casual, you know? Like, he's fun. Like, he's *very* fun, but he's... I mean, I know he's your friend, so I don't mean to sound... but you know. It's not like he's exactly *boyfriend* material."

Oh. I don't like her. "How do you mean?" I pry.

"Well, you *know*," she falters, "I mean, he's sweet... but he's *Kevin Wasserman*. Everyone knows what he's like. There are so many rumors... it's hard to take him seriously. I heard his dad saying once that he takes after his mom that way. Charming as a snake, and just as trustworthy." I force myself not to cringe. Wow. I really don't like her. "God, you must think I'm a bitch. It's just what I've heard," she covers. "Like I said, he's super sweet, and we have a good time... I guess he's just not the kind of guy I can see myself with, in the long run."

I nod and say *totally* and *makes sense,* but really, I'm just tired and ready to stop pretending that she and I were ever actually going to be friends.

Kevin is making himself lunch when we get back, and Hailey gushes to him about how amazing I am, and I sit in the living room and watch him make a sandwich and tell her he knows. After what seems like forever, she kisses him on the cheek, and says to have a good trip, and seriously thanks for last night, and to text her when he's back in town if he wants to do something. And then she's gone.

He pads into the living room and plops down across from me. He has this look on his face that I can't place, and he goes, "You have a good time?"

I squint at him. "Did *you?*"

"She got pretty drunk at the gala actually," he answers. "I brought her back here because she left her car up the street, but there was no way she was driving home." I nod. "I slept out here," he adds.

The air in the room is too thick, hazy with something I'm doing my best to ignore. "She's nice," I offer, and he nods too, and I have no idea what we're doing. I'm bouncing my knee, and he takes a bite of his sandwich and chews, and we watch each other with the kind of focus you watch a spider you're trying to catch.

And then, like he's commenting on the weather, he says, "So, I'm in love with you."

And all I can think to say is, "yeah."

"Kind of a lot, actually," he says next.

And I just say, "yeah," again.

I don't know when we started having a staring contest, but I can't remember the last time I blinked.

"I wasn't gonna say anything, because I know we're not supposed to be doing this. But then, last night, I started to get this panicky feeling like if I didn't tell you, I might die or something."

I try to swallow my laugh, but it's out before I can catch it. "Oh, please don't die," I say, and it's mostly a joke, but then I also really mean it.

"I've never done anything like this before, Mack."

"I know."

"Made a point *not* to, honestly."

"I know."

His eyes are glassy, and I hope he doesn't cry because that'd be too much, and everything is already a lot. Like he heard me think it, he blinks and looks at the floor. Composes himself.

"I was a mess when we were in school. You were… you were the first person I said I loved and meant it," he says quietly. "I couldn't handle what that meant then, and I used to think I wasn't cut out for this kind of thing. I wasn't. I'm not. But I think I have to try anyway."

We're back to staring.

"Kev."

"Are you in love with me?"

I try to get a deep breath and feel distinctly like now *I'm* going to cry. And I say the only word I can think of, "*Obviously.*"

I promise myself never to forget the way his face looks in this exact second.

"Fuck," he says, but he's beaming like he was at the beach and I feel fluorescent. Like I'm blown glass, and he's the neon that lights me up from the inside. "I want to kiss you."

"Please don't," I say because even though my heart has liquefied, kissing can only make things worse.

And he says, "Okay."

We watch each other another minute, everything in the room friction and heat, and it's impossible to think about anything except how we could be kissing if I weren't so stubborn. So, finally, I say, "Nevermind. Please do."

Kev grins as he stands up, and I meet him in the middle of the room. He leans down, his nose grazing mine, and my breath catches, and then he kisses me. First, it's this very tender and chaste thing; I feel him smiling, and I say, "You taste like mustard." He laughs and pulls me closer, his mouth sliding open, catching my bottom lip in his teeth, and I lean further into him. It's not how I'd have thought it'd be. It's sweeter. Brand new in a way kissing hasn't felt since I was a teenager. His mouth moves along my jaw, slips onto my neck, and I lose track of time, lose track of needing air. I dip my chin and catch his mouth on mine and want to dissolve on his tongue. And it feels so easy. Too easy. Like being us would fix having to be me.

I pull back, pushing him off gently and feeling the space he leaves behind so acutely that I know it was the right thing to do, no matter how much I hate it. "I'm sorry, I just... *fuck.*"

"You okay?"

"I like you *a lot.*"

"Yeah," he smirks. "I think the I-love-yous covered that, more or less."

"No, I mean, I just... I like you so much. And maybe you're ready to try now, but I'm not," I say, shaking my head. My knees get weak, and I sit on the edge of the couch. "I don't want us to get this wrong, and I will. This place I'm in... I can't love anyone well from here. I don't know how."

He gets quiet, and my heart is too loud. But then I hear him say my name and, when I look up, his face is all soft innocence and he says, "Can I hold you?"

I swallow a rush of saltwater and nod, my cheeks already wet. He sits beside me, gathering me up in his arms, and rests his chin on top of my head. He has this inescapable calm about him that envelops me. Steadies my heart.

"You already love me better than anybody, Adams," he says gently. I close my eyes and let my breath fall into rhythm with his.

"But what happens if I try my best and it turns out it's not enough? And I lose you?" My throat aches at the thought. "Because

I can't afford that. I don't ever want to know you're somewhere else trying to forget me."

His arms tighten around me. "I'm not ever gonna forget you, Mack," he says, with a tenderness reserved for the people he trusts, for me.

"Even if it was possible to know that for sure..." I say, meeting his eyes, "I need to figure out how to be a person again. Without anyone I'm trying to save, and without anyone else holding me together. I... I have to be sure I'll remember myself."

Kevin kisses my temple, and I settle against his ribs as, outside, it makes up its mind to rain.

That afternoon, in the storm, we pull over near the bridge. I pull on one of Gerald's sweaters, and walk barefoot from the car to a lookout point. We each take handfuls of ashes and watch them catch in raindrops, slicing down into the bay. We are vandals and vagabonds, and we don't care.

*

Gerald—

Did you get the invitation? I wasn't sure the best mailing address for you, but then I ran into Harry Ennington at the deli, and he said he could get these to you. Guess sometimes he sees you over at The Oyster. Now that I think of it, I guess I don't know how true that really is. Maybe he just took the letter for himself, and that was the end of it. But it's a wasted thought now. If you're reading this, then you must have got the invitation too, and maybe Harry isn't a total shit. Even though you always said he was a total shit. And you would know. Anyway.

I wasn't sure if Mackenzie would have told you. Or if she did if you'd know you were invited. And ~~I felt like I owed you an explanation~~ you deserve to hear it from me.

I'm getting married.

You'll hate getting this in a letter. I suppose I should have just told you, but the thing was that I didn't want to fight. You know how things are.

Oh Ger, I think you'd really like him actually. Not now, of course, but maybe in some other world if you two came across each other... I think you might have actually had a couple laughs. But what do I know?

You know, for everything, you were my very best friend for a long time. And you're still my family too, you and Mackenzie and I will always be a family. I didn't think things would be this way. But you know that, don't you? I wasn't sure for a long time if there was any way for me to have another start. Not while still loving you. And I do love you, Gerald. I hope you'll believe that somehow. But in any case, it seems like here I am—starting over again. Happy. What a kick.

It was Jimmy's idea to invite you. That's his name. Jimmy. You met him. Mackenzie told him you'd light the invitation on fire. Use it to roll a cigarette. If that makes you happy, I hope you do it.

I never know for sure with you how much of the man I married is still in there. Or if he's even in there at all now. But if you run into him, god, would I love for him to be at my wedding.

I hope you're well, Gerald.

Please do take care of yourself. We love you so.

Liz

*

September 12th

States and motels blur into each other. We agree to pretend like nothing really happened, and then we agree to pretend it's working. I distract myself with curiosities about the life I'm idling toward. I think about wood stains, tile patterns, and other non-essential dilemmas that keep adults busy. It's only a handful of times that I catch myself studying Kevin. The slack in his right arm when he rests his wrist on the steering wheel. The vein that strains in his neck when someone merges without a blinker. And the way he shifts his jaw when he realizes I'm staring. I pull one leg up to my chest and lean into my window, watch fields roll by, take a deep breath and say "horses," and wait until he says, "oh, yeah. Horses."

Lexington, Kentucky, is the last stop before we get to Waterford. I am about to say that I can't believe we actually made it this far when Kev pulls into the parking lot of a Homeaway Inn Express.

"What the fuck are you doing?" I say, not caring that this is the first unrestrained sentence either of us has spoken in almost a week.

"Getting us beds for the night," he answers like that's an answer.

"Not here."

"Come on."

"Not here, Kevin. No."

"Yes, here. Okay? Yes. Here."

"You don't get to decide that."

"You think it's a graveyard, but it's just a Homeaway Inn. You owe it to yourself to learn the difference."

"Stop trying to be cute."

"Stop trying to stay broken."

The lobby smells the same. The way a department store smells when you're a kid. Like grown-ups and perfumed magazine pages. Kitten heels on linoleum. Polyester blends. I get in the way of the staff, and Kevin checks us in. I expect them to recognize me, but they don't because this is Kentucky.

Our room is on the fifth floor. Elevator works just fine. The room has two queen-size beds and a couch, bigger than Gerald's. Executive suite. Kev's idea of a compromise. I push the drapes open and look out into the parking lot. The Dodge is too big and takes up two spaces, but there's no demand for spots. Just us, a couple mini-vans, a Dodge Neon, and a Chevy Trailblazer.

"What can I get ya?" Kevin says, swinging open the mini-fridge. "Gummy worm?"

"It's strange to see one of these rooms clean," I say. But I don't take my eyes off the window.

I hear the fridge close, and I can feel Kevin as he comes closer. He puts a hand on my shoulder. "Sit down. I'll make you a drink."

I don't sit, but he pours anyway. Clinks the spoon around the glass just to hear noise in the room.

"Alice paid for his room," I say.

He doesn't say anything for a minute. Then all he says is, "shit."

"For five years."

"That must've cost—"

"Almost four years tuition. Less about $7,500."

"*Jesus*. Did she tell you that?"

"She gave me the leftovers. To get me settled in Virginia."

He sits. "You can't make this shit up."

"No," I say. "But who would want to?"

He nudges my side, hands me a whiskey coke, and I sit next to him, and sip it. It's too strong.

"I kind of hate that we're drinking in here."

He winces. "Yeah, fuck. Sorry."

I only shrug. "When she gave me the check, she said I get to decide what the Adams legacy is going to be."

"Fucking A, Alice."

"I hadn't realized I'm the only Adams now. That's weird, isn't it?"

"I'm sure there are other Adamses."

"You know what I mean."

Kevin lays back on the bed and looks at the ceiling, resting his drink on his stomach. "If you'd asked him, what do you think he'd have said his legacy was?"

"I don't know," I answer. But then I lay back too, close my eyes and try, without shying away from it, to picture my dad. To remember him as the very best version I knew. Standing up straight, tall and proud and happy, and the way his eyes shone when he laughed. The way it felt to walk up the street at his side when I was little—like I knew a superhero in real life. And now, with his ashes a trail of breadcrumbs between me and home—with my whole life flayed open, stinging in the open air and too bright daylight—lying here in a Homeaway Inn Express in Lexington Kentucky, next to a boy I wish I knew how to hold, I think how ironic it is that, probably, Gerald would have wanted his legacy to be joy.

Kev rolls onto his side, "Any ideas?"

I think about telling him, but I don't. Instead, I shrug.

"Well. I'd really like to hold your hand for a while," he says. "You think that might be okay?"

The question makes me blush it's so benign, and I can't figure out how to say yes, so I just nod, and he twines his fingers in mine.

"Sometimes my palms sweat," I warn. "Just...like, in case."

He chokes back a laugh under a mouthful of Jack Daniels and grins at me.

"Mackenzie *fucking* Adams."

September 14th

"I'll give you two some time to think about it."

We are standing under a whirring ceiling fan in a renovated guesthouse on a Virginia estate. Jean, the realtor, in kitten heels and over-starched blazer, has made herself scarce after Kevin asked if this house was "for the slaves, you know, historically."

I like it, I think. It has real wood floors and a big enough kitchen for the no cooking I do. I like that it's not an apartment, but that it still comes with neighbors in the form of a cute family who lives in the main house. I keep walking through all the rooms, trying to imagine what kind of life I'll have here. Kevin just watches me. His flight is in like four hours, and he keeps saying he should probably go soon, but here he is.

"You like it," he guesses.

"I don't know, maybe."

"You do. I can tell." He's right. "It's nice. Picturing you living here."

"I wish you hadn't said that about this house being slave quarters."

"You're the one moving to Virginia."

Maybe it's the fresh paint or the unscuffed welcome mat, but despite what Kevin thinks, the thing I love most about this place is that it *doesn't* feel haunted. It's fresh, without expectations that I'll be anything in particular. I wonder if that's also because we washed the last of Gerald down the shower drain of a Kentucky Homeaway Inn Express yesterday.

I had sort of thought being rid of the last of the ashes would feel more final than it does. Kevin offered to burn the box in the parking lot, but we just recycled it. It's amazing how quiet the end of a person can be, even when their life was so loud.

"I'd love to fill out an application," I tell Jean the realtor when she pokes her head back in.

Kev says he's going outside to make some work phone calls, but when I finish filling out the application and look out the window, he's just staring at the trees. So, for a while, I just watch him watch the wind.

We wander to a coffeehouse on a main drag, where it'll be easy to meet Mom and Alice who've just landed. Alice is already texting on fifteen-minute intervals to let me know their whereabouts: de-planing, still de-planing, bathroom, baggage claim, taxi stand, etc.

Kevin is getting more adamant about how he really should get going, and I know sooner or later, he really will.

"What're you having, Adams? My treat."

I order an iced chai and a blueberry scone to pick at while we pretend this isn't the end of a weird, almost nothing. A small everything.

"I think you'll get that place. I had a good feeling about it." He doesn't sound like himself, and I squint at him, so he knows I know, but he shrugs me off. I crumble off some scone and put it on my tongue like I know how to savor good things.

"Thank you for doing this, Kev. I haven't said that enough."

"Don't mention it."

"No, I want to mention it. Thank you for coming back to Seattle, and thank you for driving me across the country. I honestly don't know if I would ever have done this alone. The ashes and everything... you didn't have to, and I just feel like I owe you—"

"Mack. Come on."

His voice is just above a whisper, but it holds. I can't think of anything to say that seems like enough. He steals a couple bites of scone, and I slide it to the center of the table. My phone buzzes, interrupting our silence, so I do a dramatic reading of Alice's text message to break the tension.

"'In Lyft now with driver Jalen, a very friendly young man who lives in neighborhood! ETA 13 minutes. Silver Toyota Rav 4.' So *that's* good. I have a friend in the neighborhood already," I mock, shaking my head.

He humors me with a short half-laugh before scooting his chair out from the table, and my heart jumps.

"Alright. I really should go. I'm cutting it close now, and if I stay, Alice'll talk til I miss my flight."

I nod even though I feel like there's no blood left in my body. I watch him call a Lyft.

"You're really going," I eke out.

"Yeah, I really am."

I swallow hard and nod again. He comes over and squats next to my chair, his hand on my knee.

"I wish we had better timing," I say, and he laughs.

"One of these days, Adams."

I take his hand and squeeze it. If I look at him too long, I'll fall apart.

"I hope you get a chance to know yourself, Mack. My life is certainly better for knowing you."

I look away to blink back tears. "Shut up. You say that to all the girls."

"Nah. I wish." He stands and leans in to kiss my forehead. "I love you. But you know that." I don't want to let go of his hand.

"I hate being friends with you sometimes," I tell him.

"It's the fucking worst," he grins. He kisses my knuckles, and then he's picking up his bags, and then he's getting in the back of a silver Honda Civic, and then the Civic is down the street and around a corner.

It feels like hours, but it's only a few minutes before Mom and Alice burst through the doors. Alice is immediately at the counter explaining their trip to the barista and asking if they have mountain spring water. Mom is barreling toward me.

"Sweetie! You're in one piece! Oh god and look at how much you've grown! Hi, my baby! Doesn't she look older, Alice?" She folds me up in one of her hugs, and I lean into it.

"Kevin left," I tell her.

"Oh, did he? Oh, what a dear he is. I've always liked that boy, you know."

"Yeah," I say. "Me too."

September 20th

Two days ago, I signed a lease, and yesterday we hung a mirror in my new bedroom. Ever since, I find I lose hours sat on my bed just looking in it. I want to believe I look as grown-up as Mom keeps saying I do, but it's hard to tell. I feel uncomfortably light, even though in the last few days, I've been eating more than I have all year. But still, my body doesn't feel like it's landed here. I feel empty the way it feels after an exam that took up the months before it with studying. No one prepares you to mourn your obstacles. I am the only thing left between me and whoever I want to be next. But that doesn't feel like freedom at all.

Virginia is still humid in September. The thickness in the air only reminds me how far from home I am. How far I ran to wind up here, alone with myself. I'm always sweaty here, so I have license to complain about feeling uncomfortable, though I know it's got nothing to do with the heat. There is a 24-hour blues station that Gerald would have loved, and I leave it on in the background even when the twang makes me bristle. I wonder if there'll ever be a time when I don't crave his company, the way it used to be. I almost hope not.

I want to believe I am doing more than just going through the motions of making a life. But the more days go by that I can't tell apart, the harder that is. Mel says moving always has a longer adjustment period than you want. She says when she first moved to New Haven, she didn't feel settled at all. She says she's still not all the way settled in, but I know that's a lie. I follow her on Instagram. I've Facetimed with her happy face.

It's late, and I can't sleep.

I do a few laps of the house, close my eyes and listen to the floor creak beneath my feet. I open the front door and watch fireflies flicker around the yard. Inside the main house, all the lights are off. I imagine them tucked in. The books with cardboard pages that they read aloud to their little girl until her imagination is sated. It'll be so easy for her, life. I picture her growing up in a pretty pink bedroom, writing in her diary about all the people who love her, and about how she couldn't choose which best friend to sit with at lunch. I hate myself for being jealous of a four-year-old girl, but I lay awake in it for hours.

In a few days, Alice and Mom will take the truck back to Seattle. In a little while, work will start. I've been telling myself again and again that this is a choice I made on purpose. That sooner or later, it'll feel that way—that I will wake up one day and look different…*better.*

I flip that word over and over in my mind. Think of all the times this year I've heard it, aspired to it, longed for it. All these months later and I still don't really even know what it means. Better than what? The truth is still true, even if you're smiling when you tell it.

When I don't watch myself in the mirror, I watch the ceiling fan—both of us chasing ourselves in circles.

September 30th

It is true that when you go somewhere new, you're still you when you get there. It is true that grief will keep finding new outfits when it outgrows sadness. It is disappointingly untrue that time heals all wounds.

Gerald's name just comes out of my mouth sometimes now. Thankfully it's mostly when I'm home alone. I hear myself say it just to remember how it sounds. Just to remind myself that this life used to be different.

The last few days before they left, I let Mom and Alice do everything. They cooked and unpacked, I even let Alice hang some tacky craft art she found at a local home store. I was there, I laughed along with them, and I feigned opinions about which cabinets should be for what, but really it all only reminded me of the way Alice had overhauled Mom's house after Gerald moved out. The way she'd plastered over that hole in our family with quilt art and Live, Laugh, Love decorative plates. I'd resented it then, but this time I'd just closed my eyes and prayed it would work somehow. Now they've gone I find myself walking through the house looking for people. Wishing for ghosts.

The unfamiliarity of this place would make it so easy to pretend I was someone else, and I think if I'd had my way—if I'd come here on my own like I'd planned—I would have. I could have said my father had been a professor or a surgeon. I could have said his death had been years and years ago. I could have said he was still alive and merely living abroad. The limitless possibility of every alternate universe I might've spun to escape myself does something funny to my heart. Twists it tight, so dense and heavy that carrying it starts to feel like a chore.

I'm dialing Mel before I know exactly how I'm going to tell her everything I need to say.

"Hey Kenzo." It's Luke's voice instead.

"Oh," I startle.

"Sorry, Mel went for a run, left her phone… we'd just been talking about you this morning, and I thought—"

"No, it's good. It's nice to hear your voice," and it is. "Hi."

"*So,*" he says warmly. "What do you think?"

I sit down on my bed and watch myself think over the answer. "He's still dead in Virginia," I say after a while.

"Mmm," Luke sighs. "I'd wondered about that."

"I don't know. I feel like I've spent most of my life apologizing for him. For talking about him, and looking like him, and acting like him, and being like him. But, even if I keep my mouth shut, as soon as anyone sees me with my mom, there he is too. He's part of the story, even if we try to act like he's not. He's part of me I can't hide, like—"

"He's your *dad,*" he says, and it's so blatantly right.

"He's my *dad*! And now that I'm away from everything, there are a million explanations I could make up about who he was or what our relationship was like…but I don't—"

"You don't want to have to lie."

"I'm tired of pretending things weren't what they were. And I don't know who I'm pretending for anymore."

"You want my opinion?"

"Desperately."

"People are never gonna be comfortable with you, sis. You're smart, and you're strong, and you're Black. Being light-skinned'll probably make some folks treat you like you're 'one of the good ones' or some shit, but at the end of the day, you're still Black. So, even if your dad's story was a cute or easy one, it probably wouldn't change as much as you think. There'll always be people who want apologies just for you being yourself. You just have to make sure you're not one of 'em."

I soak it in. "That's a good opinion," I tell him.

"Isn't it?" He chuckles. "Hey, any burning crosses in your front lawn yet?"

"Not today," I say.

"See? Sometimes I'm even right, and things *work out*—Oh, hey, baby."

Mel is home. I hear her ask who's on the phone and then, in an instant, her voice is in my ear.

"I was gonna call you today," she says, still catching her breath a bit from her run.

"I miss you," I tell her.

"Aw, Kenz. I miss you too. All the time. What's happening? How's the American South?"

"It's good. It has fireflies." She breathes a laugh. "Mel. There's a lot of stuff I haven't told you," I say.

"I know," she says. "Do you wanna tell me now?"

So, I tell her... because I want to be done faking, especially to my best friend—because that's why I called. I tell her about the panic attacks with Neil. I tell her about going to group and about Lydia. About the weeks in the basement, and how I was sure lying about it would be easier than everyone knowing the truth. I tell her about the last day I saw my dad, and about the money from Alice. I tell her that if Kevin hadn't shown up, I might've just let myself disappear once I got to Virginia. That I want so much to do better, but I don't know where to start. And I tell her I'm sorry, again and again, that I wasn't brave enough to tell her all of it sooner.

"I don't want an apology, Kenz," she says, exasperated. "Just tell me what I can do to help." I love her the most of anyone in the world, and I tell her so, and she says, "We're soulmates. That's how this works."

"I've been thinking maybe I should try again," I say. "Talking to someone."

"Wait... like, *therapy*?" I roll my eyes at the mock surprise in her voice.

"Yes, Melanie. Like therapy."

"Oh my *god*," she teases. "Mackenzie Adams. Valery would be so proud of you."

"I don't like you."

"Feelings! We all have them! Share yours!"

"I'm hanging up."

"No! Don't, don't," she squeals. "I'm sorry. But, seriously... you keep saying that you haven't been brave, but... it doesn't sound that way at all to me. I'm really proud of you."

We spend another hour on the phone looking at therapists for me online. In my discomfort, I make fun of their websites and tell Mel that I think the word "healing" is kind of bullshit, and she just sends me a link to another one. There's a grief group that meets every week, not even that far away from me, and I promise Mel I'll go.

"Call me more," she urges before we hang up.

"I will," I say, and I think that I really will.

"And, Mackenzie? Will you send me Kevin's address, please? I want to send him... I don't know. Flowers or... *something*."

October 7<u>th</u>

It's a local elementary school gymnasium with folding chairs in a circle. My shoes squeak on the over-waxed floors, and I have to remind myself more than once that this was *my* idea. There's Hi-C fruit punch and donuts on a card table along the back wall, and I make my way over, trying to look comfortable. A small bald man with metal frame glasses smiles at me.

"The glazed ones have jelly inside. Think it's meant to be strawberry," he warns as I reach for the donut tray.

"No good?"

He shrugs, bobs his head side to side. I smile and stick with the fruit punch.

"I'm Alan." He extends a hand.

"Mackenzie."

"I know it doesn't look like much." He gestures at the chairs. "Iggy says we're going to get a better venue someday. But," he sighs, and his eyes close, "these people have saved my life."

The group leader, Iggy, is a dark-skinned, bird-like man with a lot of downy grey hair. He has an endearing lisp, and he speaks gently without trying.

"I know it's coming up on a difficult time of year for many of us," he says when we're all assembled. "You can always tell it's a difficult time of year by how many new faces are in the room." He chuckles. "I see at least three new faces today, so to those folks, welcome. I am proud of you for being here tonight and making a step toward healing. And to those of you who aren't new, welcome back. Let's all take a deep breath in and out together."

I'm surprised how little I hate it. People share, not just about their grief, but also just about their lives. Some of it is heavy, and some of it is mundane and charming.

"I'm going on a first date tomorrow night," a woman named Louanne blurts. She's probably in her mid-forties, and the way she laughs at herself as she says it makes me think she never thought she'd go on a date again.

"Is this the guy from the library?" Alan wants to know.

Louanne nods, bashful. And she tells us what all they have planned.

"Well, how do you feel?" Iggy asks.

"I can't believe it, but I think... I'm *excited*." Louanne gushes at long last, and several people in the circle cheer.

"I'm jealous," I find myself saying out loud.

Iggy turns to me and beams. "I'm so pleased you feel comfortable enough to share tonight," he grins. "Remind us of your name, dear?"

"I'm, um, I'm Mackenzie. Sorry, I don't mean to ruin the moment. I just really appreciate how Louanne is feeling. It's hard to get there. And, I don't know, I guess I've sort of felt for a long time like I don't know how to be happy again really... or... if I ever have been... as an adult, actually. God, that sounds awful, doesn't it?"

Louanne's face softens, and she shakes her head.

"There's no judgment on it from us," Iggy says. "If that's how you feel, that's how you feel."

"My dad died this year," I explain. "He was a lot of things. Most of them were less than great... but we used to be close—when I was little. He was my best friend for a long time, actually. And then he was a burden mostly. And then he wasn't anything... and now he's dead, and... for the first time people ask me all the time how I feel about him, and if I miss him, and I get angry because I wish they'd asked before... that there'd been more space to grieve him before he was dead because all he ever did was leave—a million times. I've been heartbroken over it for most of my life. It doesn't feel fair that he had to die for that to be valid."

"But you know—or maybe you don't—it was valid every time before now, Mackenzie. Every time you felt some part of him had died, your grief over that was valid," Iggy smiles. "*Do* you know that?" I look into his kind eyes and shrug. "It's true," he says softly.

"I've felt it can be hard," Alan chimes in. "It can be hard to know what to do with joy when it does come. When it's always been such a foreign thing… I almost think my body tries to reject it. Like a virus."

"I try," says Louanne, "to think of it like immersion training. Maybe if I just spend enough time with joy, I'll learn the language. It's not very comfortable sometimes. I think I stick out like a sore thumb amongst the locals." She chuckles at this, and a handful of others do too.

"It takes time. Knowing how to allow yourself to experience your life as it happens," Iggy says. "Joy is a brilliant thing, but like everything else, it comes and goes. People have this idea that we should always be happy and that when we feel grief, it somehow disrupts the ecosystem. But we need it just as much as we need joy. It's all part of living, whether others know how to make space for it or not. We're not broken because we feel grief. We'd be broken if we didn't. What we all deserve is to know variety."

On my walk home, I text Kevin: *I don't know if it's too soon for us to be texting like friends… but, I miss you. Tell me what you're doing?*

And he writes back: *just thinking about this girl I know who stole my heart and then moved to Virginia. It's pathetic. Distract me.*

And then a second later, he sends a photo of a massive floral arrangement on his kitchen island. *Also, you know anything about these?*

<u>October 28th</u>

The job is, so far, more clerical than I daydreamed it. I spend most of my days trying to figure out how to use this new software so I can start to set up an efficient database to track submissions coming in and store reader reports and evaluations. Andrea has promised me that once the catalog is up and running, we'll get to do more of the fun stuff, but even the busywork is a welcome change of pace from my other new full-time job: slogging through my emotions.

In addition to group sessions, I've started seeing Iggy one-on-one. Aside from rent, it's the only way I've felt okay spending Alice's money since she and Mom left. Iggy's office is lined with books and plants. He drinks iced tea by the gallon, and sometimes as part of our sessions, we'll do watercolors or oil pastels while we talk. He says there's a lot you can learn from shapes and color, and, he adds, the business of drawing helps people to take their minds off all the honesty. There's a gentle drawl in his tone that reminds me sometimes of Alice, and I'm surprised how comforting it is.

"All reds to start," he said this week, pulling out a sketchpad. "Let's see where that takes us." And, as we sketched, I told him about a shade of lipstick they retired that Alice still special orders from Beijing. About a beanie Gerald used to wear to take me to the park. About the way it felt on an afternoon when he forgot to pick me up from first grade, and I had to go to the teacher's meeting until Mom could come after work. About feeling so angry at life sometimes that I couldn't sleep, and about the color of Kevin's eyes when the sun is coming up. While I talked, I drew something sturdy, that might've been the shape of a house, and Iggy asked who I thought lived there, and I laughed when I told him that maybe I did once, and then we moved on to blue.

It's nothing like I thought it'd be, doing all this work on myself. It's not nearly as romantic as Hollywood made me believe. About 100% less Javier Bardem. Most of the time, it feels a lot the same as just being alive, but now in unsettlingly sharp focus. Some days I think I'm making progress toward something better, however small, and other days I get hit with a wave of nostalgic depression so immense I can hardly move my limbs to tread water. But then, there are rare mornings like today, when I wake up, see myself in the mirror and think, not that I look new or improved, but instead that I look almost familiar. Like someone I knew years ago, coming home after all this time.

October 31st

It always felt like a cosmic joke that Gerald's birthday was on Halloween since I spent most of every year either afraid *of* him or afraid *for* him. His birthday was, without fail, his worst day of the year. An excuse to celebrate and terrorize, all wrapped into one day. I've never liked October. When I wake up, I already have two texts from Mel, one asking me how I'm holding up, and then a picture of a dog dressed as a ghost, with the caption ***DON'T FORGET YOU'RE MY BOO.*** I work myself into tears twice on my way to work.

Andrea is wearing a witch's hat when I get to the office, and she's disappointed that I'm not dressed up. I manage an apology, mumbling about how I've never really gotten into Halloween, before ducking into the bathroom to clean myself up.

"I've always loved Halloween. You know, when I was younger," she says, following me into the bathroom and standing at the next sink over, "it was like, right around when the *Thriller* video came out… And I actually thought that Halloween was when the dead came back to life to dance." I shudder out a laugh and discreetly try to fix my mascara. "I remember I actually looked up a spell that I'd say to myself whenever we drove by the cemetery."

"You looked up a spell?"

"Yep. Found some book called *Magic for Teens* at the local library, and it became, like, a bible for my girlfriends and me in middle school. We used to pretend to cast all kinds of spells from that book. Remember before the internet?" She slides some make-up remover from her purse and a pocket pack of Kleenex across the counter to me. "The paper towels in here are super harsh. I scratched my cornea once."

"Oh, that's—I'm okay," I lie.

"Look, I get that we don't really know each other yet. But let's at least agree to notice when one of us has been crying."

I look at her, and the tears are back. "I'm sorry, it's just… my dad died," I say on a shaky exhale. Her face goes white.

"Oh my *god*, Mackenzie. Today?"

My eyes and nose are still running like a faucet, but now I'm laughing so hard I have to sit down. "No, not today," I reassure her. "No, he died in January. I just—today would have been his birthday."

"Oh. I'm so sorry," she lays down some paper towels and sits next to me on the floor.

"He was… a lot… it's not… it's complicated." I garble and then add, "I'm in therapy," like it'll mean I'm somehow less crying on the bathroom floor of our office.

She only nods. "Did you get to say goodbye?"

"I scattered his ashes. And… he wrote me a letter. Not in that order."

Andrea studies me a moment. "Did you write him back?"

I raise my eyebrows.

"Yes, I know how it sounds. But I used to write to my grandpa sometimes after he passed. I don't know. It was… nice."

I can't think what I would even say in a letter to Gerald, but I smile thinking how much I bet Iggy would like the idea, and how much the girl I was a year ago would hate it. "Maybe," I say after a while. "Thank you."

"For what?" She smiles and starts to get up. "And, Mackenzie? Take the rest of the day. There's nothing you can do today that can't wait until Monday."

"Oh no, I don't mind," I stutter.

"I insist." She trashes the paper towels she was sitting on, washes her hands, and goes back out into the office.

The day spits me out onto the sidewalk in the lingering autumn heat. I walk past two princesses, a cat and a mummy playing four-square at recess. I see a teenage batman helping an old woman cross the street. I try to just go home, but as soon as I'm inside the door, it's oppressively lonely. So instead I grab a notebook and call a Lyft to the first graveyard Google shows me.

Getting out of the car and wandering through the gates, I'm a little aimless. I've never spent time in a graveyard before. It's weird to say I don't know anyone buried, but it's true. I drift around the plots. All the stones look more or less the same, which feels a little bleak. Everyone was someone's mother, someone's grandfather. Some stones have fresh flowers. Others are overgrown with weeds. I start to think this is too morbid, even for me, and then it happens. GERALD ADAMS, 1912-1998. Our Beloved Friend.

"You've got to be fucking kidding," I say to a field of caskets, but no one answers. I look at each of the letters so long the shapes stop meaning anything. I should probably head home, but I'm glued to the spot. "You won't believe this," I hear myself explaining to Our Beloved Friend, "but Gerald Adams was my dad's name. Today was his birthday. He would've been fifty-four today." OBF doesn't say anything. "Young. That's what they told me when he died. But I think he was older than he could stand… eight-six, though. Eighty-six is a good life." Without thinking, I'm laying down, resting my hand on the face of the stone. "This is exactly his sense of humor. Finding a gravestone with his name on it on his birthday, all the way across the country from home… he'd love this shit."

The clouds are bright today, postcard clouds, and they drift by like everything is a dream. "I made it," I sigh. And it actually feels a little bit true.

*

Gerald,

Happy birthday. Beth gave me your letter. I met Beth. She wears your ring. I'm sure you must hear from her.

There's so much I want to say, but everything feels wrong. Like I have so much to tell you and also nothing. I miss you. There's a man who works at my grocery store now, who wears those ties with the prints of different viruses and bacteria under the microscope. And, while he's bagging people's groceries, he announces which disease it is that day. Last time I was there I watched him shout "Chlamydia" three times at an old woman who was hard of hearing. I wish you could've seen it.

I know you think you did your best with me. Maybe you did. I did my best with you too. You might not believe that, but it's true. If it weren't, would I have picked up a rock on the beach in California for you? I put it with your cigarettes, so you won't lose it.

Most of the prayers I've ever said in my life have been for you. I hope you get them all. I used to be afraid to be too much like you, but as I get to know myself, I come across these little pieces of who you were. Pieces that I loved so much that I used to miss when you'd go. Thank you for leaving those things with me.

I met another Gerald Adams today, right here in Waterford. If you run into him, you can ask him about me. He's an easier Adams to talk to than we are. He's a better listener. He helped convince me to write this letter.

Mom says hi, I bet. And happy birthday. She'd want you to know she made the spareribs you liked, and she even cried when I played Graceland like you asked. You were so loved, Dad. Even when you tried not to be.

You still are.

You don't have to write me back. I still hear your voice all the time. And whatever's left in this life we started, it's all mine now to figure out. I'm trying to do better than we did. I think I have to.

I love you, I love you, I love you. That's the truth.

Please, if you think of me, remember me smiling.

- Mac

*

Before I know it, it's getting dark, and I'm starving. I consider ordering Postmates to the cemetery, and then I think I am a self-indulgent asshole and decide to just go home. I tear the letter out of my notebook, fold it into a paper airplane and let it go on a breeze—another handful of Gerald, gone on the wind.

On the ride home, there are herds of kids in the street waddling door-to-door. I run into my neighbor family, leaving to trick-or-treat as we're pulling up. The little girl is dressed as a caterpillar, and her mom and dad are dressed as a flower, and a leaf, each with bite marks munched out. Sweet.

I smile and wave to them before going inside, turning off all the lights and putting out a bowl of candy with a sign that says I'm not home.

I reheat pasta in the dark and then sit on the counter eating it. My mind flips back through Halloweens before; nights I spent anxious by the phone instead of out with friends, petrified, awaiting a call about what'd gone wrong.

And then my phone rings.

It's Mom.

"Sweetie!" she chirps when I pick up. "I was just thinking about you, and I wondered if we should talk today. How are you? It's a difficult day, isn't it? I've always found this to be a difficult day."

Her empathy catches me off guard. "You have?"

"Don't sound so surprised. Of course I have, Mackenzie."

Her tone is almost indignant, and something like rage burns the back of my throat at the audacity of it. Maybe it's the release of having written that letter, or just a renewed refusal to let her so easily off the hook after so many years of denial, but I suddenly swell up with the courage to say, "Don't sound surprised? Mom, where were you? If you found this so difficult, why were you never home with me when Dad was getting in fights, or passing out downtown?

"I—"

"Because I know you got a divorce, but *I* didn't. He stopped being your husband, but I was still your kid, and he was still my dad. And you never missed a chance to make me feel like that was somehow my fault. Do you know how embarrassed I felt that I missed him? How bad I felt about myself because I still loved him?"

"Mackenzie." Her voice comes down to its real tone, and for a second, I think I remember a night ages ago when she tucked me in for bed. "I loved Gerald so much I thought it was going to destroy me sometimes. There was so much good in him, I don't know if *he* ever saw that, but... You know, he was always determined to live his own way, no matter the cost, and I... for a long time, I thought it was worth all my fear and frustration, just to be close to him. Until, one day, it wasn't anymore." She breathes out like she's bracing for pain. "But then when we got divorced— Mackenzie, you were so angry at me when he moved out... I thought you wouldn't ever forgive me. You two always had a bond that I only saw from the outside. I hated taking that away from you... but I didn't want you to turn yourself inside out trying to get through to him like I did."

"But I did," I choke out under a blanket of tears. "I did anyway, Mom."

"Oh, honey."

"And you were never there. You were never ever there, and you wouldn't talk about him to anyone but Alice. You both always acted like you hated him. And I understood how you would but... no one ever said it was okay to still love him too." I feel myself getting younger and younger, smaller and smaller, crying out for my mom.

She sniffles into the phone. "I think I convinced myself you'd never forgive me. Because I knew how much it hurt to lose him. And so I just stayed away, and when I could, I tried to help him... when I thought it might help you both. But I know I got things wrong a lot of the time. This summer, I thought I might've gotten it so wrong I was going to lose you too."

I shake my head but can only cry and cry. Can only listen while she does too. And I suddenly realize that a stranger can be a person you've known your whole life. The way he was suddenly missing from her vocabulary, it had never occurred to me that that could have cost her something too. And now we don't have the language to say all the ways we've broken each other's hearts. I think of her and Alice, and all their conversations behind closed doors. Whole lifetimes spoken in hushed voices about a love I never saw. I wonder if Mom and I did sketches of how Gerald slammed through us... would our pictures align? Mother and daughter stretched thin across telephone lines and three thousand miles. Maybe we are both performing in roles we've never rehearsed.

"I'm still here, Mom. I'm figuring out how to still be here. But... I don't want things to go back to how they were. I can't do that anymore."

"You got so much of the best of him," she says after a long time. "I miss him the most when I'm with you."

I take a deep breath. "I'm sorry."

"No, sweetie. Don't be," she says. "It's such a relief to get to miss him."

November 4th

This week, grief group convenes at a local Italian restaurant because the school is undergoing some building maintenance. I'm sat between Erin, a single mom whose husband died from a major stroke, and Alan, who I've learned lost his daughter and son-in-law in a car accident on their honeymoon. I think how common tragedy is at our table, and my heart swells in my chest when the dining room fills up with our laughter.

Reaching for more garlic bread, I listen while Iggy leads us in a small utterance of thanks and prayer for anyone who wants it. Erin raises her glass of wine to the fact that she found a sitter for the evening so she could have linguine and clams, and I clink my Lambrusco with hers.

"Okay," I say once everyone's ordered. "I have kind of a heavy question for the group."

"Let's hear it," Iggy says.

"I don't know. I talked to my mom the other day… and I guess I'm sort of trying to get my head around… what it actually means to love someone well? In a way that isn't secretly selfish or just doomed to fail. Like… does that even happen?"

There is some munching around the table while everyone considers. Louanne is the first to weigh in. She says she always imagines love like gardening: the sweet well-intentioned notion that we can control and care for something as unknowable and indeterminable as nature. She says it's an exercise in patience, gentle tending, and listening. Accepting that some things won't make it no matter how much you try, and that's part of the process. There are days when the weather's no good, and you'd rather do anything else. And that's part of it too. "With time, things will bloom," she sighs, "and fade... and bloom again."

Erin agrees and says she thinks, to love someone well, you have to release the idea that their life is about you loving them. She says her kids are constantly reminding her that they're their own people with dreams that won't always line up with the fact that their mom just wants them to be safe. "And that's okay," she adds. "Them being who they are is exactly why I love them. It wouldn't be fair to ask them to be another way to make it easier for me."

The food arrives, and Alan slurps through his fettuccine while he explains that love isn't all that hard. It's basically just about showing up.

Bridget, who lost her mom to Alzheimer's, adds that showing up isn't quite the whole of it. "You have to show up ready to do the work too. You can't coast on simply being there," she says, defiantly biting into a meatball.

"We can all get caught up," Iggy muses, "in thinking that love is going to look a certain way. So many of us have expectations from childhood about what love is, how it should be in our families, how it should be with our friends, with our partners. But in my experience, love is different every time. It depends on the people sharing it. And that's what makes it so exhilarating and... mortifying: that there's not a single way to do it that's guaranteed. And none of us is going to consistently get it right." I roll my eyes, and Iggy laughs.

"You can't have really thought someone would just fork over a manual, Mackenzie," he teases.

"No." I duck my chin to cover that I *had* actually kind of been hoping someone would do exactly that. "It's just that, even when everyone thinks they have the best intentions, it can go so wrong. I mean I've had it go *so wrong*. So many times."

Iggy smiles. "Being able to love someone in person is a privilege of happy circumstances that we don't always get. If we're lucky enough to get that chance, all we have is the best we can do, and, of course, the gamble of forgiveness when we screw it up."

"Well, that's not very comforting," I whine.

"You didn't ask about comfort," Iggy says into a forkful of spaghetti. "You asked about love."

November 12th

Mel has arranged for them to come down for Thanksgiving. Luke is off school, and since campus will be pretty dead over the break, the store is taking a longer holiday as well. I find out she's making a Pinterest board especially for Friendsgiving menu ideas, and when she sends me a recipe for a pie in the shape of a turkey, I tell Luke he's doing a bad job keeping her expectations low.

In the background of today's phone call, I hear Luke say, "Why don't you just ask her?" and then Mel gets weird and mumbly.

"Ask me what?" I push.

"I don't wanna peer pressure her," she whispers at Luke.

"Don't love this, guys. Ask me *what*?"

"Luke had mentioned…" and I smile when I hear Luke disagreeing with this statement, "*Luke had mentioned,*" Mel doubles down, "and I agreed… that maybe you would want to invite Kevin. To Thanksgiving."

"Oh." It isn't the first time I've considered it. I've thought about it most of the time every day since Mel suggested a Virginia Thanksgiving. But it's highly inconvenient for my indecision that Mel has inexplicably become Kevin's biggest fan.

"Did you hang up?" she says into my silence.

"No," I say. "Not yet."

I listen while she takes a breath to boost her confidence to keep going. "I know you're scared. It's scary. I mean, you've been in love with this person for approximately a trillion years. But you wanna know something?"

"You're gonna tell me anyway."

"I think you're aren't as scared that it won't work out, as you are that it *will*. And I know you don't have a ton of experience with this, but not every good thing is a trick, Kenz. I promise."

My lungs fold themselves in half. "What happened to not wanting to peer pressure me?"

"I stand by that… but also… *I really want to meet him.*"

Once we're off the phone, I pace through the house straightening things on shelves and cleaning dust out of corners. Anything I can do to keep from dwelling on Kevin and his face. Kevin and his laugh.

Kevin and his hands and his teeth, and the dip at his hipbone, and the way he says my name like he's getting drunk on it.

"Okay," I say adamantly aloud to no one. "*Okay.*"

*

TO: khwasserman11@gmail.com
FROM: mackenzadams1377@gmail.com
SUBJECT: a thing maybe
SENT: November 12 2018 11:48:16 PM PST
hi for no reason, *hypothetically*, do you have thanksgiving plans?
xo mack

_____

TO: mackenzadams1377@gmail.com
FROM: khwasserman11@gmail.com
SUBJECT: Re: a thing maybe
SENT: November 12 2018 11:59:27 PM PST
You still have my phone number, correct?
No plans as yet. Intrigued. *Hypothetically*, of course. xx
K

_____

TO: khwasserman11@gmail.com
FROM: mackenzadams1377@gmail.com
SUBJECT: Re: a thing maybe
SENT: November 13 2018 12:03:48 AM PST

sorry, but if i hear your voice, i'll chicken out. forgive me? so, pretty much, i love you. like very much for real. and maybe more to the point i miss you. and i don't want to be your friend. i mean i do, but i also very much don't because i want the whole thing for us. and that is very scary because we are both emergencies mostly, but i'm working on mine. and i would rather be an emergency next to you than anyone else anyway. so. mel is coming here with her boyfriend for the holiday, and she wants to meet you. and even though so many things are changing for me all the time lately, how much i love you never seems to be one of them. so if you wanted to come and eat a turkey with me… i have a bed you could sleep in.

*

November 13th

It's only a few minutes later that my phone buzzes.

"You're calling me at midnight."

"You sent me a love letter."

"It wasn't a love letter," I feel myself blush.

"Um, it *definitely* was. And I needed to be sure the invite was still good once you heard my voice," Kevin says. "And now you've heard it… you still want to eat turkey together?"

I breathe a laugh. "Yeah."

"Okay. Then I'm gonna buy a plane ticket now."

"Okay," I say. "Please do."

November 25th

I told Kev I'd pick him up at the airport, which is useless because I don't drive. So really, I just take a Lyft to the airport and then wait for him at baggage claim so he can drive me home in his rental car. I tell myself it's the thought that counts, but truthfully, I just couldn't sit around at home and wait.

"Is this gonna be weird?" I asked him last night on the phone.

"Why would it be weird?"

"I don't know, because it's us... and I haven't even seen you naked."

"Is that what you're worried about? If you want me to send a picture of my dick, you have to ask, Mack. Maybe you've forgotten, but I'm a gentleman."

"And then there's the fact that you're actually the worst person."

"Mmm, yeah. That must be difficult for you."

This morning I was feeling very confident about this choice, but now, standing at baggage claim two days before Thanksgiving, the stakes feel precariously high. I put on about nine hundred outfits before going with the very original combination of a sweater and jeans. And even with all my costume changes, I'm at the airport a solid thirty minutes before his flight lands. I overestimated the traffic. I text him though I know his phone will be off. My stomach is on a spin cycle. What if he sees me and he tries to kiss me, and I go for a hug or a handshake, and we do one of those romantic comedy head butts? What if he sees me and is like, *"oh wow, I just realized I'm super over it?"* I worry that I didn't brush my teeth recently enough. I tell myself it's only one weekend, and if it's terrible, he can just go back to California, and we can wait several years until someone else dies, and we can try this again. Shockingly, that doesn't help.

I watch other people meeting up—couples, grandparents and their grandkids, and cousins and aunts and uncles and siblings and lifelong friends. I must look like a creep just shaking like a nervous wreck and gawkily smiling at them.

I get caught up watching the baggage handlers moving the remaining couple suitcases to the wall so they can clear the carousel for the next flight, and, when I turn, there he is—standing just inside the door from the gate, looking at me. Distressed black jeans, a soft chambray shirt over a white t-shirt, and his same white Chucks. His eyes crinkle, and he waves. I wave back and laugh, a platter of nerves in a suddenly too-hot sweater. I can feel my heart all the way down to my feet. I beckon him to come to me, and he does the same, so I give in and make my way toward him.

"What're you doing?" I say as I get within earshot.

He shrugs, "I wanted to play this super cool," he says. "But then I saw you, and my heart stopped."

"Shut up."

"No, I'm serious. You kill me, Adams. Are these the same freckles, or are there also new ones sent to destroy me?"

I sling my arms around his neck. "You're here."

"I am, can you believe it? Came all this way just because you asked. What's that about?"

"I don't know. Should we get your bag?"

"I just need like three more minutes here," he says, his eyes moving over my face like he's trying to memorize it. "I missed you."

I lean up to kiss his dimple, how I've always wanted to, and tell him, "We're those airport people I hate now."

And he laughs, hugs me to his chest and says, "Get used to it."

He throws his bag into the back of the pick-up truck he's rented for the weekend.

"You're such a romantic," I say, climbing up into the cabin beside him.

"I don't know what you're talking about," he smirks, starting the engine.

On the drive home, I point out every landmark I've learned in the months since he was here last, more eager than I realized for him to like it.

"It's not floor to ceiling windows, but it's mine," I say, pushing my front door open.

"I knew you'd get this place," Kev says, setting his stuff inside the door, and falling comfortably onto my couch. "It's nice." He looks around the room, then back to me. "You have a quilt on your wall."

"Yeah, Alice got that. It's supposed to make the room feel cozy."

"Sure, yeah, no. I feel it," he grins.

I smile back at him, at how well he fits here amongst my things. It's so effortless in this instant that I don't know why I spent so much time worrying.

I wander over and sit at his side on the couch.

"So," he says, his eyes flashing heat through his face in that devastating way they do, and I bite the inside of my lip. "I'd pictured some sort of a big romantic moment here," he says.

I shake my head. "I kind of don't think we need it."

"Oh, thank god," he exhales, and I laugh, but the end of it gets lost in his throat. It's a steadier kiss than our first, deeper, and less uncertain. I can feel the time between us: the patience and the hope we've each held under our tongues. It shouldn't be so easy, sliding into place along the edge of him for the first time, but it's like muscle memory leftover from a dream.

We make out hazily forever, or just for a moment, and I drift into his lap. His hands inch up my thighs, and somehow, he's standing, carrying me back through the kitchen, toward the bedroom, my legs wrapped around his waist.

"The layout of this house makes no sense," he groans, pulling my shirt off over my head. I glide my hands up his back. My mouth at his throat, as he pushes me up against the cabinets, strips out of his shirt. My teeth graze over his bare shoulders, my breath hot enough to fog up his skin like a mirror. I'm all goosebumps. Every place he kisses feels like it's never been touched before. The hair on my arms stands on end. He starts to unbutton my jeans, and I hold my breath.

"Breathe, gorgeous," he whispers into my collarbone, sliding his hand between my legs. His eyes meet mine, and I stutter over the air between us. "Just breathe," he smiles, his fingers finding a slow rhythm.

I feel my cheeks burn, and he kisses me again.

"What," he wants to know when I half-giggle into the corner of his grin.

"It's just… it's nothing. It's just… it's *you*." My breath fights its way out of me, but I know I'm done for. His hand slides further under me, and I gasp his name.

"*Kev.*"

"Tell me."

I drop my head back, helpless, and he brings his mouth to my neck. I bite my lip and lose track. His gaze is fixed on me, relishing every twinge that shakes through me, every quivering breath. Kevin is so fucking pleased with himself; it'd be infuriating if it weren't so. Damn. Good.

My legs go weak, and I grip my fingers on his arm, stilling his hand. "Too many clothes. Wrong room," I manage over a stunted moan.

"Do we need condoms?"

"IUD. So…not unless you have something I don't want?"

"Nope. Healthy." He is almost comically too proud of this, but I let it go.

Sliding off the counter into his arms, I push him back through the doorway and into my bedroom. He falls readily back into my bed, and his face shines up at me.

"God, you're so fucking *pretty*," I sigh. He laughs gently but loses the plot when I slide my jeans down and crawl toward him.

He's so warm and sweet under me, and I have this inescapable urge to destroy him. My fingers find the button of his jeans, the zipper; I make quick work of them. "What happens if I put my mouth here?" I ask, my tongue soft at his earlobe.

He doesn't make words, fumbling at the clasp of my bra.

"What about here?" I say, at his solar plexus.

"Mack," he rumbles.

"Here?" I drag my tongue to a kiss at his navel. My eyes dart back to his, and I bite my thumbnail, shrugging my bra straps off my shoulders, and chucking it off the bed behind me.

"Look at you," he rasps.

"You have no idea," I purr, sliding his briefs down his hips.

His fingers grip in my hair, and he's all sticky profanities and half-prayers. I sink fingers into his waist, trying hard not to be too greedily desperate for more of him.

"Mack," my name breaks through his lips. "Come here. Please. I want you."

I look up at him, and my heart unravels against my ribs. I climb back up his chest and kiss him. I let it be as sweet as it wants, let him hold me, let us be here together on purpose. "I love you," I hear myself whisper in his ear, my thigh draped across his stomach. He rolls onto me, and the weight of him feels familiar, comfortable like I'd trained my whole life to bear just this much. My back arches off the bed, and I can feel the small beads of sweat forming on my stomach. "Don't make me beg you," I say.

"Oh Jesus," he collapses a moment into the crook of my neck, weak. "Don't offer to beg."

And I laugh into his hair and whisper, "*please.*"

I lift my hips to him, and when we meet, my mind hums. Everything blurs, a collage of his skin on mine, seamless. I want to slow down time, so I don't miss anything, but I can hardly focus, every inch of my body spiking hot and cold at the same time under his fingers. I think I will be anywhere as long as he is there. It's impossible to have too much of him; we cannot get too close. It's simple as nothing at all, but I know we're quietly inextricable from each other now. There's not a future for me that doesn't hold him, even if I'm not sure how. And after, when he charts my freckles with his fingers, when I kiss the palm of his hand, and it tastes like that day at the ocean, when he wraps me in his limbs, and the smell of him closes around me, he says, "I love you," and I don't even need to hear it, because every part of me knows it already.

November 26th

"You're nervous," Kevin says to the tip of my nose as I wake up.

"Hi," I peel my eyes open, and he's frowning sweetly at me. "What's happening?"

"You've been grimacing in your sleep for like twenty minutes," he says, kissing my forehead, and when he does, I realize it's furrowed. "You're nervous."

"Could've been a bad dream," I hedge.

"Mmm. Was it?" He tries to sound genuinely curious, but he knows he's right.

"Fine," I cave. "I've never had to introduce Mel to a boyfriend before. Not since, like, high school, and even then, she knew them from class and stuff already." He rolls his head back onto his pillow and smiles his obnoxious, irresistible smile at the ceiling. "What?"

"I was sure you were gonna wake up in tears about how this was a mistake."

"Oh. No, god, sorry. Very much, no. Hi." I kiss him, and then again.

"Also," he says, his hand on my cheek, "I've never really been someone's boyfriend before." My heart goes quick and wobbly. "Wasn't full sure you were gonna let me be yours, so... I'm just... happy." I kiss him a third time because it's impossible not to, and he rolls me onto his chest.

"We need groceries," I say, coming up for air. "For tomorrow. So," one more kiss before I wrestle out of his arms and out of bed, "get dressed, please."

The grocery store is nearly picked clean, but we're able to scrounge up the few ingredients Mel left under my supervision.

"She doesn't trust you," Kevin snarks, looking skeptically at the sparse haul in the cart he's pushing while I turn down the spice aisle. "She left you in charge of whipping cream, a shallot, and what, oregano?"

"She put me in charge of *dessert* actually," I brag, and he raises an eyebrow. "But I picked up pies from a bakery in town before you got here. They're at home... this is just the list she sent me of stuff she forgot to pack."

"Ah," he says. "Mark me as awed by your domestic prowess then."

I roll my eyes at him. "We're breaking up."

He shrugs. "Predictable."

That night, we're on either side of a pizza box in my bed, and I'm distractedly watching him fold his slice in half and eat it like a taco when he presses a greasy finger into my thigh.

"Where's your head, Adams?"

"I don't know. It's weird to feel this happy when I'm still so sad," I say after a while. "I feel sort of like I might split down the middle... I don't know how to describe it. My lives feel so far apart."

He takes a deep breath and nods. "Can I help?"

"I sort of don't think so. You do help. You being here helps. It makes it worse, but also it helps."

He hands me another slice, and I wish Gerald could have known him—even if he wouldn't have liked him, and would've tried to intimidate him out of ever going out with me. It would have been nice, I think. To see both of them together, just for an afternoon. To see the way Gerald's face would light up at how much Kev makes me laugh. For him to know, I'm happy.

"You would've liked him," I say to Kevin.

"Your dad? Without a doubt. And you would've hated me for it."

I shove the box out of the way, and sprawl out, resting my head on his thigh.

"Also," I chew on my crust first, "no pressure or anything, but you have to be perfect tomorrow because Mel is a little bit primed to hate you if you're not, like, very much a dreamboat. And Luke has already offered a couple times to beat you up for me."

"Oh, excellent," he laughs.

"I promise they're really harmless."

"Fuck off. You've never loved anyone harmless a day in your life," he declares, and I try to look incredulous, but I think he's probably right. "Lucky for you, people always like me."

"Ew. I don't," I tease.

"No, you poor thing." He drags a finger over my collarbone. "You love me."

November 27th

At 6 AM, when the doorbell rings, we are very much greasy and unpresentable, and I don't know why I let myself believe Melanie was joking when she sent me their itinerary.

"Go shower," I urge Kev awake, but he just pulls a pillow over his head, and I'm too tired and jealous to fight him on it.

I stumble into his t-shirt and a pair of sweats and waddle to the door.

The view through the peephole is Melanie, Luke, and an enormous frozen turkey.

As soon as the door is open, Mel clobbers me in a huge hug, and even half-awake, I squeeze her as tight as I can. It's so good to see her. Luke waves to me over her shoulder.

"Hi! Did we wake you up? I was worried that we were way too early," she says as Luke sneaks around us into the living room, setting the turkey down on the coffee table.

"She wanted to leave early, so there'd be enough time to cook."

"I totally woke you up, didn't I?" She lets me go and passes me to Luke, who folds me in another hug.

"I was about to get up," I lie. "But, uh, Kev is still asleep." And as I'm saying it, I remember that I hadn't actually ever found the right time to tell them that he was coming. I didn't know how things would be with us when he got here, and then by the time I *did* know, it seemed maybe better to delay Mel's expectations. Her face now says otherwise.

"He's *here*?"

"Little bit, yeah."

Luke laughs a big laugh, and shoves me back at Mel, shaking his head. "Where's your kitchen, Kenz?" I point through the dining room, and he picks up the turkey and disappears.

"*Babe?*" Mel calls after him, managing to recover her jaw from the floor, "Will you unload the rest of the groceries while I talk to Kenz a minute?"

"Copy that," Luke snickers.

She drags me by the elbow out onto the front porch, and we wind up sitting in the bed of the rental truck in the driveway under an oak tree.

"I thought this thing must belong to the family in the main house," she says, gawking.

"I was going to tell you. I swear," I say.

"This isn't my first impression outfit," she deflates a bit. "But, it's okay."

"He'll love you, outfit, or no outfit," I reassure her. "And if he doesn't, we'll banish him." Her face crinkles a bit toward a smile, but she doesn't get all the way there. She's staring at me intently, and I can't quite tell what's happening behind her eyes.

"You seem different," is what she finally says. "When I left Seattle—I really wanted to believe you could find a way to be happy, with Neil and everything—"

"Me too," I offer.

She shakes her head, dissatisfied with herself. "But *this* is you. Looking at you now… I can't remember the last time I saw you happy like this. Maybe when we were kids? I'm so disappointed in myself that I didn't see it before. I wish I'd been there this summer, Kenz."

"It's not your fault." I clutch her hands.

"I should've been there. I shouldn't have left."

"No." I hold her gaze. "Even if you'd come home, even if we'd still been roommates and you'd never left… it wouldn't have changed how I felt about myself. It would just be a different filter on the same shit. I'm pretty sure there aren't any shortcuts when it comes to stuff like this. I promise. I looked."

She hugs me again, and this time, holding her tight in my arms, I can feel her heart settle.

"Virginia is cute," she says.

"It is, right? I'm still adjusting to the idea, but I think I really like it."

"And now Kevin's in there."

I nod.

"*The* Kevin."

"My boyfriend."

Mel's eyes go huge, and she swats my knee.

"I still have absolutely no fucking idea what I'm doing," I confess. "Like, not even close to an idea. But I'm starting to think maybe that's okay? Maybe the goal isn't knowing exactly how life works so you can get ahead of it. Maybe the goal is not knowing how any of it works and being okay with that."

"I might've been wrong," Mel smiles. "You might be a good Alice."

I laugh out loud. "She always says people want to know the steps for everything: happiness, loss, love. But there aren't ever going to be steps that work for everyone. Just the things you choose and the things you don't. So, I'm trying to see what happens when the first thing I choose is myself."

"Alice knows best."

"So I've heard."

"*Darling*," I turn to find Kevin, hanging lazily in the frame of the front door. "I do hate to interrupt, but we may need your help in the kitchen." He drops a hand into a small wave. "You must be the much-adored Melanie."

"Oh my *god*," Melanie says under her breath to me, taking him in for the first time. "Like, my *god*."

"No, I know. It's vulgar and very unfair," I agree, validated to have her appraisal after all this time.

"Later," she whispers. "You're going to fill me in on *all of the things*." And when I nod, she shakes it off, hops out of the truck, and bounds up to the front porch. She takes Kev's face in her hands and kisses him on the cheek. Unlike himself, he blushes. "You fuck this up with Kenz, and I'll stuff your dick in a blender, but I'm so excited to meet you *finally*! Do you cook?" He shoots me a mildly terrified glance over his shoulder as she pulls him inside, and I just smile at him.

A morning breeze brushes past, and I breathe it in.

"Happy thanksgiving, Dad."

It won't always be this good, but right now—right at this moment—life is *so* good. Luke and Kevin spend a good two hours researching best practices for defrosting a turkey, while I sit on the counter next to Mel's cutting board and she preps everything. The house is buzzing with the voices of people I adore, and I remember how easy it was to forget that it could ever be like this. By noon, Kev is mixing a holiday cocktail he made up that he calls The Gravy, which at first tastes terrible, but then is kind of okay, and then is really very delicious.

Iggy is always saying that the lie we believe about grief is that when it comes into your life, you just have to put everything on hold and wait for it to leave. But I'm learning that acceptance doesn't signal the departure of grief. It just means there's room for other things to move in alongside it. For some days to be painfully beautiful. For some things to be inexplicably good even if others are still bad.

Joy is hard, I text Louanne. And she says she knows, to take breaks if I need to.

I put myself in charge of setting the table so I can get some unsaturated space.

After a while, Mel flounces into the dining room, slathered in stuffing up to her elbows, and buzzed on The Gravy. "I really like him, Kenz," she whispers, surprised. I try to smile and find I'm close to tears. "Oh, no!" She puts her sticky fingers on my arm. "Kenz! You okay?"

I nod, but when I open my mouth, I can only cry. I brace myself on the back of one of the dining room chairs.

"What can I do?"

"I'm good. It's just a lot. I just need a minute," I say softly. "Maybe I'll take a shower?"

She nods, and I push back through the kitchen into the bedroom and to the bathroom. I slouch out of my clothes and catch my reflection in the mirror. I look soft, some of my weight coming back at last, and my face less dulled from exhaustion. After everything, I'm so grateful to this body for surviving, to myself, for believing in some dimly lit corner of my mind that one day I'd be glad to be here again.

The water is warm and crisp and, when I allow myself to think it, there is something almost holy about it today. I don't picture myself rinsing away down the drain but instead think maybe I am worth the care of soap and water. When I shut off the shower, I sit a while on the edge of the tub, fastening the memory of this feeling in my mind.

The house smells divine when I open the door, roasting vegetables and butter. I find an old sort of orangey shirtdress and throw it on before joining the team in the kitchen. Mel is in the zone as the meal is really coming together now, Luke and Kevin are delightfully drunk at this point, taking turns picking songs, dramatically lip-syncing into wooden spoons, with Luke stepping in as Mel's sous chef as needed.

I look at the table I set, with place settings Kev and I picked out at Target yesterday, and I wonder if there is some ritual to setting traditions or if all of them start when no one is really thinking about it. I don't own enough serving dishes, and Mel has to repurpose Tupperware, and I know she doesn't like it, but she smiles anyway and says it adds charm. Luke nudges me in the ribs over the gold-brushed decorative gourd sitting at the center of the table, and I tell him Kevin insisted on it yesterday because he said it was a seasonally responsible purchase.

There's gentle bickering over who is sitting where, even though it's only the four of us, and once we're all seated, Mel proposes we each go around and say something we're grateful for. I wince mildly at the earnestness of her suggestion, and Kevin catches it, shaking his head softly to keep me from backing out of a perfectly good moment.

"I'll start," says Mel. "I'm grateful for my friendship with Mackenzie, which has lasted since we were twelve... when we used to wear those matching striped polo shirts from The Gap...I'd never have survived all this time without you. Seriously. I'm so proud of you, Kenz. And I'm so lucky to get to be here celebrating this very bad and problematic holiday with you."

I bite down on my cheeks and force myself to make eye contact with her, though the sincerity surges in my system and makes me squirmy.

"I love you, Mel," I manage, and squeeze her hand across the table.

"Babe," she says to Luke. "You're up."

"Okay, shit," Luke grins. "I'm grateful.... I guess, I mean, I'm grateful to be here. Y'all are... It's special, you know? To find people who don't expect you to be anything except like... *you*. And I'm so lucky to have that with Melanie... but then it's dope to have met Kenz, and to have met you too, Kevin... just like... more people doing their best to be here, like, alive... and to just figure shit out. And to not take shit too seriously. Like, I'm grateful to know that Kenz fucking hates this gratitude circle, and I'm grateful that Mel is making us do it anyway."

He laughs, and Mel smirks, shaking her head at me.

"I don't know," he says. "I guess, yeah. I'm just grateful for y'all."

"This is emotional," I whine at Mel, and she just shrugs.

"You're up," she says to me.

"Oof," I start, looking around at them. "I am… grateful… for… I guess for unconditional love?" I say it before I even know I've thought of it. "I don't think I really knew what that was like before I knew you all. It sort of always seemed like everyone wanted something back for loving me, or for caring about me. And this year has been… I used to think that I wouldn't ever be able to do enough to earn as much love as I felt like I needed, I guess. And the three of you have been so fucking insistent on loving me, even when I've been a total pain in the ass. And you never asked me for anything to earn it from you… you didn't blame me when I acted in ways that didn't deserve you… I don't know if I will ever be able to thank you for that. You loved me when I didn't. And I know firsthand how hard that is to do. Just… thank you. Thank you all so much for doing that for me."

I'm all teary by the time I get through it, and I glance up to see Mel is too. Luke has his head bowed, listening like it's a prayer. I turn to Kevin, and he smiles at me, wiping under my eyes with his thumb. I sniffle and pull his hand to my lips, kiss his knuckles.

"Your turn," I say, and he laughs, raking a hand through his hair.

"All right, let's see. I, uh… so, I'm obviously the newest addition here," he looks nervous, biting his lip and glancing down into his lap to think. "Gratitude is weird, you know because lately, I have so much of it… like sometimes, Mack, I look at you, and I have so much of it… it's like I can get lost in it. It gets hard to even identify where it starts… or what triggers it. But I can say… this morning, when you woke me up at the crack of dawn—when everyone first got here… I woke up looking at Mack's drool-crusted face making demands and just generally freaking out… and I thought, thank god, this girl is real. Thank god I didn't dream her."

"I love you so much," I interrupt, and he lets out this bash-ful laugh.

"I've never had anything like this before," he says, looking at Mel and Luke. "I've never been part of a group of friends that gen-uinely felt like a family. I've never even been part of a family, really. So… thank you. For this."

Melanie hasn't been able to shut off the waterworks this whole time, and by now, she's fully leaned into Luke's shoulder, just gushing tears. Luke smiles broadly at me, rubbing her shoulder.

"Is that good, Melanie? Should we drink?" Kev laughs, raising his glass, my hand clasped tightly in his other palm.

Mel nods, with a gasping laugh over more tears. She scrambles to refill her glass before raising it.

"Fucking cheers," Luke says, and my cheeks burn from beam-ing so damn hard.

Luke carves the turkey with confidence, and there is a small round of applause. We eat and eat and eat, and there's still more food, and I haven't laughed so much since I can't remember when and at some point Kevin says "Fuck, I really love these people," and I am so happy to see him so at home that I almost can't stand it.

Mel halfheartedly offers to find a hotel if there's not room for all of us, but Kev takes her phone away and asks her if she's kidding or just too drunk for good sense. We pull the quilt off the wall and make her and Luke a makeshift bed on the living room floor out of couch cushions and decorative throws, and they overdo it raving about how comfortable it is.

I'm over-full in every sense and hardly ready for the day to end, but Kev is half-asleep standing up. He's blinking very intentionally, trying to stay awake long enough to check in with me.

"How are you doing?" he asks as we roll ourselves into bed.

"This level of joy is very off-brand for me," I say.

"Mm. For me too," he says over a yawn. "What do you think? Should we call it off?"

"I don't think I have a choice," I sigh. "Sorry."

"No, I'm glad you said something. I was starting to think I might have to do something drastic, like pick up my life and move here." I freeze. My heart has for sure stopped beating but, somehow, I don't die. I roll onto my side and look at him. His eyes are closed, but he's grinning.

"How serious are you being?"

"I don't know. 78% and climbing?" He opens his eyes, and they fall on mine. "Aw, look at your nervous little face. I'd get my own apartment."

I couldn't swallow my smile if I wanted to. "It's been two days."

"Sure, Adams. But it's also been like six years." I look up at the ceiling and try to breathe. "So, if you're serious, and you're ready to try this... I mean, if you think this might be what you really want... then I guess—I don't know. I guess I have to move to fucking Virginia."

"You've thought about this."

"You don't have to decide anything right now. I'm just saying. I'm in if you are."

But it's the easiest thing to decide. So simple, it doesn't even feel like a decision.

"I'm in," I say. "I am so very irreversibly in."

PART FOUR

December 2018

MACKENZIE'S CHRISTMAS WISHLIST, AGE 8

- *A normal mom and dad*
- *A new diary with a lock*
- *The Powerpuff Girls backpack*
- *A canopy or four-poster bed with a pull-out bed underneath for sleepovers*
- *A PET!!!!! (must be cute)*
- *To get my ears pierced lip gloss (not gross organic chapstick PLEASE)*
- *Be Normal*

*

December 25th

There are five Christmas trees in Alice's living room. Four fake decorative ones in each corner of the room, and one enormous real tree right in the middle. They all have twinkle lights. It's like being at a holiday rave.

Nathan and I are together on the couch, while the adults fuss over who can bring out what from the kitchen.

"Merry Christmas," he produces, without looking at all in my direction.

"You too."

"Is it weird? You know, because your dad is dead?" I stare at him a moment. Some people say it's nice having brothers. I have no idea why.

"Where, um, where's your girlfriend? Lana, right?" I deflect.

"Oh, she volunteers on Christmas. It's a hard day for orphans. That's why I asked about your dad. Sorry if that was rude."

"No, it's… yeah. It's a little weird."

"Yeah," he sighs. "That's what I thought."

Mom appears first with a tray of sugar cookies.

"We frosted these at the Dear Alice holiday party. This one's my favorite, the little Rudolph? I think that one's supposed to be a snowman, but if you ask me, Charlotte was a little lax with her decorations."

"They look great, Mom." I take the globby snowman and bite its head off. Nathan looks disappointed and wanders out of the room.

"I have something I wanted to give you, sweetie," Mom says, sidling up next to me on the couch.

"Let's wait for everyone else to do gifts," but she's already under the tree sifting through packages.

"This one's just between you and me." She hands me a large flat rectangular package. It's heavy.

"Mom—" I say, but she just waves for me to open it. I peel the paper back, and there it is, a big silver frame, an enormous white matte, and right there in the center, the sun-speckled photo of me on Gerald's shoulders. It makes me smile so wide my face aches.

"Oh," I say. "Oh, this is… *wow*. Thank you."

She kisses my temple and rests her head on my shoulder, and we both just look.

"I thought," she sighs, quietly, "I thought, let's leave room around the edges for everything else we know was there too. But for now, let's choose just to look at what was right at the very center."

I nod, tears running down my face. "This makes all the stuff I got you look like crap," I confess. She swats my arm, then hugs me close.

Alice glides in from the kitchen. "EGGNOOOOOOG," she belts. She appears to be a sixth and final Christmas tree, head to toe red and green polyester, and a twinkling light necklace. She's even got her own topper in the form of a bedazzled headband. The woman is unrivaled.

She foists overfull cups of eggnog into our hands and shimmies herself down right between us.

"You know something, ladies," she says, wrapping an arm around each of us, "if we had the chance to do our whole lives all over again, I'd choose y'all to be my family every single time. I sure would."

And I think—even though the eggnog is sticky and over spiked, even though I can smell Walter's aftershave coming into the room before I hear his voice, even though Jimmy's sweater says COOL YULE on it, and Nathan is watching Minecraft videos on his phone during carols—I would too.

<u>December 28th</u>

"I thought this apartment would be less obnoxious now that I'm your girlfriend," I say, looking out at the Bay.

"But?"

"It's worse, somehow? It's like now it reminds me that you're an asshole, and it also makes me feel like an asshole by association."

"Oof, that *is* bad," Kev laughs. "You want wine or something?"

"Yeah, I'd drink wine." I sit down at the island and watch him pour. I am waiting for the joy of just looking at him to wear off, but if it never does, I won't mind. "No boxes, I see."

"So, here's a gross thing to admit, but, uh, it came like this?" I snort. "So, I kind of just leave it like this," he shrugs. "I mean, unless you wanna steal something."

I scope out the place, try to imagine any of this stuff alongside Alice's quilt.

"Hey. Merry belated Jesus' birthday," he says, clinking my glass.

"Happy belated *birthday* birthday," I lift a toast in his honor.

"Only two weeks late."

"Well, I'm here now. I'll make it up to you," I tease, and then get caught up in the view again. "You're sure you don't want to be in San Francisco anymore?"

"Why? You backing out?"

"No, stunningly still very into you. I just—you're always just giving me stuff like it's easy. You know, like, just showing up for me when I need you... and I don't want you to move your whole life just because it makes my shit easier. Like, I know I'm a jerk, but I don't *not* like this apartment. Or... I do but, I guess what I mean is... I like Virginia, but I could move my life for you. I'd do that, you know." His cheeks pink up, and I love him all over again. He takes my face in his hands.

"I act like it's easy to give you stuff because it is," he says, and I like that answer, but I also don't.

"Come on, don't be cute. I'm serious."

He takes a deep breath and pulls up the barstool next to me, bracketing my knees with his. "All right, look. So, for a long time, it felt really easy to do the stuff that looked like what adults do. I went to the same school my dad went to, studied the same stuff, graduated with honors just like him so that I could work in his office, date everyone and no one. He tells people I'm like my mom, and maybe I am... but everything I did was modeled after him.

"And it wasn't like... it wasn't one of those sob stories about kids who think they have to live up to their parents' example. It was just... what I understood best how to do. And then... when you had this thing happen that broke everything open, I realized, like... I had no clue how to actually be an adult. It wasn't even just that I didn't know how to help you. It was like I started to realize I didn't know how to do anything as myself... How few decisions I'd ever really made."

I take his hand in mine; hold it in my lap.

He pushes on. "I started to think... my mom probably left because she never chose the life she wound up in. She just did what I'd been doing, all the things she thought adults were supposed to do.

And she got in over her head. Didn't figure out 'til way too late that it wasn't at all what she wanted."

"She missed out on knowing you," I say.

He smiles. "Mack, leaving San Francisco—I'm not walking away from my whole life. There's not a whole life here to walk away from. When I got on that plane to Seattle just to see you, that was the first real choice I made to be someone I'd never seen growing up: someone who chooses things because they feel right—not just because they're easy. And that's the life I want. All I'm doing is walking away from the person who would never have let himself have something like this."

I brush my fingers across his cheek. It still feels impossible sometimes that he's really mine to love.

"Okay," I breathe. "I guess you can come to Virginia, then." He smiles, leaning in and kissing me. "And let's steal that rug. For sure."

December 31st

Mel squeals the entire elevator ride up, and it's nice, I guess, for Kevin to finally get to show off. Luke doesn't squeal, but he does shoot a look at me when he pushes the PH button, and again when the elevator doors open right into the living room. The four of us agreed to one last hurrah at Kev's place: New Year's Eve.

"That's the BAY," Mel runs in and presses her face right to the glass. She's tipsy from two cocktails with dinner, so I help Luke get their suitcases in the door.

"Shit," he says as the elevator doors glide shut behind us. "Remind us again why you don't want to live here, Kenz?"

I laugh. "You mean, aside from it being a grotesque and unnecessary display of wealth?"

"She refuses to be swept off her feet," Kev answers, putting the leftovers from dinner in the fridge and taking out a bottle of champagne. "How're we doing on time, gorgeous?"

"It's almost 11:45 now. Fireworks should be right at midnight, yeah?"

"Yeah. Grab some glasses, would you?"

"The *actual bay* is right there," Mel says again, and Luke laughs.

I brush past Kevin in the kitchen, and he leans into my ear, "You doing okay?"

I nod, "I'm okay," and press my lips into his cheek, but my heart is shaky.

Another New Year. Another first.

"Should we do resolutions or something?" Luke asks, as Kevin snakes his arm around my waist.

"Ooh, yes! I want to," Mel chirps. "Is there paper or something?"

Paper and pens are dug up for everyone, and we camp out in front of the window with our champagne. I watch while they all scribble and cross out prospective hopes. Even if I wanted to write a list this year, I have no idea what'd be on it. So many things I accomplished this year that I never planned on—never could have planned on. So many things I'd dreamed of that I'm so lucky I never got.

So instead, I make a list of people I'd still like to thank for the year I survived.

I write a thank you for Neil. For Lydia. For Beth.

I imagine how each of them might ring in the New Year and hope none of them feel they're going into it alone. I look out at the water, rogue fireworks already erupting in small corners of the sky. And now it's now. I close my eyes as Kev, Mel, and Luke countdown.

10. I am Mackenzie.

9. I am twenty-five years old.

8. I am tall.

7. I am softer than I thought.

6. I am stronger than I thought.

5. I am part of a family.

4. I am loved.

3. I am in love.

2. I am here.

1. I am still here.

ACKNOWLEDGEMENTS

With a project as long in the making as this one, it feels like there are a million people to thank, and not ever enough space to thank them all. I wrote this book because it's the story I needed growing up. Writing it has helped me to process so much of my own grief, and I hope it can offer some of that same comfort to others. So, before I get specific, thank you to every person who has touched this book, who sees themselves in these pages and characters, who understands the strength it takes to pull a broken heart back together. This story is for you, and I love you.

Okay. Onto the specifics. Thanks, until the end of time, to my friends, for reading, loving, and encouraging this book into being. Thanks especially to Abigail, Anna, and Tia, who have been reading and re-reading this story for me since the beginning, and without whom Mackenzie would never have made it this far.

Thanks to my mom and my older sister, Tanya, both of whom have been tirelessly advocating for me all my life and have listened to me talk about this book since before it started. Thanks to my incredible friend & editor Kenna Kettrick, who caught all my mistakes and redundancies and made this book shine. Thank you to Kelly Forsythe who so generously offered me insights into the world of marketing and publicity for this project. Thanks, from the bottom of my heart to my therapist Christina, without whom even imagining an ending for this story would've been impossible.

Thank you to all the Kevins I've loved before.

And a tremendous thank you to my father Tyrone Davis, whom I love with all my heart, for teaching me so much about grief, about love, about loss, and about life. This book could not be without you.

ABOUT THE AUTHOR

Author photo by Anna Czosnyka, © 2016

Nicky Davis is a novelist, playwright, poet, and screenwriter from Seattle. As a queer, biracial Black woman, she is passionate about telling honest stories that represent all shades of humanity in its complex dysfunction and beauty. She likes music turned all the way up, iced chai and croissants for breakfast, and as many queer romance novels as she can get her hands on. She also makes a pretty spectacular lamb curry. She currently lives in Los Angeles with her best friend, Anna, their fake dog Ernold Lisa, and their 30+ houseplants.

You can find Nicky on Instagram @nickydavis13,
on Twitter @NickySDavis, or on her website
www.theconversationalite.com